D0122476

PAINTED HANDS

PAINTED HANDS

JENNIFER ZOBAIR

THOMAS DUNNE BOOKS
St. Martin's Press
New York

This is a work of fiction. All of the characters, organizations, and events portrayed in this novel are either products of the author's imagination or are used fictitiously.

THOMAS DUNNE BOOKS.
An imprint of St. Martin's Press.

www.thomasdunnebooks.com
www.stmartins.com

Library of Congress Cataloging-in-Publication Data

Zobair, Jennifer.
Painted hands / Jennifer Zobair.—First Edition.
pages cm
ISBN 978-1-250-02700-9 (hardcover)
ISBN 978-1-250-02701-6 (e-book)
1. Muslim women—Fiction. 2. Muslim women—Conduct of life—Fiction. 3. Boston (Mass.)—Fiction. I. Title.
PS3626.O23 P35 2013
813'.6—dc23

2013003762

St. Martin's Press books may be purchased for educational, business, or promotional use. For information on bulk purchases, please contact Macmillan Corporate and Premium Sales Department at 1-800-221-7945 extension 5442 or write specialmarkets@macmillan.com.

First Edition: June 2013

10 9 8 7 6 5 4 3 2 1

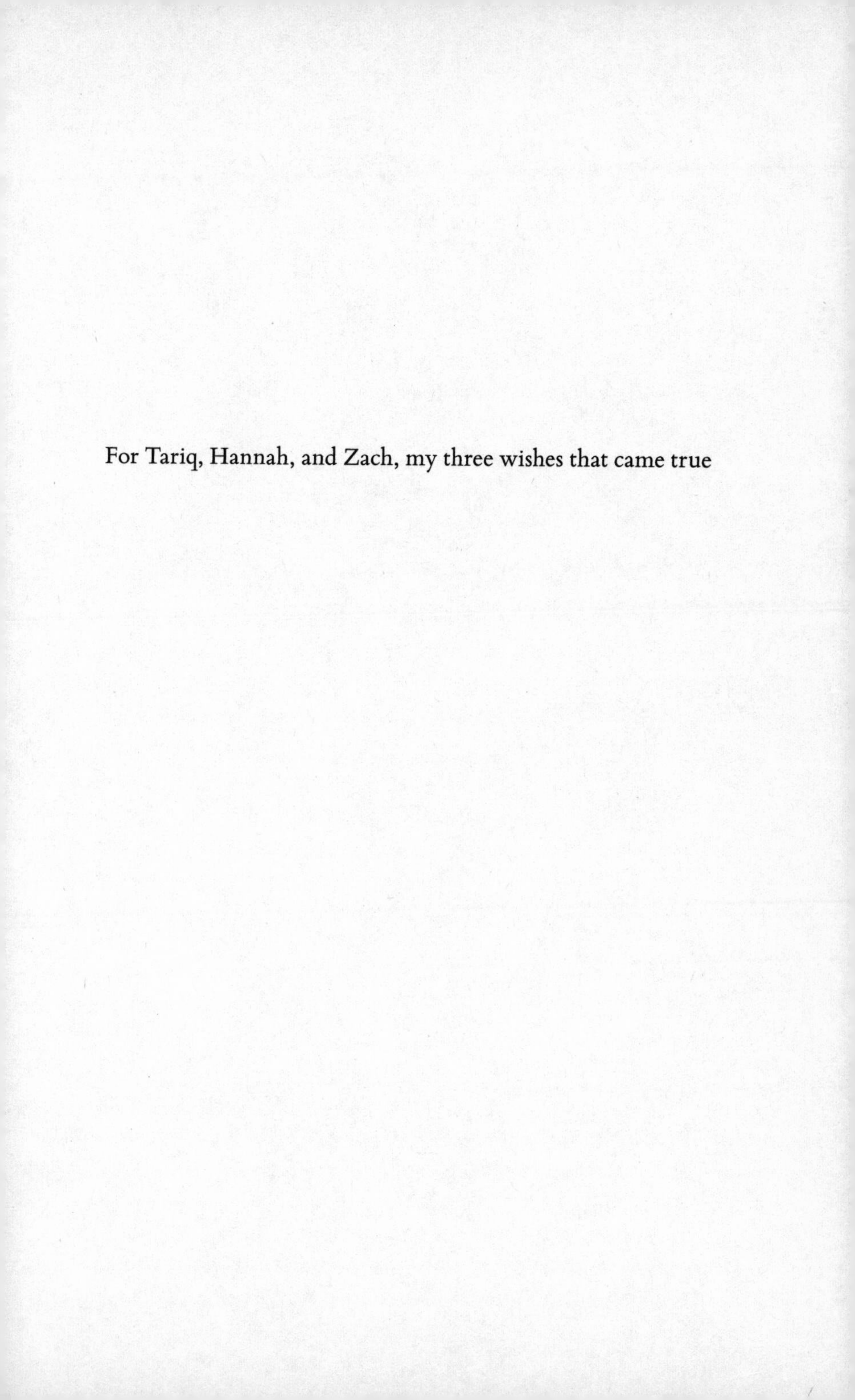

For Tariq, Hannah, and Zach, my three wishes that came true

Acknowledgments

I am deeply indebted to my agent, Kent Wolf, who believed in this novel and understood it in ways that touched me profoundly, and to my editor, Toni Plummer, who called the book beautiful and then made it better. I'm also grateful to Angela Gibson for the careful eye during copyediting and to everyone at Thomas Dunne Books/St. Martin's Press for their wonderful work.

I owe more than I can express to those who read and commented on the manuscript: Kristan Smith-Park, without whom this novel would not exist; Mary Jo Hochsprung, who bravely and gently read very first; Sarah Hina, who was thoughtful and *sure* and with whom I will someday watch a *Seinfeld* marathon; Brian Ziska, for a thousand doubt-quelling teatimes; Sarah Hochsprung, who embraced these characters with such affection; and Blake Moore, who is proof that what you think of someone in high school can be completely wrong. I'm also thankful to Wendy Russ for creating a beautiful Web site for the novel and for much laughter and hand-holding along the way.

I am especially grateful to my family: my husband, Talha, who encouraged me to tell this story and always asked what he could do to help; his family, for the ways they welcomed me into their rich culture; my parents, Kathie Scott and James Ziska, who allowed me to find my own path; and my grandparents: Lucille Benson, who made magic with a kiln in her basement and taught me that artistic pursuits can light a life, and Don and Betty Knight, who, for reasons that will forever elude me, thought I walked on water and who always felt like love and home and happiness to me.

And finally, my children: Tariq, who shines brighter than all the stars in the sky; Zach, who knows more than I do about almost everything and whose cute powers will always work on me; and Hannah, my beautiful, strong Muslim daughter who believes she can be anything, even president of this country.

I do, too, sweetheart. I do, too.

PAINTED HANDS

1

THEY HAD TALKED about marrying a white man, but Amra never thought they were serious, not even when fed up with the proposal-slinging aunties who showed up at weddings and holiday celebrations with wallet-sized photos of eligible doctors and engineers, their particulars scribbled on the back (*5'11", MIT, owns home* or *Stanford Medical, 33, professional wife okay*). It was simply a way to vent. Because sometimes she and her friends needed to say *something* after the Ramadan parties and family celebrations, where the men always ate first and never helped clean up. It was just a bluff, the threat to marry outside of their culture, or so Amra thought until the Friday after Valentine's Day, when Rukan rushed into Khao Sarn twenty minutes late—Amra and Zainab had already finished their *miang kum* and were attacking the fried tofu—and, without taking off her coat, flashed an enormous diamond ring.

Amra didn't know what to say. All she could think of was the Home Shopping Network and a laboratory. Which, unfortunately, opened the floor for Zainab.

"What the hell is *that*?"

"Nice, Zainab," Amra said. "What would her father say if he could hear you?" Rukan's father did not tolerate women who swore.

When they befriended her that first earnest year at Smith, despite Zainab's prodding, Rukan couldn't even say "crap" until the second semester.

Zainab nodded, like she was glad Amra had asked. "I think he would say, 'What is that ring doing on my daughter's finger and it better not have come from that goddamned *kafir*.'"

"Adam isn't a *kafir*," Rukan said. "He's an Episcopalian."

Zainab rolled her eyes.

"It counts," Rukan insisted. "You know, People of the Book? Christians and Jews. And Sabians." Rukan frowned. "What even is a Sabian?" Amra shrugged. Zainab shot Rukan a look suggesting it couldn't possibly matter, at that moment, what a Sabian was.

"Rook, even if it counts," Zainab said, "it doesn't help you. In your father's world, Muslim *men* can marry Christians and Jews. Not Muslim women."

"Some scholars say that women can, too."

"Name one."

Rukan sighed and turned to Amra. "How bad do you think it will be?"

"With your parents?" Rukan nodded. Amra searched for the right words. "I think they'll be caught off guard."

Zainab laughed. "Really, Amra? You think?"

Rukan slumped in her chair. "Well, they'll just have to deal with it. I'm getting married."

"To Adam," Amra said.

"Yes, to Adam. Should I agree to some arranged marriage instead? To some guy who's only after my father's money?"

"Of course not." It was a false dilemma, Amra knew, the idea that those were Rukan's only choices. "It's just so . . . sudden."

"Please. You go to weddings all the time where the bride and groom have spent all of three hours together." Rukan took off her coat, finally, and pushed it over the back of her chair. She seemed to notice the food for the first time and spooned some Chinese broccoli onto her plate. "It's been almost three months," she said. "That's practically a lifetime in our community."

Amra didn't disagree. But Adam was not from their community. "I'm sorry," Amra said. "You're right. Three months is more than enough time to fall in love." Rukan nodded and took a sip of her water, staring at the wall on the other side of the restaurant.

"So," Zainab said, "when do we get to meet the *kafir*?"

Amra didn't check her voice mail until she was back in her office. Her mother had called twice and sent one text during lunch: *Salaam, Beti. Where are you? Please call, ASAP.* Amra had discreetly texted back, asking if it was an emergency, while Rukan talked about reception venues and tiered cakes. *It is not emergent,* her mother replied, *but urgent.*

She smiled at her mother's precise response. Growing up with her mother, an English professor at NYU, meant not being allowed to say "snuck" instead of "sneaked" or "ironic" to refer to a coincidence. It did, however, mean scoring a perfect 800 on the verbal SAT.

Amra closed her office door and dialed. Her mother picked up on the first ring, and Amra could picture her in her study, her hair pulled into a loose bun, her black reading glasses perched on the end of her nose, making comments in careful, slanted script on her students' papers. The entire wall behind her mother's desk was covered with a sea of books arranged by subject—gender studies, politics, linguistics. On the antique end table near the door, she displayed a signed first-edition copy of Virginia Woolf's *A Room of One's Own* in the original cinnamon cloth. The wood floor of her mother's office was covered with a maroon Tabriz rug, on which Amra played as a child while her mother graded papers and prepared her lecture notes. It was where she learned that women's work mattered, that a mother was also someone who did interesting and important things outside of the home. Amra grew up wanting to be just like her and had tried to forge a similar space in the spare bedroom of her Back Bay condo. Somehow, it fell short.

"*Beti,*" her mother said, "what are you doing the weekend of March tenth?"

Amra didn't need to check. "Working."

"I knew you were going to say that. I have a better idea. Why don't you come home for a couple of days? Let me pamper you. All those long hours. You need a break."

"I can't. I have two deals closing that week and Eric is going on vacation."

"Eric," her mother scoffed. "The man who cannot bother to learn your name after four years?" It was true. Eric still mispronounced her name, rhyming the first syllable with "Sam" instead of "sum," giving it an odd, southern twang even though Eric was from Scarsdale. "It's pronounced Umruh," she'd tried to explain during those first grueling weeks and then given up.

"If that man can go away for seven days," her mother continued, "surely my overworked daughter can take one weekend off." Amra looked at her desk—the neat piles of manila folders, the stacks of merger and acquisition documents, the pink message slips her secretary placed in the tray as Amra had instructed (urgent ones on the left and in descending order of importance)—and wished it worked that way. Amra wasn't up for partner for two years, and until then she was yoked to Eric's slightest whim. But Amra knew such explanations would only upset her mother further.

"Maybe I'll come over the Easter holiday," she said. "Things should settle down by then."

"Easter? Amra, I need you here on the tenth." Her mother's tone became less conversational and more infused with purpose.

"Why?"

"The Syeds will be in town."

"Which Syeds?" Amra knew about fifty Syeds.

"Don't you remember? From our first apartment on Ninety-first

Street. Dr. Syed and his family. You used to play with their daughter, Maha."

Amra remembered. Who could forget Maha with her little notepads, watching the other children, scribbling furtive notes. Once at a wedding, Zainab grabbed Maha's yellow tablet, stood on a chair, and read its contents. It turned out to be a list of various children's names and a chronicle of their indiscretions. Maha had cited one boy for staring at a girl, Zainab for swearing, and Amra for "acting like she is better than everyone on the planet." "You're recording our sins?" Zainab had asked incredulously. Maha just shrugged and said the angels were doing it anyway. It was at Maha's house, years later, that Amra got her first period and the ever-prepared Zainab led her to the bathroom for a crash course in tampon wearing. Maha caught sight of the white tube and told her father that the girls were smoking. Because of Maha, Amra had to endure Dr. Syed banging on the bathroom door while Zainab held it shut long enough for her to get her pants up. Amra had been mortified, but Zainab simply deposited the cardboard applicator in Dr. Syed's hand as they passed him and said, "I think this is what you're looking for." The only good part about Maha was her brother Mateen, with his Shahid Kapoor good looks, but he was several years older than the girls and never paid them any attention.

Amra sighed. "I doubt that Maha cares much about seeing me."

"Don't be ridiculous," her mother said. "She worshipped the ground you and Zainab walked on."

"She had a funny way of showing it."

"Yes, well, children can be funny. Shall I make your shuttle reservation or will your secretary take care of it?"

2

SHE SAID *WHAT*?"

On the corner of Columbus Avenue and Stuart Street, Zainab set her briefcase at her feet, balanced her phone between her ear and shoulder, and searched for "Eleanor Winthrop-Smith" on her BlackBerry.

"Pros-ti-tu-tion," Ben repeated, as though speaking to an uncommonly slow child. "Didn't you know? It's been seriously overlooked by the job-seeking crowd."

It took less than twenty seconds to find the story. Ben, unfortunately, wasn't joking:

> Massachusetts Senatorial candidate and former CEO of her eponymous corporation Eleanor Winthrop-Smith asserts that prostitution should be considered a legitimate career option, for either gender.

"Shit, shit, shit." Zainab leaned her head back and exhaled hard. *"Shit."* A woman pushing a small child in a yuppie stroller made a wide berth around her.

"Zainab?"

"That explains the five hundred messages I got during the meeting." Zainab sighed. She had spent the past hour trying to persuade two dozen nurses—who'd been expecting Eleanor but had to settle for Zainab when Eleanor got stuck in D.C.—that Eleanor's willingness to fight for increased workplace safety for medical workers made up for her less than desirable position, in the nurses' eyes, on licensing. The nurses weren't buying it. And now Eleanor had served up this little treat.

"You've got a ton of messages here, too," Ben said. "Some talk-radio clown has been calling nonstop. Like seriously every half hour. Plus—"

"What?" Zainab said. "Plus *what*?"

"Jim hasn't started the St. Patrick's Day speech yet." Ben cleared his throat. "Any chance you can blow through here for a few minutes on your way to dinner?"

Zainab checked her watch. She was supposed to meet a *New York Times* reporter at Temple Bar in forty-five minutes. "Plenty of time," she said, and hailed a cab.

Zainab tried to reach Eleanor on the way to the campaign office, but the private number went straight to voice mail. She didn't bother leaving a message. The comment sounded like something Eleanor would say, and if she said it she meant it. There would be no retraction, no apology, just Zainab clarifying. She could hear Eleanor now: "This is what I hired you to *do*."

Zainab knew she was lucky to have her job. At the age of twenty-nine, she was the communications director for the first serious Republican Senate candidate in Massachusetts in years. Eleanor, with her hedge fund fortune and cozy Beltway relationships, was the kind of professional contact that could change a person's life regardless of the outcome of the election. Still, Zainab had been skeptical when her former Women and Public Policy professor and occasional yoga partner, Linda Erlich, had proposed the interview with Eleanor. The suggestion came in the middle of a Bikram class when they were drenched in sweat, opening their hearts and lungs in an intense *bhujangasana*. "I know her from Princeton," Linda said as they arched their spines. "The two of you are a perfect match. Except for one thing." After the teacher made a stern "tusht" noise in their direction, Linda mouthed, "She's a Republican." They moved from the cobra pose into the locust, balancing on their stomachs, raising their arms and legs, and Zainab almost laughed. Whether they slithered or swarmed, she was no fan of Republicans. But she trusted Linda, and Eleanor turned out to be a fierce libertarian with an incisive intellect and a seemingly congenital inability to skirt difficult issues. By the end of their two-hour interview, Zainab was professionally smitten and Eleanor must have been impressed, too, because she offered Zainab a job on the spot.

The car dropped Zainab in front of the Court Street campaign headquarters. Ben met her at the door, dressed in his ubiquitous faded jeans and vintage tee shirt, and followed her to her office. "I assume you've spoken to Eleanor," he said dryly.

Zainab shot him a look. It was common knowledge around the campaign that there was an inverse relationship between the urgency with which someone needed to speak to Eleanor and the ease with which she could be reached. Zainab sat at her desk and sorted through the chaos of memos and handwritten messages as she spoke. "Here's the deal. Until I can reach Eleanor and flesh out an official statement, our position is that Eleanor has strong libertarian leanings but that prostitution is settled state law that has nothing to do with the United States Senate campaign. Spin it as an inconsequential personal opinion. Say that no one is suggesting any changes to any law concerning prostitution."

"Right." Ben nodded. "Are you sure about that?"

Zainab leaned back with a small, stipulating groan. "Of course not. But when I talk to Eleanor, I'll convince her that a policy based on her opinion would be untenable to Massachusetts voters." She gestured at the doorway. "Tell Jim I've got five minutes."

"Yeah, about that."

Zainab narrowed her eyes. "He's not here, is he?"

"I told him you were stopping by, and he suddenly remembered an appointment he had to keep."

"Right. An appointment." Zainab shook her head. "Soon, Ben. We have to check his résumé *soon*."

Ben nodded. "So, are you excited?"

"About?"

"Your big interview."

"I'm thrilled."

"Come on," Ben said. "This is huge."

"They should be interviewing Eleanor."

"She's quite the gunner."

Zainab frowned. "Eleanor?"

"Darby Tate. The woman from the *Times*."

"You know her?"

"I met her today. She came in earlier."

"She what?"

Ben waved his hand. "You know, to talk to the staff."

"That's just perfect." Zainab closed her eyes. "What did she want to know?"

"Just your deepest secrets and most embarrassing moments."

"Ben."

"I'm joking. You know we're all loyal as puppies to you. But she's very impressive. And tall. Or maybe it was just the boots. She wore some truly kick-ass boots. Now that I think about it, the two of you are going to get along fine."

Zainab ignored Ben's comment. "Call Jim. Call until he actually *answers*. Tell him I need a copy of the St. Patrick's Day speech before he so much as thinks of going to sleep tonight. I don't care if I get it at four in the morning. If I don't get it, he doesn't sleep." Jim Gertz was the son of a friend of Eleanor's from their Wharton days. Eleanor had hired Jim directly before there was anything Zainab could do about it.

She picked up the schedule for the next three days, marked with Eleanor's scrawl, and wondered again why she had agreed to the interview with Darby Tate. Zainab spoke to reporters all day long, but always about Eleanor's position on late-term abortion (yes, up until the very second of birth) or equal rights for gays (of course, and if you really wanted to be an idiot about it, no, she could not care less if it led to "people coupling with animals, domestic or otherwise") or aid to Africa (a "lovely impulse" and private citizens should donate to their hearts' content, but "America is not the world's personal checking account"). Zainab had fielded so many off-the-wall questions and been forced to explain a host of seemingly absurd but actually rather coherent positions that she could almost do it in her sleep.

But what Zainab did not do, ever, was talk about herself. Her job was to promote the candidacy of Eleanor, period. When a snarky local blog named her one of Boston's most eligible bachelorettes, she faced the office staff with a closed-mouth smile to suggest she was humoring the matter. When the *Globe* called her style effortless and referred to her as the Grace Kelly of Eleanor's campaign, she laughed it off. But when she'd apologized to Eleanor for the distractions, Eleanor had simply said that if they were talking about Zainab, eventually they'd be talking about the campaign, and wasn't that what they wanted? When Zainab mentioned the *New York Times* piece and indicated she'd be perfectly willing to decline, Eleanor looked perplexed. "*The* newspaper of record?" she'd said. "Why would you do that? You're young, you're brilliant, you're glamorous. It's a sexy public interest piece. Enjoy the attention, dear." And so Zainab grudgingly agreed to the interview.

Zainab packed her briefcase and looked at her watch. If she was lucky, she'd only be fifteen minutes late. She climbed into a cab.

"Temple Bar. On Mass Ave.," she told the driver and checked her e-mail. She had forty-seven new messages, including one from Rukan inviting Amra and Zainab to meet Adam at her parents' home. A politely worded plea for support. Zainab was relieved that date was still weeks away. She skimmed a few more e-mails and saw Amra's text: *Thought you'd like to know that this morning I spoke, at some length, to a NYT reporter. Don't forget me when you're famous.* It was followed by a second text: *P.S. Looks like we get to meet the kafir!* Zainab took a deep, cleansing breath and noticed the driver stealing furtive looks at her in the rearview mirror.

"Kya aap Pakistani hain?"

"Half," she said. "And half Indian."

"But you are Muslim?"

Zainab thought about telling him that it was none of his business, but he was old and thin and he looked as though he had lost or suffered something. "I was raised Muslim, yes," she said.

"You are married?"

"No."

"Engaged?"

Her sympathy evaporated. "No." She turned back to her phone, hoping to end the interrogation.

"Your parents are looking?"

Zainab sighed and bit the inside of her cheek. *My mother is dead and my father's trophy wife has abandoned him to dementia,* she wanted to say. But she just said, "No. No one's looking."

The driver nodded. "I have a son. He is a good Muslim boy, smart, very smart. He has a medical degree from Johns Hopkins."

Zainab laughed. "I'm sure he's very nice, thank you. But I'm all set."

The hostess led Zainab to a small booth in the middle of the restaurant. Darby had arrived and was sipping a glass of white wine. She wore her platinum hair in a stiff, chin-length bob that she tucked behind both ears. Her face was tight and tan, which made it difficult to tell her age. Zainab guessed mid-forties. Darby stood to greet her, revealing a short black skirt and the boots Ben had mentioned. They were knee-high with impossibly tall, impractically thin heels, reminiscent of the boots Condi Rice had worn at Wiesbaden Army Airfield several years earlier. Darby towered over Zainab's five-foot-six frame, even though Zainab wore black pumps. She coveted those boots.

"Zainab, thanks so much for coming. It's a pleasure to finally meet you." Darby extended her right hand. "I hope the traffic wasn't horrible. We should have picked someplace closer to your office."

Zainab wondered if it was a dig at her late arrival, but Darby's smile seemed genuine. "No, this is great," she said. "I love their food."

Darby nodded. "They're supposed to be good for vegetarians."

"You don't eat meat?"

"Actually, I do." Darby made an apologetic expression, something short of a wince. "But I don't have to eat it in front of you."

"No, I don't mind. I was just curious." Zainab adjusted her jacket on the seat next to her. "But how did you know—"

"That you're a vegetarian? You'd be surprised at how much I know about you."

Zainab shifted. "I'm sure."

"It makes you uncomfortable, the idea that I've talked to people about you." Darby seemed to study her. "I want this to be a complete profile. The real Zainab Mir."

"Wouldn't you rather write something about Eleanor? Maybe her latest declaration that we should tax overweight people because they take up more space?"

"Or that women should sell their bodies to the highest bidder?"

Zainab eyed the door. She could be on the street in less than thirty seconds. In a cab, if timed properly, in under a minute.

Darby smiled. "I think we're getting off on the wrong foot here.

I'm not a gotcha type of reporter. But you are a fascinating player in the political scene."

"I don't know about that."

Darby shrugged as though it were obvious. "I think this will be great exposure for your career as well as for the campaign."

Zainab was saved from responding by the waiter's appearance. When Zainab ordered the white truffle pizza, Darby said she'd have the same. A small détente.

As they talked, Zainab tried to turn the conversation back to Eleanor. When Darby asked about her fastest mile time, Zainab mentioned Eleanor's commitment to preventative medicine, and when she asked about Zainab's vacation in Indonesia three years earlier, when she'd actually had time for a vacation, she pointed out that Eleanor was well-traveled and had a firm grasp on international affairs.

After their food arrived, Darby took a bite and cocked her head. "She didn't really say that about overweight people."

Zainab laughed. "No, she didn't really say that."

"You know," Darby said, "you're more charming than some people may have indicated."

"I'm not sure if that's a compliment."

"It's meant to be." Darby smiled. "It can't surprise you that others might be jealous of you. Or that there might be catty people in politics."

"Catty, yes. Jealous, not so much."

"You don't have to be humble on my account."

Zainab adjusted her napkin. She wasn't sure where this was going.

"So there's the whole jealousy thing," Darby continued, "and then there is the fiercely loyal-to-the-death vibe I encountered."

"Amra."

"Your best friend. Yes, her, and also people at your office. Even someone from the Harshbarger campaign."

Zainab had volunteered for Scott Harshbarger's gubernatorial campaign when she was in college. "Who *didn't* you talk to?"

"I told you, I'm thorough."

"Right. But it's not like I'm Mary Matalin."

"Of course not," Darby said. "You're far more interesting."

"Mary Matalin is pretty interesting."

"In her own way, yes. Mostly because of her marriage," Darby said dismissively. "To be perfectly frank, politics isn't known for an abundance of attractive men and women. You're familiar with *The Hill*'s most beautiful people list? After the first few, it's all kind of a stretch." Darby took a sip of her wine. "Now couple your looks with your background—if I may be blunt here, your religious and ethnic background—and let's just say that's what made my editor say yes to this story."

Zainab forced a smile. A high-profile piece making a big deal out of her religion wasn't going to be helpful in certain Republican circles.

Darby changed the subject. "So why Eleanor? I know you had other offers."

"Yes. I had other offers." Zainab nodded. "But none like Eleanor. Does she say provocative things? Yes. Absolutely. But she *means* those things. Eleanor knows exactly who she is and what she believes. And she's completely unafraid to put it out there. Do you know how rare that is in this business? Part of why she can get away with it, of course, is because she's brilliant. But part of it is that she just genuinely doesn't care what you think of her." Zainab waved her hand. " 'You' as in collectively, of course."

"Of course." Darby frowned slightly.

Zainab continued. "When I graduated from college, the commencement speaker said she hoped we'd take part of Smith with us. And I actually cried, because I thought, how could we not? And in case none of the thousands of people you interviewed mentioned it, I never cry. But even though she didn't go to Smith—didn't even go to a women's college, for God's sake—Eleanor has more Smith in her than most of the people I graduated with. She probably has more in her than I do."

Darby shook her head. "I doubt that."

Zainab took a breath and realized that she had just bared her soul to a reporter from *The New York Times*. And essentially called her boss eccentric. She was about to ask if it was too late for her little diatribe to be off the record when she noticed Darby flagging down the waiter.

"Is everything okay?"

Darby nodded. "Yes. Absolutely. I know this is terribly unprofessional of me, but I just remembered a call I have to be on."

When the waiter reached their table, Darby pushed her credit card at him without looking at the bill. Zainab asked if it was something she'd said.

"Not at all." Darby paused. "Look, I'll follow up by e-mail if I need anything else, okay? It was great to meet you. I'll be in touch."

Zainab watched in the oversized mirror on the far wall as Darby crossed the restaurant to the copper bar and tapped the waiter on the shoulder. She signed the receipt and rushed out of the restaurant without looking back.

In the cab on the way to her office, Zainab considered warning Eleanor that the article might not be as favorable as they'd hoped. But what could she say? That she'd admitted Eleanor said outrageous things and Darby bolted? She focused on what Eleanor had said earlier: As long as they were talking about Zainab, they were talking about the campaign and Eleanor's candidacy.

At the office, Ben informed her that Eleanor had finally been in touch. "She was just making a point about prostitution. Apparently, she'd said it in passing to some *Boston Herald* reporter at the airport."

"Right," said Zainab. "And what was the point she was trying to make?"

"She didn't say. She just sort of laughed it off." Ben patted Zainab's arm. "So good luck with that. But, in the spirit of balance, Jim's speech is on your desk. He delivered the hard copy himself."

Zainab spent two hours reworking Jim's speech. He still couldn't step into Eleanor's head or capture her voice. His speeches read as though he were channeling John McCain. Eleanor would never say "my friends." Or quote Ronald Reagan. When Zainab was working on the closing, her phone vibrated. It was an e-mail from Darby:

> Sorry for leaving so quickly. Let me make it up to you. I have tickets to the Correspondents' Dinner in Washington in April, and would love to bring you as my guest. I'll send a copy of the article soon. Best, Darby

Zainab smiled. She had, apparently, not offended Darby or done any harm to the campaign. Plus, she'd just scored a ticket to the most coveted political event of the year.

"Ben!"

He appeared in the door with a PETA mug in one hand and his BlackBerry in the other. "Yes?"

"Guess who's going to the White House Correspondents' Dinner."

"You and your favorite assistant?"

"Ha," she said. "You wish."

He gave a conceding shrug. "But how?"

"My new BFF, Darby Tate."

"You must have made quite an impression."

"It would seem," Zainab said. "See if you can get me on the latest possible shuttle that Saturday and try for a reservation at the Willard or the Hay-Adams. Work your magic."

"I'll get the wand."

"Oh, and Ben?"

"Yes?"

"Celtics-Lakers tickets if you find out where I can get a pair of those boots."

3

It was after midnight and Amra still had to pack. In the end, she'd agreed to an overnight trip to Manhattan, long enough to have dinner with the Syeds and pacify her mother, short enough to bookend with Saturday-morning and Sunday-night hours at the office. She plopped the suitcase on her bed and noticed how lately a feeling of loneliness had seeped into her state of being alone. The new feeling had coincided with Rukan's announcement. It wasn't just concern, although Amra *was* worried about Rukan and how her family would react. Her parents had been fielding proposals for years, all from FOB men who knew nothing of how sweet Rukan was, how she'd scouted *halal* chicken soup for Amra and Zainab whenever they were sick at Smith or placed gifts outside of their doors before exams—mugs of hot chocolate, neon-colored stress balls, cookies from La Fiorentina's. Ignorant as they may have been about Rukan's loving nature, her suitors knew much, Amra was sure, about her father's medical-supply empire. It didn't help that Rukan's *phupi,* her father's sister, always told Rukan how lucky she was to have a well-connected father to facilitate such offers. "What she means," Rukan wailed the night she met the obese engineering student with the pockmarked cheeks, the one who asked repeatedly about her *biryani* and whether the meat always stayed on the bone, "is that for someone like me, my father's money is my charm." Amra and Zainab told her that she was being ridiculous, that she had everything going for her. "I'm sweet and funny," Rukan conceded, "but they all want someone who looks like the two of you."

As other, less altruistic feelings associated with Rukan's wedding surfaced, Amra placed a long black skirt and white blouse in her suitcase and reminded herself that she had a plan. Her parents had been adamant about her completing her education before she got married. Once Amra started working, her mother had asked circumspectly if Amra wanted help meeting a potential spouse. The aunties were in full swing by then, complaining that her parents had waited too long, but Amra didn't have time to meet anyone and figured that wouldn't change until she made partner. Now, with Amra nearly thirty years old, the aunties had given up. Besides, what *desi* man was going to put up with a wife who routinely came home after midnight and hit the gym before dawn?

Her packing completed, Amra stacked the pillows on the bench at the end of her bed and folded down the white duvet cover. She secured her hair in a high ponytail and tried to read an asset purchase agreement, but as she stared at the seller's representations and warranties her eyes refused to focus. She leaned back and looked at the other side of the bed. The only man who had ever slept next to her was Will, and, in a show of respect, he'd worn all of his clothes and stayed on top of the covers. She'd met him at Columbia, drawn to his sheepish smile and tousled hair, and the self-deprecating way he acted like he wasn't completely brilliant. His name turned up in the alumni bulletins from time to time, and in the last one Amra had read that he and his wife were expecting twins. She felt a mix of happiness and the tiniest pocket of regret. Will had said he was willing to convert for her, if it would make things easier with her family. He'd even gone to a mosque in Brooklyn once but found it fully segregated, filled with solemn, long-bearded men, complete with a lengthy sermon delivered in Arabic. Afterward, he looked unsettled. Amra pressed him until he admitted it was different from the books he'd read. She'd given him Feisal Abdul Rauf's *What's Right with Islam* and Reza Aslan's *No god but God,* only to realize she'd been stacking the deck. When she asked him if he'd still convert if they broke up, he didn't answer. And when they finally went their separate ways a week before the bar exam, their nerves shot, their patience strained, she wasn't surprised to find that the sadness in his eyes was also mixed with relief.

Amra gave up on the merger document. She told herself that she could sleep on either side of the bed, that it was all hers, but when she turned off the light and closed her eyes she didn't move so much as a limb past the middle of the mattress.

"*Beti,* I have some new saris for you to look at," her mother said. "Perhaps you'll want to wear one tonight."

Amra had taken the three o'clock shuttle to New York, and as she sat at the oversized island sipping her tea and watching her mother rinse the cilantro to make chutney, she felt a rush of gratitude for her mother's persistence. She always loved being in the kitchen while her mother fussed about, marinating meats, browning onions, and she realized she was glad to be in the only place that felt like home.

"I'll look in a minute," Amra said. "Are you sure there's nothing I can do to help?"

"*Nahin.* It's all been done. Now hurry with your tea and go pick an outfit."

Amra stared at the saris. There must have been a dozen of them covering her old bed, a brilliant rainbow of turquoise and pink and even a deep maroon one that looked so much like a bridal outfit with its extensive gold *zardosi* work that Amra eliminated it immediately.

In fact, they were all a bit on the formal side. She finally settled on the royal blue one with the simple beadwork. Her mother had arranged bangles and a matching necklace on the dresser. She dressed quickly, wrapping herself in the sari, twisting her hair into a bun. Finally, with a lipstick borrowed from her mother, Amra painted on a ridiculously bright shade of red, the kind of color she would never wear to work.

Dr. and Mrs. Syed arrived promptly at seven. Mrs. Syed hugged Amra, clasping her tightly to her chest, where Amra was forced to breathe in her heavy floral scent. After a quick tour of the apartment, Amra's father and Dr. Syed retreated to the balcony while the women perched in their formal clothes on the living room couches.

"Huma," Mrs. Syed said to Amra's mother, "your Amra has grown into such a beautiful young woman, *masha'Allah*." She looked at Amra. "Your hair is like silk. Do you straighten it with one of those irons? No? Well, lucky you. Maha would kill for such smooth hair. And those eyes, as wide as Medjool dates, and that perfect nose! From the profile you cannot even notice it, I sneaked a look, is it wrong to admit that? I suppose it is. But you know how some of them just pop off the face and it's all you can see. And that complexion, Amra. You are like a porcelain doll." Mrs. Syed smiled while Amra felt like a cow at auction.

"And so smart, too," Mrs. Syed continued. "Your mother has filled me in. It is no small thing to make law review at a school like Columbia. No, it's not Harvard, or Yale, or if my *U.S. News and World Report* research is correct, not really Chicago or Stanford either—" She laughed. "But it is very solid, Amra. Very solid indeed." Mrs. Syed took a sip of her tea. She turned back to Amra's mother. "Huma, you must be overwhelmed with proposals for this one. From here and back home."

While her mother smiled what Amra considered to be a very generous smile, Amra tried to change the subject. "*Ammi* tells me you're in Florida now. How do you like it?"

"We miss certain amenities of New York, of course," Mrs. Syed said. "But you cannot beat the weather."

Amra nodded. "And what's Maha doing now?"

"Oh, you know Maha, always the overachiever. The easy path was not for her, no, not in any of it. She's at the London School of Economics. She graduated *summa cum laude* from Georgetown with a degree in international relations. I wouldn't be surprised if she is an ambassador someday." Mrs. Syed set her tea down. "She really would have loved to have seen you."

"Would have loved to—but isn't she joining us?" Amra had assumed she was arriving separately. She looked at her mother. Wasn't Maha the reason she was in New York at this very moment instead of in her office marking up merger documents? Her mother did not meet her glance.

"Maha? Oh my, no! She's in London, dear. Didn't I just say that? She sends her *salaams,* of course." Mrs. Syed slid the face of her gold watch to the top of her wrist. "But Mateen should be here any minute. He had to make a call from the hotel, but he promised it wouldn't be more than one half hour."

Amra's face burned. Mateen, as in Maha's brother. The good-looking older sibling who never gave them the time of day. Most of the girls they'd grown up with had crushes on Mateen at one time or another. Maha often teased them about it, saying that her brother was too good for any of them.

And here Amra was, at her parents' home, dressed in a fairly elaborate sari and wearing red lipstick, ready to be displayed for proposal-snaring purposes. It was beyond mortifying. Her mother was not normally so conniving, and yet there had been the full-court press to get Amra to New York for this dinner, and the roomful of traditional outfits, and the carefully selected jewelry. Amra was sure of only one thing: She needed to change her clothes, no matter how odd it would appear to Dr. and Mrs. Syed, before Mateen arrived.

As she was plotting the retreat to her bedroom, the doorbell rang. Amra closed her eyes. *Of course.*

Her mother answered the door and led Mateen into the living room, where Amra and Mrs. Syed sat, and where the two fathers suddenly reappeared. Amra stood to offer her *salaams* and willed her face not to redden. *It's just an outfit,* she told herself. *He's used to women dressing traditionally.* Mateen, of course, was wearing western clothes, a white button-down shirt and navy blazer. And jeans. He was taller than Amra remembered. And more serious, somehow, as though he were an adult and she were still a nervous child. When Mrs. Syed said, "And you must remember their daughter, Amra?" his gaze took in her outfit and his mouth turned up in a small smile.

"Of course I remember. You used to play with my sister, right?"

Before Amra could answer, Dr. Syed cleared his throat. "Your call was okay, I trust?"

Mateen nodded. "More than okay. I think we're ready to close the deal."

Dr. Syed did not smile at his son's apparent good news, or comment on it. Instead, he just adjusted the cuffs of his shirt, looking every bit as imposing as Amra remembered from when they were kids. If his father's reaction bothered him, Mateen didn't let on.

"Huma Auntie, Parvez Uncle," Mateen said, "your place is amazing. A little different than Ninety-first Street." Her parents laughed appreciatively at the reference to their first apartment, where they'd lived when her father was still in medical school. It was a one-bedroom, small enough that Amra had slept first in a crib at the foot of her parents' bed and later on the sofa in the living room. They'd lived there until they could pay cash for a larger place.

"Amra," her mother said, gesturing at the balcony, "why don't you show Mateen the view?"

Amra was mortified by the suggestion. Was wearing a sari not obvious enough?

Her father chimed in. "Yes, *beti*. Go on," he said, and then turned to Mateen. "It's a bit different than our view on Ninety-first Street, too. Have a look. I think you'll like it."

With her father apparently in on the conspiracy, Amra had no choice but to lead Mateen to the balcony under the unwavering gaze of four seemingly satisfied parents. She opened the door and stepped into the cool night air.

"Your father was right," he said. "The view is incredible. I didn't realize you were so close to the park."

She nodded. "If you walk three blocks you come out near the zoo."

"Do they still have the polar bear exhibit?"

Amra had no idea. She hadn't been there in years. "Probably."

He nodded. "So, you're all . . . grown up, I guess." He laughed. "I remember you as this quiet kid hanging out with my sister. And that other friend of yours. What was her name?"

"Zainab."

"Right, Zainab. The two of you were inseparable. My friends thought she was your sister." He looked out over the city lights. "And you're working in Boston now?"

"Yes."

"As a lawyer?"

"Yes," she said. "I don't think my mother told me what you do?"

"Venture capital." He waved his hand dismissively. "What kind of law do you practice?"

"Corporate. Mostly M and A."

He raised his eyebrows. "Impressive."

"What did you think I was going to say? Family law?"

"I guess I deserve that." He smiled and then bit his lip. "But you know, now I have to ask what you really want."

Besides you, she thought, and then shook her head to push the thought away. The sari was clearly getting to her. "I'm sorry?"

"Every lawyer I know secretly wants to be a writer or an artist or a teacher. You know, something else. I'm wondering what your something else is."

Amra paused. "I want to be managing partner of my firm."

He nodded, and she watched his eyes wander slowly from her hair to her eyes, to her lips, and back up again. When he spoke, his voice was low and penetrating. "So, Amra Abbas. Do you always come to New York when your parents host old family friends?"

"I do sometimes. I mean no, not usually." She realized she was stammering. And possibly blushing. "*Ammi* said that Maha was coming."

"Ah, Maha." He took a step back. "And here I thought you came to see me." His eyes locked on hers playfully. She searched for the right thing to say, but was saved by her mother calling them inside for dinner.

Her mother was a talented cook, everyone always said so, but as Amra ate the lamb *vindaloo* and the chicken *korma,* she tasted nothing, not a speck of coriander, not a pinch of red pepper. She may as well have been eating soda crackers. Mateen spoke mostly with her father and his, discussing the bursting of the housing bubble and the tightening of the credit market. He had not addressed Amra directly since she'd said she'd come to New York to see his sister. She hoped there would be plans the next day, perhaps brunch at the Syeds' hotel, but when her father asked about Mateen's schedule, he said he had a 9:00 A.M. flight to Dubai.

At the door, as the Syeds were leaving, Mateen's look lingered on Amra, but all he said was that it was good to see her again after so long. When she helped with the dishes, Amra was sure her mother would say something about the evening—apologize for bringing Amra under false pretenses, perhaps ask if it would be okay to pass along her phone number. But her mother went to bed without saying a word about any of it. It was possible, Amra was forced to consider, that there had been no plot at all and that her mother had been just as surprised as Amra to see Mateen walk in the door. Somehow, the absence of a scenario that had only hours earlier made her blood boil now filled her with a nagging sense of disappointment.

On the flight home Amra told herself to snap out of it. Nothing had changed. She was still two years away from making partner. She would still head straight from the airport to the office, still get home after midnight and get up before dawn. There was no time for Mateen Syed, even if he'd wanted her to make time for him, and there was no indication that he did. Still, when she stared out the window all she could think of was the deep brown of his eyes, the way he looked when he studied her face, the sound of his voice in the cool night air.

At her office, Amra spent an hour dealing with her e-mail and then headed to the sixth floor to see if Hayden wanted anything from Pho's Asian. Hayden, a fellow fourth-year associate, was knee-deep in a restructuring deal about to fall apart and was putting in preposterous hours as well.

Amra found Hayden at her desk, her chair turned halfway toward her window, staring at the patchwork of lit offices across the street. No one wore business attire into the office on the weekends, but she was surprised to find Hayden in a sleeveless sequined top.

"Hayden?"

Hayden turned, revealing black smudges under her lower lashes. "God, Amra. You scared me."

"Sorry. I just wanted to see if you wanted to order Chinese."

Hayden shook her head.

"Are you okay?"

"Sure."

Amra hesitated. Hayden did not look okay, but delving into her latest heartbreak was likely to cost Amra at least thirty minutes of work, probably more. She hedged her bets by remaining in the doorway while asking if Hayden was sure nothing was wrong.

"Well, other than the fact that I was just stood up, yeah. I'm fine." She shrugged. "You know how it goes."

Amra did not. Nor did she particularly want the details, which previously had included descriptions of a man who drew on Hayden's stomach and thighs with a Sharpie marker to indicate her "problem areas" and one who, after sleeping with her, tried to fix her up with his old fraternity brother. Amra used to share the stories with Zainab until she realized Zainab was enjoying them a little too much. By the time Amra became more circumspect about Hayden's difficulties, Zainab was already referring to her as "the doormat."

Amra discreetly looked at her watch. "I'm sorry, Hayden. But you have to remember that it's his loss." Amra realized she didn't even know to which "he" she referred. She walked over and gave Hayden a quick hug. "I need to get some work done," she said, "but come get me if you want to talk, okay?" Hayden nodded, and with a mixture of relief and guilt, Amra returned to her office.

Twenty minutes later, when Amra paid the delivery man, her phone vibrated with a text from a 310 area code. She clicked on it and nearly dropped her *ma po* tofu. It was Mateen, saying that he was stuck at Heathrow, that his connecting flight had been delayed. She smiled. And thought of her tight-lipped mother, who had clearly given Mrs. Syed her number after all. Amra put the food down and leaned against the lobby wall. She replied that she was sorry about his flight and that it was nice to hear from him. There was a delay and she wondered if he'd had to board his flight. She took the elevator back to her floor, holding her phone gingerly. As she reached her office, he responded.

So I was wondering . . . would I have to bring Maha if I wanted to visit you in Boston?

Amra read his text three times and then asked if it was a hypothetical question.

You first, Counselor.

She held her breath, and then typed *no.*

No, you won't answer first?

No, you wouldn't have to bring Maha.

Good answer.

Amra smiled. *Your turn.*

Unfortunately.

Unfortunately it's your turn?

Unfortunately, it's a hypothetical question.

Oh.

What would you say if I told you I'm working on it?

I'd say good answer.

Then I'm working on it. Sweet dreams, Amra.

He assumed she was at home. Of course. Who wouldn't be at home at 10:30 on a Sunday night? The urge to be in her bed, not to text him but to have him call, to hear his voice, overwhelmed her. She let her mind go a little further before stopping. The thought of actually being with Mateen made her dizzy. She typed *you too* and then picked up the "Agreement and Plan of Merger by and among Bank Corp and Sector Financial Services Corporation" and started to read.

4

HAYDEN WAS TIRED. And not just because of the fourth martini or the seven-day workweek. It was a deeper exhaustion, as though the air around her had thickened, and even the slightest movement took a grudging effort.

And so when David sat across from her at City Bar and, within easy earshot of the power couple next to them—the woman with her Christian Louboutin handbag and the man with some sort of 379 Club manicure, the couple who by most definitions of space and seating were at the *same* table as they were—said that he thought they should take a break, that it had nothing to do with Hayden, it was just where David *was at* with it all, she just stared. And did a little inventory. She had already overlooked the delightful collection of magazines he displayed with no apparent shame on the coffee table of his Somerville apartment and the fact that he routinely had "lunch" with his ex-girlfriend, a redheaded administrative assistant with cat eyes and a surgically enhanced chest. Yes, David was good-looking. He knew the right places to go and looked like he belonged in them. He could even, she had to admit as she looked at the modern gray leather furniture and walls around them, pull off City Bar. But if she looked closely enough, she was sure his hair was as highlighted as hers—it was March in Boston, for God's sake—and once or twice she'd wondered if he'd already had plugs put in. He had a decent job, although his firm was not in the same tier as hers, nor had he gone to comparable schools: Her Northwestern trumped his Emerson and her Stanford Law blew his Hofstra out of the water. She was certain she made more money than he did. By most measures, he wasn't even in her league. And *he* wanted to take a break from *her*. Which meant that he thought he could find someone better.

"You can't, you know."

David looked confused. "Can't take a break?"

Hayden frowned. "What? Oh, sorry. No, you can take a break. *Obviously*." She laughed a choppy little laugh that even she could tell was tinged with some indication of poor mental health. "I meant that you can't find anyone better than me."

He smiled, but his eyes became sterile. "I guess we'll see."

She noticed how anorexic he looked in his white button-down shirt with his shoulders sticking through the cotton like the ends of a wire hanger. She wanted to slap his unseasonably tan face. She stood abruptly, bumping the table, sloshing their drinks. He reached out to steady her, but she yanked her arm away. "Just to clarify," she continued, "it's not that there isn't someone better than me out there, someone with better facial structure or a smaller nose"—she waved her hand—"because of course there is. What I meant is that *you,* little Hofstra Law David, with your fake tan and scrawny shoulders and apparently uncorrectable overbite, and maybe most importantly your limited earning potential, cannot find someone better. There's only so far a guy like you can go. This was your ceiling. I imagine it's quite depressing to realize that every woman you date from now will be a bit fatter than I am, or have thinner hair or big feet. Or maybe she'll carry a pleather purse and wear drugstore makeup. You know the type, right? Yes, I bet you do." Hayden smiled knowingly at David.

He recoiled as though she were diseased and shrugged at the adjacent couple as if to say, *I barely know her. She's just some chick I was trying to screw.*

Hayden held it together in the cab and through the lobby of her building. She entered her apartment without turning on the lights or removing her coat. She dropped her keys by the kitchenette and went to the farthest corner of the living room, near the window overlooking the small, snowy courtyard. It was as private as she could get. She hugged her knees and let the sobs come, jerking her body, until even the neck of her shirt was damp.

"You win," she whispered to the city and knew she would leave it all as soon as possible.

5

SIX MONTHS AFTER he'd arrived in Boston as a fellow at the Institute on Prosperity and Fairness, a nascent "new Keynesian" economic think tank, Chase Holland struck gold. In the goddamned *New York Times,* of all places. Even after reading the article about Zainab Mir a third time, he still felt the urge to high-five his producer. This sophomoric impulse triggered a smile—he still couldn't believe he *had* a producer. One week earlier, he'd been asked to sub for Ed Henrick, right-wing talk-radio giant, holder of the lead-in spot to Rush fucking Limbaugh. Henrick was embroiled in some sort of extramarital situation—the most-often-repeated rumors included the words "threesome," "underage," and "Rohypnol"—the kind of thing that didn't go over well with his conservative, pro-family audience. When Henrick announced that he would be "spending more time with his family," the station manager called Chase, and Chase accepted on the spot.

It wasn't just the money, although what they'd offered him was double what he was making at the institute. What Chase really wanted was the exposure. He'd been pursuing it, the white-hot celebrity—although at this point, he'd settle for notoriety—that would finally get his book published. It was a minarchist, somewhat scathing critique of prominent politicians who claimed to be conservatives, calling bullshit on their claims to support a limited government, written in a sort of Bill Maher, "New Rules" tone of voice. He'd penned it four years earlier while pursuing his Ph.D. in economics at Iowa. In his fourth year, he'd taken a leave, doing a stint as a staff economist at the Council of Economic Advisers, conducting statistical analyses during the day and writing at night. By the end of the year, his book was finished and so was his academic career. He found that he liked the political realm more than the academic one, that he'd rather publish a commercially viable book than serial scholarly articles about optimal policy with commitment, or recursive game theory. And if he was completely honest, the idea of fraternizing with politicos and media personalities appealed to him far more than the thought of ministering to his undergraduate students as they slogged through Real Analysis and Multivariable Calculus, asking, with cloying repetition, how to get into Harvard.

Chase dropped out of the Ph.D. program, freelanced for a bit, living essentially on credit cards, deferring his considerable student loans. Eventually, he had enough published pieces that his byline, Charles Holland III, became recognizable in certain circles and generated something of a following. He applied for and received a fellowship at Cato in 2005 and did some commentary on CNN and Fox News during the 2006 congressional races. Still, when he approached agents with his book, the response was always the same, an instruction to come back when he had reached Ann Coulter or Dick Morris status. When the opportunity came up to join a vibrant, well-funded new think tank in Boston, one that promised access to the movers and shakers in conservative circles, he'd jumped at the chance. The Henrick gig, with its large, syndicated audience, was simply Reagan-flavored icing on the cake.

By the third day in Henrick's shoes, Chase was on fire. He had to be, if he was going to make it permanent. Everyone knew Henrick wasn't coming back; the spot was Chase's to lose. Fortunately, the

Republican senatorial primary was heating up and a certain feminazi crackpot named Eleanor Winthrop-Smith, who was challenging the far more conservatively credentialed Fred Whitaker, promised to make things very easy for Chase. Besides the fact that she didn't stand a chance with her views on abortion and drug legalization, Winthrop-Smith said whatever was on her mind, no matter how outrageous or indefensible. She never apologized and rarely clarified. Chase had planned to hit that angle hard, highlighting her many gaffes, like her recent outburst glorifying prostitution, and when his producer handed him the article from the *Times* about Winthrop-Smith's communications director, Zainab Mir, Chase nearly kissed him.

With a thick yellow marker, Chase highlighted the pertinent parts of the article, written by Darby Tate, a known leftist reporter. Apparently, Zainab Mir was raised as a Muslim by her Indian father and Pakistani mother. Chase thought about that. Very likely, she still had relatives in Pakistan. Maybe a good question for Ms. Mir, which of course Darby Tate neglected to ask, would have been something about her loyalties in the war on terror. Whose side was she on, did she have sympathies for the Taliban, that kind of thing. The article concluded by stating, "If the measure of a candidate is in any way linked to the people with whom she surrounds herself, Zainab Mir is a convincing reason to support Ms. Winthrop-Smith." Chase almost laughed. Darby Tate had certainly left open the door for the reverse conclusion as well. He only had the print version, which was too bad. He would have loved to have seen a picture of this Zainab Mir. Darby Tate called her "a beacon of timeless style," which Chase assumed referred to some sort of head covering.

"Ladies and gentlemen," he began, "did you see this? Did you get a chance to look at the *New York Times* piece on Eleanor Winthrop-Smith's right-hand woman? Of course not, because it's *The New York Times,* and you probably had something better to do, like, say, inserting a fork into your ocular cavity. So let me summarize it for you. Eleanor Winthrop-Smith's communications director—the one controlling the message of the campaign and, let's face it, likely shaping some of that message—is a Pakistani Muslim." He paused to let it sink in. "Now I'm all for giving people the benefit of the doubt. But excuse me. Are we not at war? Are we not fighting against Islamofascists? I'm pretty sure that we are. And I'm pretty sure that Fred Whitaker is. But let me tell you who apparently is not: Eleanor Winthrop-Smith. So give me a call, Boston, and let me know what you think about *that*."

Chase left the studio flying. The response had been incredible, and, surprisingly, the female callers were the most jacked up of all. If Eleanor Winthrop-Smith was hoping to capitalize on some sort of crossover women's vote, she'd better think again.

In his car, he checked his messages. The first was from Savannah, something about her flight being delayed. He paid little attention; he wasn't meeting her at the airport, and she had a key to his condo. His desire to see her lately was inversely proportionate to the number of times she would mention getting engaged. It wasn't all Savannah's fault. He knew her parents had been pressuring her since she'd graduated from GW Law a year ago. He and Savannah had been dating for two years, and her parents, who had welcomed him with eager arms in the beginning, were starting to look at him with obvious irritation. Things came to a head when Chase accepted the position in Boston. Savannah was putting in long hours at her firm, hours suited to a partnership track that, she'd made clear, she did not want to be on, and she was looking for some indication that Chase intended to settle down, buy a four-bedroom home in Arlington, and have the children that would give her a respectable reason to quit her job. When he'd announced the position at the institute, even her parents had grown alarmed. They were evangelicals from Charleston, willing to look the other way when he and Savannah took trips together or when he was present at her apartment at suspicious hours, only because they were sure a ring was forthcoming. It had taken two weeks of "talking about it" and a phone call to her father, during which Chase emphasized the limited duration of his appointment, to calm everyone down.

The next voice mail garnered Chase's complete attention. It was from Fred Whitaker, Eleanor Winthrop-Smith's Republican primary opponent. "Great show today, Charles. Appreciate your support. Would love to meet you sometime. We're looking for some capable economic advisors on the campaign. I'll be in touch." It would have been slightly more exciting if he'd left a return number, but Chase wasn't going to complain. A week earlier he'd been plugging away at an article on VAT. Now, he had the ear of thousands of listeners and an in with the Whitaker campaign. For the briefest of smart-ass moments, he considered sending Zainab Mir a bouquet of flowers.

6

AMRA HAD KEPT exactly three secrets from Zainab in her life. First, when they were eleven and Zainab thought her parents were divorcing, Amra said she thought it would be fun, pointing out that Zainab would get two sets of presents for every Eid and birthday. The truth was that Amra couldn't imagine anything worse. Of course, in retrospect, a divorce would have been a blessing.

Second, she never told Zainab about getting into Dartmouth or Brown or Williams. Zainab had applied to one school: Smith College. There was no backup plan, no shoot-for-the-stars dream school, only Smith. Zainab had made up her mind by the time they were fourteen and would not be sidetracked with frivolous talk of "Ivy League" this or "Wellesley is ranked higher" that. In the end, Amra chose Smith because Zainab chose Smith. Her parents reconciled themselves to her decision for their own reasons: Her mother had a feminist spirit the size of the Hindu Kush teeming inside of her, and her father knew what teemed inside of college boys, figuring Smith was as good a bulwark as any. Plus, her parents adored Zainab and considered her their second daughter.

The third and final secret was Mateen, that Amra had seen him in New York, that he had texted her. She was not ready to tell anyone, not her mother, not even Zainab. It still had about it the sense of something floating, like a bubble, and she was afraid saying it out loud would cause it all to disappear. Plus, she hadn't heard from him since his text from the airport.

So when she met Zainab for a run at the Common early Friday morning and Zainab asked how the trip to her parents' had gone, how "that little witch, Maha" was, Amra told her the truth, that Maha hadn't come, but left it at that. Fortunately, Zainab didn't seem to remember Mateen, or at least didn't ask about him.

"I have some news," Zainab said as they stretched.

"Oh, *God*."

"Oh, God?" Zainab laughed. "Why, 'Oh, God'?"

"Because, as you well know, the last time someone had news, it was Rukan." Amra sat down, extended her legs, and grabbed the toes of her shoes.

Zainab nodded. "Right. But this is actual good news, not horridly bad news masquerading as good news."

"Is that what Rukan's engagement is?"

"Yes. Probably. You know, since he's most likely a total prick."

"Zainab."

"What? How many American guys do you know who are in such a rush to get married?"

Amra didn't want to think about that. "Fine. But what's with all the name calling?" she said. "It's not even six in the morning."

"Sorry to offend your delicate sensibilities. I didn't know you were so protective of Maha and Adam."

"I'm not. I just think you're being a little harsh."

Zainab nodded. "It's probably all of the right-wing talk radio I've been listening to."

"The *what*?"

"You know, Rush Limbaugh kind of stuff," Zainab said. "I'm doing recon. Some local punk has decided to make me a campaign issue. It's actually quite riveting."

"I don't even know what to say."

Zainab shrugged. "Ready?" Amra nodded, and let Zainab set the pace. "Maybe I am being harsh," Zainab finally said as they turned onto Tremont Street, "but you tell me what the chances are that Mr. *Kafir*-face there isn't after Rukan's trust fund just like all the home-boys ready to hightail it over here on the next PIA flight."

Amra didn't like the chances. "Okay, this conversation is depressing me. Didn't you say you have some news?"

"I did," Zainab said. "I'm going to be in *Vanity Fair*."

Amra stopped running. "Are you kidding?"

Zainab circled back. "I'm not."

"But how? Why?"

"I'm going to assume you don't mean that to sound as insulting as it does," Zainab said. "They called a few days ago. After the piece in the *Times*. And here's the best part: There's going to be a photo spread. I get to wear Vera Wang."

"I love Vera Wang."

Zainab nodded sympathetically. "I know."

"Will you be upset if I'm insanely jealous?"

"Not at all."

"Good." They started to run again. As they passed Park Street Church and the Granary Burying Ground, Amra felt unsettled, as though Zainab were moving away somehow. She shook her head. She was being ridiculous. It was just a magazine. There was no reason for anything to change. They were sister friends, forever. As they turned onto School Street, Zainab picked up the pace, her long legs pushing hard. Amra dug deep and stayed with her the entire way.

Eric appeared in her doorway as Amra was getting ready to leave for the night. She was on her way to meet Hayden at the Institute of Contemporary Art for a Children's Hospital function. Hayden had taken clients, an apparently raucous bunch of bankers, all men, all married, and had made a furtive call to Amra from the ICA bathroom begging her to come, saying that one of the men was hitting on her.

"Amra, I'm glad I caught you." Eric's pale face was peppered with red blotches, a look Amra knew well. It was worse when he actually sweated. "I scheduled a conference call with the attorneys from Piper for tomorrow morning at eight. I need you on that call."

"Sure." Amra tried to sound upbeat. "No problem."

"They're sending comments sometime tonight. I told them to e-mail you directly."

She knew what that meant: She had plenty of time to go to the reception before she'd see a single comment.

"So you're on top of it? I'm counting on you." She nodded, and Eric left without thanking her.

Amra entered the museum and was surprised at the turnout. The line at the coat check was ridiculous, but she had no intention of carrying her heavy coat and her computer around with her. She sighed and got behind a woman in a black sheath dress.

"Hey," Hayden said, coming up behind her. "What took you so long?"

"Eric."

"Oh, sorry. Do you need to go?" Hayden sounded sincere. She knew all about the wrath of Eric.

"Not yet." Amra looked at her watch. "But in an hour, I turn into a pumpkin."

"Okay," Hayden said. "Until then, don't leave my side." After Amra checked her belongings, they stopped in the ladies' room, where Hayden rolled her skirt twice at the top, raising the hem a good four inches above her knees, sprayed her hair, and rattled on about the "skinny, balding old guy" pursuing her. Amra nodded as patiently as possible. When they emerged from the restroom, Hayden's clients were nowhere to be found. They got drinks from a temporary bar that had been set up along the window on the first floor—a white wine for Hayden, a sparkling water for Amra—and considered how hard to look for the clients. When two blond-haired men approached, Amra looked at Hayden and raised her eyebrows. Hayden shook her head. Not, apparently, the clients. As the men started their introductions, Amra's cell phone rang. It was her mother. "Excuse me," she said, and stepped onto the terrace.

"*Assalaamu alaikum, beti*. Where are you?" It was typical for her mother. She always needed to know where Amra was, although usually it wasn't the first thing out of her mother's mouth.

"I'm at a museum. The modern art one I took you and *Abba* to last year."

"Oh, yes. The Anish Kapoor exhibit. Simply breathtaking," her mother said. "Tell me, *beti,* what is the name of the museum again?"

"The ICA."

"That's it? It must stand for something."

"The Institute of Contemporary Art."

"Yes, that's it," her mother said. "And how long do you suppose you'll be there?"

"I'm not sure. Not too much longer. Why?"

"Just an estimate, Amra," her mother said. "Do you think you'll be there at least thirty minutes?"

Amra rubbed her forehead. "*Ammi,* I'm at a reception. Is there something you need?"

"*Nahin, beti*. I was just checking in. *Khuda Hafiz*."

Hayden was not where Amra had left her, so she made a sweep of the perimeter, weaving through the crowd. She tried Hayden's cell unsuccessfully. Fine, Amra thought. One trip through the museum. If she couldn't locate Hayden, she was going home. On the second floor, she walked through rooms housing various installations—rows of identical beds with foam mattresses depressed where bodies might have been; a collection of pantry items comprised of cracker boxes, Jell-O packets, and jars of nuts; some typed pages hanging by black clips—and understood none of it. She'd brought Zainab along with her parents the year before and watched the three of them gush over metal sheets intersecting large spherical shapes or chains of silver bangles hanging from the ceiling. Her parents nodded while Zainab spoke of "universal themes of absence" and "the crushing weight of patriarchy," but Amra could only shake her head. "It's because you never bothered with art history at Smith," Zainab had said, pityingly, and reminded her of the Sean Kelly Gallery in New York, when it was still on Mercer Street, where they'd gone to see Marina Abramović's *Luminosity*. "It was a naked woman," Amra said. "On a bicycle seat. How is that art?"

Amra came to the back of the museum, near the floor-to-ceiling windows overlooking the harbor, and spotted Hayden. She was sitting on a couch kissing one of the two blond men who'd approached them earlier. The other man appeared at Amra's side and asked if he could get her a drink. His breath smelled like beer, sour and assaultive.

Amra backed up. "No thanks. Hayden?"

Hayden looked up and wiped the corners of her mouth with her thumb and middle finger. "Sorry. I didn't know you were back."

"Back" isn't really accurate, Amra wanted to say, *since I did not leave you in this corner making out with some guy you barely know.*

"Hayden, I need to get going. I have that early conference call?" She paused. "I think you should come with me."

Hayden nodded. "I think I'll stay for a while."

"Are you sure?"

"Yep. I'll talk to you later."

Amra leaned down to hug Hayden. "Call me when you get home, okay?"

Hayden laughed. "Okay, Mom."

. . .

Amra collected her coat and bag and exited out the back of the museum, walking along the boardwalk to the parking lot, where she hoped to find a queue of cabs. The wind had picked up, but she didn't mind. It felt redemptive, capable of wiping away unwelcome images: Eric giving flushed, unreasonable orders, Hayden kissing a stranger with dubious motives. In the distance, she noticed a man in faded jeans and a sweater, his shirttails sticking out, his hands in his pockets, leaning against the railing staring at her. She pulled her bag tighter and veered closer to the building, which was well lit and reassuringly populated.

"Amra?"

She stopped and looked. "Mateen?" She tried to control her smile. "What are you doing here?"

"I told you I'd work on visiting."

"I know but I assumed—"

"That I'd give you some notice?" He laughed. "Sorry about that. I'm just here on a layover. My flight to L.A. leaves first thing tomorrow. I made the change in Munich, and called my mother, who called your mother."

"I just spoke to her."

Mateen looked sheepish. "I hope you don't mind."

Amra wondered if he was insane. "I don't mind."

"Good," he said. "I thought maybe we could go somewhere to talk."

The cab dropped them near Faneuil Hall. Mateen said he'd only seen it on TV, when John Kerry delivered his presidential concession speech. They walked through Quincy Market, pushed together by the crowds, an amalgam of students in Abercrombie gear and tourists in Red Sox paraphernalia standing in line for food. When the crowd closed in on them, Amra walked ahead. It was possible that she felt Mateen's hand resting lightly on the small of her back, but with her coat she couldn't be sure. She pushed thoughts of Eric out of her head. She did not care that she would be up literally all night to prepare for the conference call.

They crossed to Long Wharf and headed down the pier, past the whale-watching boats and the aquarium. Mateen told her about his time at Kellogg and how he'd joined his start-up straight out of business school. She was afraid she asked too many questions, but she was suddenly ravenous for information about him. He asked her questions, too, about law school and her job, and laughed when she did an impersonation of Eric. She didn't tell him about the conference call. There was no reason to telegraph that she was a workaholic. Not yet.

At the end of the pier, next to the million-dollar yachts, they were quiet, but Amra was surprised at how comfortable it felt, how there was no awkward attempt to fill the silent, salty air. After a bit, she made a futile effort to tuck her blowing hair behind her ears and turned to Mateen. He was staring at her, and didn't pretend not to be. What she saw in his eyes, she wanted to keep.

It was nearly one o'clock when Mateen said he should get to his hotel. He hailed a cab and asked the driver to wait while he walked her to her door.

"Thanks for this. For spending some time with me," he said, smiling. "You know, on such short notice."

"Thanks for coming." His face was so close to Amra's that she could see the flecks of gold in his brown eyes, the careful arch of his brows, a small scar below his left eye.

"This is hard for me," he said.

"What is?"

"To know how to think of you."

"I don't know what you mean."

"Don't you?" He searched her eyes. "I'm trying to figure out if you're the girl from the community my mother is pushing for, or the impossibly beautiful woman I just spent the last few hours with." She knew what he was asking. But she was torn between the two as well, and so she didn't move, didn't erase any of the small space between their lips, but didn't expand it either.

"I should go," he said, and swallowed. For a moment, he didn't pull back. But then he said, "I'll call you from L.A." and rushed toward the cab.

7

ZAINAB AGREED TO meet Darby in the lobby of the Mayflower Hotel. She'd caught a later shuttle than she'd intended and found herself ironing her red *lengha* with one hand and taking notes during her last-minute call with Eleanor with the other. The skirt was speckled with gold beadwork, the shirt was tight and, if she moved at all, exposed some of her stomach. She conceded it was something of a risk. When she'd told Amra what she was wearing, Amra asked if she was sure it was the right thing to wear to the Correspondents' Dinner.

"Because it's revealing?"

"No. Well, maybe. I mean, it is practically a camisole. And so *red*. Isn't this dinner a little more . . . conservative?" Amra said the last part with her nose wrinkled.

"Don't you ever watch the news? Ludacris has gone. More than once."

"Right," Amra said, "but I bet he didn't wear *desi* clothes. You could wear a little black dress and still look like a woman of the night."

Zainab laughed. "A woman of the night? What are you, seventy?"

"I'm just not sure that Eleanor wants you to play up your ethnicity."

"Eleanor is not Eric," Zainab said, which had ended their conversation a bit more abruptly than she'd intended.

Still, as Zainab juggled a searing-hot iron and a cell phone, she wished Amra were there. They got to spend so little time together lately, between the campaign and the tyranny that was Eric. Zainab looked at her watch, put Eleanor on speakerphone, and got dressed. She slipped on a dozen gold bangles and a pair of gold earrings that dangled almost to her shoulders. By the time Eleanor let her go, she'd already applied fire-red lipstick and lined her eyes with kohl. She grabbed her clutch and headed to the lobby.

Darby stood in front of the concierge in a sleek black pantsuit, her hair pulled into a clip at the back of her neck. She wore pearl earrings and a matching choker. She was tapping on her BlackBerry as Zainab approached.

"Darby. Sorry I'm late."

Darby looked up. "Wow."

"Too much?"

"Absolutely not." Darby shook her head. "But I think I'm going to need a drink."

The dinner was a blur of red-carpet frenzy, tame Rich Little jokes, carnivore-friendly food, and the pretense of not being completely starstruck. Darby introduced her to Rachel Maddow from MSNBC and a bunch of *New York Times* reporters. Amy Poehler sat two tables away, and Zainab spoke for four stunning minutes with Jane Lynch in the ladies' room. During dessert, Darby asked Zainab if she was interested in after-parties. "There's one at the Argentine embassy," she said. "It will probably be killer." She did not look thrilled at the prospect.

"But?" Zainab said.

"It's just that it will be totally frenetic. All about seeing and being seen." Darby took a long drink of her wine—if Zainab had counted correctly, it was her fifth glass—and shrugged. "That's kind of the point, though, isn't it?"

"We don't have to go anywhere," Zainab said. "I can just go back to my hotel."

Darby shook her head. "There's no way I'm letting you go home early. I'm just trying to figure out where we want to be. There are quieter parties, too. Not soporific, but a little less 'I'd cut my left arm off to get in'–ish."

Zainab laughed. "I'll defer to you. Whatever you want."

"Perfect."

By the time the limousine dropped Zainab and Darby at the Argentine embassy, the line snaked nearly to Nineteenth Street. As they waited, shuffling forward a few steps at a time toward the tented party, they munched on fried pickles and sweet potato fries passed out by the unflappable service staff. Darby's mood had soured considerably since leaving the dinner, and by the time they made it inside, amid the pulsating music and the beautiful people, she was somber, almost irritable. Zainab was losing patience. And developing a headache.

"Look," Darby said blandly. "It's Rosario Dawson."

Zainab sighed. "Darby, have I done something to upset you?"

"No. God, no. It's not you. It's me."

"I'm not sure what that means."

"It means," Darby said, "that I brought you here under false pretenses."

"What are you talking about? You invited me and I came. There weren't any pretenses." Zainab opened her clutch, hoping she'd find some aspirin.

"Yes. There were." Darby swallowed. "Zainab, have you ever looked me up online? Or asked anyone about me?"

Zainab shook her head. She felt around the bottom of her purse. A single Motrin would suffice. "I'm a little busy these days."

"Right." Darby looked around, as though she wanted to say something. "Listen—"

Zainab glanced up; she'd located two loose Tylenols, dating from God knows when. "Yes?"

"Nothing. I'm going to get going. I'll be in touch, okay?"

"Sure." She watched Darby disappear out the door and then pulled on the arm of a waiter. "Where can I get something to wash these down?"

At the bar, Zainab chased the potentially expired analgesics with cranberry juice before typing "Darby Tate" into her phone's browser. The search yielded dozens of articles with Darby's byline, a Wikipedia entry, a couple of links to Wonkette, and several to Gawker. She clicked on the Wikipedia link, but was interrupted by a man with graying hair and deep-set wrinkles leaning across what could only properly be considered her bar space to order a vodka tonic. Zainab moved, noticeably she hoped, to her left.

"Sorry, didn't mean to run you off the bar," the man said, making a show of staring at her chest. "Although I can't say I would mind running off *with* you."

Zainab glared.

"What's the matter, babe, cat got your tongue?"

Zainab shook her head. "No. I'm just wondering what it's like to be as old as you clearly are—I'm guessing, what, sixty? sixty-five?—and to still be so pathetic."

"Ah, we've got a feisty one here." The man swilled his drink. "Don't worry, I've had a couple of you South Asian girls before. That is the politically correct terminology these days, I assume? Although it cost me a few rupees an hour, if you know what I mean."

"Oh, I know what you mean," Zainab said, and leaned toward him. "Now let's see if you know what I mean. Get the fuck away from me or I'll send the recording I just made of our little conversation to every news outlet I can think of and let them figure out who you are." She gestured with her phone. The man seemed to size her up, and then backed away. A younger guy who'd been on the other side of him smiled and shook his head.

"So can anyone enter?"

"Excuse me?"

"You know," he said, "the contest for worst pickup line of the night. Although it looks like you may just have had the winning entry."

Zainab looked at him. She guessed he was close to her age, with the kind of brownish hair that probably streaked in the summer and eyes that might be considered blue or green, depending on the light. He wasn't her type at all, but she still had to admit that he was attractive, as she might say to Amra, for a white boy.

She bit her lip. "Sure, take your best shot."

"Okay, give me a second." He crossed his arms and stared at the strobe-lit ceiling. "Nothing. Obviously, I'm going to have to get back to you." He shrugged his shoulders. "Which means, of course, that I'll need your phone number."

Zainab narrowed her eyes. "You find yourself very charming, don't you?"

"That's meant to be an insult, right? That between the two of us I'm the only one who finds myself charming?"

"Interpret it however you want."

"Fair enough." He smiled. "So. Are you a reporter or a special guest?"

"Guest. And you?"

"Sort of both," he said. "Where's your host?"

Zainab waved her hand. "Gone. Abandoned me."

"Wow. And it's not even midnight. You must not be nearly as interesting as you look."

This time she laughed. "Thanks."

"Seriously, what was the emergency?"

"What makes you think there was an emergency?"

"Because there is no way someone would willingly leave a woman like you, in a dress like that, all alone." He took a sip of his drink. "Barring a death in the family or a ruptured spleen."

She didn't know what to make of him. "Actually, I'm not sure why she left."

"She?"

"Darby Tate. Do you know her?"

Before he could answer, her phone rang. She excused herself and turned away from him. "Zainab Mir."

It was Ben. "Eleanor marked up the teachers' union speech again," he said. "She needs a revised copy ASAP."

"Jim included her final edits. I signed off on it yesterday."

"I know. But she says those were her *prefinal* final edits."

"Fine, but perhaps there is a speechwriter or two on our staff—"

"She specifically told me to get you. I think she's starting to trust you more than anyone else here."

"Lucky me." Zainab rolled her eyes. "Fax or e-mail?"

"E-mail and courier," Ben corrected. "Eleanor handwrote the comments in microscopic script that only partially scanned. Frankly, I couldn't read half of the original either, which, therefore, will be at your hotel in an hour."

She hung up and turned back to the reporter-slash-guest, not sure if she even owed him an explanation. Her mind was already two steps ahead, anticipating Eleanor's changes. She knew they'd been too vague about tenure. "I have to run," she said.

"I heard."

"It was nice to meet you—" She smiled politely. "I'm sorry. I don't even know your name."

"It's Chase," he said, looking slightly dyspeptic, similar, now that she thought of it, to the way Darby looked before she made a run for it.

She shook his hand. "I'm Zainab. It was nice to meet you, Chase. Take care."

In the cab, she tried unsuccessfully to decipher the e-mailed speech revisions on her phone before remembering the Wikipedia article. "Oh my God," she said when she read it, loud enough that the driver eyed her in the rearview mirror. It all made perfect sense, and she had been an idiot.

Chase walked along Embassy Row, heading toward the Dupont Circle fountain. He needed some air before he went back to Savannah's. At first he thought he'd misheard, that she had not actually answered her phone "Zainab Mir," that he'd morphed whatever she'd said into a name he'd been repeating fairly often on his show. But then, when he'd given his nickname, she'd confirmed it: *I'm Zainab.*

He turned onto Connecticut Avenue and tried to shepherd the events of the evening into some coherent narrative. First of all, he was lucky to be at the Correspondents' Dinner. At the last minute, the radio station said Fox News was looking for younger conservatives—the word *hip* may have been used, but Chase chose to push that out of his mind—and he was given two tickets. Second, he shouldn't have been at the goddamned party. He was a nobody, by after-party standards, but then he'd met the head of the RNC at the dinner and it turned out that he'd read some of Chase's work. After a couple of drinks, while Savannah pouted, he said he could get him into any party he wanted.

Which of course led to Savannah. He was at the dinner with his *girlfriend,* for Christ's sake. His long-term, waiting-for-the-ring, home-in-the-suburbs-coveting girlfriend, who had, it turned out, genuinely believed that Chase was going to propose that night. After sitting petulantly through the dinner, they'd endured a silent ride to the Argentine embassy. She did look stunning, all southern sorority girl, and the pout only enhanced the effect. He'd seen it a million times when she didn't get what she wanted. But tonight, it bothered him. A lot. Like every single important occasion existed only to provide an opportunity to get engaged. He'd told her, not very graciously he could now see, to knock it off. She'd claimed not to know what he was talking about.

"Savannah, let me save us both some time here," he'd said. "I don't have a secret Tiffany box in my pocket. I don't have one in my suitcase. I'm not proposing tonight. What I am doing is trying to enjoy my first White House Correspondents' Dinner. It's kind of a big deal? I could have brought anyone. A celebrity. A sports figure. I could have invited Paul fucking Pierce. But I brought you. Because I thought we'd have fun." He sighed. "But we're not having fun. So here's my question. Can you put aside the whole 'when will he propose' thing, just for one night?"

Savannah told the driver to stop and that one of them was getting out of the car. Chase couldn't let her walk around the city at night, so he'd departed and, after considering for all of about thirty seconds whether to follow her home, caught a cab and headed to the Argentine embassy.

He understood everything up until that point, but he still wasn't sure why he'd flirted with Zainab. (*Mir.* He couldn't even think her first name without adding her last.) It's not like he and Savannah had broken up. He wasn't even thinking of breaking up with her. He was just trying to figure out how to delay committing the rest of his life to her.

But then he'd seen her at the bar. Zainab Mir. He'd noticed her at the dinner as well. Who could have missed her? It wasn't just the red Bollywood dress that she wore like a Hindu goddess or the flash of skin that appeared when she leaned in to kiss the cheek of whatever lucky bastard she was meeting. Or even that incredible, almost feral torrent of hair. It was something about the way she carried herself. Chase got the feeling, to borrow shamelessly from that Elton John song, that Zainab would hold herself while those around her crawled.

He'd watched as that older prick had approached her and then crashed and burned so spectacularly. He'd been pissed off on her behalf, and filled with admiration when he'd heard what she'd said to him. This was no shrinking violet. This was no southern belle waiting to be rescued. Still, he hadn't planned to talk to her, but there he was, when he played it back in his head, with the lame pickup line, hitting on Zainab Mir.

He walked the seven blocks to Savannah's and let himself in with the key she'd placed on his key ring herself. He tried to get into bed without waking her, but she sat up, amid the puffy lavender comforter and the mountain of pillows. After the perfunctory apology and requisite cuddling, Savannah settled into his embrace and fell asleep. But Chase couldn't even close his eyes. He kept replaying the scene over and over in his head: "I'm Zainab. It was nice to meet you." It would have been funny, the last part, if it had happened to someone else, if one of his buddies had shared the story over a couple of beers. But it wasn't funny. He'd felt protective of her at the bar, though she didn't seem to need it, and he was surprised to find that he felt that way still, like she needed to be protected from Charles Holland III, which of course meant from *him*. And it would not, he knew, be "nice" to meet him. It would be infuriating. The irony. The absolute fucking irony. He'd almost told Savannah. She listened to all of his shows online. She would know exactly who Zainab Mir was. The words almost escaped his mouth. He could picture it perfectly: "After you left, I met Zainab Mir." But he was afraid that that simple statement of fact would reveal everything else as well.

8

AMRA ARRIVED AT Rukan's parents' house before Zainab. They lived in Lexington in an oversized historic home that had endured several additions over the years, so that the large modern kitchen was two rooms away from the dining room and one of the bedrooms was right off of the living room. What it lacked in cohesion, it made up for in size and style. Rukan's mother, Mrs. Masood, had decorated the home in period style, purchasing the rugs and much of the solid, heavy furniture from India and the accent pieces from various New England antique stores.

"*Assalaamu alaikum,* Amra," Rukan's mother said when she answered the door. She was wearing a black *salwar kameez,* which struck Amra as unnecessarily bleak: the clothes of a mother who had imagined something different. She kissed Amra on each cheek and waved her in. "The others are in the living room."

Amra followed Mrs. Masood into the foyer and removed her shoes. She could see Rukan's father sitting in a Winchester leather chair, stiff-backed and somber, his legs crossed and arms folded, staring at the coffee table in front of him. Rukan and Adam sat silently on the couch, facing him. Rukan looked beautiful in a turquoise tunic and jeans. Her long, spiraling hair was loose and her cheeks were flushed. She gave Amra a nervous smile and smoothed the hem of her shirt. Adam had one leg over his knee, leaning his head against the back of the couch. His dark hair was cropped short and gelled up in the front. He wore a wrinkled white shirt, unbuttoned to reveal a Celtics tee shirt and a braided twine necklace. He looked like some of the fraternity boys who trawled Smith on the weekends. He had not, Amra noticed, removed his shoes.

Rukan jumped up. "Amra, this is Adam." Amra moved toward him but he did not get up.

"Hey, what's up," he said, sticking out his hand. Rukan let out a nervous laugh. Her father cleared his throat. Rukan's mother told Amra to sit, pointing at the love seat. For a time, no one spoke and then, as though there had not just been a several-minute pause after Rukan's introduction, Mrs. Masood said, "It's a good name. Adam. It's actually a Muslim name, although we pronounce it differently. With an 'ah' at the beginning. Ah-dum."

Adam stared at her. "You're kind of making me want to change it."

Mrs. Masood nodded. "We can talk about that afterward."

"So," Amra said, in a possibly foolish attempt to ease the tension, "Rukan tells me you're in real estate?"

"Yep. I work with my uncle."

"That must be nice."

Adam rubbed his chin. "Yeah, I'm sort of in the apprentice stage right now."

Amra nodded, slowly. "Great. That's wonderful. I didn't realize there were realtor apprentices." Amra hoped Rukan didn't notice the forced lilt in her voice. "So how long does that last?"

"However long it takes for me to pass the licensing exam."

"He had a cold the last time he took it," Rukan explained.

Amra pressed her lips together. She'd taken the Massachusetts bar exam the day after all four of her impacted wisdom teeth had been removed, doped up on prescription painkillers, her cheeks swollen to twice their normal size. She'd had to bite on tea bags during the lunch break to control the bleeding, and still she'd passed with flying colors. And Rukan knew it.

The doorbell rang and Mrs. Masood jumped to her feet. Amra looked at her watch. It wasn't like Zainab to be so punctual. But when Mrs. Masood returned, it wasn't with Zainab. Instead, she led a tall man in a white *kurta* pajama and a matching *kufi* and introduced him as Imam al-Fayed.

"*Assalaamu alaikum!* Rukan, what an auspicious occasion. *Mubarak!*"

Amra could not believe it. Rukan was marrying a non-Muslim and the imam was here to congratulate her? And thought it was an auspicious occasion?

Rukan did not return his smile. "*Ammi,* can I see you in the kitchen, please?" Before Mrs. Masood could respond, the bell rang again.

"That must be Zainab," Mrs. Masood said. "Amra, *beti,* can you let her in?" The imam took Rukan's mother's seat, reached in his bag, and pulled out a gold-embossed Qur'an. Amra excused herself and made a beeline for the front door.

From the foyer, Zainab took one look at the scene in the living room and shook her head. "What the hell is going on?" she whispered to Amra.

Amra raised her eyebrows and shrugged. "Nice boots," she said. Zainab held out her left foot for Amra to admire, unzipped the boots, placed them next to the wall, and followed Amra into the living room.

"*Assalaamu alaikum,*" said the imam enthusiastically. "I don't think I've met the two of you. I'm Imam al-Fayed."

Zainab looked from the imam to Rukan and back again. "*Wa alaikum Assalaam,*" she said, hesitantly. "I'm Zainab Mir. And this is Amra Abbas. We're friends of Rukan's from college."

"A pleasure to have you with us on this blessed occasion." The imam indicated that they should sit. Mrs. Masood left the room and returned with an armful of scarves. She handed one to Amra and one to Zainab.

"Oh, I'm all set," Zainab said. Mrs. Masood's eyes could have cut stone. Zainab took the scarf.

Rukan found her voice. "Why," she said, pointing at Imam al-Fayed, "is he here?"

Mr. Masood cleared his throat again, but this time he spoke. "He is here to administer the *Shahada* to Adam."

Rukan's face turned red. "He's here to do *what*?"

"Rukan," Adam said, "what is he talking about?"

"Oh my God." Rukan shook her head. "You thought you could just sneak him in here, that we would just go along with it? That Adam wouldn't *notice*?"

Adam pulled at her sleeve. "Wouldn't notice what? What are they talking about?"

"*They*," Rukan said, waving her hand at the lot of them, "think you're going to convert to Islam. Right here and now."

The imam pointed at his Qur'an. "Rukan, surely you didn't think you could marry this young man without his accepting Islam?"

"Um, hello?" Adam interrupted. "You're talking like I'm not sitting right here. First of all, I'm not converting to *anything*. And, second, since she's walking around with a good chunk of my hard-earned cash on her finger, I'm guessing that, yeah, she thinks she can marry me."

Mr. Masood rose to his feet. "Young man, you will not speak to the imam in this way and you will not speak in my home in this way." He shook his finger at Adam. "And you will not marry my daughter. I forbid it."

"You forbid it?" Adam shook his head. "She's twenty-eight."

"She's a good Muslim girl. She will obey her father."

"I wouldn't be so sure about that." Adam stood. "Come on, Rukan."

Mr. Masood took a step toward Adam. The imam put his hand on Mr. Masood's sleeve. "Brother Ali, you must remain calm."

"Yes, *brother Ali,*" Adam said. "Or wait—are we going to have an honor-killing situation on our hands here? Is that where this is headed?"

The imam looked like someone had told him his child had been injured and was unlikely to survive the night. In a soft voice, he told Adam it would be best if he left.

Rukan's father looked at her. "I suppose you have a choice to make." Rukan closed her eyes and wiped under her eyelashes. Without a word, she followed Adam out the front door.

9

HAYDEN KNEW SHE wasn't carrying her part of the conversation. She'd dragged Amra along, promising her a box of her favorite chile-limón truffles from Beacon Hill Chocolates, to avoid being alone at lunch with the remarkably boring and slightly imperious potential lateral hire. His name was Hank Rutherford, and he had all of the boxes checked: law review at the University of Michigan, four years of commercial lending experience at a top Chicago firm, solids recs. His wife had accepted a job at Goodwin Procter and his firm was, apparently, supportive of his job search. Or maybe they were relieved. After spending the entire morning ushering him in religiously timed thirty-minute intervals from office to office in the corporate wing of their firm, Hayden found Hank lacking in anything approximating a social skill. And Hayden, who normally could make conversation with any guy, was flatlining.

They'd chosen Sel de la Terre for lunch, an old standby. After they ordered, Amra stepped up to the plate. "So, Hank," she said, with a best-effort smile, "what did you think of your interviews this morning?"

Hank nodded. "They were great. I think I nailed most of them."

Amra raised her eyebrows. "Really? Nailed them? That's great.

Did you hear that, Hayden? He thinks he nailed them." Hayden forced a smile. Amra frowned a bit and turned back to Hank. "I saw your résumé. Very impressive. All the extracurriculars, Meals on Wheels, Habitat for Humanity, even during law school. I barely had time to eat and sleep." She laughed, but Hank just stared at her.

"You're joking, right?" he said. "I mean, after the initial adjustment, it's a piece of cake."

Hayden watched Amra closely. The small, deliberate breath, the brief but unmistakable pressing of the lips together. She wondered what it would be like to see Amra, whose smooth black hair was never out of place, whose suits never wrinkled, lose it in the middle of Sel de la Terre, scream that she had gone to Columbia Law, and point out the obvious: that she was just being nice.

But of course Amra didn't lose it. She simply nodded and said that it was nice for Hank that school had been so easy for him. And then she asked him a host of questions prompting answers that included something about Hyannis, Ethiopian food, and—could Hayden have misheard?—SpongeBob. But Hayden was listening without listening, knowing that Amra would carry the conversation and ask Hayden about it later.

It was not Hayden's fault. She was planning to leave Boston, with its commitment-phobic men in their insufferable Nantucket Reds and their parents' BMWs, and return home to Colorado. And, at the moment, it was all she could think about.

As she watched Amra navigate the lunch so gracefully, she felt the familiar mix of envy and pity. Amra was perfectly put together, but had she really lived? Had she, for example, ever watched a hundred guys stare at her hungrily while she placed second in a wet-tee-shirt contest in Cabo? Hayden guessed not. Amra was not a strict Muslim. Still, Hayden had never seen her drink, at any bar or party or firm function, anything stronger than seltzer. And while Amra listened to Hayden talk about her many dates, Amra herself never spoke of any boyfriend, past or present. When Hayden was completely wasted at the firm's holiday party two years earlier, she'd asked Amra if she was going to have one of those arranged marriages where her parents had promised her as a child to some guy twice her age. They hadn't talked for a while after that. But they worked together with the kind of long hours that fostered solidarity, and one night a few months later when they'd both changed into jeans and were buried in marked-up documents, they'd made up over *prik king* shrimp.

Looking at her colleague now, Hayden couldn't help but feel like it was half a friendship, like she'd overstepped by sharing so much and misread Amra's apparent kindness.

They deposited Hank in a cab and agreed that the burst of sunshine was too nice to do anything other than walk the six blocks back to their office. After a few minutes, Amra asked what was wrong.

"What do you mean?" Hayden slowed her pace, removed a pack of mints from her handbag, and offered one to Amra. Amra shook her head.

"Hayden, please. You barely said a word during lunch. And he was *your* interviewee."

"I know. I'm sorry. I just have a lot on my mind. But I appreciate your carrying the load. Seriously." Hayden nudged Amra's shoulder with her own. "Plus, you get chocolate."

"I almost forgot."

"So we're good?"

Amra sighed. "Yes. Of course. But I still wish you'd tell me what's wrong."

Hayden thought about it. She felt the weight of the words rising in her and could imagine what it would feel like to set them free. But it was not the sort of thing you told a half friend before you told your boss.

"I will. Soon. I promise," she said, and quickened her pace.

10

AMRA WAS KNEE-DEEP in deals. The days ran together, a rush of document review, conference calls, insipid fights with opposing counsel over minor changes, protracted arguments over major ones. Eric hired the smug Hank, which should have lightened Amra's workload, but there was something about Hank that made her not want to delegate too much to him. Like the way Eric lunched with him. The first and last time Eric had taken Amra to lunch—just the two of them, no clients and not counting the hundreds of times he made her pick up sandwiches before a closing—had been on the first day of her first year. It was quite possible, Amra realized, that she was working *harder* now that Hank was there.

The high point of her day was the e-mail or text from Mateen. It had started simply enough, a quick note to tell her what he had for lunch that day or where he was traveling, or a funny anecdote about the people on his deals ("Is it still acceptable, and I don't mean this in any way other than simple curiosity, for women to wear bows at the top of their button-down shirts?"). Soon, they were e-mailing back and forth every night—with the time difference, he thought calling would be too late after he got home from work. Of course, Amra was usually still at the office. She would get his e-mails and practically have to sit on her hands to stop from responding. Once, when he e-mailed at midnight, she'd lied and said she had insomnia and responded right away. When he called, she'd pretended to be at home.

Some of their communication inevitably turned to their childhood: Sunday school, Eid gatherings, the weekly dinner parties. "Do you remember," Mateen once asked, "how the parents all trusted us to be downstairs? How they separated by gender upstairs and never thought twice about the young teenagers they left downstairs?" She had thought it was odd, too, but of course no one asked their parents about it; no one wanted it to stop. When Zainab was there, inevitably a game of truth or dare broke out, although the boys spent most of the time pretending to ignore them. One night, while they talked, Amra asked Mateen if he'd had a crush on Zainab.

"She was so much younger than I was. It was obvious that she was exceptionally good-looking—everyone thought so—but there was something about her. An edge or something. Like she wouldn't give an inch. I don't know. It detracted from her looks, at least for me."

Amra joked that he probably didn't even remember her. He was quiet for a minute and Amra thought his cell had died.

"Mateen?"

"I remember the first Eid after I started college," he said. "Your family stopped by during the day. I was busy with my friends but I remember trying to joke with you. Of course, you were pretty shy back then. Later that day, I saw you at someone's house. Maybe the Baigs'? Anyway, I remember saying to myself, she's really going to be amazing when she grows up."

She laughed. "You're totally making that up."

"Amra Abbas, are you calling me a liar?"

"I am."

"Well, you're going to feel really bad about that in a second."

"Why?"

He cleared his throat. "You were wearing a peach-colored *salwar kameez* with a rather elaborate *dupatta* that kept sliding off your shoulders. Your lipstick was the same shade as the fabric, and I was surprised that Huma Auntie let you wear makeup. Your hair was pulled back into a long ponytail, and you had a peach rose stuck into the side of it. It wouldn't have been right to consider you beautiful yet—your face was still too childlike—but I knew you were going to be."

Amra swallowed. She remembered that day, the outfit, her first lipstick. She was fourteen. Mateen would have been eighteen or nineteen. "Okay, I feel bad for calling you a liar."

"How about this. You tell me what I was wearing that day and we'll be even."

Amra knew exactly what he was wearing, how his hair was longish, touching his collar, how he'd worn khaki pants and a blue button-down instead of traditional clothes, but there was no way she was going to reveal that much. "I guess we're not even."

"I thought so," he said. "I guess we'll have to find another way for you to make it up to me."

Amra finally confided about Mateen, amid the desserts and dancing in the Taste of the North End tent, to Rukan and Zainab after they'd sampled chocolate cannolis and shell-shaped sfogliatelle while seated at a small white-clothed table. She'd explained to Rukan who Mateen was, with Zainab's help—"we *all* had crushes on him"—and told them how her mother lured her to New York to meet him, how he'd surprised her at the ICA, how they were in contact every day.

"I knew it," Zainab said, narrowing her eyes. "I knew you were preoccupied with something other than that little boy toy of Eric's."

Amra sighed. "Can we please not talk about Hank? It's been so nice to have something else to focus on."

"Fine," Zainab said. "So is Mateen still as good-looking as when we were younger?"

Amra felt her cheeks redden. "More so."

"It's just so romantic," Rukan said. "I mean, it's like you were destined for each other."

Zainab rolled her eyes. "Grab hold of the reins there, Rook."

"What? It does seem like fate has taken over."

"Right," Zainab said. "That, or the aunties."

Rukan turned to Amra. "So, are you . . ."

"Am I what?"

"I don't know." Rukan laughed and made a face. "I mean, you'd tell us if you were engaged, right?"

"Oh my God." Amra shook her head. "Yes, I'd tell you. And no, I'm not."

"They just reconnected a couple of months ago," Zainab said, before appearing to remember Rukan's situation with Adam. "I mean, I'm sure she'll let us know."

They switched to talk about Rukan's wedding. Her parents had agreed to a civil ceremony, hoping that the Islamic one would follow and, Rukan thought, laboring under the belief that she would not consummate anything until it was done "properly." When Rukan spoke, Amra noticed a tightness in her voice but hoped it was just nerves.

Later, at home, Amra made tea, settled into the oversized chair in her living room, and listened to her voice mail. Mateen had called an hour earlier, when she was still with Zainab and Rukan. She could have listened on the way home, in the backseat of Rukan's car, but she'd wanted to savor it. She skipped through the work messages until she reached his.

"*Salaam,* Amra. It's Mateen. So I'm sitting here at dinner wishing you were with me, and thinking about how you are, in fact, three thousand miles away, with your life there, and how my life is here. And how I'm falling for you pretty hard. And I guess I'm just wondering, given our bicoastal lives, what we're doing here."

Amra swallowed hard. She'd known it was coming. He was thirty-four. He was *desi*. He wasn't looking for a fling, not with her, not with their parents involved. No one had said a word about it, not Mateen, not her parents, not even, miraculously, Zainab, but she knew they were all thinking it: *What would Amra do about her job?*

She wasn't ready to answer.

She took advantage of the fact that he was at dinner and sent him a text. Instead of addressing his question, she asked him to come to Rukan's wedding. She breathed in short, shallow half breaths until he responded—that he'd do his best—and went to bed.

11

ZAINAB WAITED FOR the young blond thing to finish powdering Eleanor's face, which was now decidedly more orange than when they'd arrived. With her short whitish hair, the contrast was impressive. Zainab was torn about whether to make an issue of it. She wanted Eleanor to look good on television, but she also needed Eleanor to review her talking points. And to have Eleanor swear on Betty Friedan's grave that she would not say a word about prostitution.

Zainab cleared her throat. "Her face looks orange."

The blond thing kept powdering. "It's bronzer. She needs it for the camera."

"I know what it is. But she doesn't need to look *orange*." Zainab didn't understand what it was with white women and the whole fake-tan business. She wanted to say, "You're white; you're privileged; come to terms with your pasty skin already."

"Give me a mirror," Eleanor said. She looked at the left side of her face, then the right. "I think it's fine, Zainab. It makes me look relaxed."

"That might not be the look we're going for. We don't want them to think you've been lying on the beach somewhere."

Eleanor nodded. "Do you remember Nixon in the debate with Kennedy?"

Zainab, of course, was too young to have watched it live. "I've seen the video."

"For purposes of this analogy, I'm Nixon and Fred Whitaker is Kennedy."

"He's really not that much younger than you."

"But I'm a woman," Eleanor said. "There is a higher standard. If they think I've been to Bali, fine. Better than thinking I look like a feeble old lady."

Zainab conceded the point. They had more important matters to discuss. "Eleanor, I'm sure that some reporter is going to bring up the abortion thing."

Eleanor closed her eyes. "The Paglia comment."

"Yes," Zainab said. "The Paglia comment." The previous week, Eleanor had said she agreed with Camille Paglia's position that, while abortion should properly be considered murder, the state does not have the right to interfere with the decisions a woman makes about her body. "Steve Clemson from the *Bay State Review* was on the list of questioners, but there are any number of people who might ask. Someone from the Independent Women's Alliance, for example. They've got one of their minions here." Zainab flipped though the papers she was holding. "Monica Beck. And don't forget our local talk-radio fan, Charles Holland. *The Third*."

"Charles Holland is an insignificant troll."

Zainab sighed. "My point is that you'll almost certainly be asked."

"So let them ask. I said it, and as you know, my dear, I usually mean what I say."

Zainab bit the inside of her cheek. "Yes, but you're running in the Republican primary." *Hello,* Zainab wanted to scream. *Pro-life platform*.

"So my comment requires some nuance. Republicans can be

nuanced. Well, some of them. Not the evangelicals. But they aren't going to vote for me anyway." Eleanor settled back in her chair. "Therefore, I can't imagine why it matters."

Zainab took a seat toward the middle of the hall, hoping they'd start on time. She'd agreed to speak later that evening to a group of Muslim youth about public service careers. At a mosque. Zainab hadn't been in a mosque since her mother died and the men, many of whom didn't know her or her mother, refused to let her go to the burial. But the woman on the phone, Leila something or other, had told her she would be a real inspiration to the kids in the community, "especially the girls," and that "we need more Muslims to get involved," which Zainab didn't dispute—it was better than remaining insular and complaining—so she'd agreed. But between the debate and the debriefing with Eleanor afterward, she would be pushing it to make it on time.

During the introductions by a local TV reporter, Zainab checked her e-mail. The man next to her regarded her disapprovingly. Zainab shifted away from him and continued to scroll through her messages, including one from Darby Tate. She was glad she and Darby had cleared the air. She was flattered, incredibly so, she'd told Darby, but she was straight. She could see how Darby might have gotten the wrong impression—her research into Zainab's life had not turned up any husband or boyfriend. She was simply focusing on her career now, she explained. Darby had been equal parts gracious and apologetic, which Zainab appreciated.

Eleanor and her opponent, Fred Whitaker, each had two minutes to make an opening statement, with Eleanor going first. Zainab had written Eleanor's, but when Fred began speaking, she put her phone away and paid full attention. He was a tough-as-nails conservative, with a 100 percent favorable rating from the religious right, gun owners, and pro-life groups. She wanted to see how it would fly in a state like Massachusetts. Unfortunately, his remarks were vague and inclusive, revealing none of his extremism.

The first three questions posed were about taxes. The candidates' positions were similar, except that Whitaker favored sin taxes. Next, a small, anorexic-looking woman from the *Boston Times* who introduced herself as Jill Gill—*Jill Gill?* Zainab thought. *Really? Did they let mothers drink in the hospital before signing the birth certificate?*—stood and tapped on the mic. She looked about twelve years old.

"Ms. Winthrop-Smith, recently you quoted Camille Paglia on the issue of abortion." Zainab leaned forward. "Specifically," Jill Gill continued, "you stated that abortion is murder but that it should be allowed. Can you please tell the voters of Massachusetts which other types of murder you condone and which ones you might work to decriminalize if elected to the Senate?"

Eleanor smiled. A genuine, relaxed smile. Zainab thought someone should tell Jill Gill to duck.

"Ms. Gill," Eleanor began, "this is the sort of hyperbolic idiocy that ensures nothing changes in Washington. It is not *part* of the problem. It *is* the problem. And I suppose we can trust people to make the appropriate assumptions about your role in that problem, and your motivations." Eleanor tilted her head in one subtle, accusatory motion. "As for your question, please indulge a condensed tutorial. The vast majority of murders fall under state jurisdiction, so even if it was my innermost desire, which I suppose I must explicitly state that at this time it is not, to legalize 'other types of murder,' as you put it, say of vapid, attention-seeking reporters, there isn't much I could do about it." The crowd laughed. Eleanor continued to smile. "Now, if you want to ask me a grown-up question, I'm more than happy to give you a mulligan." She leaned forward, like there was nothing more she wanted than to hear Jill Gill's next question.

Jill Gill glared at Eleanor. Red blotches had formed on her cheeks. Frankly, Zainab thought, she could use a little bronzer.

"With all due respect, Ms. Winthrop-Smith, you said it. You said that it's murder and you're okay with it. And most Republicans in this state—most *Americans*—would find that abhorrent."

Eleanor nodded. She raised her eyebrows expectantly.

Jill Gill looked confused. "Well?"

"Oh, I'm sorry, dear. Was there a question in there?" The crowd laughed again.

Fred Whitaker interjected. "I'd be happy to answer the question. Abortion is murder and I will do everything in my power to make the commission of it illegal."

Eleanor rolled her eyes. "I see Fred could use the expanded tutorial." Zainab smiled. Eleanor had the crowd eating out of her hands.

The moderator moved to the next question, a technical issue about the medical workplace safety legislation. Zainab held her breath, hoping that licensure wouldn't come up. It did not. While the next reporter adjusted the microphone, Zainab made a note to follow up with Eleanor, to see if there was some wiggle room there. Nurses, who labored under almighty, God-complex-suffering doctors day in and day out, might just find the ever-outspoken Eleanor refreshing, as long as they didn't think she was in favor of diluting the value of their R.N.s.

"Ms. Winthrop-Smith, Mr. Whitaker, I'm Charles Holland from WXS Radio. I'd like to go back to the abortion issue, if we could."

The insignificant troll. Zainab craned her neck. And then realized the troll was the guy who had tried to hit on her at the party after the Correspondents' Dinner. She didn't hear the rest of his question or either candidate's answer. She could only replay that night—his pathetic pickup line, and how he'd only given a first name, and not even his real one, when he'd introduced himself. For the smallest of moments she recalled how he'd looked at her when asking why Darby left. She had to hand it to him. He'd played his role flawlessly. All for what? To sabotage Eleanor's campaign? As if Zainab wouldn't have figured out who he was. As if she would have gone out with him.

Zainab breathed in through her nose, counted to ten, and exhaled slowly through her mouth over and over until she was able to listen to the rest of the debate. When it was done, people swarmed the candidates. Eleanor would be expecting Zainab to appear at her side, but she had something to take care of first.

She caught up with him in the Fred Whitaker line. "I thought you said your name was Chase."

A look flashed on his face, a mixture of surprise and, she was almost certain, the attraction she'd noted the night they'd met. "It is. Chase Holland."

"You mean Charles Holland," Zainab said, "the *Third*."

"It's a nickname. You know, short for Charles."

"According to whom?"

"I'm sorry?"

"I don't think most people would get Chase from Charles."

"Okay," he said, "but your incredulity notwithstanding, my friends call me Chase."

"I'm not your friend."

"I don't remember saying that you were." They were being jostled by the crowd, and his face was uncomfortably close to hers.

"So what was your grand plan that night?" Zainab asked, taking a step back. "To seduce campaign secrets out of me? Or were you just looking for fodder for your show?"

"I didn't know who you were until you answered your phone."

"Right."

"I swear."

She laughed. Like his swearing meant anything. "Well, even if that were true, once you knew who I was, you still hid behind your nickname. Why?"

"I don't know. Shock? Self-preservation? Or maybe it was just easier than explaining, since you were rushing off to deal with the latest Winthrop-Smith campaign crisis."

"So you're a coward at heart. Got it. And now you'll have to excuse me while I rush off again." She started back toward Eleanor.

"Hey, Zainab," he called after her.

Zainab stopped and closed her eyes before turning around. "What?"

"Why don't you give me a call sometime." He held out a business card. "I'd love to have you on the show."

"When hell freezes over."

He laughed and put the card in his pocket. "Fair enough. See you around the campaign trail."

Zainab stalked off, found Eleanor, and ushered her through the crowd. When she looked over, Chase Holland was gone.

She arrived at the mosque twenty minutes late. It was a nondescript brick building with latticework rising in the shape of a crescent. Its plainness paled in comparison to the grand architecture of the mosques she'd visited in India and Indonesia. Inside the door, two men in *kurta* pajamas and *kufis* eyed Zainab warily.

"The ladies' entrance is in the back," one of them said. She ignored him and walked toward the next set of double doors. "Excuse me! Sister! You must go to the rear of the building."

"I'm not your sister," she said, and opened the doors, revealing the prayer space. The imam was reciting *Surah al Falaq* in Arabic, which she recognized from her childhood days with Mrs. Baig, sitting on the floor in her living room, swaying back and forth, reciting. She knew it by heart, even now, although she had no idea what it meant. She stepped back into the hallway, where the two men regarded her with open hostility. Soon, a sea of men exited the prayer hall, parting to move around Zainab as though she had some contagious disease. Finally, a woman peered around the corner at the end of the hall.

"Zainab? Is that you?" She was short and rosy-cheeked and wore a black pantsuit and a white headscarf.

"It's me." Zainab smiled wearily. "And you must be Leila."

"Sorry, the prayer took a bit longer. We've had a great turnout. People are very eager to get involved, to hear from Muslims who've established themselves politically." She smiled brightly. "Come, we've got a space set up."

As they entered what appeared to be a classroom, Zainab noticed that the men sat on one side and the women on the other. She was tempted to address it, to explain that this gender nonsense was going to prevent meaningful forays into the American political scene. But it was obviously a conservative mosque. Zainab wasn't going to change anything with one speech. She greeted them and began her discussion of her career path, the courses she'd taken, the work on various campaigns, the time at Harvard, and finally the position with Eleanor. She concluded by saying that by bringing all of that experience to the table, she'd been given more responsibility than her job title suggested and had become a critical component of the campaign, "even in these crazy times." She then opened it up for questions.

A woman in a full-length coat and headscarf stood, introduced herself as Fareeda, and said that, while she noticed that Zainab was wearing a pantsuit today, she had seen pictures of her in "less Islamic attire" and wondered if she'd felt pressure to compromise her religion to get ahead.

Zainab almost laughed. After everything she'd said, they were stuck on the covering issue. She looked at the woman for a moment. "No. Next question?"

The woman put up her hand. "I'm sorry, sister. I don't feel like you've answered my question."

Zainab smiled an Eleanor smile. "And I feel that I have. Next question."

Leila gave a nervous laugh, signaling they should move on. Zainab looked at the young members of the audience, the guys and girls who looked to be in their late teens. The former had adopted bored looks, as though there was nothing they could learn from her. The girls looked interested, but none raised her hand. Zainab had rushed from the debate for this?

Finally, a tall, thin man stood. His graying beard worked a patchwork across his jaw, squaring off his bare cheeks, distorting the shape of his face. It was the kind of beard worn solely for religious reasons and with no apparent regard for how it looked. Zainab took a breath and prepared for incoming.

The man took the microphone and motioned with his hands for the audience, which had started to murmur, to quiet. "Sister Zainab, with all due respect, I am aware that you are friendly with a female reporter who is a known lesbian. I'm sure you know to whom I refer and we shall not mention her name here. I am also aware that you traveled out of town with her last month, attending the very public White House Correspondents' Dinner, giving at least the appearance that you are involved in a romantic relationship. I would like to register my protest to your appearance here at our sacred *masjid* and ask that the community not consider you a role model or something to aspire to." The murmuring returned as people leaned forward and spoke behind cupped hands. The man started to sit but seemed to think better of it. He tapped on the microphone, which emitted a loud, huffing sound followed by a high-pitched tone. "And sister," he said, "it would behoove you to spend more time in a *masjid* so that you can appreciate why we have separate entrances."

Zainab wasn't sure whether to laugh, or scream, or bolt.

"If I may respond," she began, and waited for the room to quiet. "First of all, I didn't come here as a role model. I came here to speak about my path to a career in public service. I came to inspire young people to get involved. Because sitting around in conservative mosques—which, as this one appears to be, are usually segregated not just by gender but by country of origin—complaining about how Muslims are treated at home and abroad is no way to participate in this country's democracy. In other words, I came here to *help*. And as for my personal life"—Zainab paused and for a second she was not sure what would come out of her mouth—"it's none of your business."

Leila offered rushed concluding remarks and followed Zainab out the door. In the parking lot, she apologized. "It was a more conservative audience than we'd planned. Possibly because it was right after the prayer." She frowned thoughtfully and gave a little shrug. "We really do appreciate your participation, and if you ever have openings for interns, we hope you'll keep the youth of our *masjid* in mind."

Zainab shook her hand and thought, *Fat chance.*

12

On the way to Rukan's *mehndi* ceremony, Amra told Hayden about the henna.

"It's a way to break the ice. To help with shyness in an arranged marriage. The bride gets the groom's initials written somewhere in the design, and when they're alone together, he looks for them. It's an excuse to start touching."

"That's sweet," Hayden said. "In a weird, innocent kind of way."

Amra laughed. "I know it must sound strange to you. But imagine all the pressure of that moment. I think it's probably good for them to have a distraction, to forget that they're actually touching for the first time."

"Why would you want to forget *that*?" Hayden shook her head. "I mean, here you've been, pining away for this person, no one has let you anywhere near him, and it's finally okay. I say, focus, people."

The decision to invite Hayden, Amra conceded, had not been particularly well thought out. Hayden had asked Amra if she wanted to do something that weekend, maybe go to City Bar or grab something to eat in the North End. When Amra said she was busy with Rukan's wedding, Hayden looked forlorn, and Amra found herself inviting Hayden to the festivities, hoping Rukan wouldn't mind. And that Zainab would behave.

"So what do the other people write in their henna?" Hayden asked. "The nonbride people."

"They don't usually write anything. They just get the design," Amra explained. "But my friend Zainab and I—you'll meet her tonight—we usually write something that we hope for. It's just a silly thing we started when we were kids."

Hayden nodded and Amra thought back to the many weddings, parties, and holidays when she and Zainab wrote their deepest wishes, in small, secret script, onto the palms of their hands. When they were eight, Amra wished for the Dream Date Barbie, and Zainab, a black kitten. Sometimes, feeling philosophical, they wrote things like "world peace" or "true love." When they were in college, Amra once wrote "Harvard Law," while Zainab wrote "the presidency."

"So," Hayden said, "what are you going to write tonight?"

Amra shrugged casually, as though she hadn't given it a second thought.

They entered the hall and found it filled with women dressed in bright colors, mostly *salwar kameez* but Amra spotted the occasional *lengha* and even a couple of *ghararas*. She scanned the crowd for Zainab. "She's probably running late," she said to Hayden, and led her through the crowd to Rukan. Amra hugged the bride-to-be, kissing both of her cheeks. "You look beautiful," she said, then introduced Hayden.

"I feel so out of place." Hayden gestured at her black dress. "Like I brought the funeral."

"Don't be silly," Rukan said. "You look great."

They watched the younger girls dance, a sensual, hip-slinging sort of belly dance to some techno-Pakistani music, and fed Rukan fried dough soaked in syrup. When it was time for the henna, Zainab finally showed up. They watched the henna artist do Rukan's hands, and then Amra grabbed a cone. She looked at Zainab and said, "Well?"

"I don't know. Just write 'U.S. Senate.'"

"That's not really your wish," Amra said. "It's more for Eleanor."

"Right, but if she wins, I go with her."

Amra hadn't considered this. She wrote it in tiny lettering, hoping if she made it small enough Zainab would not get her wish, or go away.

Hayden declared she wanted her hands done, too. Zainab raised her eyebrow and looked at Amra.

"Have you told her how long it lasts?" Zainab asked.

"It's okay, she works for Elise."

"So?"

"She's civilized."

Zainab drew an intricate design with paisley and dotted lines and small flowers on Hayden's hand.

"What about my wish?" Hayden said when she'd finished. Zainab frowned and for a minute Amra was afraid she'd be mad. But Zainab just said, "Do you want to do it or do you want me to? I mean, is it a secret?"

Hayden thought for a minute. Then she said: "Just write 'home.'" Zainab and Amra exchanged glances. Before Amra could ask Hayden what she meant, the music started up again, pulsating from a speaker a few yards from where they sat.

Amra took the henna tube and wondered if she was about to jinx everything. She thought about writing "partner" as she had at every wedding and holiday for the past four years. But their unwritten rule was that it had to be what they wanted most. She took a slow breath and, just above her wrist, where her suit would cover it, wrote "Mateen."

13

ZAINAB FELT GUILTY for attending the talk. And for lying to Amra and Rukan about why she would be late to the wedding. Research, she told herself. She was a fierce advocate for knowing what she was up against. It was why she had scouted other competitive runners in college and why she listened to Chase Holland's show. And why she now fidgeted in her seat as she waited to hear Nadia Asad, the darling of neoconservatives and S. F. Addington Scholar in Religion and Public Policy at the Religious Freedom Institute, a Christian-right think tank, speak. Nadia was hawking a new book, *Calling a Duck a Duck: The Perfidy of Islam*. Zainab refused to plunk down the $24.95 to purchase the book, but she had read a handful of reviews and excerpts online, enough to turn her stomach and raise her blood pressure.

The book contained the usual litany of sensational claims. Essentially, from what Zainab pieced together, Nadia Asad recounted her upbringing in a fundamentalist Muslim household in Dearborn, Michigan, and argued that all of Islam was stained with her parents' sins. According to the excerpts, Nadia was promised, at age four, to an older uncle, who would wait until she turned the statutory age to officially marry her. However, the "Islamic" marriage took place when she was twelve. To avoid attracting the attention of authorities, the uncle moved into her parents' home, where, apparently, he had at her.

In the book, Nadia claimed that Muslims did, in fact, hate America for its freedoms, that there was no such thing as a moderate Muslim, that a war to defeat Islam worldwide was not only justified but necessary, and that the sooner such a war took place, the better.

Zainab sat in the back, behind the rows of white people—the men in khaki pants and the women with stiff bangs. Outside, protesters carried signs declaring "Hate Speech is Un-American," or "Nadia Asad wants to bring back the Crusades," but inside it appeared to be a rather supportive audience. Zainab felt self-conscious of her henna from the night before, fearing that someone might whip out a camera and snap her picture for *National Geographic.*

A small, bird-like man stood up to introduce Nadia Asad. "Ladies and gentlemen," he said, "we are truly honored to have with us tonight one of the most courageous voices in the Muslim world." Zainab smirked. The idea that Nadia was part of the "Muslim world" was laughable.

When Nadia got up to speak, the room hushed. She was small, shorter than Zainab would have thought, and slight. The tone of her voice was surprisingly gentle, belying the things she had written and was certainly about to say, in a way that made the audience lean forward to hear her.

"How many of you know what a fistula is?" Nadia began, scanning the audience. "A fistula," she continued, though several people had raised their hands, "is formed when a hole develops between either the bladder and the vagina or the rectum and the vagina during childbirth. Fistulas are often caused when there is trauma during sexual intercourse, or when a young girl gives birth. In my case, both conditions were present." Nadia let it soak in before launching into the story of her home birth, describing how "no one wanted to take a twelve-year-old who has been impregnated by her forty-nine-year-old uncle to the hospital" and how she'd suffered in labor for days before the baby was delivered dead and her insides had ripped apart.

"I share this with you not just to get your attention, though if I'm honest that is part of my motivation. And I share it with you not just to repulse you, but I hope that you are, in fact, repulsed." She looked around the room slowly. "But the main reason I share it with you is to illustrate the horrors of a life lived Islamically. To illuminate how differently Muslim parents view their children. To show you what we are up against."

Zainab was sure she was going to vomit. Part of it was the graphic description. Who would not be horrified by that? But it was also the insidious conclusions Nadia had drawn. Zainab stared straight at Nadia Asad, willing her to make eye contact, wanting her to know that unlike the rest of the head bobbers in the room, she wasn't buying it.

When Nadia finished, the host brought microphones to the center aisles and instructed audience members with questions to form two queues. The first questioner was an older woman with sculpted hair and a lavender sweater set.

"Ms. Asad, my dear thing, I'm so sorry for your pain," the woman said. "Your parents should be in jail and all of the people who follow their cult should be deported." A flutter of applause rippled through the room. The woman held her hand up. "My question is, How can we get them to leave?"

Zainab sighed. In fact, she almost smiled, because the woman's statement was so hyperbolic that even Nadia Asad would have to point out that many, many Muslims were American citizens. Many were converts. Many were African Americans. There was no place to "deport" them to.

But Nadia just nodded. "Well, that's the hard part. Muslims like to hide behind our free society and our beloved Constitution, a document that means nothing to them. Democracy is counter to their entire ideology, but they will happily use it for their own ends whenever possible. So it will probably take, unfortunately, another terrorist attack and the suspension of certain rights, coupled with a Republican president's emergency powers, to deal with this population."

Deal with. Zainab turned the phrase around in her mind, feeling along the edges of the hope for another terrorist attack and the implications of being "dealt with."

Someone yelled out, "Then what can we do?"

"An excellent question," Nadia said. "I have to be a little careful here. But if it were me, if I were just sitting around thinking about what I could do, I would remind myself that Muslims are all around us. They are in our schools, our workplaces, our neighborhoods. You can't always pick them out by their dress." As she said that last part, Zainab was sure Nadia looked at her. "But they are *everywhere*. And I would consider it nothing less than my patriotic duty to watch every move they make and take whatever action the situation requires." And at this last part—this ominous call to, what, physical force?—Nadia Asad finally met Zainab's gaze, staring straight at her long enough for the moderator to ask if she was ready for the next question.

On the street, Zainab told herself to calm down, that she had come willingly. Still, Nadia's chilly stare at the end felt like a threat. Not from the woman making it—she was too small—but maybe from the others in the room who'd been whipped into a frenzy.

"Zainab!" She turned to see Chase Holland descending the stairs, two at a time.

Zainab sneered. "What a surprise, Chase. Or is it Charles? You must be a big fan."

He caught up to her. "I don't know about fan. I know Nadia from D.C. Just trying to support a former colleague."

"How admirable."

He grinned. "Well, obviously you don't think so."

"No. I find it repugnant that you support her. But not surprising."

"Hey, slow down. I just wanted to say hello, not start a war. I don't necessarily agree with everything Nadia says, but doesn't she have a right to say it?"

"I never said she didn't have the right," Zainab said. "I just think it's horrifically irresponsible."

"In what way?"

She wondered if he was really that obtuse. "I have to go," she said. Unfortunately, he followed.

"You're always running off. I'm going to start to take it personally."

Zainab kept walking.

"Look," he said, "some of Nadia's conclusions might be a bit out there, but maybe there is some truth there, too? Some Muslim women are oppressed. At least she's talking about it."

Zainab stopped and turned. "Yes, thank God for the one brave soul who will talk about how oppressed Muslim women are! Where would we be without Nadia Asad, our savior? Who would ever tell the story?" Zainab was aware of the venom in her voice. For a moment, when Chase stared at her sheepishly, she almost felt bad. Almost. "Nadia talks in generalities. She says *all*, not some. Like every Muslim parent is a monster who will pimp her daughter out to the nearest relative. I wasn't raised like that. No one I know was."

Chase nodded. "But maybe you and your friends are the exception."

"Or maybe *she's* the exception." Zainab sighed. She was too tired for this conversation. She needed to get home to change for the wedding. Still, for some reason she couldn't let his assumptions stand. "Do you know any Muslims, Chase? Do you ever hang out with any Muslims in between working on state secessionist movements or pushing anti-evolution curricula or hunting kittens, or whatever it is you do for fun?"

He laughed. "First of all, you do know that you're arguing against stereotypes of Muslims while stereotyping conservatives, right? And second of all, no. I don't really know any Muslims." He gave a small shrug. "Other than kids I went to school with."

"I didn't think so."

"I'd like to get to know you."

"I'm sure."

He looked at her and shook his head. "Are you always this bristly?"

"Around intolerant conservatives? Yes." She couldn't help it. In the past few weeks she'd been called a tramp and a lesbian by Muslims at a conservative mosque and dangerous and evil by Nadia Asad.

"Fair enough." He bit his bottom lip. "So, how about a cup of coffee?"

"You're joking."

"Think of it as outreach."

"Tempting as that sounds, I can't. I have to get home and change for a wedding, which"—Zainab looked at her watch—"I'm already going to be late for."

He gestured at her black suit. "You look great. So skip the whole changing thing and, voilà, you have time for coffee."

"I can't go like this." She couldn't believe she was still in the middle of this conversation. "It's a Pakistani wedding. Here's a cultural factoid for you. We don't wear black to weddings. We actually wear colorful clothes. Probably a throwback to some third world—"

"Okay, okay." He put his hands up. "You need to change. Got it. But don't you have time for one quick cup of coffee? Half a cup? A shot of espresso?" She noticed the way his eyes mirrored his smile, not at all how she pictured him when she listened to him on the radio. Of course, his voice was different, too, lighter, *younger*. He sounded so old on the air. Like he was two different people. Charles and Chase. Barring some untreated psychiatric disorder, one of them was an act. She tried to focus on Charles, to summon anger about the comments he'd made about her, but he didn't look like that person. He looked like the guy who'd hit on her in D.C. A guy whose mind could be changed. And after what she'd just sat through, changing someone's mind, anyone's mind, started to take on the characteristics of a duty.

"I can give you fifteen minutes," she said, and wondered how long it would take her to regret it.

Seated at a nearby coffee shop, Zainab asked what he wanted to know.

"Well, for starters, how's your coffee?"

She flashed a one-second smile. "You're the one who said, you wanted to get to know me."

"Yeah," he said, "as a person. Not an interview. Are you always this tough?"

"I think you already asked me that," she said. "And yes."

"Right. I did. And good."

"Why is that good?"

"I kind of like it."

Zainab added some more cream to her coffee and wiped the constellation of droplets off the table with a napkin. "In that case, I'll have to rethink it."

"Maybe that was my strategy."

"For what?"

"To take down the Winthrop-Smith campaign by softening up her go-to woman."

She looked at him. "What exactly is your problem with Eleanor?"

"She's not a real Republican. She's got no business seeking the nomination."

"Isn't that for the voters to decide?"

He nodded. "But for them to make that decision, they need perfect information."

"Which you are kind enough to give them."

He grinned. "So you understand."

Zainab looked at her watch. He leaned forward. "Just a couple more minutes? I promise not to talk about the campaign."

She sighed. "Fine."

"Okay, let's see . . . no campaign issues, no political debates . . . religion? Clearly not going to wade into that minefield."

"Why not?" Zainab took a sip of her coffee. "You seem rather preoccupied with my religion on your show. Surely you must want to ask me something."

He seemed to consider it for a moment. "Okay," he finally said. "Do you drink?"

"Alcohol? Not ever."

"Because of your religion?"

"Because I choose not to poison my body."

"So the fact that your religion forbids it in no way informs your decision to abstain?"

"I didn't say that."

He nodded. "So it's partially the reason."

"I wasn't raised around alcohol. I didn't grow up watching adults drink wine at dinner or guzzle beer during football games. That probably makes it easier for me to see it as a harmful substance. But the fact that someone says I can't is not why I don't."

"Isn't the someone here supposed to be God?"

"Lots of people purport to speak for God."

"Good point." He tapped his fingers on the wrought iron table. "So, let's see . . . the headscarf. Why don't you wear one?"

"I don't think it's required."

"Would you, if you thought it were?"

She shrugged. "Probably not."

He laughed. "So you're not particularly orthodox. But you identify as a Muslim."

"Yes."

"Aren't you ever uncomfortable with that? You know, being associated with all of the violence done in the name of Islam?"

"I'm not associated with it."

"Right," he said, "but other people associate you with it. There's nothing you can do about that."

"Exactly. So what's your point?"

"I don't really have one. I'm just asking if that's hard for you."

"Hmmm," she said. "Is it hard for me to hear a certain radio talk-show host call me an enemy of the state? To imply that Eleanor shouldn't have let me come within ten feet of her campaign? That my participation is somehow less American than someone else's? Is that what you're asking?"

He winced and ran a hand through his hair. "I deserve that. And I'm sorry. I haven't done it again, not since we met."

"Your restraint is admirable." She retrieved her wallet in spite of the hand he raised in protest. "Let me see, Chase. How to put this in terms you'll understand. You're familiar with the story of the Last Supper?"

"Of course."

"If I may paraphrase: Before this is all over, you'll betray me again." She dropped a ten-dollar bill on the table and left without looking back.

Chase sat there, staring at Zainab's mug. He pulled it closer. No lipstick stain. Her lips couldn't really be that color. But maybe they were. They had definitely been a deeper shade of red in D.C. On the one hand, he was glad that she didn't seem so high-maintenance—Savannah couldn't so much as go to the mailbox without spending forty-five minutes with her industrial-strength blow-dryer—but he was also disappointed that she hadn't left anything behind.

He was trying harder than he should have, given Savannah. Although clearly there was nothing for Savannah to be jealous of. Whenever Zainab smiled, now that she knew who he was, it never reached her eyes, not really, not if he was looking. And Chase wasn't just looking. He was on a goddamned search party for some indication that he'd broken through that cool exterior, that she might be willing to separate his professional life from his personal one and forgive what he'd said about her.

That he would see her again.

He *had* been careful not to mention her by name on the air again, even though his producer constantly tried to goad him into it, slipping him notes quoting anti-Muslim activists and Web sites. But he couldn't stop criticizing Eleanor. Zainab had to understand that. It wasn't so much that Eleanor would be a disaster for Massachusetts. If he were honest, if he reached back to the reasons he became a conservative, which had everything to do with personal responsibility and fiscal conservatism and nothing to do with abortion or gay marriage, he could imagine a scenario in which he actually supported Eleanor. But his audience could not imagine it. Eleanor's social liberalism kept his listeners up at night, worrying about what was happening to this great nation. If Chase was going to make a real name for himself and get his book published, he had to act like it kept him up at night, too.

He'd backed off the personal attacks and, as much as possible, the comments about Muslims. But he could not be expected to ignore national security issues. Surely Zainab couldn't take offense if he criticized Al-Qaeda or the Taliban. And if his listeners could quote from the Qur'an to find the seeds for terrorism, who was he to argue? He wasn't a religious scholar. Still, when a caller went on a particularly vitriolic rant, it gave him pause in a way that it hadn't before the Correspondents' Dinner.

But really, how often could Zainab listen to his show?

14

THE WHITE PEOPLE, it was clear, didn't know what to do. The *desi* guests had mostly separated by gender, even though Rukan wouldn't have wanted it that way. Force of habit, Zainab knew. Even at gatherings held by not particularly conservative people, it often ended up that way.

She made her way toward the table near the front where Amra sat. The music was blasting and she could feel it in her head. A few children gathered around the dance floor, shyly attempting a couple of moves before retreating in fits of laughter to the safety of the crowd.

Adam and Rukan had agreed on a half-Pakistani, half-American wedding. Or so they said. To Zainab, it seemed more like twenty-eighty: The music and Rukan's dress would be Pakistani; the food, the justice of the peace, and the bulk of the guests were American.

"Hey," she said, touching Amra's arm. "Am I that late?"

Amra shook her head. "No. We still have time to go see Rukan."

They took the elevator to the seventh floor, where Rukan was getting ready. Amra knocked twice before Rukan's cousin Reema came to the door, peering tentatively through the three-inch crack.

"Yes?" she said.

"Reema, it's us," said Amra. "Amra and Zainab. Can we come in?"

"Let me check." Reema closed the door.

"Okay," Zainab said, "how rude was that?"

Reema opened the door again. "It's fine. She wants to see you."

They found Rukan on the bed, dressed in her crimson bridal *gharara,* her hair flayed, her face blotched, the skin around her eyes puffed. She smiled a half smile and then burst into tears. Amra and Zainab rushed to her, sitting on either side, looking to Reema for some clue as to what had happened. Reema just kept shaking her head.

It was a good twenty minutes before Rukan could talk. She said that Adam had called—*"called!"*—and told her that everything was happening too fast, that he needed time.

"But he's the one who rushed it," Amra said. "He's the one who proposed after only three months."

Rukan nodded. "I know." She looked at her ring and started to cry again.

Amra handed her another tissue. "It doesn't make any sense."

"It was my father!" Rukan waved her hand. "He went to him with a prenup. He told Adam he could not support the wedding but that at least he could protect his daughter. He said if Adam didn't sign it, he'd cut me out of his will. Can you believe it? So Adam took it and said he'd bring it today. But he just called and said I should have 'controlled my family' and that my father needn't have bothered with the agreement because there wasn't enough money in the world to make him marry into *this*." Rukan looked at them with eyes that made Amra embrace her and Zainab want to kill someone.

Hayden scanned the hall for Amra. She'd said six o'clock. And that she'd be wearing "tea pink." Hayden had to look that up. Apparently, there was a tea recipe that called for baking soda that turned the color light pink. When she'd asked Amra what she should wear,

Amra said nothing too revealing. Hayden had settled on a red, floor-length evening gown with spaghetti straps. It showed a bit of cleavage, thanks in part to the built-in push-up bra, but she figured the length of the dress balanced it out sufficiently.

She saw plenty of light pink outfits, but no Amra. She considered her options. There were several tables of women near the front, a fairly equal number of all-male tables on the other side of the hall. Interspersed among these were mixed-gender tables, but most of them were already full. Hayden took a seat at an empty table in the back and took out her phone in an attempt to look busy and less like someone with whom no one wanted to sit. She texted Amra but got no response.

For a bit, she people-watched. Some of the women covered their hair, a few with tight-fitting scarves, others with loosely draped shawls. Hayden was struck, again, by how colorful the women's attire was. And how much it contrasted with Adam's side, where most of the women wore black.

She continued to watch the door for Amra, or her friend Zainab. Hayden had been blown away and more than a little intimidated by how beautiful Zainab was. Amra was pretty, of course, but there was something very controlled about it. Zainab was in an entirely different league. Hayden would never say the word out loud, of course, but who wouldn't think it looking at her: *exotic*. Her skin was darker than Amra's, her eyes more Asian-looking. And her figure. Zainab could easily have been a swimsuit model. If Amra was *Town and Country,* Zainab was definitely *Maxim*.

Hayden sighed. What would it be like, she wondered, to look like that? To not have to try, to not have to spend hours getting her hair just right, applying makeup like a mask to make sure no one saw what she really looked like. Hayden had to spend a full ninety minutes each morning to look "naturally" beautiful. She got her hair colored every four weeks to mask her true mousy brown. She sipped coffee for breakfast and ate a can of tuna and an apple for dinner so she could eat normally with her colleagues at lunch. The worst was when everyone ordered dessert; to avoid standing out, Hayden would sample a piece of cheesecake or Mississippi mud pie and deal with it later. She couldn't make herself vomit. Instead, on the days she indulged, she would take a handful of laxatives and tell herself that if it came out fast enough, nothing would stick.

A couple of young women in headscarves sat down at the other end of Hayden's table. They smiled and said hello, but they began speaking a language she didn't recognize. Hayden sat in an uncomfortable silence. Though it would surprise the people who knew her now, she'd struggled in high school with an inexplicable and sudden onset of shyness, an anxiety so extreme that answering a question in class would cause her palms to sweat and her voice to quiver. By college, the classes were so large that no one spoke much, and by law school she seemed to grow out of it. At least in class. Social settings were more hit-and-miss. She recalled several times when she was forced to socialize with a date's friends and she could think of nothing clever enough to say to make them like her. And her dates' friends *never* liked her. She would sit and tell herself to say something, anything, but her mind would get caught in a loop and her voice hid somewhere far away and she would remain mute.

Her phone vibrated. It was Amra. Finally. *Small crisis with the bride. Maybe more than small. Will be there soon hopefully. Sorry!* Great, Hayden thought. Not-so-small crisis with the bride. She put her phone back in her clutch and thought about leaving. Or at least hiding in the ladies' room for a bit.

"Excuse me, are you saving these seats for anyone?" Three young men stood before her. They looked Pakistani, like Amra, but were wearing regular suits. The one who spoke had his hands in his pockets, his tie already slightly loosened, and gestured at the empty seats with his shoulder. Hayden realized that the room had filled up rapidly, and now there were only a handful of seats in an odd, patchwork pattern among the tables. Her table, with only herself and the two other women, was one of the emptiest.

"Yes. I mean, no. Not all of them." She assumed Zainab would be joining them, although Amra hadn't really said. "I only need to save two spots."

The man smiled. "Great. Thanks." He took the seat one away from her on her left side, and the other two men sat on the other side of him. One of the head-covered women scooted closer to her friend, even though there was still a chair between her and the male guest.

The man next to Hayden smiled and leaned toward her, lowering his voice. "I guess we've got cooties. You'd better not get too close."

Hayden smiled. "Thanks for the warning."

"I'm Fadi, by the way. I'd shake your hand, but I might start a riot."

"I'm Hayden," she said. "Nice to meet you." She thought that would be it, that he would turn back to his friends. But he kept looking at her and, at least once, the area below her neck.

"So you're with the groom?"

"No, the bride. Actually, with a friend of the bride's." Hayden looked around the room. "She said to meet her here, but I haven't seen her yet." Hayden didn't mention the crisis with the bride.

"Oh yeah? Who's your friend? Maybe I know her."

"Amra Abbas."

"Amra Abbas," he repeated. "Nope. Doesn't ring a bell."

Hayden nodded, noticing his warm smile and relaxed demeanor. And the lack of a cheesy pickup line. He was good-looking enough to be a player, but somehow he didn't give off that vibe. He seemed genuine. Of course, she wasn't necessarily the best judge of that kind of thing.

"So, Hayden, what do you do?"

"I'm a lawyer."

He shrunk down in his chair, dropping his shoulders. "Of course. My archenemy."

She laughed. "So you're a doctor."

"Resident. Anesthesiology. At Brigham and Women's."

"Wow."

"I know, you're impressed, right?" He grinned.

"No, I was just thinking that there's a lot of room for lawsuits in anesthesiology."

"Ouch." He laughed. "Just tell me you're not a trial lawyer."

"I'm not a trial lawyer."

"Good. I thought maybe they were going to have to separate us."

Hayden smiled. But her stomach fell, too. She barely knew him, but somehow she felt a twinge of sadness at the idea of being separated from him. She nursed a tiny, selfish thought: Maybe the not-so-small bridal crisis could balloon just enough to keep Amra busy for a bit longer.

Amra watched Zainab announce that the wedding had been postponed. It was a lie, of course, but it was the explanation Rukan felt would spare her the most shame. When the crowd rumbled, Zainab said that dinner would be served, making a joke about its having already been paid for. "Please," she said, "enjoy yourselves."

Amra looked around. No one seemed to care about the devastation seven flights up. She spotted Hayden at a table near the back of the room talking to some *desi* guy and assessed the buffet line to see how long it would take to get something to eat before checking on her. Too long. The guests had swarmed the tables from both sides, as though the delay had been just long enough for famine to set in. Amra wished Indian food had been part of the bargain; she could have used a heaping plate of *korma* right about then.

She started toward Hayden's table and then saw him: Mateen. He stood, leaning against the double doors in a dark suit and striped tie, watching her. He held one arm behind his back. When she met his gaze, he raised his eyebrows and smiled, as if to say, *I'm here*. Hayden would have to fend for herself. Amra made a beeline for Mateen.

"You came," she said, surprised at how strong her sense of gratitude was. He produced a bouquet of light pink roses from behind his back. She smiled; she'd told him about the color of her outfit weeks ago.

She wanted to explain what had happened, but she didn't want to betray Rukan. She simply repeated Zainab's words: "The wedding has been postponed." He nodded somberly, and she knew he understood that there wasn't going to be any future date for Rukan's wedding.

"How's Rukan?"

"As well as can be expected," Amra said, and shook her head. "Don't you hate it when people say that? What does that even mean? Why doesn't anyone say 'as bad as you would think'? Why doesn't anyone tell the truth? That the person is a mess. That she is crumpled on a bed in some random hotel, embarrassed and angry, and that no one knows for sure when she will be okay again?" Amra bit her lower lip. She hadn't meant to say so much. She didn't want Mateen to think she was a basket case herself.

But he just ran his finger along her cheek. "They should," he agreed. "They should say all of that. And I'm sorry that Rukan has to go through this, but she'll be okay. She's got great friends to help her." He tilted her head up gently. "And what about you? Are you okay?"

She nodded. "I am now." She hoped it didn't reveal too much. But he just smiled and asked if they could go for a walk.

The air was cool and he put his blazer over her shoulders, keeping his hand on the small of her back as they walked along Boylston Street.

"So," he said without looking at her. "Why am I so nervous?"

It was hard to believe that he could be—larger-than-life Mateen, running million-dollar deals. She was tempted to play dumb, to say, *Nervous about what?* But it was too important for games. She leaned in against his side, hoping to reassure them both.

"Amra, have you ever been to L.A.?"

"Once. For a seminar."

"What did you think of it?"

"I never left the hotel."

He laughed. "Not the answer I was looking for."

"What was the answer you were looking for?"

He stopped walking and looked in her eyes. "That you loved it. That you could see yourself living there."

"Mateen." How could she explain how hard she'd worked at her firm, how many hours she'd put in, how many tedious dinners and parties and sporting events she had endured to make contacts and forge relationships with her clients? "My job is in Boston."

"I know. But we do have law firms in L.A."

"But I'm so close to making partner here."

"Well, I assume you'd go in as a lateral, right? So you wouldn't really lose anything."

"But I would. I would lose the relationships I've built. The connections you need to make partner. At a new firm, I'd just be another associate. It would set me back years."

"Is it everything? Your career? What about a family and kids? Are you going to work these hours when you have a baby, Amra?"

She almost laughed. He didn't know the half of it. "Hopefully, I'll be a partner by then. I'll have more leverage. But if I go to a new firm now, I won't have any leverage." He stiffened and took a step back from her. She felt it steal her breath, that step.

"So I guess my question stands. What are we doing here?"

She tried to make her voice light. "You could move to Boston."

"I wish I could." He did not, she noted, feel the need to justify his position.

Mateen stared at the sidewalk and then he shrugged. "I guess we should head back." They walked in silence to the hotel entrance.

"Aren't you coming in?" Amra asked.

He stuck his hands in his pockets. "I don't think so."

She couldn't let his words—the import of them—in. Not there, not when she had to go back into the reception. She nodded and slid his coat off her shoulders.

"Keep it. You might need it later." But she didn't want it. The idea of his empty coat in her condo, she knew, had the potential to bring her to her knees. She handed it back to him.

He took the coat without protest, holding it with both hands in front of him. She wanted to ask where he was staying, when his flight was, whether they could talk the next day. But a single rotation of the earth wasn't going to change their conversation. He'd come to ask her something, and she'd given the wrong answer. There wasn't anything else to say. And they both knew it. She smiled a flat, pressed-lip smile and pushed through the glass doors.

15

WITH A FEW well-placed calls, Hayden tracked down his contact information. "Fadi," wedding guest and anesthesia resident at Brigham and Women's Hospital, was Fadi Amin, M.D., in his third and final year of residency. She guessed he was around her age, perhaps a year or two younger, depending on whether he'd gone straight through school. She studied his name, which she'd written on a white legal pad, and swiveled in her chair, facing the rain-streaked window of her office. The question was what to do with the information.

She briefly considered enlisting Amra's help. It was possible that Amra knew of him, even though he hadn't recognized her name. Unfortunately, by the time Amra had found Hayden at the wedding, Fadi's restless friends had convinced him to leave. He'd barely had time to say good-bye to her as they pulled him out the door. Amra's friend Rukan must know him. He was a guest at her ill-fated wedding, after all. Hayden didn't cross the Amra option off her list, but for some reason, she wasn't quite ready to bring Amra into it.

The most obvious and direct path to her goal would be to call Fadi at the hospital. Hayden abhorred the thought. It reminded her of Sadie Hawkins Day dances in high school, and even then, when the girls were supposed to do the inviting, it hadn't felt right to her.

Still, she could easily fabricate an excuse to phone Fadi, perhaps concerns about a grandmother who needed anesthesia for some surgical procedure, accompanied by an apology for bothering him, but that she had, fortuitously, remembered him from the wedding. She felt there was about a fifty-fifty chance that he would see right through it.

Hayden took a deep breath and dialed.

"Brigham and Women's," the receptionist said.

"Hi, I'm trying to reach Dr. Fadi Amin."

"What department?"

"Anesthesiology."

"Hold please."

Hayden watched the clock. After eight minutes and thirty-nine seconds, a different woman came on the line. "Anesthesiology."

"Yes, I'd like to speak to Fadi Amin."

"Are you a patient?"

"No. I'm an acquaintance. I met him at a wedding last weekend. I have some questions about my grandmother."

The receptionist paused, and then asked if her grandmother was a patient.

"Not currently."

"He's in surgery right now. Can I take a message?"

Hayden gave her name and cell phone number and hung up, wondering what she had just done.

By the time she left the office, Fadi had not returned her call. Hayden stuffed her briefcase with extra force. Just who did Dr. Fadi Amin think he was? She thought back to the wedding, wondering if she had imagined his flirtatiousness. It wouldn't have been the first time. But he had seemed so attentive, ignoring his friends to talk to her. She told herself that he probably had a busy schedule. It *was* surgery after all. He couldn't just leave some poor patient on the table to call her.

In her apartment, she stood under a hot shower until her skin was patched with red spots and her fingers tingled. She thought back to the pasta she'd had at lunch and decided to skip dinner. She made a cup of green tea and checked her voice mails. The first was from a Jones Day guy about a new deal. She made a note on the back of her grocery list while she hit PLAY on the second message.

"Hayden, it's Fadi. From the wedding." She thought she heard a smile in his voice. "I'm returning your call about your grandmother." Had he paused before "grandmother"? She couldn't be sure. "But since I have your number now, I'm going to kill two birds with one stone and see if you'd like to have lunch on Saturday."

Hayden let out a squeal. She had to play the message back to hear the end, that he'd try her the next day, and sit on her hands to keep from calling him back that minute.

They made plans to meet at the Isabella Stewart Gardner Museum café for a late lunch on Saturday. He'd called the next day, as promised, saying he didn't have much time at the moment but that he'd be happy to answer her questions on Saturday, "unless they're of a serious nature?" She'd said Saturday would be fine.

In the cab, she smoothed her hair and cursed the humidity. Even after forty minutes with the flatiron, it would only cooperate for so long. She wished he'd suggested somewhere else for lunch; even though the café garden was romantic, it was, of course, outdoors. Her outfit had been another matter. She didn't want to be too dressed up, but she definitely wanted to wear heels and show off her legs. After a frenzied wardrobe session that lasted slightly more than an hour and saw the contents of her closet emptied onto her bed—if there was going to be something more after lunch, it would have to be at his place—she'd settled on a short, sleeveless dress with the Jimmy Choo heels that she'd put on her credit card for exactly this kind of occasion.

She arrived before Fadi and was led by the hostess to a small table, where she sat fidgeting with her hair until he finally appeared.

"Hayden, great to see you." He was even better looking in broad daylight. He wore khaki pants and a white button-down shirt with the sleeves rolled up past his elbows. He filled out the shirt perfectly, and even when he sat his stomach remained flat. His dark hair looked damp, as though he'd just showered, a thought that made Hayden's own stomach seize, and his jaw, which was slightly squarer and stronger than she recalled, was covered in a faint five o'clock shadow.

He adjusted his napkin on his lap and picked up the menu. "So, tell me about your grandmother."

"I'm sorry?" Hayden stopped ogling him long enough to focus. "Oh, yes, my grandmother." She paused. She'd planned out what to say, researching geriatric anesthesiology, and had even written down some questions on a lined index card in her purse. But as Fadi looked at her with those dark eyes and that open, generous smile, she changed her mind. "My grandmother is eighty-one and in perfect health."

"So she's not, imminently, having a surgical procedure."

Hayden shook her head.

"That is the best news I've heard all day." Fadi smiled. "I mean for your grandmother, of course."

Hayden's smile faded. "Of course."

"And for me as well."

"It is?"

"It is." He leaned in. "Because I think it means that you wanted to call me as much as I wanted to call you."

She felt her cheeks redden. "Did you really want to call me?"

"I did. And I tried like hell to remember who you said you knew at the wedding, to see if I could hunt you down. But I couldn't remember her name."

"Amra Abbas."

"Right, but you see, now I don't need to know." He gestured to his cell phone. "Because I've got your number right here."

Hayden nodded and opened her menu. Fadi recommended the "incredible" roasted Atlantic salmon, making her wonder how often and with whom he'd dined at the café. She wrinkled her nose and said she couldn't eat fish, something about the texture, but that the thyme and sweet onion quiche sounded delicious. In the end, he ordered the quiche as well—"Making you nauseous on our first date wasn't exactly my plan"—and proceeded to ask about her job and her friend Amra and what she'd thought of that crazy wedding. As they talked, he revealed that he was, in fact, a year younger than she, at twenty-eight, and that he'd grown up in New York but planned to settle in Boston permanently. For the first time in months, Hayden thought that maybe she would stay in Boston, too.

After their coffee had gone cold and the waiters were starting to clear their throats, Fadi took the credit card receipt, which he'd signed a half hour earlier, and pulled out her chair. He apologized for not having more time, saying he wished they could spend the afternoon together. Outside, he hailed her a cab.

"I'd really like to see you again," he said, taking her hands.

"Me too."

"Good." He leaned down and kissed her on the cheek, his face lingering close to hers before he pulled away. She wished they were somewhere more private, that there weren't so many people on the street walking past them.

In the cab, her heart fluttered like a schoolgirl's. *You always feel like this in the beginning,* she scolded herself. But even she, with all of her poor judgment and misplaced affection, could tell this was different.

At home, she took a tall glass of water to the bathroom and swallowed six laxatives. There was no way she was going to let a high-calorie lunch ruin this for her.

16

Zainab wondered if it was time for some sort of intervention. For the third Sunday in a row, Amra had rebuffed her invitation to go running. She said she was fine, that she was just swamped at work, but Zainab wasn't buying it. First of all, Amra sounded like she had a cold, her voice thick, her ending syllables muted, and Amra never got sick. Even more worrisome was the music: Zainab had been prepared to look the other way when she'd heard "It Must Have Been Love" playing in the background and even "Nothing Compares 2 U." But this time Zainab was sure she'd heard "Mandy," by Barry fucking Manilow. If that wasn't a cry for help, she wasn't sure what was.

Frankly, Zainab didn't understand the big deal. It was Mateen from when they were kids, the same guy who'd played video games with the other boys in their parents' basements. Yes, he was good-looking and successful, but he clearly had no respect for Amra's career, thinking she would just walk away from it like it was nothing, like she hadn't worked her ass off for the past seven years—eleven if you counted Smith—making law review at Columbia, living on Diet Coke and takeout Chinese food, laboring under Eric's untreated narcissistic personality disorder. What was the point of all of that? she wanted to ask Mateen. So she could quit, marry him, and have his babies?

Zainab grabbed her phone and headed toward the Common. When she rounded Beacon Street, she got a call from Ben announcing that Jill Gill had struck again. For weeks, Jill had been asking questions about Eleanor's business dealings in Thailand, harassing the board members of Eleanor's former corporation, her personal accountant, and even her adult daughter. Eleanor assured Zainab that no one was talking. But now, according to Ben, Jill had e-mailed an article she planned to print reporting that Eleanor was quietly buying up sweatshops in Thailand. The article was titled "Senate Candidate Advocates for Women—Unless She Stands to Profit." Jill was looking for the campaign's comment.

Zainab had known about the purchase from the beginning. It was one of the many issues Eleanor disclosed during their initial meeting, a debriefing of sorts, where they separated out things that Zainab was free to discuss should they arise during the campaign (her drug use in college; the fact that she had once, briefly, been a member of NOW; her bout with melanoma) and things that were likely to come up but that under no circumstances, and with the threat of swift firing and potential legal action, was Zainab to discuss (the fact that her husband had been unfaithful and her plan to quickly buy up sweatshops and turn them into guarded dormitories before the local pimps had a chance to notice what was going on). When Zainab pointed out that people would be investigating her and such a purchase was likely to be fair game in the campaign, Eleanor said the purchase could be acknowledged, but the plans could not. "Not without jeopardizing the workers," Eleanor said. "It has to look like just another greedy American investor." When Zainab said that might not be the best PR move, and could even cost her the election, Eleanor raised her eyebrows and said, "So?"

And now Jill Gill had decided to make it an issue. Zainab needed a trusted neo-con voice. And an oversized coffee. She adjusted her headphones and headed for the Starbucks on Winter Street.

Ben cleared his throat. "Zainab?"

"I'm here. Tell Jill that we acknowledge the purchase by Eleanor; that it is a business transaction, plain and simple; and that we won't have any further comment. And get me Chase Holland's number."

"Who?"

"Sorry. Charles Holland. The right-wing radio guy."

"You're kidding."

"Ben!"

"Okay, okay. Hold on."

Chase answered on the first ring. "It's Zainab Mir," she said, hoping her forced smile would reflect in her voice. "How are you?"

"Great. I'm great. Hey, this is unexpected."

"I'm sure. Listen, much as it pains me to admit this, I need a favor."

Silence. And then: "From me."

"Yes," she said. "Implausible as that may seem."

"Quite a bit, actually," he said. "But that's fine. Shoot."

"I was hoping to talk in person."

"Oh. Well, I have a couple of things I need to do this afternoon. But I could meet you somewhere around six. Does that work?"

"Six is fine. But I think it might be better if we don't meet in public."

"How Deep Throat–esque."

"Nothing that important, I promise. If you don't mind, could you just swing by my condo?"

"Are you making dinner?"

"Unlikely."

"Okay, I'll bring something."

"Really, it won't take that long. Just a few minutes—"

Chase cut her off. "Look, you've got to eat, I've got to eat. Give me your address and I'll see you at six."

. . .

At 5:30, Zainab stood in front of her closet, deciding if she was actually going to try to appeal to Chase's apparent attraction to her. She decided that no job, no campaign, was worth pimping herself out for and, with more than a little disgust, threw on faded jeans and a SHIRLEY CHISHOLM FOR PRESIDENT tee shirt. She twisted her hair into a bun at the back of her neck and left her face bare except for the smear of kohl under her eyes.

The bell rang promptly at six. When she opened the door, Chase stood in the hall holding two paper bags.

Zainab frowned. "That's a lot of takeout for two people."

"It's not takeout. It's groceries."

"You brought me groceries?"

"Us," he said. "I brought *us* groceries. Since you so rudely refused to cook for me, I'm going to cook for you."

She didn't know what to say. He stepped inside and looked around, taking in the matching white couches, the espresso-colored floors, the large loop sculptures, and said it was like something out of a magazine. He placed the grocery bags on the kitchen island overlooking the living room. From his legs—what she could see of them in his long khaki shorts—she guessed he was not a runner. Running did great things for a woman's legs, but Zainab thought it made men look emaciated and somehow frail. His looked more like the calves of a tennis player. So he had nice legs. Zainab still bet she could take him in a 5K.

"This is really nice," she said, "like above and beyond nice. And unexpected. And a bit odd, actually." She lost her train of thought for a moment, thinking about just how strange it was that this man who had essentially called her a terrorist and a traitor on the radio was standing in her kitchen about to cook dinner for her. "It's really not necessary. I just need a few minutes of your time."

"Right. So where do you keep your skillets?"

She waved. "In the bottom drawer. Chase, you're not listening to me."

"No, I am. Really. And I would find a cutting board where?"

She pulled one from under the sink and looked at the items he'd set on the smooth concrete countertop: cheese, mushrooms, Swiss chard, pumpkin.

"What are you making?"

"Pumpkin-ricotta ravioli."

"That sounds amazing."

"We can hope, right? Now, where do you keep your blender?" She started to protest but gave up, pointing at the cupboard.

While Chase cooked, he talked nearly nonstop, telling her that he'd grown up in the Midwest, also in a single-parent household, that his mother had raised him the best she could but that he'd moved out before he graduated and had little contact with her after. When Zainab asked how he became such a raging conservative, he shrugged and blamed his major. He'd been more of a progressive, he said, until he started taking econ courses and realized, "to oversimplify it, that life is full of trade-offs" and that "the market was as good an arbiter of the whole efficiency/equality question as any bought-and-paid-for politician." She asked what that had to do with issues like abortion and school prayer. He stopped stirring for a moment and said, "Not much."

"So where does all that come from?"

He shrugged. "Just an externality, I guess."

Before Zainab could respond, Eleanor called. "I have to take this," she said, and retreated to her room. When she looked at the clock, she noticed that it was after seven. So much for a quick ten-minute conversation with Chase.

When she finished her call, she found him in the dining room looking at the framed artwork on the far wall.

"Those are pretty amazing paintings," he said.

"The Gulgees? They're my favorite."

"The what?"

"Ismail Gulgee. He's a Pakistani artist. He's quite famous actually."

Chase raised his eyebrows. "They're originals?"

"Yes."

"Wow. Where did you get them?"

She paused. "I got the two blue ones at Sotheby's. The beige one I purchased directly from a private seller."

He whistled. "Eleanor must pay you well." Zainab let that go. It was none of his business how she'd gotten the paintings. Chase moved closer, squinting. "I like the movement in them. Sort of that whole action-painting vibe."

Zainab looked at him. "You speak art?"

"A bit. I took a few classes in college."

She nodded and then remembered that it was Chase Holland standing in her dining room. "Is dinner ready?" He nodded and motioned for her to go ahead. The island was already set for two. Chase spooned the ravioli onto their plates and waited for her to take a bite.

"This is fantastic," Zainab said, wiping her mouth. "Where did you learn to cook like this?"

"My mom wasn't exactly a whiz in the kitchen." He shrugged. "So you wanted to talk to me about something?"

Zainab nodded and took a small breath. "We just found out that Jill Gill is about to go public with a story that places Eleanor in something of a bad light."

"So what else is new?"

"This is different. It's partly true, but it's not the whole story."

"So tell the whole story."

"I can't."

"Why not?"

"I can't tell you that either."

He laughed. "Okay, honestly? I have no idea what you're talking about or what it has to do with me."

She got up and handed him Jill Gill's piece. He read it and then shook his head. "'Bad light' might have been a bit of an understatement."

"Right, but that's just on its face."

"I'm still not sure what this has to do with me."

"Well, that's the thing," Zainab said. "I want you to defend it."

He choked on his water. "I'm sorry?"

"I want you to give the pro-sweatshop argument."

"You want me to do what?"

"You know, the whole Paul Krugman argument that we can't judge these things from a first world perspective, that in third world countries what we call sweatshops are actually *desirable* jobs, better than a lot of other jobs. Or starving." She got up and grabbed her briefcase off the couch. "I have a stack of articles you might want to read."

"I'm familiar with the argument," he said. "I just wouldn't have pictured you as a proponent." He took a bite of his pasta and wiped his mouth. "If you've done the research and it's your candidate actually buying up the sweatshops, why don't you float the argument? Just explain that Eleanor doesn't think it's exploitative."

"That would be easier," she conceded. "Except it's not true."

He leaned forward in his chair. "So what you're saying is that Eleanor thinks sweatshops *are* exploitative, but she's going to operate them anyway."

"Well, that's off the record, of course. And there is more to the whole situation, as I said, that exonerates Eleanor."

"I think you're going to have to tell me what that is."

"I can't." Zainab sat back down. "Not even off the record."

"And I'm just supposed to take your word that there is some redeeming explanation that you can't share with me, and go put forth a defense that technically doesn't even apply here."

"Ideally, yes."

"Why would I do that? I don't support Eleanor. From my perspective, anything that makes her look bad helps Fred Whitaker."

"I know. I realize that." Zainab sighed. "But I'm asking for a favor here. For you to believe me when I say this isn't the issue you want to focus on, that there's an important reason for this, beyond the campaign."

It moved between them, her request and its implicit dependence on his trusting her. She could see that he believed her. It both surprised her and didn't at the same time.

He folded his napkin and placed it over his plate. "And that's why we couldn't meet in public, because people are going to be scrambling to know why I would take this position, why I of all people would defend Eleanor, and if we were seen together, they'd think . . . well, we both know what they'd think." He leaned back and stared at her. She felt it at that very moment, like one of the paintings on her wall—a bold, sweeping *shift*.

"So you'll do it?"

At first, he didn't answer. Then he nodded. "I'll do it. Under one condition."

"What?"

"Next time, you make dinner."

17

HAYDEN COULDN'T GET over the nagging feeling that something wasn't right. In the seven weeks she'd been seeing Fadi, except for their initial lunch, they had never had a date on the weekend. At first, when she'd let him do all the asking—after all, she'd made the bold first move and, feminism notwithstanding, she didn't want to appear desperate—she'd told herself that she was dating a doctor, and she needed to be understanding about his schedule. When people asked if they had plans, she'd say, "No, he's on call," or "You know how crazy physicians' schedules are," and try not to sulk. But when she asked him why he always had to work on the weekends, he said he didn't, that there was a rotation and he only had work one or two weekends a month. She'd grown quiet, walking through the Boston Common, and stayed that way as he put out a plaid blanket and unpacked their lunch.

"Hayden, what's bugging you?" he'd finally asked.

"Nothing."

"Come on. What is it?"

She paused. She didn't want to be one of *those* girls. But still, if he wasn't working, where *was* he all of those weekends? Finally, she blurted out, "Why don't we ever go out on the weekends?"

He laughed and took her hand, kissing the fingertips. "Because I go to my parents' house on the weekends. In New York."

"Every weekend? You go to your parents' house *every* weekend?"

"When I'm not working, yes."

"Why?"

"I guess I've never really thought about it. I just do."

"You must think about it. You have to drive there or fly or whatever. That's a decision, right?"

"I have a large extended family," he said. "There's usually some big event or gathering. What can I say? They like me to be a part of things."

At the time, Hayden let it go. It was just his family. How much fun could they be? Once they got more serious, she figured he would start sticking around Boston on the weekends. Or maybe he'd start taking her with him. It wasn't like he didn't want to be with her. During the week, she was spending most nights at his place in Cambridge. When she asked why he couldn't spend the night at her apartment, he explained that he was closer to the hospital in case of an emergency. Eventually, she learned the real reason: the morning phone calls from his mother, which came early enough to find them still in bed, pressed together. The first morning Hayden had been there, Fadi raised his eyebrows and held up a hand to quiet her. Apparently, his parents were old-fashioned. Hayden complied, staying silent as a mouse, because she didn't want to make a bad impression before she even met his mother. When he got off the phone that first time, he kissed her deeply and thanked her for being so good. But sometimes the conversations went on forever and Hayden grew restless. Once, she'd started to run her hand up his leg, but he scowled and left the bed.

On Sunday nights, he would call from his car and tell her to meet him at his place. "I really missed you," he would say, with enough catch in his voice for her to know he meant it. He always returned with plastic containers of spiced meats and vegetables, often lamb *vindaloo* and chicken *biryani*. "Souvenirs," he would say, although they both knew that the food was not for her, that his mother didn't even know she existed.

And now it had been almost two months, and Hayden wanted to bring him to the firm's summer associate boat cruise in a couple of weeks. It was on a Friday night, and Hayden didn't want to look like she couldn't get a date. Several of the women in the summer class wore impressive engagement rings, and at least one had the Yale undergrad degree and top-Manhattan-law-firm fiancé that suggested a wedding announcement in *The New York Times* would be forthcoming. During the perfunctory lunches with these women, their smug gestures with their left hands were not lost on Hayden.

When she asked him about the boat cruise, Fadi shook his head. "I'm going to New York, silly," he said, and tapped her nose in a way that he must have thought was cute but was intensely annoying to Hayden.

"Can't you just stay here that weekend? Just this once?" She regretted the last part. She wanted him to stay *every* weekend.

"I really can't. There's a party I said I'd go to. It would be rude to just not show."

"I'm not asking you not to show. You could call and say you're busy. You could even say you have to work. It's not like they're going to check."

"I wish I could, Hayden."

That night, at his place, she'd tried more exacting ways of persuasion. When both their shirts were off and he was breathing hard, she whispered it in his ear again, a plea to come with her. But he just pulled her closer without responding.

Hayden finally caught Amra for lunch near the end of July. Amra hadn't been herself in weeks, looking tired, and, while not exactly disheveled, somehow off. Whatever was eating her, she refused to discuss it. Hayden knew Hank had been giving her a hard time, so maybe it was just that. She didn't want to bother her, but she really needed Amra's opinion.

When she finished explaining the odd nature of her relationship with Fadi—the weekends alone, the furtive phone calls from New York that usually ended in an abrupt, muffled good-bye, the morning conversations with his mother, when he practically gagged her to keep her quiet—Amra sighed.

"Well?" Hayden said.

"I don't know him, so this is merely speculation," Amra began. She dabbed at her mouth with the linen napkin. "But it sounds to me like he must have a pretty traditional family. He's probably not supposed to be dating."

"What do you mean, not supposed to be dating?"

"Conservative Muslims don't believe in dating. Particularly not white, non-Muslim women."

"What is this, the eighteen hundreds?"

Amra flashed her a look.

"Sorry. So are you saying that this relationship isn't going anywhere?"

"No. Not at all. Muslim guys marry non-Muslim girls all the time. But usually the girls convert." Amra shrugged. "And even then, some families accept the situation and some don't."

Hayden couldn't process it all at that moment, the idea that Fadi's family might never accept her.

"You just need to talk to him," Amra said. "Ask him what his intentions are, what the situation with his family is."

"What if it's not good?"

Amra nodded. "Better to know sooner rather than later."

In the Eastern Religions section of the bookstore, Hayden found titles about Zen this and meditation that, a handful of books about

Hinduism, one about Sikhism, and several ominous copies of Robert Spencer's *The Politically Incorrect Guide to Islam (and the Crusades),* complete with a masked gunman on the cover. In a gesture of solidarity with Fadi, she placed the Spencer books facing backward on the bottom shelf. Finally, she settled on Suzanne Haneef's *What Everyone Should Know about Islam and Muslims,* because the Western first name was reassuring to her, and a copy of the Qur'an, translated by Ahmed Ali.

As she stood in line, it dawned on her that, aside from Fadi and Amra, she knew no Muslims, nor did she really know what they believed. She remembered Amra saying once that there were important similarities between Christianity and Islam, but she had no idea what they were. When she thought of Islam, she thought desert, camels, and covering. She had some vague sense that it was not a great place for women to be, and yet Amra was so normal and had a job and didn't wear that headscarf that so many of the Muslim women on television wore.

When she'd told her mother about Fadi, she'd emphasized the doctor part and played down the Pakistani part. But her mother, a high school AP History teacher, was geopolitically aware enough to ask about his religion. When Hayden disclosed it, her mother had been silent for a long while, before telling her to watch the Sally Field movie *Not Without My Daughter.* Hayden laughed, having seen the movie in college. "Mom," she'd said, "the man in that movie was *Iranian.*" When her mom continued to protest, Hayden told her not to worry, that no one was moving to Iran. Later, she felt that maybe she shouldn't have implicated the entire nation of Iran, that perhaps she was as bad as her mother. She was glad that Fadi would never know she'd said it. But it had seemed to end the conversation with her mother, so Hayden couldn't fully regret tossing the Iranians under the bus.

She read the Haneef book first. It was fascinating to learn of the similar rituals and the prophets in common. The book said that dress and other customs were often the result of cultural differences. And yet it suggested that a woman's hair must be covered. Hayden thought about that for a long time, even going to her closet to pull out the ubiquitous Burberry-patterned scarf that she'd purchased with her summer associate money years earlier. She took a deep breath and put the scarf over her head, tying it underneath her chin. Her blond hair peeped through at her forehead. She looked more like an old-fashioned movie star about to take a weekend trip in a convertible than one of the Arab women she'd seen on TV. She pulled it lower on her forehead and tied it tighter. Then she pulled it off quickly. Fadi wasn't conservative. The last thing he would care about was whether she covered her hair.

18

CHASE READ THE e-mail from his self-declared fan: *Since you've been letting the Paki from the Winthrop-Smith campaign have it, here's a freebie. So much focus on not offending, but they are so ass backwards!* The "fan" had pasted an article into the e-mail about HIV and a practice called *watta satta,* a tradition in Pakistan where a brother and sister from one family marry a brother and sister from another family. Chase had to read the article a second time to understand. Apparently some woman had contracted HIV, likely from her drug-using husband, which was not as uncommon in Pakistan as one might think, and couldn't tell anyone because her family was connected to her husband's family through sibling marriages. She wasn't receiving any medical care and the signs, particularly the skin lesions, were becoming noticeable.

Chase put his hands in his head and felt like he was going to vomit. He took a deep breath and reread the e-mail for any indication that it had something to do with him, that this person had been digging around in his past. His first thought was how Savannah and her Bible-thumping parents might react if they learned the truth. He told himself to calm down. There was no reason for anyone to be investigating him. He wasn't running for anything. His book hadn't been published yet. And on its face, the e-mail did seem to be nothing but a cheap swipe at Zainab.

He put his finger over the delete button, holding it there for several minutes, but in the end he couldn't bring himself to push it. He printed the e-mail and placed it inside his leather bag. Just in case.

19

AMRA DROPPED HER briefcase by the door and stepped out of her shoes without putting them in the closet. She stripped off her nylons on the way to the kitchen, leaving them on the living room floor. She tossed her jacket on the couch and untucked her blouse. She stood in front of the open refrigerator, surveying with little interest its contents: a plastic takeout container from Chef Chow's, organic soy yogurt, broccoli florets. She closed the door and riffled through the delivery menus. Finally, she settled on a pint of cookie-dough ice cream, eating it from the carton with an oversized spoon. She walked to the French doors, went outside on the balcony, and slumped in her Adirondack chair.

She thought about Hank and how he was undermining her with Eric, questioning her negotiating style, implying she wasn't tough enough. When she'd explained to him that she picked her battles, often giving in on inconsequential changes in order to fight for more critical issues, he called it a "defeatist attitude." *You have no idea, Hank,* she thought. Except she felt worse than that, like someone who had taken a stand for the sake of taking it, only to find out it was the wrong stand after all. This—working with Hank and Eric—is what she had said no to Mateen for. The hours, the exhaustion, the frustration. Eating ice cream for dinner, alone on her balcony.

She wondered what Mateen was doing. He was probably out to dinner with some new *desi* woman, someone his mother thought had better credentials. Or someone who was actually willing to compromise to make a life with him.

Her own mother had been careful not to bring it up after the one time Amra had asked if she talked to Mateen's mother. "No, *beti,* it wouldn't be appropriate for Safa and me to talk," her mother had said. Instead, she asked if there was anything Amra needed.

She shivered, a combination of the ice cream and the cool night air. She trudged inside, picked up her nylons and jacket, and put her shoes in the closet. She knew she should mark up the acquisition agreement she was working on. But she was tired. Didn't she deserve a break? She could set her alarm for 3:00 and have two hours before she went to the gym. Or three if she skipped it. She thought about the ice cream dinner and scratched that idea. She couldn't let herself get fat. How on earth would her parents get her married if she were a fat, middle-aged spinster? And then she laughed at herself, heated some tea in an oversized mug, and dug out the agreement.

Just before midnight, her phone vibrated with a text. Her heart skipped, even though she didn't want it to. She picked up her phone.

Are you awake?

It was Mateen. She closed her eyes and opened them again to make sure she wasn't imagining it. Barely breathing, she responded that yes, she was awake.

Good. Do me a favor. Look up my company on the Wall Street Journal's website.

Amra almost cried. She'd hoped he was contacting her to tell her that he loved her, that he couldn't live without her. Instead, he wanted to share news about his company and the career that kept him three thousand miles away from her.

Mateen, I'm really tired and I've got work to do. I'll take a look tomorrow, ok?

It will only take a second. Please?

Fine, she thought. It was only her job. She told him to hang on while she looked. At first, she couldn't find it. Then, as she scrolled down, she saw the headline. His firm was opening an office in Boston. She skimmed the article, reading about their recent leasing of office space in the financial district, how they were planning to be up and running by the fourth quarter, how "Mateen Syed, former Director, newly promoted to VP," would spearhead the new endeavor. Amra tried to call Mateen but it went straight to voice mail. She texted back.

Mateen!!!!

So you read it?

It's definite? You're moving to Boston?

I guess you read it.

I can't believe it.

Me either. Now do me one more favor, okay?

Anything.

Look outside your door.

She got up slowly. It couldn't be a package. No one delivered this late. She went to the door and, holding her breath, opened it.

Mateen was on one knee, his eyes solemn, staring straight at her. In his right hand, between his finger and thumb, he held a diamond ring. Before he could say a word, Amra started to cry. She shook her head and put her hand over her mouth.

"Amra, I thought I could leave you here in Boston. I thought I could return to my life in L.A. and just move on, find someone else. But there is no one else. There's only you. And if you need to be here, on this coast, in this city, then I need to be here, too." He took her hand. "So, since I've rearranged my entire life—" He smiled, and Amra laughed through her tears. "Will you marry me?"

She couldn't find her voice. Not if her life depended on it. She just nodded. He put the ring on her finger, stood, and embraced her. Behind his shoulder, she held up her hand and said a silent prayer of thanks.

20

Zainab sat in her bed, the phone still in her hand, notes about health care and insurance trusts and public options scattered around her, her laptop's screen blackened. In the mirror on the opposite wall, she could see her brows knit into a small, surprised frown. First Rukan, and now Amra. Maybe because Rukan's engagement came with the family drama and interfaith condemnations, because it had been sufficiently *distracting,* Zainab did not recall even a moment of this feeling—something approaching disappointment—when Rukan had announced her engagement. It wasn't that she was jealous. When she had stated for years that she didn't want to get married, she'd meant it. It was not a "Smith thing," as some slighted Yale grad had said when she didn't want to "get serious." And it was not, as the aunties speculated, a reaction to her parents' painful marriage. No one ever considered that it might actually be her choice. That Zainab simply felt sure there was no man who would fit her, not truly, and not in the important ways that would allow her to contemplate notions of *forever.*

Amra understood Zainab's position as much as anyone could. "You think the *desi* guys are too traditional, even the liberal ones who say they're not, and the American guys will never understand how much being *desi* is part of your identity, even if they pretend to respect it," Amra had said, as though the only fissures were religious or cultural, as though there were not other, equally valid divisions, like the gulf between people who had to blame one of their parents for the absence of the other and those who couldn't even imagine such a thing. When Amra had said, gently, that Zainab still needed to consider the possibility that there was someone out there, Zainab shook her head. Why did she need to consider that possibility? The idea that someone would fit into the absurdly small center of her personal Venn diagram was laughable.

Later, when Amra said she didn't want her to be alone, Zainab joked that she had Amra, which, of course, made Amra cry and promise to always be there for her. And now Zainab realized that exchange, and the not-even-remotely-joking sentiment underlying it, was the genesis of her sadness. She did not want to lose Amra. Fortunately, Amra was too jacked up on her good news, with Mateen apparently right there in the flesh, to notice any hesitation in Zainab's voice. And when her phone rang again, startling her out of her selfish reverie, she took a breath and committed herself to sounding happier. But it wasn't Amra. It was Chase Holland, announcing that he was "cashing in."

"You're what?"

"Let's just say I need your help this time," he said. "And you know what that means."

She groaned. "Dinner."

"Bingo."

Zainab scooted the papers out of the way and straightened her legs. "Small problem."

"Let me guess. You don't cook."

"I don't cook."

"Right," he said, "but isn't that sort of the point of a Seven Sisters education?"

"Careful."

"And didn't *Julia Child* go to Smith?"

"You're talking a lot of trash for someone who said he needs help."

"Good point." He gave her his address in Cambridge. "Eight tomorrow? I'll take care of dinner."

Zainab arrived twenty minutes late. When she knocked, Chase yelled, "It's open." She entered a modern-looking loft with exposed brick and ductwork and dark wood floors. She found him in the kitchen, stirring a wok on the gas stove, surrounded by rising steam. "God, it smells good in here," she said. "Personality issues notwithstanding, you might just be marriage material." She realized what she had said and quickly added, "You know, for the right woman."

"Of course." He shook the wok with both hands and added tamari sauce in concentric circles. "And who would that be?"

"I don't know. There must be lots of gun-toting, immigrant-hunting, Phyllis Schlafly types to choose from."

He laughed. "Now that's an image."

"Quite." She took a seat at the small table and watched him transfer the contents of the wok into a square wooden bowl. The table was set with matching square plates and wineglasses filled with sparkling water.

"Fork or chopsticks?" he asked.

"Either."

It was *pad thai,* and it tasted as good as it smelled. Not too much garlic, just enough ginger. Of course, she hadn't had a chance to eat all day. She gestured at her plate with the chopsticks. "It must be a pretty big favor you need."

He didn't smile. "Do you want to eat first? You seem . . . hungry."

"No," she said. "It's okay. Go ahead."

"Okay. If you're sure?" She nodded. He took a long drink of water. "I need to get some money to someone in Pakistan."

"What on earth for?"

"Let's just say, medical issues. And I don't just need to get the money there. I need to find a doctor who will keep the whole thing quiet."

Zainab set her chopsticks down. "Chase Holland, did you get some *desi* girl pregnant?"

He laughed. "I did not. But thanks for the vote of confidence."

"Okay, then I'm totally lost."

He got up and handed her the hard copy of an e-mail. "Read this."

When she finished, Zainab shook her head. "That poor woman."

Chase nodded.

"And you want to help her?"

"Yes."

"No offense," she said, "but why?" He shrugged. She stared at him for a minute and then pointed at the e-mail. "Why not use this to 'let the Paki have it'? I assume that's a thinly veiled reference to me."

"It is, and I'm sorry. The guy's an idiot."

She nodded. "So what do you need me for?"

"I need someone who speaks Urdu. To contact the doctor in the article and see if he can arrange for her treatment in secret, or if he knows someone who can. I'll pay up front." He leaned back. "You're the only one I could think of who might be able to help."

"The doctor might speak English, you know."

"I just assumed—"

"I know, that we're all backward."

"That's not what I was going to say."

She waved her hand. "I'm just giving you a hard time."

"So you'll help?"

"Are you going to tell me why you're doing this?"

"I wasn't planning on it."

"So, what? It's payback for not telling you Eleanor's secret?"

He shook his head. "No. It's not payback."

"You know, I keep secrets for a living."

He smiled wearily. "Maybe someday, Zainab. But not tonight."

She nodded and ran her fingers over the e-mail. "She's in a bad place."

"Yes," he said. "And?"

"And I'll help you. Under one condition."

He grinned. "I promise; I'll always do the cooking."

21

HAYDEN THOUGHT THE lunch with Fadi and Amra was going well. Amra's engagement had transformed her mood; even Hank didn't seem to be getting to her as much anymore. Over salmon and salads at Legal Seafood, Amra asked polite questions of Fadi, who, though he'd been a bit uptight at first, seemed to have loosened up. When Fadi told Amra his parents lived in New York, she said hers did, too, and that she was going there that weekend to tell them about her engagement.

"You are?" Hayden frowned. "But Friday is the summer associate harbor cruise." She didn't look at Fadi. It was still a point of contention between them.

"I know. Unfortunately, I'm going to miss it."

Hayden tried not to pout. She'd been planning on tagging along with Amra. "I invited Fadi, but he's going to his parents' this weekend, too," she said, which may have been responsible for the awkwardly silent end to their lunch.

Still, as Hayden walked Fadi to the T afterward, she felt a small, if fragile, wave of contentment, as though her future might actually be unfolding before her, that maybe on the boat cruise the following year, *she* would be one of the women sporting a diamond ring. Fadi had finally met someone from her life, and while she still hadn't met any of his friends or family, she felt sure that she would soon. And that perhaps it was time to broach the elephant in the room.

"So I've been reading about Islam," she said tentatively. She watched Fadi to gauge his reaction. "It's a little confusing, really."

"How do you mean?"

"Well, there are all of these strict rules, and yet the Muslims I know don't really seem to follow them."

He stepped behind her to allow an elderly couple to pass them. "Do all Catholics shun birth control? Do all Jews avoid bacon? Come on, Hayden, you can't be that naive. So some Muslims observe every little law and some look to the bigger picture. And some don't practice at all but still identify as Muslims."

Hayden felt instantly better. The book about having to wear a headscarf had thrown her. "And what about you? Which kind are you?"

He leaned close to her. "Isn't that obvious?"

"But you go to the mosque sometimes."

"So?"

"So you're like a Christmas and Easter Catholic?"

Fadi laughed. "I guess so."

"And your family?" She held her breath. So many questions about their future seemed to turn on his answer.

"They're more conservative."

"But they accept you how you are?"

He frowned. "Sure."

"So where do you go on Eid?"

"You mean which mosque?"

"Yes."

"Well, if I have the time off, I go—"

Hayden cut him off. "Home to New York," she said, rolling her eyes.

"Yes, home to New York. Eid is like Christmas. It's not that unusual that I would want to be with my family."

They neared his T stop. Hayden needed to get to the point. "Okay, so where do you go if you don't have time off?"

He looked puzzled. "There's a mosque in Wayland that I like, but depending on my work schedule sometimes I go somewhere in Cambridge." He stopped and looked at her. "Why are you asking me all of this?"

"I was thinking maybe I'd go with you sometime. To see what it's like." She thought she saw concern on his face, possibly even alarm. "I'm just tossing it out there, Fadi. It was just a suggestion."

He seemed to recover his composure. "No, it would be great. I'll keep it in mind."

22

AMRA SMOOTHED HER skirt and paced the foyer of Mateen's condo. Every now and then she sneaked a look at her ring and smiled. She couldn't wait to show her mother. She didn't feel like she could make a single plan until her parents knew, and she didn't want to tell them over the phone. They'd had to wait two weeks, until Mateen had moved to Boston and she could arrange her work schedule accordingly.

She looked at her watch. If Mateen didn't hurry up, they were going to miss the shuttle.

"Relax," he said, coming up behind her. "If we miss the flight, we'll just drive. It will be fine." And she knew it would.

Her mother opened the door and gasped. "Amra! And Mateen? What on earth—" She stopped when Amra held out her hand. "*Alhamdulillah,*" she whispered before calling out to Amra's father. "Parvez, come, quickly!" She waved the couple in, embracing Amra and smoothing her face, and then did the same to Mateen.

Her father shook hands with Mateen. "*Mubarak*. Welcome to our family, *beta*." Amra could tell he was pleased. "What did Safa and Hassan say?"

"We haven't had a chance to tell my parents yet," Mateen said. "We were hoping to do it in person, but I think now that we've told you, we'll have to go ahead and call them."

Her mother nodded and said they could use the phone in her study. After Mateen told his parents and Amra talked to his mother, who cried and said she'd been praying for this day, they returned to the living room, where Amra's mother was pouring tea.

"It's so good to have you here," she said. "I'm wondering, though, if you have plans for tonight."

"Plans?" Amra shook her head. "*Ammi,* we came to see you and *Abba*."

"I know, and that's so lovely of you. Such a precious, precious surprise. And we have so much to talk about. But—" Her mother looked at her father.

"But?"

"Do you remember Fatima Badir? From Sunday school? Her father is the emergency-room doctor who saw you when you broke your ankle in gymnastics?"

Amra nodded impatiently. "Of course."

"Well, she's recently engaged as well. I haven't even had a chance to speak to her mother yet, which is really quite rude of me." Her mother took a sip of her tea. "In any case, her parents are having a small party tonight to announce the engagement. I'm afraid we've committed to going."

"Oh." Amra couldn't help it. She was disappointed. This was supposed to be *her* moment and her parents were leaving to celebrate Fatima Badir's? "Well, Mateen and I can see a show or something, I suppose."

"See a show? Don't be silly! You and Mateen will come with us, of course." Her mother clapped her hands as though it were decided.

"But we don't have anything to wear." Amra was thinking of

Mateen. She, of course, had a closet full of saris and *lenghas* and *salwar kameez* in her old room.

Her mother nodded. "Hmmm, yes. Mateen, I don't suppose you'd fit into one of Parvez's suits?" Mateen laughed. He had a good five inches on Amra's father.

"No worries," Mateen said. "I figured we might do something special tonight, and I always come prepared."

"You have a suit in that duffel bag?" Amra was incredulous.

"I do." If her parents hadn't been there, she would have hugged him. "Just point me to the iron."

"Don't be silly," her mother said. "I'll have it pressed in no time." She hushed Mateen with her hand when he protested. "We're all set. An engagement announced at another engagement party. God has smiled upon this evening."

"You look amazing," Mateen whispered in her ear in the cab. Her father was in front, with the driver. Amra sat in the middle between Mateen and her mother. She'd decided on a fitted *choli* top in pale green, with a matching slim skirt. As she'd changed, all she could think about was that soon, when she and Mateen visited her parents, they would share the double bed in her old room.

They entered the Hilton ballroom, decorated with streamers and bold floral displays. A dais had been placed at one end of the room and covered in rose petals. Although the hall was only half-full, all of the tables were set; it looked as though they were expecting a few hundred people.

"A small party?" Amra whispered to her mother. Her mother shrugged as if to say, *You know how these things are*. They took a table near the front. Amra saw Fatima sitting in the middle of the dais on an ornately carved chair. A matching chair awaited her fiancé.

When the music started, everyone stood and faced the door. The fiancé's relatives entered first—the aunties and uncles and small children carrying gifts for Fatima. They filed in in small clusters until Amra was reminded of the circus clowns in the small car. *How many relatives can you fit in the lobby of a hotel?* And then, finally, Fatima's fiancé entered, flanked by his parents. The guests strained to see him, pushing people in front of them, craning necks. Amra didn't get a good look at him until she and Mateen were in line to greet the couple. "Oh my God."

Mateen touched her elbow. "Amra? Are you okay?"

Amra shook her head and tried to turn around, but the crowd behind her was too thick. She had no choice but to continue forward until she was standing in front of Fatima Badir and her fiancé, Dr. Fadi Amin.

Amra couldn't sleep that night. She tossed and turned, wishing Mateen were next to her. She replayed the events of the evening, especially that initial moment of recognition. She should have found some way out of that line, some route of escape. Once she realized she was trapped, she'd hoped to just kiss Fatima quickly and move on, but Fatima had been so excited to see her that she had cried out, "Amra Abbas!" and then "introduced" her to Fadi. It took a second, but she knew the exact moment the recognition washed over Fadi's face. Later, he'd approached her near the dessert table and asked her to let him be the one to tell Hayden. He said he'd been trying to find a good time, that he didn't want to hurt her. Amra said she couldn't promise anything.

"I don't want to cause her any more pain than necessary," Fadi said again, and Amra wanted to spit.

And now she didn't know what to do. Hayden would be devastated. She thought they would get married. How could Amra just sit on this, waiting for Fadi to get the nerve to tell her? And then, what, act surprised when Hayden came to cry on her shoulder?

The other thought haunting Amra was what to do about sweet

Fatima Badir. Her family was very conservative, and Amra had never heard anything about Fatima dating. And even if Fatima was prepared to accept the fact that Fadi had dated before their engagement, and that was a rather large if, she was sure her tolerance would not extend to dating someone, and presumably sleeping with her, during her engagement.

She wanted to ask her mother, but she was sure that would result in a phone call to Fatima's parents. She remembered the bride's radiant smile and wondered if she could really be the one to bring it all crashing down.

She fell into a fitful sleep, waking every couple of hours. By the time morning came, it was a relief to get out of bed.

"Screw him," Zainab said. "You don't owe him anything. Hayden is your friend, and you know something horrible that guy is doing to her."

Amra stretched across Zainab's bed, folding and unfolding the edge of the duvet while Zainab organized her closet. She and Mateen had taken the noon shuttle, and Mateen dropped her off at Zainab's before heading to his office. "His name is Fadi."

"Whatever. You don't have a choice. Did you want to know about his sordid, cheating ways? No. Of course not. Did you snoop around or do something questionable to get this information? No. All you did was go to a stupid engagement party and, surprise, the groom-to-be is your colleague's boyfriend."

Amra rubbed her eyes. "I know all of that."

"So what's the problem? That people will be upset? Not your fault." Zainab pulled a black silk skirt off a hanger and dropped it into her donate pile.

"She thought they were getting married."

Zainab laughed. "Well, she was half-right."

"Zainab."

"Sorry."

"She even told her parents. She said her dad made a comment about how she was turning out to be the kind of woman men fool around with but don't marry, and Hayden told him there would be a wedding within a year."

"Her dad said that? No wonder she's so messed up."

"I know," Amra said. "And what about Fatima? Am I supposed to ruin her life, too?"

Zainab sighed. "Why are you doing this to yourself? *You* didn't do this. *He* did it. What would be better, Fatima calling off her wedding now or finding out later that her husband is a total dog?"

"I don't know."

"Really? You really don't know?" Zainab shook her head. "Well, think about it. And in the meantime, get some sleep. You look like hell for someone who just got engaged to her dream man."

Amra called Fadi after leaving Zainab's and gave him one week to tell both Hayden and Fatima the truth. He'd seemed grateful, saying that it would feel good to come clean. She didn't believe a word of it.

On Monday she barely had time to breathe. Hank had raised some issues behind her back with one of her clients, resulting in two pages of last-minute changes to a merger agreement, and on Tuesday she was at a closing all day. On Wednesday she asked Hayden if she wanted to have lunch. Hayden said she already had plans, but her mood seemed fine. That night, Amra asked Mateen at dinner if she'd been wrong to give Fadi so much time.

"Relax," he said. "It's not your job to save the world." She told him he sounded like Zainab. He joked that he'd have to swear like a sailor to sound like Zainab.

When Amra got to work on Thursday, Hayden's office light was off. Sometimes, particularly if Hayden had been out drinking the night before, she would call and ask Amra to turn on her light and make her desk look like she was already there. But Amra didn't have any messages from Hayden. "She's out sick, hon," Hayden's secretary informed her. "Stomach bug."

Amra called Hayden's cell and home numbers, but they both went straight to voice mail. On Friday, at lunch, she went to Hayden's apartment, knocked, and said she wasn't leaving until Hayden opened the door. Hayden finally did, revealing her blanched face and flat, matted hair. Amra hugged her, then sat her on the couch and made her some tea.

"He's getting married," Hayden said. "Fadi. He's already *engaged*."

"I know."

Hayden set her tea down. "What do you mean, you know?"

Amra sighed. "Remember when Mateen and I went to New York to tell my parents we were engaged?" Hayden nodded. "They took us to an engagement party they were invited to. It was Fadi's party. I've known his fiancé since I was in grade school."

Hayden didn't react. Amra continued. "I thought he should be the one to tell you. I said I'd give him a week. To tell both you and Fatima."

"Who?"

"Fatima. His fiancée."

"Oh," Hayden said, "right. *Fatima*. So did he?"

"Did he what?"

"Tell her."

"I don't know." Amra frowned. "Does it matter?"

"Maybe they'll break up?"

"Maybe. I mean, she'd have every right to leave him. But I don't think you should worry about that."

"I know, I shouldn't. Except what if he was pressured into the marriage? What if I'm the one he really wants, but he didn't know how to tell his parents? Because of all the cultural stuff you talked about."

Amra thought back to the engagement party. How sweet Fatima

was, how Fadi had looked at her. "It's possible, Hayden. But you need to think about what you really want, not what he wants. About what kind of person you want for yourself."

"Right." Hayden was quiet for a minute. "What did your parents get you for your birthday this year, Amra?"

Amra couldn't imagine why Hayden wanted to know. "Pearl earrings."

"That's a nice gift. Do you know what my dad offered to get me?"

Amra shook her head.

"A nose job."

"I'm sorry, Hayden."

"It was before Fadi. He said it seemed I was having trouble meeting someone. He said he was trying to help."

Amra didn't know what to say.

Hayden shrugged. "You're lucky, you know. It all worked out so easily for you."

"What did?"

"Mateen. Your parents practically handed him to you. Instant dream fiancé."

Amra decided to let that go. "I have to get back to work. Promise you'll call me if you need anything?"

Hayden said she would, but it came from a distant place, like she was already gone. As Amra let herself out, she was glad it was Friday. The weekend would do Hayden good, give her time to put everything in perspective. By the following week, she was sure, Hayden would be ready to move on.

23

CHASE FINISHED THE book and still wasn't sure what he'd gotten himself into. He'd been excited when he learned James Walden was trying to reach him. James was a huge player in Republican circles, the head of a powerful political action committee, famous for his fund-raising ability. When they'd finally connected, James had a request. After saying that he'd heard good things, "great things, actually," about Chase and that he did his "damnedest" to catch his show "straight from the lion's den of Taxachusetts," he got to the point. "The reason I'm calling," James said, "is that the college Republicans up there want to host a little debate. Harvard has some hotshot visiting professor, a Mr. Taj Fareed, running loose, complete with one of those 'blame America first' kind of books. People are worried about indoctrination."

"I've heard of him," Chase lied. He didn't know who the hell Taj Fareed was.

"Well, good. Then you probably know he's the Muslim jihadist version 2.0. Young and cool, a real smooth talker. Clean-shaven, Brooks Brothers type. Doesn't look like he just rode in on a camel, you know?"

Chase thought he knew where James was going. "Harder to see a movement as dangerous when the spokesman is the boy next door."

"Exactly. But it's just lipstick on a pig. And we've got to wipe that lipstick off. And you're going to help us."

"Me?"

"Yes, you. We've decided you should debate him."

"Why me?"

"Think about it. You're young, you're a rising star on our side. And I've read some of your scholarly work. You're sharp as a tack. We think you can decimate him."

Chase wondered if James meant the part about the rising star. "I appreciate that."

"Plus, we were looking for someone equally, how shall I put this, easy on the eyes. Nadia Asad assured us that you fit the bill."

He was surprised. He hadn't seen Nadia since her speech, the day he'd persuaded Zainab to have coffee with him.

"What, are you blushing over there, son?" James laughed. "I tell you Nadia thinks you're a looker and you go all quiet on me."

"No, I was just thinking lipstick on a pig might apply in this case as well."

James was silent for a moment. "I hope you don't mean Nadia."

"No. God, no. I meant me."

"Relax. I'm just pulling your leg. But we both know who the pig is here. So, we can count on you?"

As soon as Chase got off the phone with James, he ordered Taj Fareed's book. And now, as he finished it, Chase knew he could take him. He had some nagging sense that he should call Savannah, offer to fly her up to watch. But all he could think about was that the debate provided the perfect excuse to contact Zainab.

The day of the debate, Chase started to get nervous. There'd been more publicity than he'd expected. Harvard had done a PR whirlwind, and the leftist students were riled up. But even with all of the attention, he knew that a good part of his anxiety involved Zainab. She'd agreed to come, and he'd been so focused on seeing her again that he had failed to consider that the very reason he'd had an excuse to invite her, the subject matter of the debate, might also be the thing that alienated her once and for all. If forced to choose sides, he didn't want to think about where Zainab would end up.

Chase spent the day reviewing his notes, the copious, penciled quotes from Taj's book, along with his own rebuttals. He knew Taj's weakest points—his tendency to gloss over problematic verses of the Qur'an and his insistence that any nondemocratic tendencies were merely cultural—and planned to hit him repeatedly on those issues. But in the back of his mind, he couldn't shake the awareness that Zainab would be hearing it all, that in an auditorium likely to be standing room only, he might as well be speaking only to her.

The debate, or at least the first three quarters of it, was a civilized affair. Chase had gotten Taj to admit that if enough people believed a particular interpretation of the Qur'an, even if it was a misinterpretation, it could reasonably be considered a defining belief of Islam in the current political environment. Chase could have pressed harder on the treatment of women—he could hear James Walden begging him to wipe that lipstick off—but overall, he felt good. He was winning without hitting below the belt, and there was a good chance Zainab might still be impressed, or at least not offended. All that was left was the issue of cooperation with law enforcement and Chase could declare victory, maybe even convince Zainab to celebrate over a friendly dinner.

Taj gave a rather perfunctory tribute to constitutional notions of privacy and the presumption of innocence. Chase was practically chomping at the bit by the time it was his turn.

"But here's the thing," Chase said. "Why wouldn't a Muslim American, assuming that he's done nothing wrong, that he's a loyal citizen, why wouldn't he want to feel safe, too? And why wouldn't those dual impulses of loyalty and the desire for security make him want to do whatever he can to assist the government in rooting out terrorists?"

Taj smiled. "I am the exact type of Muslim you just described. I was born and raised in the suburbs of Washington, D.C. You don't get much more American than that. I am of Indian descent, just as I am sure you are of, what, Irish descent? Maybe a hint of German? That dirty-blond hair is hard to pin down." There was some laughter. "But if you ask me what I am, it's simple. I am an American. I do want to be safe. And you know what? I feel pretty safe. But you clearly don't. So tell me, what am I doing or not doing that affects your personal level of security?"

Chase could not dispute that the guy had charisma. "Well, it really isn't so personal. And it's not just one person. Why aren't more people willing to talk to the FBI? Why aren't mosques more open? Why so much in Arabic? And if it came down to it, would you advocate Muslims registering with the government?"

"First of all," Taj said, "Muslim Americans cooperate with the government all the time. They meet with the FBI and law enforcement regularly. They provide tips and report suspicious behavior. Second, a lot of Muslims happen to be Arab and that is the language of our holy book, so it's not surprising that some of our services would be in Arabic, just as the Catholic Church used to conduct Mass in Latin." He smiled. "And it's not a secret code, you know. Anyone is free to learn Arabic and come and listen. They even offer it in some high schools now." There was more chuckling.

"As for procedures like registering, I'm not sure how that would work or why. Should we all wear a symbol like the Nazis forced Jews to wear? Does knowing my religion really tell you anything that you need to know about me?"

"Yes." Chase nodded. "I know it's not politically correct to say it, but yes. It might. It creates a pool. Not everyone in that pool will commit an act of terrorism, but an act of terrorism is likely to originate from that pool. It makes more sense than strip-searching old ladies at the airport." There was a burst of applause at his last point.

Taj waited for the audience to quiet. "Do you really think a terrorist is going to register?"

"Maybe, if he was afraid not doing so would bring attention to himself. But the real question is, How far are American Muslims willing to go? If I were a Muslim and completely innocent, I would gladly identify myself to the government. I'd say, Here I am, investigate me, watch me, I have nothing to hide. So my question is, Would you?"

"No."

"Well, I think that's pretty telling."

Taj nodded. "Maybe. But what you're suggesting requires a perfect system free of bias. Which of course we don't have."

"We have the best system in the world."

"I doubt that Girvies Davis would agree."

Chase didn't know what the hell he was talking about. "I'm sorry?"

"Girvies Davis was a twenty-year-old African American man with a record of petty crimes who was accused of killing an elderly white man. He was convicted on the basis of a written confession and put to death by the state of Illinois in 1995."

"I'm not sure what your point is."

"Mr. Davis was functionally illiterate. He couldn't read. He signed a confession, under duress, possibly at gunpoint, that he literally could not read. African Americans were purposely kept off the jury, which is, as I'm sure you know, illegal." Taj paused. "America is a great country, but you'll have to excuse Muslims for fearing they might be accused and possibly convicted of things they did not do. Or if being forced to identify themselves as Muslims officially and publicly might make them feel a bit precarious."

"There are mistakes in any system," Chase said. "But the impulse for justice is stronger in America than anywhere else. Yes, our system has given us cases like the one you cite, and those cases are tragedies. But it's also given us the Innocence Project."

Taj nodded. "The Innocence Project is inspiring. But it wasn't a governmental creation. It was formed by private citizens in response to death penalty abuses."

"Our government, Mr. Fareed, *is* our citizens. By and for the people. It doesn't exist in a vacuum. It's not a dictatorship or a monarchy."

"But it can be corrupted by powerful interests."

The moderator interjected, saying that they would have to leave it there, but that he hoped the debate would lead to more, not less, conversation.

Taj leaned over and shook Chase's hand enthusiastically. His smile seemed sincere. "Great debate, Charles. I enjoyed it." The audience members formed two lines in front of the stage. Many of the people in Taj's line were holding copies of his book. Chase tried not to think of his own unpublished work. Instead, he focused on how events like the debate would bring him closer to getting published. He also tried not to care which line Zainab would join. Still, he was relieved when she remained sitting, talking to a couple of women next to her. James stepped forward to congratulate Chase, telling him he'd done a great job, and pointed out some areas where he could improve next time. "This is just the start, son," James said. "We're going to promote the hell out of you." When Chase looked up, Taj had left the stage and made his way to the third row, where he looked quite comfortable leaning against the back of a chair, talking to Zainab.

So Taj had sought her out. Chase didn't think they knew each other. Surely Zainab would have mentioned it when he'd invited her. Or would she have? It's not like they told each other everything. In fact, they hadn't really told each other much of anything, exchanging barbs and favors, forging a strained peace.

He slowly packed his briefcase, watching out of his peripheral vision. A few others loitered, but the room was clearing out. When he could stall no more, he descended the stage.

"Chase, hi," said Zainab. "Great debate. Fascinating."

"Thanks."

Taj looked back and forth between Chase and Zainab. "You two know each other?"

"Yes, Chase and I go way back," Zainab said. "Ever since he ripped me a new one on the radio."

Taj raised his eyebrows. "Brave man."

"Or stupid," Chase said.

Taj nodded. "Or that."

For a moment, no one spoke. Finally, Zainab stood and put out her hand. "Taj, it was a pleasure to meet you." Taj held her hand longer than Chase thought necessary. Zainab gestured with the book in her other hand. "I'm looking forward to reading this. Thanks for signing it." Chase would have given his salary at the institute to know what the inscription said.

"No problem," Taj said. "I'd love to hear what you think of it when you finish." He handed her his card.

"Of course. I'll be in touch."

Taj returned to the stage to get his things. Chase walked Zainab out.

"So are you going to thank me now or later?" he asked.

"For what?"

"For introducing you to Mr. Wonderful."

Zainab laughed. "Actually, you didn't introduce us. He introduced himself."

"But I provided the opportunity."

"That you did."

The traffic on Massachusetts Avenue was frenzied, affecting Chase's bearings. "So I should get a little credit."

"Is that what you want?"

He could not tell her the truth—that he didn't want her to see Taj, or to read his book or "be in touch."

"Seems only fair," he said, hoping she didn't hear the catch in his voice.

She nodded. "Right. *Thanks,* Chase. See you around, okay?"

She turned and walked away, leaving him alone on the street, knowing he'd blown it.

Zainab texted her delay to Amra, who, no doubt, was already at Tamarind Bay with Mateen, snacking on *pappadum* and sipping mango *lassi*. If Taj Fareed hadn't introduced himself, she would have been on time. Of course, there was that odd little exchange with Chase—was he actually trying to fix her up with Taj?—but that had only lasted a matter of minutes.

Zainab found Amra and Mateen exactly as she'd predicted, minus one sweetened yogurt drink. "I've got to think about fitting into my wedding dress," Amra said.

"Give me a break," Zainab said.

"That's what I keep telling her." Mateen smiled and shook Zainab's hand. "It's great to see you again after all of these years, Zainab."

"You too."

"I hope so. I'm sure I wasn't that nice to Maha's friends."

"We didn't care. We were too busy having crushes on you."

"Zainab!" Amra laughed. "You're going to embarrass him. Or me."

"You can tell me more about that later. Particularly about Amra's crush on me," Mateen said as the waiter approached. They ordered and began to reminisce about their childhoods.

"That's back when Amra used to be fun," Zainab said. "Now she's all work, all the time." A look crossed Mateen's face, but Zainab couldn't place it. Maybe he was defensive about someone teasing her.

Amra changed the subject. "So, Zainab, what's new with you?"

"Well, work is work. Eleanor is half-crazy, as usual. I knew there would be a degree of damage control when I took the job, but some weeks, it's all I do."

"Do you think she has a chance?" Mateen asked.

"On the record? Of course." Zainab sighed. "But just between my best friend and her super discreet fiancé? It's going to be tough. The women she should appeal to are often diehard Democrats. And frankly, she makes most men nervous. But enough about that. I just met Taj Fareed."

Amra put her water down. "*Met* him, met him?"

"In the flesh."

"Where?"

"Do you remember that right-wing radio guy? Charles Holland? The one who said Eleanor was sleeping with the enemy by hiring me?"

Amra nodded. Mateen looked confused. "Wait, some guy said *what*?"

"He said we're at war with Muslim fascists and that she shouldn't have hired me." She waved her hand. "Anyway, we're good now—"

Amra interrupted her. "What do you mean, you're good now?"

"Chase and I—that's his nickname—have run into each other a few times. He's really fairly harmless."

"He called you an enemy of the state," Amra said. "He traffics in bigotry."

"Well, some of that is hyperbole."

"Some of it . . ." Mateen mumbled. "Does that make it okay?"

"Hold on," Amra said. "What does this have to do with Taj Fareed?"

"If you would let me finish, I was trying to explain that. Chase invited me to watch him debate Taj Fareed at Harvard. I just came from there. And afterward Taj came over and introduced himself."

Amra leaned forward. "Okay, we'll get back to the Chase-invited-you thing in a second. So Taj just came over out of the blue?"

"He did."

"Taj Fareed. America's Muslim golden boy?"

Mateen cleared his throat. "Still here, ladies."

Amra laughed. "Sorry. You know if more people knew you, you'd be the golden boy."

"Right." Mateen spooned some chutney onto his plate. "I almost believe you." He turned to Zainab. "So what was Mr. Fareed doing, hawking his book?"

"He was signing copies, yes, but that wasn't the point of the debate."

"I'm sure," Mateen said. "I saw him interviewed on some talk show a while ago. Frankly, I wasn't that impressed."

Amra turned and looked at him. "You're kidding, right?"

"He seems a little too slick. Like he's trying too hard to get non-Muslims to like him."

Zainab put her fork down. "Would that be a bad thing?"

"If he's selling out."

Zainab took a breath. "Personally, I thought he did great in the debate. I mean, he was going against a right-wing wack job—"

"You mean your new friend, Chase," Amra interjected.

"—*and* he was dispelling stereotypes. Which I think is sorely needed."

"Right," Mateen said, "but it's a question of degree. How much should he have to pretend to get approval?"

"What do you think he's pretending about?"

"Well, for example, take the *hijab*. It's one thing to say that no one should be compelled to wear a scarf, but it's another thing to say that it's not scripturally required."

Zainab raised her eyebrows. "Let the *fatwa* throwing begin." Amra looked away. Mateen set his jaw. "Joking, guys. Lighten up." She made a mental note to call Amra later to make sure that she and Mateen were on the same page about things. Better to find out sooner rather than later if your fiancé was a closet *mullah*.

"So," Zainab said breezily, "anyone up for some *rasmalai*?"

Later, at home, she realized that, thanks to Mateen's little trip down Sharia Lane, she never told Amra about actually talking to Taj Fareed. She changed her clothes, washed her face, and got into bed with Taj's book.

. . .

At a quarter to one, Zainab turned the last page and ran her fingers over the cover of the book. She was impressed. She hadn't sensed any of the pretense to which Mateen referred or discerned any Uncle Tom impulse. It was thoughtful and well-reasoned, if a little esoteric. (She was more than a little chagrined that she didn't know what *Ijtihad* and *Ijma* meant.) Just as she was sure she would never find someone she wanted to marry, Zainab had given up looking for a comfortable fit in her community. Sure, she knew about the Fatima Mernissis and Amina Waduds of the world. But those were just scholars writing books, not people she knew in real life. Until now. Here was someone she'd actually met, who articulated a vision of her faith that she could embrace. She dug Taj's card out of her bag and composed a quick e-mail:

> Taj,
> I finished your book. I'm not sure I'm ready to talk about it yet. Or, wow.
> Zainab Mir

Within five minutes, to her surprise—although not complete—he wrote back.

> Zainab, I was hoping to hear from you. Thanks for the "wow." Seriously. Would you be interested in getting together sometime? I promise not to make you talk about the book. Taj

Zainab smiled. So he wasn't just interested in her thoughts on his book. She'd have to tell Chase he was right. When she thought about Chase, something pulled at her stomach, a strange, sticking homesick feeling. She shook her head to clear her thoughts. Chase had mocked her faith and said people like Nadia Asad had important contributions to make to the nation's political discourse; Taj made her feel good about her faith. Maybe she would suggest to Taj that he debate Nadia.

She e-mailed back that she would love to see him.

Taj asked if they could do something touristy, since he'd never spent much time in Boston. "Something historical." When Zainab asked if he wanted to walk the Freedom Trail or maybe visit Lexington or Concord, he confessed that he'd always wanted to visit the Salem witch museums.

"Really?" Zainab said. "It could be a bit morbid."

"It's still an important part of our history," Taj said, and Zainab had agreed to go.

On route 128, sandwiched between cars heading north for the weekend with bikes hanging off the back or kayaks strapped on top, Taj asked about her job. "I imagine that working for Eleanor Winthrop-Smith keeps you on your toes. She's a very interesting candidate."

"I hate that word. Interesting. It's almost always a euphemism for something bad."

Taj inched into the far left lane. "You're absolutely right. What I meant to say is that she's a piece of work."

Zainab laughed. "Maybe we should stick with interesting."

"I'm kidding. She's very forthright and says some provocative things, but that's sorely needed in politics. It's refreshing."

"I agree."

"And I assume she's got your back?"

"How do you mean?"

"I read some of the stuff people have said about you. The hacks on the far right. They've been brutal."

"Some of them."

"Like the guy I just debated."

"Chase."

"You mean Charles."

"Yes," Zainab said. "Chase is his nickname."

Without looking at her, he nodded. "So you know him pretty well."

"I wouldn't say that. We seem to run into each other a lot and he did me a favor once." She didn't mention that she had also done him one, before the debate, getting in touch with the doctor in Karachi to arrange for the care of the HIV-positive woman. Instead, she heard herself say that was why she went to the debate. "I figured it was the least I could do."

"So are the two of you even now?"

"Even?"

He looked at her and then back at the road. "I'm just wondering how much I need to worry about Charles Holland."

Zainab stared at the red Honda Civic in front of them. "I wouldn't worry about him at all."

They stopped on Washington Square near the Salem Common. At his request, she took a picture of Taj next to the large statue of Roger Conant. When they reached the Dungeon Witch Museum, he looked at her with his eyebrows raised. "Shall we?"

"Your call."

He paid for the tickets, saying it was the least he could do since she'd agreed to be his tour guide, and they entered the gloomy building. They watched a short reenactment of a witch trial, and then filtered down into a musty dungeon meant to simulate the area where the accused were held. Zainab found the mannequins hanging from the ceiling disturbing and the figure representing Giles Corey, pressed to death under heavy boulders for refusing to enter a plea, downright repugnant. She felt like she couldn't breathe, either from the musty air or the macabre surroundings. "I need to get out of here," she whispered to Taj. He frowned, but followed her out of the museum.

On the street, in the bright sunlight, they stood, blinking, silent.

"Okay," Zainab said, shaking her head. "I was not expecting *that*."

"What do you mean?"

"The mannequins. You didn't find it hard to take?"

He nodded. "I think that's the point."

"I know, but didn't you think it was a bit . . . morbid?"

"How so?"

Zainab felt like they'd been in two different museums. "It was like puppets hanging from the ceiling. You could *touch* them."

"Who would touch them?"

"No one intentionally." Zainab shuddered. "Did you see the kids in there? They couldn't have been more than nine or ten."

"Maybe they'll grow up recognizing persecution when they see it."

"If they can ever sleep again."

He laughed. "Okay, so it was a bit much." He took a deep breath and blew it out. "So, do you want to get some ice cream or something?"

When he dropped her off, he apologized. "I just wanted to explore Massachusetts with you, not give you the creeps."

"It's not your fault," she lied.

"We should have gone to the aquarium."

"Probably."

"Would it still be okay if I called you sometime?"

Zainab knew it wasn't a casual question. Taj Fareed was not a casual guy.

"I'd like that," she said, and got out of the car before she could change her mind.

24

IN THE END, according to Amra's mother, Fadi confessed all to Fatima and her family. After the initial fallout, Fatima forgave him and said she intended to marry him as planned. Amra broke the news to Hayden, who reacted with a catatonic stare. After that, Hayden took a short leave from work, returning as a more somber version of herself. Her suits all became gray or black. The sheer silk blouses were gone, replaced by white cotton shirts, buttoned to the top. The three-inch heels had been replaced with sensible loafers. Amra asked around, to see how she was doing at work. According to her secretary, Hayden was working harder than ever. "I don't know what's up, hon," she said. "She seems to be holding it together, but then she shuts herself in there a couple of times a day with strict orders that I don't let anyone disturb her. And yesterday, she asked for a lock. A *lock*." She leaned forward. "You don't think she's going to do something crazy, do you? Because they don't pay me enough to find the body."

Amra assured her that Hayden wouldn't do anything crazy. But truthfully, she had no idea what Hayden might do. The request for the lock was concerning. They'd only put one on Amra's door to accommodate her need to do the ritual prayers. She'd explained to Eric and HR that once a Muslim begins one of the five daily prayers, she isn't allowed to stop, barring an emergency. Amra was afraid someone might walk in and become confused if she ignored him. Eric, who loathed knowing anything personal about his associates, shifted in his seat the whole time Amra was talking. When she'd finished, he waved his hand and said, "So get her a lock. Are we done here?"

Hayden knew about the lock. She'd joked that she might put it to good use with one of the more attractive associates late at night. And if the firm had given Amra one, Hayden probably figured they'd have to give her one, too. Although Amra wondered if the firm would consider mourning a guy she'd only dated for a matter of months sufficient justification for installing a lock.

Amra invited Hayden to lunch for a week before she said yes, with the caveat that it had to be seafood. Once seated at the marble bar at Neptune Oyster, Amra said she was surprised at the choice.

"Why?"

"Because you hate seafood," Amra said.

"I'm learning to like it. Otherwise, it's hard to find something low carb I can eat."

Amra wasn't sure what she meant. Perhaps her stomach was giving her trouble because of Fadi. Amra had had a hard time eating when she and Mateen had broken up. Although fish was not high on her list of stomach-soothing foods.

"Hayden, are you okay?"

"Absolutely. Why do you ask?"

"I don't know. You seem . . . different. Your clothes. The lock." Amra motioned at the menu. "Your eating habits. I'm just wondering if you're—"

"Depressed?"

"Well, yes." Amra was relieved that Hayden had said it first.

"Quite the opposite, actually." Hayden tapped the counter with her newly short nails. "I suppose there's no reason not to tell you."

"No reason not to tell me what?"

"I converted to Islam."

Amra raised her eyebrows. "You *what*?"

"It's not what you're thinking. It has nothing to do with Fadi." Hayden fidgeted with her flatware. "Well, that's not true. It has a little bit to do with him."

"I don't understand."

"Well, for a while there when I was young and naive"—Hayden stopped and laughed—"I thought Fadi was going to marry me, so I started reading about Islam. To prepare."

Amra nodded. "But you're *not* marrying Fadi."

"I know. But I'd already sort of adjusted my thinking that way, you know? It's hard to just change course." Amra looked at Hayden's bare face and gristle-colored suit and thought that Hayden had changed course rather easily. "So anyway," Hayden continued, "when I first found out about Fadi and his engagement, I was mad. More than mad. I was *pissed*. So I thought about ways to get back at him. Call his fiancée and tell her everything, call his parents, something. But the thing is, I loved Fadi and I wanted him back. So I decided that if I converted and sort of infiltrated his community, he'd see that I was the one he wanted and that there wasn't anything Fatima had that I didn't have."

Except dignity and common sense, Amra thought, but she let Hayden continue.

"So I went to the mosque in Wayland. Did you know they prefer that you call it a *masjid*? That the Spanish started calling it a mosque as a derivative of mosquito? Anyway, I went and I liked what they had to say, and I found myself asking how to convert. And they asked me some questions and if I was sure and then had me repeat some words in Arabic and, voilà, instant Muslim." Hayden gestured at their surroundings. "Which is why I'm eating *halal*."

Amra took a long drink of her sparkling water, unsure how to respond. "I think that's a myth, actually. About the origins of the word *mosque*."

"Well, that's what they told me." Hayden crossed her arms. "Is that all you can say?"

Amra shook her head. "I'm not sure what to say."

"How about welcome to the club?"

"Of course." Amra attempted a feeble smile. "Welcome to the club."

25

IT WAS CHASE's first time at the Tennis and Racquet Club, and he was getting killed. After dropping the first squash game, he tied the score in the second at seven and then proceeded to hit the fucking tin three times in a row.

"Hey, Chase," John said.

"What?"

"You know it's not racquetball, right?"

"Just serve the ball."

John did, launching a rally that went twenty-nine shots—Chase counted—and ended with John making a nick shot. Chase watched the ball roll off the wall and shook his head. Chase had never made a nick shot in his life. He bent over with his hands on his knees and tried to catch his breath.

"You okay?" John said. "Because if you need some sort of medical attention, I'm willing and able. But you should know that you're embarrassing the hell out of me at my new club."

Chase raised his right middle finger and got in position. He'd met John in D.C., through a friend of a friend, when Chase was renting a room by the month in an old, possibly senile woman's Georgetown home. After a couple of happy hours at Chadwick's, John mentioned he was looking for a roommate, and Chase, who was tired of waking to the sound of the kitchen television at four in the morning and having to be quiet after eight at night, handed him a deposit on the spot. John was doing his residency at Georgetown then and had recently taken an infectious disease fellowship at Mass General. He was Chase's first close African American friend.

Chase won the first three points in the next game. "Smells like a comeback," he said.

"You wish." John returned the next ball, and the rest of the match became a war of attrition. Chase made a few good shots, even moved John around the court a respectable amount, but his shots became looser and John's stayed tight, and in the end Chase owed John a burger and a beer at Jerry Remy's.

"I don't get it," Chase said, slumping against the wall. "Isn't a fellowship supposed to be some sort of living hell where you make hugely consequential decisions on fifteen minutes of sleep? Do they know you're playing this much squash?"

John sat down next to him. "What makes you think I'm playing that much?"

"You joined the Tennis and Racquet Club."

"It has other amenities."

"I noticed."

"*Anyway,*" John said, wiping his forehead with the bottom of his shirt, "speaking of illustrious careers, I've been listening to your show. What happened to you?"

"What do you mean?"

"The whole far-right thing. You know, social issues. Gays, immigrants. Abortion. When did you become so down with the 700 Club?"

Chase shrugged. "I guess when I figured out how much it pays."

John laughed. "At least you're honest. Do you even like Whitaker?"

"What's not to like?"

"He's kind of a tool."

"Well, they're *all* kind of tools," Chase said. "It's him or the feminazi."

"Or the Democrat."

"God forbid."

"You know, I get the whole fiscal conservative thing. But the rest seems like a bitter pill to swallow."

Chase nodded. "Look, for the first time in my life, I have serious money. Not just 'I can pay my bills' money. Down-payment-on-a-house money. Vacations-to-Europe money. I might actually get my book published. It's not like you with the medical degree. I don't know how long this will last. It's quite conceivable to me that I could be dog-shit poor"—he didn't say *again*; John only knew the for-public-consumption version of his past—"at any time. Who doesn't make compromises for his career? There are some lines I won't cross, but I can't really get too worked up about supporting, say, a pro-life candidate. What's the worst thing that will happen, a baby will be born?"

"What if that baby is born to a fourteen-year-old girl who was raped by her father?"

"How many of the millions of abortions in this country do you think fit that fact pattern?"

"Wouldn't one be enough?"

"To justify a million other babies not being born?"

"Fetuses."

"Word games, my friend."

They were quiet for a minute, as though John also knew there was nowhere good for the conversation to go. Finally John spoke. "It's all moot anyway."

"How's that?"

"You're going to vote for the feminazi."

"You're certifiable." Chase spun his racquet on the floor. It fell, logo up. The same way John had gotten the first serve.

"I guarantee it."

"And why would I do that?"

John grinned. "Two words. Zainab Mir."

Chase felt like he'd been sucker-punched. He had never mentioned Zainab to John. He never mentioned her to *anyone.* Except of course his enthusiastic listeners. "What about her?"

"Well, at first I thought you were just picking on her to please your base of crazies. You know, the rabid, xenophobic—"

"Got it. My base."

"But . . . then I happened to see a picture of Ms. Mir in *Vanity Fair.*"

The evening gown shot. Zainab in a black dress with skinny straps, filled out in all the right places. "I don't know what you're talking about," Chase said.

"Of course you do. Zainab Mir is a successful, apparently brilliant, incredibly sexy woman, and you spend half your show poking her with a stick."

"Sounds like someone has a crush on Ms. Mir."

"Exactly."

"She works for the candidate I despise. She speaks; I react."

John nodded. "It's all very first-grade."

"And I don't even attack her anymore."

"Maybe, but you still mention her a lot."

Chase sighed, leaned forward, and put his head in his hands. He looked up through his fingers. "Is it that obvious?"

John shrugged. "Apparently."

"I've had dinner with her twice."

"Holy *shit.*"

"Not like that. They weren't dates. And by the way, no one knows."

"No one like Savannah?"

"No one period." Chase shook his head. "Maybe in a different time or place . . ."

"How *Horse Whisperer* of you."

Chase shot him a look. "*Horse Whisperer*? Seriously?"

"I watched it with Jenna."

"Sure you did." Chase laughed. "Anyway, it doesn't matter. It would be career suicide. And I'm pretty sure she's seeing someone."

"As are you."

"Yes." Chase grimaced. "As am I."

John stood and reached out a hand to pull Chase to his feet. "So. What are you going to do?"

Alone, showered, with two pieces of cold pizza in his stomach, Chase sat on his balcony, drinking a beer, bouncing a tennis ball against the glass door, and tried not to think about his conversation with John. It was self-preservation. Because if he were honest, he would admit that that last question, the "What are you going to do?" had given him hope. The notion that there were still options, that there might be something to *do*. Of course, there wasn't. Zainab was, in all likelihood, seeing Taj Fareed. For a woman who wasn't a practicing Muslim, she sure rolled over quickly for the first good-looking Muslim guy to come along. He bet Taj didn't have to do her a favor in order to dine with her. He pushed that image out of his head and tried to focus on Savannah, how cooperative she'd been in their nightly phone calls, *not* asking about their future (in what he was sure was some mother-advised reverse psychology), and how she didn't deserve a snake of a boyfriend who sat around thinking about another woman. He tried to use his sense of honor to blunt the disproportionate pull he felt toward Zainab, this Muslim woman of Pakistani descent who, exchange of favors notwithstanding, probably didn't even consider him a friend. He told himself to stop the characterization there, to not round the corner to the rest—the sharp, take-no-prisoners tongue, the way she shook her head and bit her lower lip when reading the article about the woman in Pakistan, the hint of vulnerability that flashed in her eyes when he'd joked about how she'd been able to afford her artwork. How she looked at the Correspondents' Dinner.

Hell, how she looked in jeans and a tee shirt.

He finished the rest of his beer in one long drink and told himself to grow a pair. He'd been easy on her and look where it had gotten him. Watching her flirt with Taj Fareed right under his nose. He needed to go back to the beginning, when Zainab was nothing more than a political target.

He retrieved a second beer from his refrigerator and called Savannah to see if she wanted company over the weekend.

26

BEN DROPPED A copy of the *Boston Herald* on Zainab's desk.

"What?" she snapped. "What now?" She had finished her second cup of coffee before 7:00 A.M. and was halfway done with her third. Eleanor had decided to make a play for the nurses, but she wanted to meet with them immediately. Zainab was trying to rearrange her schedule and prepare talking points. As far as she was concerned, her plate was full.

Ben pointed to an article. "Read."

The article detailed local reaction to the federal hate-crimes legislation and specifically the inclusion of sexual orientation and gender as protected classes. The reporter quoted Alan Burke, the Democratic front-runner, the one either Fred Whitaker or Eleanor would run against next November, as welcoming the legislation as "long overdue." Fred Whitaker was on record as "vehemently opposing this thinly veiled attempt to criminalize thoughts as well as actions" and said that the legislation infringed on his constitutional rights to freely practice his religion. When the reporter asked him to explain that last remark, Fred replied, "Read the Bible. Sodom and Gomorrah. Nothing ambiguous about that."

Zainab was bothered by the fact that no one had called her to get

Eleanor's opinion. Eleanor was not the front-runner, but she was keeping the race close, and most reporters covered her with the same frequency as Fred Whitaker or Alan Burke. Plus, it pissed her off that a piece about hate crimes based on gender would fail to include the only viable female candidate in the race.

"Why didn't they call?" Zainab asked. "Get me the reporter on the phone."

"Keep reading," Ben said.

She skimmed down a couple of paragraphs. Sure enough, there was a quote from Eleanor: "I have always opposed any sort of so-called 'hate crime' legislation. A crime is a crime. We do not need, nor should we want, the United States government digging around into its citizens' thought processes. With a murder, thoughts are not the problem. Killing is the problem. We should punish killers. Period."

Zainab groaned. "When did she talk to them?" She pulled out her cell phone and checked the messages she'd been ignoring. There were a dozen or so from local reporters. Two from Darby hoping for, "optimistically, a clarification." And one from Chase Holland.

Zainab dialed Eleanor's private number.

"Zainab, what is it? Is it the talking points? Just e-mail them. I'm about to get on the shuttle."

"Eleanor, did you talk to the *Herald* about the hate-crime legislation?"

"The what? Oh yes, I did. A chipper young man. David something, I think."

Zainab looked at the byline. "Woods."

"Yes, that's it. He asked for a response and I gave one."

"He called you directly? And you answered?"

"Goodness, no. I ran into him at dinner the other night. Is there a problem?"

"Possibly." Zainab sighed. "We're trying to distinguish you from Fred Whitaker. To make inroads with women voters who might not ordinarily vote for a Republican candidate. To sell you as a live-and-let-live, New England kind of politician."

"Exactly."

"And on this issue, your position is virtually indistinguishable from Fred's."

"Nonsense. Fred is a homophobic bigot."

Zainab rubbed her forehead. "I didn't say his *beliefs* were indistinguishable from yours. But on this issue, you both came down on the same side."

"Well, I can't help that. I'm sure you're not asking me to assert a position with which I don't agree." Eleanor's tone lost some of its patience.

"Of course not. I guess I'm just looking for some nuance. And the voters will be, too."

"Which is what I hired you for. And now I must run and leave this all in your eminently capable hands."

An hour later, Zainab had done her best to spin the issue as a referendum on gay rights, an area in which she could legitimately point out differences between Fred and Eleanor. She put out a press release saying that, unlike Fred Whitaker, Eleanor Winthrop-Smith believed in the fundamental equality of all people and that her opposition to H.R. 1592 should not be interpreted as a slight against the gay community. On the contrary, Zainab wrote, it was because of her deeply held belief that all life is precious and equal that she could not carve out different categories. Fred Whitaker, on the other hand, believed that discrimination against homosexuals was permissible, as evidenced by his opposition to extending legal privileges to gay couples. In short, Eleanor's opposition was principled; Fred's was bigoted. She felt she had done a good job until Darby called back.

"Alan Burke's campaign has just responded to your press release."

"You're following this rather closely from New York," Zainab said dryly.

"Does that surprise you?"

"I suppose not." She sighed. "So what did Burke say?"

Darby started reading. "While Alan Burke would love to sit back and let the Republican candidates for Senate bicker among themselves, there is one misconception he must correct. Eleanor Winthrop-Smith, by her own admission, does not support gay marriage. The only candidate running for Senate in Massachusetts who supports the unfettered right of gay people to marry is Alan Burke."

Zainab closed her eyes. "Shit."

"Eleanor doesn't support gay marriage? You never told me that."

"She supports civil unions."

"How 2004."

"For everyone. She thinks marriage should be a religious institution that people can participate in if they choose. But for legal purposes, everyone should have a civil union. Gay or straight."

"She's not making this easy for herself. First, she agrees with Whitaker on the hate-crimes thing and, second, technically Burke is right. He's the only one who supports gay marriage."

"Eleanor is nuanced."

"It's hard to make nuance fly in a rough-and-tumble campaign."

"It's my job to make it fly," Zainab said. "Will you help? Talk to the reporters you know up here, try to get our side out?"

Darby was quiet for a minute. "I'll see what I can do."

Zainab saved the call to Chase for last.

"Took you a while," he said.

"Sorry. As you can imagine, I've been swamped with calls."

"Any from Taj Fareed?"

"Excuse me?"

"Just wondering who you've been swamped with."

"Reporters. You know, people like you calling for a response."

"Had to go down the pecking order. I understand."

Zainab wasn't sure what the attitude was about. "Anyway," she said, "I'm returning your call. I assume it's about the hate-crimes deal."

"It *was* about that, when I first called. Which was, well, hours ago. But now I'm interested in Burke's statement. True or false."

"True with an explanation."

"There always seems to be a footnote with Ms. Winthrop-Smith."

"Intelligent people are often complex."

"And sometimes they're an open book."

"I don't even know what that means." Zainab took a deep breath. "Do you want the explanation?"

"Sure, try me."

She repeated what she'd told Darby, that Eleanor wanted a shift toward civil ceremonies for everyone. "She thinks it's fundamentally fairer."

"That's one theory."

"And the other?"

"I guess you'll have to tune in to my show to find out."

Zainab felt the overwhelming urge to cover her ears, similar to how she and Amra had watched horror movies as children, peering between their slightly parted fingers, controlling how much of Jason or Freddy Krueger they let in. At first, she thought Chase was going to leave it alone, but just before he cut to his first commercial break, she heard him say, "And guess what? Eleanor Winthrop-Smith, an actual Republican candidate for Senate here in the Bay State, wants to outlaw marriage. Heard it straight from her Pakistani press secretary, Zainab Mir. More after the break."

Zainab muted the audio on her computer. There was no need to hear the rest. Chase had morphed, for some inexplicable reason, back into Charles Holland III, a man with no shame. She considered calling the show, but it bordered on dignifying his remarks. The only thing to do with a snake like Chase was to ignore him.

27

It was their first argument since Mateen proposed. Amra could imagine her mother correcting her, telling her it was a disagreement, not an argument, and insisting that the two were completely different things. She could also hear Zainab saying who cared what she called it and to stand her ground. Amra was trying. It was important to her to find a home in the city, but she was having a hard time convincing Mateen. She tried to push the closer-to-their-jobs angle, but he said the idea of getting away from work was what appealed to him about the suburbs. "Think of it like a retreat," he said. Although the idea of retreating each day with Mateen sounded lovely, Amra worried about the times when she would need to abandon that retreat, often on a moment's notice, and head back to the office. Mateen still had no idea how often she returned to work after they'd gone out to eat or caught a show. He'd drop her at her condo, and when he called to wish her good night, he assumed she was home in bed. "Pretend I'm tucking you in," he'd say, and Amra would look at her desk with something close to despair.

And so they sat at Peet's on Labor Day weekend, at a table too small to comfortably hold all of the residential listings Mateen had printed, color coded, and then spread between her caffe latte and his caffe con panna. She'd grown quiet when she noticed there were homes from Wellesley (green), Weston (yellow), and Newton (red) and become positively forlorn when she saw Lexington (blue). Was he planning to live on a farm? Conspicuously absent were any Beacon Hill or Back Bay listings. Or even Brookline.

"Mateen, I know you love the idea of the suburbs. I get that, I really do. But can we at least look at condos? Something near the Common would be nice."

"You'll pay a million dollars for two bedrooms," he said, and pointed at the papers in between them. "We can get a four-bedroom house for that in any of these suburbs."

"But we don't need four bedrooms. We could get by with two. We could use the extra one as an office slash guest room. That would work for now."

"Well, it would be pretty cramped when our parents came. We'd have very little privacy. And soon, when we have a baby, it won't be nearly enough room."

Amra tried not to focus on that word, *soon*. Soon, like after she made partner, or soon, like nine months after the wedding?

He seemed to sense her consternation. "Amra, beautiful Amra, with the crease between her brows. Don't fret. Of course we'll look at some places in Boston. But we can do that anytime, even over lunch. Today, we hit the suburbs." He said it with such dramatic emphasis that Amra couldn't help but laugh. She knew she'd follow him anywhere, even to bucolic Lexington.

They made their way west and then north of the city. In Newton, they looked at a charming three-bedroom on a meticulous street. Amra breathed a little easier. If she left for work early enough and stayed late enough, her commute wouldn't be horrible. She could actually picture herself living in the quaint home, taking her daughter or son by the hand to the local elementary school.

She grew a little more nervous in Wellesley, and by the time they reached Lexington, her shoulders tightened and her stomach knotted. They met with a perky young realtor in Lexington's "downtown" named Val, who had white-tipped nails, a Louis Vuitton bag, and a jet-black bob. The way Val looked at Mateen, hungrily, did little to help Amra's mood.

Val showed them several four-bedroom homes, all of them bigger than the ones in Wellesley or Newton, but also in dire need of updating. One even had olive-green appliances in the kitchen and palm-tree wallpaper in the master bath, which Amra planned to use as ammunition in the battle she was sure was coming. Once they looked at a well-kept townhouse on Beacon Street or a place with exposed brick and recycled countertops in Back Bay, Mateen would come around. But then Val, snaky but surprisingly intuitive Val, said she had one final place, "just a bit" over their price range, that she thought would be perfect.

Mateen's eyes lit up when he saw the house. Amra couldn't deny, from his perspective, its perfection. It had four bedrooms and four updated bathrooms with a kitchen that looked like something out of *Interior Design*. The family room and dining room each had French doors that opened onto a tiered brick patio spanning the entire length of the house.

"So?" Val crossed her arms and tapped her nails on her biceps. "Is it perfect or what?"

"It is pretty perfect," Mateen said. But when he looked at Amra, his smile faded. "We still need to look at some places in the city."

"You're sure? I could get in a lot of trouble for this, but I happen to know that one of my colleagues has a client who is going to put an offer in on this house first thing in the morning."

Amra wanted to call her bluff. Or if it wasn't a bluff, call her a weasel. But she looked at Mateen looking at the house and thought of how he'd moved to Boston for her, and how it would appear if she couldn't even move twenty miles for him.

"Let's make an offer," she said, ignoring the tightness in her chest.

28

HAYDEN TAPPED ON Amra's half-open office door before entering. "Hey," she said, and waited for Amra to look up from her computer.

"Hayden." Amra gave her a fake smile. "What's up?"

"I can come back."

Amra shook her head. "No, it's okay."

Hayden entered but didn't sit, telegraphing, she hoped, that she wasn't going to take up much time. "I was wondering if you were free on Thursday night."

"I have a closing Friday, so, you know." Amra waved her hand. "It will probably be an all-nighter. Why?"

"I wanted to know if you'd go somewhere with me." Amra looked slightly irritated. Hayden knew it was no time to beat around the bush. "There's a party for Muslim women I'd like to go to, but I'm a little self-conscious since I don't know anyone."

"I wish I could go with you, but I don't see how."

"Would it help if I said it was in Cambridge? We can go separately so you can leave once I meet a couple of people."

Amra sighed. She wasn't, Hayden noted, being very sisterly.

"Okay. I'll consider it my dinner break. But, Hayden, I can stay half an hour, tops, okay?"

Hayden said she would personally kick Amra out the door after thirty minutes. Amra rolled her eyes, but at least she was smiling.

They ended up taking Hayden's car so Amra could work on the way to the party. When they hit traffic, Amra clenched her jaw. After a few minutes, she said, "So who exactly are these women?"

"I'm not sure," Hayden said. "I read about it online. I called the woman and she sent me the flyer."

"The flyer?"

"Yes." Hayden motioned to her purse. "It's in the front pocket."

Amra retrieved the paper. "Hayden, it's a *halaqa*."

"So?"

"It's a religious talk."

"How do you know?"

"Because that's what a *halaqa* is!"

"I just thought it was Arabic for 'party.' "

Amra shook her head. "I have final documents to review before our closing tomorrow morning, and I'm about to spend God knows how long at a *halaqa*."

Hayden felt like Amra was yelling at her, even though she hadn't raised her voice. Was it really the worst thing Amra could do? Get a little closer to her faith? Because frankly, with all of her reading, Hayden was starting to notice that Amra didn't exactly *do* everything correctly. She told Amra they didn't have to stay the whole time.

"I never planned to stay the whole time. But it would be a lot easier to slip out of a party than a *halaqa*." Amra leaned her head back. "Sorry. I'm just stressed about work. It will be fine. As long we get out of there by eight. Okay? I absolutely have to leave by eight o'clock."

. . .

The *halaqa* was at the home of a young woman named Zahara, who welcomed them and gestured at the women milling about in the living room, picking at appetizers. "Make yourself at home," she said, waving them in. Like the hostess, most of the women wore headscarves. In fact, except for one older woman, Hayden and Amra were the only ones *not* wearing headscarves. Zahara said that "things" would get under way "soon."

At 7:45, the speaker finally arrived. Amra pressed her lips together and stared at Hayden. Hayden shrugged apologetically. The speaker, an unusually tall woman with thick glasses and a scarf worn so low that it almost touched her eyebrows, introduced herself as Mariam and proceeded to speak at length about beauty, about how God did not find supermodels or porn stars beautiful. She pointed at her long gray coat and white headscarf and said that this was what God considered beautiful. Modesty was beautiful. *Cleanliness* was beautiful. She focused on that last point for quite some time. A young mother who was nursing an infant raised her hand and asked about diapers. "Take them outside every night," Mariam instructed. "Do not go to sleep with a dirty diaper in your house. That is no way to God." Another hand went up. The woman asked about the menstrual cycle. "When the blood stains the underwear, should we throw it out?" Mariam smiled a patient smile. "When you are on your cycle, simply wash your underclothing seven times under running water, then launder. Then, it is clean."

Hayden found the talk overwhelming. She already knew to take her shoes off in a Muslim's home and to say *Alhamdulillah* after she sneezed or if someone asked how she was. But there were even more rules than she'd imagined. And she wasn't even getting Fadi out of this.

The talk ended at a quarter past nine. Amra practically dragged Hayden out of the door, before she could meet anyone. In the car, Amra was quiet, and Hayden thanked her for coming. She had to force the words out, because she wasn't feeling that grateful in light of Amra's attitude.

"Sure. No problem." Amra looked straight ahead at the road. "So, what did you think?"

"Well, there's a lot to learn, that's for sure."

Amra nodded. "You know, there are different opinions about a lot of these issues. Covering, obviously." Amra gestured at herself. "But all of the rest, too. You have to be careful. As a convert, people will have lots of advice for you. But you could think for yourself before you converted, and you can still think for yourself now."

Her words felt patronizing somehow. Lecturing. But what was Amra going to say? She was probably a bit defensive, particularly about the beauty thing. Amra and her friend Zainab were definitely the kind of women who cared about what they looked like. Hayden wished Zainab could have been there to hear the talk. It might have taken her down a notch.

She smiled at Amra, but she thought to herself that maybe she'd have to be careful about what Amra advised her as well.

29

CHASE FORCED HIMSELF over the threshold of Shreve, Crump & Low and tried not to think about what he was doing. He browsed the engagement rings in the glass case and asked the saleslady if he could get a closer look. With long, lacquered nails she extracted the ones he pointed at, offering them to him with an enthusiastic smile. He supposed he should care about cut and clarity and all that, but he just couldn't muster it.

The saleslady seemed to misunderstand his ambivalence. "If you're not sure of her size," she said, "just have her bring the ring in and we'll take care of it." Chase actually laughed. He'd known Savannah's ring size for two years. Even her mother had mentioned it once, pretending to comment on how petite Savannah's hands were.

He finally settled on a two-carat brilliant-cut ring in a platinum setting (Savannah's choice, also telegraphed repeatedly) and hoped it was acceptable. Savannah always said she never wanted to "trade up," which was supposed to sound romantic but really just meant that the first one better be big.

. . .

Chase caught the five o'clock shuttle and was at Savannah's apartment before seven. He knew he should have planned something special—tickets to the Kennedy Center or dinner at Marcel's—but when he thought about it, when he imagined sitting through a four-course meal or some tedious musical performance, he felt like a fidgety teenager without his Adderall. Extending the limbo he'd been in since he'd met Zainab at the Correspondents' Dinner was not an option. Sitting through a fucking symphony was unthinkable.

Still, standing in her apartment, Chase lost his nerve. They ended up at Ceiba, where he had three beers in such rapid succession that Savannah asked if everything was okay. He slowed down on the fourth, but only to fly under her radar. He didn't need the headache of her, years later when they were fighting about who was going to load the dishwasher or why they never had sex, asking if he'd only proposed because he was drunk.

At one point, as Savannah talked about her decision to chair her firm's annual breast cancer walk, she reached over and smoothed the collar of Chase's shirt, almost reflexively, without missing a beat in her conversation. The small gesture conjured up images of an uncomplicated life together. There would be no cultural misunderstandings with Savannah. No self-censoring bullshit.

It was enough. He pulled the ring from his pocket and took Savannah's hand. She started squealing before he got the words out—a textbook proposal that he somehow managed not to slur.

"Really?" she said.

"Really." He slipped the ring on her finger and closed his eyes, waiting for the relief to come.

30

THE DAYS LEADING up to Amra's wedding were a blur. Relatives flew in from India, Pakistan, and the UK. Amra arrived at her parents' home the Wednesday before the wedding. Her mother had asked her to come a full week before, but with the honeymoon the following week, she was pushing it. As it was, Hank had to cover one of her closings, a fact that he continued to remind her of by peppering her with unnecessary questions the week before she left. Mateen wanted to be traditional, so she'd taken the shuttle by herself. She entered her parents' apartment and was swept into a rush of aunties full of makeup suggestions and questions about the groom. Finally, her mother whisked her down the hall, covered her eyes, and pulled her into her old bedroom. "It's done, *beti,*" she said, and removed her hand. On the bed were yards of red and gold Banarasi silk stitched into a fitted top and a long, full skirt.

"It's so beautiful," Amra said. She ran her fingers over the embroidery. "It's perfect."

Her mother nodded. "And here is your *mehndi* outfit." Her mother held the outfit out over her bent arm. "Just exquisite, don't you think?" It was green with a hint of tea-pink shimmer that could only be seen when it caught the light.

"They turned out even better than I could have imagined," Amra said. "Let's hope I haven't gained any weight."

"Nonsense, *beti,* you're skin and bones. But we have a couple of days to fatten you up."

"I'm sure Mateen would love that. Here comes the fat bride."

"Impossible," her mother said. "You couldn't become fat if you ate all of the *biryani* yourself. Besides, the way Mateen looks at you, I don't think he'd even notice."

At the mention of Mateen, she remembered what the dresses were for, that soon she would be standing in front of him in the red silk, and that later he would remove it. A flutter rounded her stomach and she felt herself blush standing next to her mother. She thought she'd been pushing it by coming on Wednesday. Now, she didn't know how she would be able to wait.

"Where are Zainab and Rukan?" Amra whined to her mother in front of the bathroom mirror. "I'm not going without them."

"They're coming. Zainab called from the car. Their flight was late, but Rukan is driving as fast as she can. She said don't wait; they'll meet us at the hall."

Amra looked at herself and tried to locate the root of her anxiety. The *mehndi* outfit was perfect and the wedding gown was likely to be so, too. She refused to try it on, much to her mother's consternation, which only grew when Amra refused to say why. But there was no way she could explain to her mother that she would only put it on once and it would only come off once, by Mateen's hands, as well.

"I need to call Zainab," she said, and edged the bathroom door shut. She dialed Zainab's cell, but it went straight to voice mail. She was probably on the phone with Eleanor. She knew Rukan wouldn't answer while she was driving. She tried Zainab's number one more time before giving up and calling Mateen.

"Hey, you," he said.

"Hey, you." She closed her eyes. "I miss you."

"Me too. Hey, shouldn't you be getting your hands and feet done right about now?"

"I'm not doing my feet."

"Why not?"

"No one does their feet anymore."

Mateen lowered his voice. "I think it's sexy."

"Did I mention I'm doing my feet?"

His laughter was like salve on her nerves. "So Amra *jaan,* what's wrong?"

How could she tell him when she didn't know? "Nothing. I just wanted to tell you that you're missing out on a rather tight-fitting, potentially hint-of-midriff-showing mint-green *lengha.*"

"Ouch." He was quiet for a minute.

"Mateen?"

"I'm here. I'm just picturing you. Promise you'll wear it for me sometime?"

"I promise."

"Amra?"

"Yes?"

"I love you."

She smiled. She wished she could sneak off to see him after the *mehndi,* but there was no chance of that with the auntie patrol in the house. "I love you, too."

She fixed her lipstick and emerged from the bathroom to a sea of impatient, silk-clad women. "What are you waiting for?" Amra asked. "Let's *go.*"

Rukan and Zainab missed Amra's entrance but made it in time for the dancing. They hugged Amra and then proceeded straight to the dance floor. They didn't stop until it was time to apply Amra's henna. When Tahira Auntie held the cone expectantly over Amra's hands and asked where she wanted Mateen's initials, Amra took a small, nervous breath and pointed at her right foot.

Zainab raised an eyebrow. "Kinky," she whispered, before Rukan slapped her arm. Amra blushed and redirected the attention to Zainab. "And what about you? T.F., perhaps?"

"Ha," said Zainab. "I don't think so."

"Just checking." The rule was he had to be *the one*. "So what then? You already did the campaign." But Zainab just shrugged and pulled Rukan back to the dance floor. By the end of the evening, Amra was so tired that she forgot to ask what Zainab wrote.

Amra slept in the next morning until a quarter past nine. She had wanted to run in the park early, before everyone was up. It was too late to be the first one awake—she could hear commotion from the kitchen—but she still wanted the run. She took the cellophane off her hands and feet and rinsed the henna paste in the sink. The design left behind was auspiciously dark and beautiful. She dressed quickly, pulled her hair into a ponytail, and grabbed her shoes. In the kitchen the relatives were having tea.

"Amra, dear, come," said Fatima *Phupi,* her father's older sister. "We've got *paratha* and your father got *dosa* from around the corner. You need to eat. Goodness, what are you wearing?"

She kissed her aunt on the cheek and pulled her mother into the hall. "I'm going for a run, *Ammi*. I'll be back soon."

"A run? On your wedding day?" Her mother wiped her hands on the white dish towel she was holding. "No, *beti,* today you just relax. Let us pamper you."

"I'll be less than an hour, I promise."

In the park, she ran past the carousel and the pond and the zoo, remembering the night she and Mateen had spoken on her parents' balcony, how she knew then that she wanted him, how it had all come to fruition so fast. She'd thought there'd be time to explain about her work, but the moment never seemed right. She whispered a short prayer, asking God to make it easy for them.

. . .

Zainab and Rukan came to help her get ready for the wedding ceremony. Amra was glad she'd held her ground on the venue. Several of her aunts had pushed for the Plaza or some other traditional hotel. But she had always wanted to be married at Tribeca Rooftop, the penthouse space with the views of the Empire State Building and the Hudson River. It was a bit of a squeeze with their substantial guest list, but when her mother had called and said they had a cancellation for the third week in October, Amra had asked her to book it immediately.

In the adjacent photographer's studio her parents had rented, Rukan did Amra's makeup, lining her eyes with kohl, painting her lips a deep red to match her dress. She put on the *lengha,* which, to her enormous relief, fit perfectly. Her mother's hair stylist swept her hair into a French twist, fastening it with jeweled pins, carefully arranging the *dupatta* to fall from the back of her hair down her back. As she looked at herself in the oversized mirror, framed by the important women in her life, Amra forgot there was anything in the world other than love.

She could hear music as they gathered at the top of the spotlighted staircase. Six flower girls descended ahead of Amra, some carrying sweets and candles, the others dropping rose petals. Mateen's relatives gathered at the bottom, ready to greet Amra's family and finally Amra, who, while "Teri Ore" played, walked between her parents with her head modestly bowed. When they reached the dais, her mother and father kissed her cheeks. She saw them both wipe away tears.

Mateen stood before her in a black tuxedo. She had never seen him in one, and it nearly took her breath away. They sat in matching ornately carved wood chairs with gold cushions. Mateen leaned close to her. "I have *never,*" he whispered, "seen anyone more beautiful in my life."

The imam approached and gave a talk about marriage, about men and women being created for each other, to love and know each other. He recited verses from the Qur'an in Arabic and English, and her father and Mateen signed the marriage contract. When it was done, the men shouted "*Takbir*" and the women rushed to hug Amra. Mateen's sister, Maha, was at the front of the line. It was the first time Amra had seen her since they'd sparred as children, and Amra's back stiffened a bit as Maha hugged her.

"Funny how things work out, isn't it," Maha said, tossing her curled hair over her shoulder. "I have to say I never imagined *you* as my sister-in-law." In the spirit of the day, Amra did not take the bait. "I'm glad to be part of your family," she said, and turned to hug Mateen's mother.

With the ceremony finalized, Mateen and Amra could hold hands. Mateen squeezed hers, and then ran his thumb up and down the tender spot on her wrist until she couldn't focus on anything else. He didn't stop until their mothers brought them plates of food and they both agreed they were starving. Children danced, along with some of the less conservative guests. When they cut the cake, pausing for the photographer, Mateen leaned close to her ear. "I can't wait until we're in the car." She laughed, and whispered that the first time they made love was not going to be in the back of some car.

"It's not 'some car,'" he said. "It's a limo. With a driver. And a partition."

At two in the morning, Amra and Mateen began their escape. They weaved through the crowd, taking nearly an hour to reach the door. She kissed her parents one last time and descended the twelve flights to the waiting limo. Mateen told the driver the address of the hotel where they would spend the night before their morning flight to Goa. Then he pressed the button on the panel, raising the tinted divider. He took Amra's hands, palms up, and traced the flowers and paisleys and swirls and then stopped. "Aren't my initials supposed to be in here somewhere?" he asked.

Amra felt herself blush. She reached forward and undid the straps of her gold heels, put her legs across Mateen's lap, and leaned back. He swallowed hard. She forced herself not to move while he ran his hand down her right calf to the sole of her foot. He found his initials just below her ankle. He traced them with his finger, making a path back up her leg. He paused and then his lips found hers, softly at first and then more insistent as he slid the silk fabric out of place, until the neckline of her shirt met the hem of her skirt, bunching around her waist. His mouth warmed her secret places until she shivered. He pulled away and closed his eyes.

Amra tried to pull him back. "Don't stop."

"But at the reception you said—"

"*Don't stop,*" she said, and he was on her, whispering that he loved her. At one point he asked if she was okay, and when she nodded, pushed past it, until she forgot all about drivers and leather seats and small, protective lies about work.

31

A FEW WEEKS after Amra's wedding, Zainab wandered through Porter Square Books with Taj. He'd called the night before, saying that if she wasn't ready to discuss his book, perhaps she might like to look for another, with him. Under the "Eat, Sleep, Read" sign, Zainab tried to explain the impact his book had on her. When she finished, he nodded enthusiastically.

"You *have* to meet May al-Ansari," Taj insisted.

"Who?"

"You're kidding, right?"

Zainab picked up a copy of Ha Jin's *A Free Life* and pretended to study it. Instead, she looked at her hands, relieved the henna was gone. It was the first time she'd been unable to figure out what to write, what she wanted more than anything. And although Amra's wedding had been beautiful and a thing of joy and all of that, for Zainab, it represented a potentially grand jinxing of herself, as though in response to her failure to wish for anything the universe would say fine, take nothing.

She flipped through the pages of the book without answering Taj. Something about the way he had just asked if she was kidding made her feel stupid. And Zainab did not like feeling stupid. Of course, she hadn't had much experience with it. There was the physics class at

Smith for which, unbeknownst to Amra and Rukan, she'd consulted a tutor before the final, and every now and then Amra came up with some obscure grammatical rule she wasn't familiar with, but still, it was pretty infrequent.

"I'm actually not kidding," she said coolly.

"I just meant that I think you would be really into her work." He followed Zainab around the bookshelf. "She's doing great things on the Muslim feminism front. She's got two books out and she lectures all over the world—here, the UK, Canada, even Japan."

"I didn't know there were that many Muslims in Japan." Zainab focused on his tangent, as retribution.

"There aren't. Maybe a hundred thousand or so. Historically, a lot of Turks, but then in the nineteen eighties Asian immigrants came with the economic boom. And as contact increased, of course there have been conversions among ethnic Japanese, although I'm sure that's a smaller percentage of the Muslim population—" He paused. "You don't really care about this, do you?"

She smiled and shook her head. "But I am impressed that you know all of that."

"*Anyway,*" he said, "there's a reception at another professor's home in a couple of weeks, and May will be there. I'd like you to come."

At home, she typed "May al-Ansari" into Google. Born to Episcopalian parents in Darien, Connecticut, she converted while in college and married a Jordanian surgeon. She'd attended Harvard Divinity School and taught for a year at Yale. She lectured at home and abroad about women's rights in Islam. From the article, it sounded like May had converted before she got married. For some reason, Zainab was glad.

The night of the reception, Zainab got stuck in a meeting with Eleanor. She texted Taj for the address and promised to come as soon as she could. With the help of her GPS, she found the Wellesley home, a white colonial with a patio over the garage and monochromatic Christmas lights strung on the front trees. Inside, she greeted the host, a professor of Islamic studies at Harvard, and his French-sounding wife. They welcomed her in, taking her coat, telling her to make herself at home. She spotted Taj near the piano in the living room and watched him for a moment. The two young women he was talking to were hanging on his every word. She took a seltzer from a caterer and headed over.

"Zainab, finally." He smiled. "I'd like you to meet two of my students, Pamela and Kate." Before Zainab could respond, he said, rather breathlessly Zainab thought, "There's *May*."

She was not what Zainab was expecting. Or, to be more precise, her headscarf was not what Zainab expected. While Taj made the introductions, Zainab tried to reconcile "feminist" with the traditionally dressed woman in front of her.

"Zainab, *Assalaamu alaikum*. Welcome. It's so nice to meet you. I've heard a lot about you from Taj." May had taken Zainab's hand, and leaned forward. "It must be very sexy to work on a political campaign."

Zainab laughed. "You'd think, wouldn't you? Most days, I feel like a one-woman cleanup crew."

May smiled. "I'm sure. But from what I hear, you're very good at what you do."

"Thank you," Zainab said. "Taj has told me a lot about you, too. I'm very interested in your work. I'd love to hear more about it."

May nodded. "We should have lunch sometime."

A middle-aged man with cropped graying hair and rimless glasses approached, touched May's elbow, and whispered something in her ear. May nodded and turned back to Taj and Zainab.

"Taj, you remember my husband?" The two men shook hands. May touched her husband's chest. "Zainab, this is Nidal. He's a physician at Children's Hospital. Darling, this is Zainab Mir, communications director for Eleanor Winthrop-Smith's campaign." May winked at Zainab. "And you should be on your best behavior. Zainab is obviously going to be president someday."

Zainab laughed and shook Nidal's hand. "It's nice to meet you."

"The pleasure is mine," he said. "And, unfortunately, the apology. It seems we have an incipient babysitter crisis. Something about hamsters and a locked bathroom door."

May shook her head. "Four kids. It's always an adventure when we try to get some time to ourselves. Nice to see you again, Taj. And it was wonderful to meet you, Zainab. I hope to talk with you more sometime soon."

Zainab was struck by the palpable intimacy between May and her husband—something about the way they shared the same space—and felt an unexpectedly strong flutter of envy.

She turned back to Taj, but he was watching May leave the room. He had never, Zainab was sure, looked at her like that.

Later, when Amra called and asked her how the night had gone, she said it was fine. "May seems great," Zainab said, "although we only spoke for a minute."

"There's a 'but' somewhere in your voice."

"I don't think so."

"Zainab. Something is bugging you."

"Maybe. Do you remember how Taj kept saying I had to meet her? I think *he* just wanted to see her."

"Isn't she married?"

"Yes, quite happily it appears, to a doctor."

"So there's nothing to be worried about."

"Who said I was worried?"

"Besides," Amra said, "from what you've told me about Taj, I think you're more his type."

"I wouldn't be so sure about that."

"Why not?"

Zainab laughed. "When push comes to shove, every man loves a good girl."

32

Amra was getting fat. She was sure of it. Not bigger, perhaps, but definitely *looser.* Jiggly in places that never jiggled before. She knew why. It was the running. Or lack thereof. She'd barely exercised since they'd gotten back from their honeymoon in Goa, where she and Mateen had taken morning runs along Cavelossim Beach, barefoot and carefree.

When they returned and moved into their new home, she'd adjusted her morning routine. She woke at a quarter to five, kissed a half-awake Mateen, left in her workout clothes, and headed for the gym. Once there, instead of getting on the treadmill, she showered and got to the office before six. By working through lunch, she'd managed to leave between eight and nine, in time to have a late dinner with Mateen, watch some television, and then go to bed like a normal wife. Once Mateen was asleep, she headed to the study, where she would put in a few more hours of work. Something had to give, and so far the only thing she could spare was her workout.

She tried to do some squats and lunges in her office, with the door locked. During conference calls, she walked around her office. But by the third week back, she was so tired she couldn't even muster the energy for that. She started making frequent trips to the vending machine for caffeinated soda, at first only during her late-afternoon lull, but soon she found herself downing Diet Coke at nine in the morning. One night, while packing her briefcase and calculating how many hours she needed to put in after Mateen fell asleep, she put her head on the desk and cried. She was used to pulling all-nighters, for God's sake. During the State Street deal, she hadn't left the office for three days. And now, after one month of married life, she'd morphed into an old lady.

She unplugged her laptop and deposited it in her leather bag. In front of the elevator bank, just as she spotted Hank coming down the hall, she vomited.

"Is it possible to have something from India that didn't show up until now? Traveler's sickness? Malaria? TB?" Amra pulled out her phone to search for tropical diseases.

"I don't think you have malaria. Or TB." Mateen steered with his left hand, resting his right hand on her shoulder. "You're working too hard. You don't come home until nine o'clock some nights. You're burning the candle at both ends."

"I think I'd have a fever if it were malaria."

"It's not malaria."

"Same for TB."

"Amra. Put your phone down. When we get home, I'll make you some tea and run a bath. Everything will feel better after some sleep."

She leaned back and closed her eyes. She barely remembered getting out of the car, or Mateen helping her in the house. She fell into the bed, fully clothed. When he brought the tea, she could only open one eye, and that only for a second.

"Forget the bath," he said, and kissed her cheek. "Sweet dreams, Amra *jaan*." He took off her shoes and pulled the covers up to her chest.

When she woke, it was light out. She reached for the clock. 9:03.

She looked around the room for her handbag. She needed her cell phone. Immediately. Before she could find it, the nausea set in and she ran to the bathroom.

Mateen found her lying on the floor near the tub. "Jesus, Amra, you're pale as a ghost."

"Why didn't you wake me?"

"Because you needed the sleep."

"But I have a huge meeting with potential clients tomorrow. I have a thousand things to do to prepare. Eric—"

"I've already talked to Eric."

She sat up. "You *what*?"

"He says he hopes you feel better soon."

"Eric said that?"

"What would you expect him to say?"

"Did you tell him I'll be in later this morning?"

Mateen laughed. "Of course not. You're spending the day in bed."

Before Amra could say anything, she was dry-heaving into the toilet. When it was over, through parched lips and a raw throat, she asked Mateen to get her phone.

Eric was unusually calm. "It's fine. Hank figured you'd be out this morning, what with his witnessing the episode last night. He stayed here last night and got himself up to speed. No need to rush in. Do what you need to do."

Eric never cared about what anyone needed to do. He only cared about people getting done what he needed them to do.

"Are you sure? Because I can take calls from home this morning and be there after lunch."

Eric cleared his throat. "I guess I'm not being clear," he said. "Hank is taking over."

Mateen poked his head in the door at noon. "Hey, sleepyhead. Your mother called. She tried you at work and when your secretary said you were out, she panicked. I said you were fine, but I'm not sure she believed me."

"I'll call her in a few minutes. I'm in desperate need of a shower."

Amra let the hot water run over her and wondered how she had gotten to this point—home on a work day, her mother worrying, Eric giving new clients away. At least her stomach seemed to have settled. She dressed, nibbled on a cracker from the tray Mateen had left on the bed, and called her mother.

"*Ammi,* I'm fine," she said. "I'm sure it's just exhaustion or maybe I picked up something in Goa. It's not unheard of, you know."

"Were you sick during the trip?"

"No." She sighed. "I felt great during the trip."

"And now?"

"Just like Mateen told you. I'm tired and I have a stomach virus. It's nothing."

"*Beti.* When was the last time you were sick?"

She couldn't remember. "Why does it matter?"

"Because you don't get sick."

"Right, but I was in a foreign country."

"On your honeymoon."

"Yes, on my honeymoon."

"Amra."

"Yes?"

"Has it crossed your mind that you might be pregnant?"

Amra almost laughed. "No, because that's not possible."

"Even the best birth control is not one hundred percent reliable."

Amra squeezed her eyes shut and fingered the bedspread. "You're right. But not ovulating is a pretty sure thing. I haven't had a period in months, between the running and the erratic work schedule." As soon as she said it, she blushed. She didn't want her mother thinking that those months corresponded to the time she'd been seeing Mateen. She was pretty sure her mother would know she'd waited until the wedding, but once she said it, she realized how it sounded.

But her mother simply said that ovulation could commence unpredictably. "Why not just get one of those home tests? Don't trouble Mateen about it right now. Not until you know."

"It's really not necessary."

"You're probably right, but humor me. If it's nothing, fine. But if it's something, it's better to know now, *Insha'Allah*."

The next morning, Amra threw up with the shower running so that Mateen wouldn't hear her. She assured him she was fine, that whatever it was had been of the twenty-four-hour variety. On the way to work, she drove to the pharmacy and purchased a pregnancy test promising results as early as six days before a missed period. Later, instead of going to lunch, she slipped into the bathroom, took the test, and remained in the stall, ticking off the minutes on her watch. But when it was time, she didn't even look. She placed the stick back in the box and into her purse. She had a feeling it was the kind of thing Mateen would want to see.

33

HAYDEN SIPPED HER ginger steamer at Crema Cafe and considered how to branch out from Amra, who was still, essentially, the only Muslim she knew. None of the women from the *halaqa* had called her, even though she'd left her contact information on the sign-in sheet. And though she'd assumed Amra would introduce her around, so far it had not happened. Of course, Amra's sole purpose in life now seemed to be to get home to her new husband.

Hayden tried not to be bitter. Amra *was* juggling a lot with Eric and Hank. But it was hard for her to feel sorry for Amra, with her devoted, gorgeous husband and beautiful new home. Hayden, who now sat alone in red flannel pajama pants at a coffee shop on a Friday night, was pretty sure she could put up with a little grief at work if someone like Mateen was waiting for her at home.

Hayden opened her laptop and started reading some of the message boards for converts that she'd bookmarked. She scanned the topics, hoping to avoid the usual arguments—whether the headscarf was required, if women needed to be separated for prayer, or even, to Hayden's horror, how to deal with husbands who wanted to take a second wife.

As she read, two college-aged boys sat at a nearby table and proceeded to assess their chances of getting laid later that night.

"Here's a line I like to use," the blond one said, holding his coffee mug mockingly in the air. " 'Here's to the past two hours and to the next two years.' Chicks dig that shit. You know, love at first sight. Trust me."

Hayden felt her face burn. How many lines like that had she fallen for? More than she cared to count.

She turned her body further toward the brick wall and focused on her computer screen. Finally, through a link to a link, she stumbled across Women for Islam, a new group with an introductory dinner to be held at an Arab restaurant in Cambridge. The post said they were actively recruiting new members, including some for leadership positions, and that they planned to focus on "establishing true Islam in the hearts of Muslim women" and "providing support as we go about leading our Muslim lives." Support was exactly what Hayden was looking for. And maybe she would allow herself to be talked into an organizational role.

The restaurant was small but cozy. Hayden was a little disappointed in the turnout. It was eight women, including Hayden, not exactly a treasure trove of potential new friends. A tall woman in a black headscarf named Fareeda introduced herself as the group's founder and made some remarks about getting back to the basics of the faith.

"Our problem is that people are busy and don't necessarily want to get involved with a new group. They think, oh, there's CAIR; we don't need to bother. CAIR does fine work, but we can leave that to the men, now can't we?" She smiled with a sweetness that was not reflected in her tone. Hayden knew of CAIR. It was one of the major Muslim civil rights organizations. But she thought it included women. She raised her hand and Fareeda nodded.

"I'm a convert, obviously," Hayden began, and regretted the self-minimizing "obviously" almost instantly. "But I thought CAIR was for men and women." Her voice rose at the end, turning her "thought" into a question.

Fareeda narrowed her eyes. "Well, of course. I am just *suggesting* that *perhaps* women don't need to insinuate themselves into everything. That if we think Islamically here, really *think* about things, we *might* conclude that we would all get more done if we followed our Creator's guidance in these matters."

Hayden was not entirely sure what Fareeda meant, nor could she pinpoint the exact insult in her words. She only knew that none of the other women would meet her gaze.

"Are there any more questions?" Fareeda looked around the table. "Good. Now on to our dinner plans. We need to start thinking about a keynote speaker. We need someone who will really draw attention to us, who will sell tickets."

Hayden saw an opportunity to redeem herself in the other women's eyes. She raised her hand.

"Yes?" Fareeda said, barely concealing her skepticism.

"What about Zainab Mir? Eleanor Winthrop-Smith's communications director? She's really making a name for herself around the state, and was even in *Vanity Fair*. I would be happy to contact her on behalf of the group," Hayden said. "She's a good friend of one of my colleagues."

Fareeda crossed her arms. She sat stiffly on the edge of her chair. "My dear, I do appreciate your attempts to *contribute* here," she said. "But Zainab Mir would be a most inappropriate choice."

"But she's a pretty famous Muslim woman. At least locally."

"She wears miniskirts."

"I'm sorry?"

"She wears miniskirts," Fareeda repeated. "And dresses that look like nightgowns. Zainab Mir is no example to Muslim women. In addition to her completely inappropriate clothing choices, she also keeps company with inappropriate people, including known *lesbians*.

For all I know, she *is* a lesbian. And no doubt consumes alcohol and pork as well." Fareeda's voice had risen, making "pork" a rather spectacular crescendo.

Hayden wondered if there was a way, short of bolting, to put an end to her humiliation. Clearly, this was not the group for her. All she could do was sit quietly through the rest of the dinner and hope that she never saw any of these women again.

Fareeda mentioned the names of several women Hayden had never heard of as potential speakers. She assigned tasks to the others present, asking them to contact the women on her list and to organize the food preparation. She did not assign any tasks to Hayden.

As the women were splitting the check and gathering their coats, Fareeda approached Hayden. She put her arm around her and gave her a small, rigid hug. "Hang in there, dear," she said. "You just need a little molding. And lucky for you, I like working with raw material."

34

By march, amra had learned the best places to stop along route 128, often driving in the far right lane even when the other lanes were moving significantly faster, so that she could take an exit or, if needed, pull onto the shoulder before heaving the contents of her stomach into the plastic bags she kept in her car for that purpose. On a good morning, she would only have to stop two or three times; on the worst days, five or six. Usually it was out of her system by the time she reached the parking garage near her office. She'd asked the doctor about medication, but Mateen was worried about the side effects. He'd become more protective since she'd shared the news. That first night he wouldn't let her eat the *maacher vindaloo* she'd brought home before he called the restaurant to see what kind of fish they used (haddock) and consulted the Food and Drug Administration Web site to check its mercury level (low). Amra decided that she'd rather deal with the vomiting than risk Mateen pressuring her to take a medical leave from work. Hank would love that. And maybe Eric, too, though she tried not to think about that.

The vomiting continued and, after noticing a funny taste in her mouth for a week and only urinating twice a day during that weekend, Amra agreed to see her doctor. "The good news," she said after examining Amra, "is that I don't think we're in hyperemesis gravidarum territory quite yet, but let's not take any chances." And so Amra got three hours on an IV drip and strict orders to taper back her work schedule. "At least for this week," the doctor said, looking pointedly at Mateen.

"What can I do to get better quickly?" Amra asked, and immediately added, "for the baby's sake."

The doctor nodded. "Lots of fluids, a bit at a time. Small meals, nothing terribly fatty or spicy. Don't brush your teeth right after eating; let the food settle. Sometimes ginger capsules help. And something as simple as getting out in the fresh air can make a difference, too." The doctor touched Amra's hand. "Call me if you're not getting better. We may need to admit you."

Amra tried not to think about the damage she was doing to her career, or the boost she was giving Hank's, when she called Eric to tell him she wouldn't be in for the rest of the week. She sipped clear liquids and forced herself to keep down plain *naan* and yogurt. In the afternoons, she walked the neighborhood, and was surprised at how good it made her feel.

On Thursday, when the color had returned to her cheeks and she'd regained her sense of taste, she ran into a Wellesley graduate named Bethany jogging with her infant twins in a tandem stroller. She said she lived in the adjacent neighborhood—the one, Amra guessed, that the realtor had said was beyond Amra and Mateen's means—and mentioned the moms' group to which she belonged. She described it as an outlet for stay-at-home mothers who used to have high-powered careers. "We do a happy hour once a month, *sans maris* of course, a few golf outings in the summer, and of course we have the ubiquitous book club. In fact, we're meeting at my house next Thursday. You should totally join us."

Totally. Amra didn't know what to say.

"We're reading Zadie Smith's *White Teeth* right now," Bethany continued. "Maybe you've read it? No? Well, it's truly something, just super amazing. You won't be able to put it down."

Amra couldn't remember the last time she'd read for fun. She had piles of books she planned to get to, but there was never any time. She heard herself say that she'd love to come.

Two nights later, propped up on the pillows Mateen had fluffed for her, she finished the book and sighed.

"What's wrong?" Mateen asked. "Did the ending disappoint?"

"No, the ending is fine."

"Poorly written?"

"It's brilliant."

"But?"

"I can't put my finger on it."

"Well, isn't that what the book club is for?" he teased. "You know, to discuss the book?"

"I guess." She smoothed the orange cover of the book. "The thing is, I can't tell if I'm in on the joke, or if I'm the butt of the joke."

"Not you personally."

"No, not me personally. *Desi* Muslims. Of which I am one."

"The most beautiful one," he said, and pulled her near him, resting his hand on her stomach. "Although soon, I may not be able to say that."

Bethany's house was a large two-story colonial with a three-car garage. The yard was immaculate, with diagonal stripes mowed into still-green grass, despite the recent frost. Cars lined the driveway and the side of the street. Although with the exception of a BMW 7 series sedan and a fire-red Porsche, they weren't cars; they were enormous SUVs. To carry all of the baby gear, no doubt. Amra wondered just how big the group was.

Bethany opened the door and kissed her on both cheeks. "Amra!

Welcome. I'm so glad you could make it." The foyer was two stories and flanked by dual staircases. The paintings looked like something Zainab would appreciate.

Bethany introduced Amra to the other guests, a crowd of white women whose generic names—Brooke, Anne, Lisa, maybe a Laura?—Amra would never remember. Most of them had the same blond-streaked hair as Bethany, except for one woman with a tight black ponytail and pursed lips that could not be considered a smile.

Bethany led her to the hors d'oeuvre table and gestured at the dark-haired woman. "Don't mind her," she whispered. "Rebecca doesn't think that anyone who lives outside the immediate neighborhood should be part of the group."

The bell rang and Bethany rushed off to the front door. Amra was surprised when a darker-complected woman entered. And relieved, which caught her off guard. She usually gave little thought to ethnicity, but something about this experience was making her feel slightly off.

Bethany introduced the new arrival to Amra. Her name was Elena and she also had twins. "Two-year-olds," she said, smiling. "So you can imagine how nice it is to get out of the house for a bit."

"Elena used to be a pediatrician, but we try not to pepper her with too many questions," Bethany said.

"What's this 'used to be'? No one took my degree away, Bethany," Elena scolded.

After everyone had a drink—mostly red wine, although because of her condition, no one looked at Amra strangely when she asked for seltzer—they began. Since Bethany was leading, she gave a summary for anyone who hadn't had time to finish the book. "Spoiler alert," Bethany said in an exaggerated, high-pitched voice before revealing the ending. Amra was waiting patiently for a time to bring up her own issue with the book, whether it was, in fact, satire, when Rebecca spoke.

"Can I just say how much I enjoyed the book and how impressed I was with Smith's portrayal of Samad? I mean, she just got him, spot on."

One of the blond women nodded. "I was wondering how accurate it was. Because it is a little over the top."

Rebecca leaned forward. "No, it's actually not. That is really how Indian Muslim men are. All bottled up about sex, strict with their kids and their wives, but really, you know, sort of obsessed. How do the kids say it? *Horndogs*." The women laughed and Rebecca nodded. "Because they try to restrict it so severely."

Amra couldn't believe what she was hearing. What did Rebecca know about Indian Muslim men? Amra cleared her throat. "I actually disagree," she began. Rebecca gave her a look that was intended, Amra suspected, to make her tread carefully. "Of course you could find some Indian Muslim men like Samad," Amra continued, "but I think Smith has taken an extreme example for satirical purposes. To make a point."

Bethany nodded. "I suppose that's possible, Amra. But Rebecca was a missionary in India. She may know more about this than the rest of us."

If that were true, if Rebecca really had spent any significant amount of time in India, she could probably recognize Amra as a Muslim name. But Rebecca didn't say anything.

"Right," Amra said, "but I happen to be married to an Indian Muslim man."

The room was silent, first, and then filled with nervous coughs and averted gazes. "Let's move on," Bethany finally said. Amra left the gathering feeling less like she was the butt of the joke in the book and more like she might be one at the next book club meeting. It didn't matter. Unlike these women, she still had a career and didn't need the "moms' nights out." And as for the *sans maris* thing, Amra actually liked spending time with her husband. *My Indian Muslim husband,* she thought and, in an imaginary gesture that would have made Zainab proud, she mentally gave Bethany and Rebecca the finger.

35

If Zainab were forced to pick a word for her lunch with Taj a week before the Young Conservatives' Convention, it would have been *strained*. Taj seemed genuinely bothered by the fact that Zainab did not spend her free time grappling with religious issues and finding a scholarly basis for her beliefs, even when they reached the same conclusion. When they talked about gay rights in the context of the campaign—Fred Whitaker continued to push the issue, jabbing at Eleanor—Zainab said that she arrived at her position intuitively, that it was just her belief that gay people were no different than straight. "But maybe you were shaped by your experiences at Smith," Taj had suggested. When she said she didn't think so, he went on to explain his own thought process, including a biblical and Qur'anic study.

"I find Scott Kugle's reasoning compelling," he said, and again Zainab was forced to admit that she had no idea whom he was talking about. "I thought you might say that," he said, and presented her with a copy of Omid Safi's *Progressive Muslims*.

Zainab admired Taj's enthusiasm, and his professorial good looks, but he was starting to irritate her. She didn't pepper him with Eleanor's position papers or ask how he arrived at his support for revamping the tax code. She was perfectly fine to let Taj be Taj and did not require his approval to have her own thoughts.

She tried to explain this to him over their Phuket noodles. He said he hadn't meant to be so overbearing. "I just think that it would be good for you to have a basis for your choices. You'd take less heat that way."

Zainab thought about those two unlinked thoughts that he'd just joined together. She turned his premise and his conclusion around in her mind, trying to decide which one was more offensive. She'd had quite enough in her life of people knowing what was "good" for her, but she actually thought the second idea bothered her more—the notion that she couldn't take the heat, that she might be so lacking in boundaries that her opinions were subject to the whims of others.

She took the Safi book, knowing that she would be in no hurry to read it, that there would be no flirtatious pretense of getting together with Taj to discuss it. The look in Taj's eyes indicated that, perhaps for the first time, they were on the same page.

When Zainab arrived at the Young Conservatives' Convention in Brookline, she noticed a handful of G8-type protestors on Webster Street, dressed in black with their pant legs tucked into their socks and bandannas tied around their necks. They were handing out flyers calling for a return of "Native lands to Native peoples." Zainab took a flyer, which she promptly deposited in the trash in the hotel lobby. Eleanor was trying to reach the middle and Zainab had no time to muck about in the margins.

In between speakers, Zainab made the rounds of the various booths. She talked at length with the BU students at the Republicans for Choice table and the guy representing the Log Cabin Republicans. She had a promising discussion with some new-Keynesian types from Tufts. But beyond that, she was back in the muck. She paused in front of the "Say No to Jihad" table with its "Islam Is of the Devil" bumper stickers and the stack of gold-colored flyers "exposing the truth about Islam." The Evangelical Women's Alliance a few tables down was handing out a position paper condemning the doctrine of egalitarianism, calling it a "cancer in the church." When she finally found Eleanor, all she could do was roll her eyes.

"I know, I know," said Eleanor. "We just have to keep our eye on the ball. Reach out to the economically conservative young folks here who *don't* want to brand the two of us with scarlet letters."

When Eleanor spoke at the end of the day, she was a surprising hit, speaking without notes; telling funny, slightly sarcastic anecdotes; fielding questions as though there was nothing she'd rather be doing. Zainab looked around the crowded room. She thought she might have seen Chase at the lunch break, but light-haired preppy guys were not exactly in short supply. Besides, they hadn't spoken since their little exchange over the hate-crimes legislation, so it wasn't like they were going to grab a cup of coffee together and chat.

After she finished, Eleanor said she had to run but asked Zainab to take the pulse of the crowd, stir up interest in working for the campaign. "You're young and beautiful," she said. "Don't look a gift horse in the mouth."

By the time Zainab was ready to leave, police were stationed at the front entrance of the hotel, warning the attendees to exit at their own risk. Zainab smirked—she was not afraid of a few kids in kneesocks—and pushed through the door. She heard the chanting from the crowd first, which had grown considerably and was challenging the perimeter of policemen. When she saw the plume of tear gas, she decided that the four blocks to her car wasn't worth it. Clearly, she should have sucked it up and paid the thirty bucks for hotel parking. She sighed and headed back to the lobby to wait.

"Zainab." It was Chase Holland. "Come on. I'm parked in the garage."

. . .

By the time they reached his car, traffic was already backed up. People laid on their horns; some yelled out their windows. "They've probably blocked the exit," Chase said as they got into his black Jeep. "I think it's going to be a while. Sorry."

Zainab smoothed her hair. "It's not your fault."

"How generous of you."

She realized that she was stuck in a car with Chase Holland, possibly for hours. In retrospect, she probably should have taken her chances on the street.

Chase put the keys in the ignition and fiddled with the radio stations. He tapped his fingers on the steering wheel. "So," he finally said, "how've you been?"

"Fine," Zainab said.

"And Eleanor? Doing well?"

Zainab just looked at him.

He raised his eyebrows, mouthed an exaggerated "okay," and sighed. "How about Taj Fareed? How's he?"

"He's fine."

"Just fine?"

Zainab looked at him. "He's great."

"I'm sure." Chase nodded. "How's his vegetable *biryani*?"

"I'm sorry?"

"Nothing. So I suppose you've been showing him around Boston."

Zainab paused. "We've seen a few things."

"Oh yeah? Like what?"

"Quincy Market, Old North Church, the Dungeon Witch Museum in Salem."

"Wow." Chase laughed. "The Dungeon Witch Museum? Really? How romantic."

"Salem is very historical."

"I know, but the museum itself is a little morbid."

It was exactly what she'd said to Taj. "Parts of it are a little hard to stomach," she conceded.

"I mean, there's the dungeon which, from what I recall, smells a bit—"

"Musty."

"Right. Musty. And then those mannequins just, you know, hanging there. And that guy—"

"Giles Corey."

"—pressed to death. How does that even work?" Chase seemed to consider it. "I mean, is it a quick death?"

"I wouldn't think so."

Chase shook his head in agreement. He bit his cheek and looked at her. "You have to admit it's an interesting choice for a date."

She was about to defend it, but she didn't see the point. Instead, she turned the tables. "So, I never had a chance to congratulate you."

"For what?"

"On what," she corrected. "Your engagement. Darby told me."

He didn't say anything.

"Oh, so your personal life is off-limits?"

"No, it's not that. We've called it off."

"I'm sorry." Zainab wished she hadn't brought it up. "Really."

"It's okay. It was my decision. I shouldn't have proposed in the first place. I ended up really hurting her."

"You don't owe me an explanation," she said.

"Don't worry. I wasn't going to bore you with the details."

Zainab sighed. "I just meant that most people don't confide in their enemies." She searched for any sign of movement ahead of them.

"You're not my enemy. Far from it." Something in his voice caught at that last part, but Zainab ignored it.

"You could have fooled me."

He nodded. "I tried to. I tried to fool myself, too." Some of the cars had started inching forward, but Chase didn't seem to notice. He gripped the steering wheel with both hands and leaned against the gray leather headrest. "I can't believe I'm going to say this, but what the hell, right?" He took a breath. "Ever since that first night in D.C., I haven't been able to get you out of my mind. You were so incredibly beautiful that night." He looked at her and shook his head. Zainab didn't know what to say. He looked like the guy who had made her dinner, twice. She tried not to remember. She tried to pretend she was waiting for the other shoe to drop, for him to turn bristly and abrasive again. To steel herself against the look in his eyes. But then he continued. "And once we actually talked, really talked, you know, at your place that first time . . ." He swallowed, tightening his jaw as though downing something jagged. "Well, let's just say you've been basically all I can think about."

"Chase."

"I know. I've said horrible things. I don't expect you to forget that. Or to forgive me, even though I am sorry. I don't expect anything in return. I just needed to say it. And if you want, I'll never say it again."

Zainab tried to focus. *He traffics in bigotry,* Amra had said. It was increasing as the election drew near—the vitriol from the right-wingers, the anti-Muslim rhetoric—and he had been part of it.

"What if you didn't know me?" she said. "What if you didn't think I was beautiful? Would you still be sorry?"

"Truthfully?" He grimaced. "Probably not."

"At least you're honest." She looked at him and something gave way. She smiled. "Maybe it should be one of Eleanor's new policy positions."

"What do you mean?"

"You know, pimping out the best-looking Muslim women to ignorant neo-con men. Might just start a revolution."

He laughed. "It does have a certain Eleanor-esque feel about it." He shook his head. "But what are you going to do about the ignorant neo-con women?"

"We have good-looking men, too."

"Like Taj Fareed."

"Yes, like him," Zainab agreed. Chase looked forlorn. She let him suffer for a couple of minutes. "Hey, Chase."

"Yeah?"

"I'm not seeing Taj anymore."

"You're not?"

She shook her head. He didn't say anything. She nudged him. "This might be the first time I've seen you speechless."

"I guess I'm just wondering if it would be bad form to smile right now."

"Because it didn't work out with Taj? Probably."

He nodded. "You might want to close your eyes."

"Just because I can't see it doesn't mean it's not bad form."

"Right," he said, leaning toward her. "But it would make it easier to kiss you."

She looked at him, hard. "There's something you should know."

"Yes?"

"I'm not big on second chances."

"I figured," he whispered just before she closed her eyes.

36

EASTER WEEKEND, HAYDEN decided, was perfect. She had three days off from work and no plans. None of her friends called anymore, which was fine. They had nothing in common ever since Hayden had stopped drinking.

With her newfound free time, Hayden gravitated toward the members of Women for Islam. After that first awkward meeting, Fareeda called to apologize. "I think I was a little hard on you," she said, and explained that she was just trying to steer Hayden in the right direction. "There is so much misinformation out there. I don't want to see someone with as much potential as you go astray."

Hayden had turned the word *potential* over in her mind. In terms of her career, Hayden was already fairly successful, but she was pretty sure that's not what Fareeda was talking about. Hayden asked Amra what she thought without telling her too much about Fareeda. Amra said she wasn't sure. But then she said to be careful. "Sometimes people like to make a big deal out of converts. You know, sort of parade them around as validation."

Hayden was pretty sure that Fareeda would have told her to be careful of Amra. "Just because some of our sisters don't wear the headscarf doesn't mean it's not required," Fareeda had said once, telling

Hayden to "pray about it." Hayden already enjoyed the extra freedom she felt on the subway now that she no longer wore leg-revealing skirt suits. She also allowed herself, for the first time since college, to eat more than one full meal a day. She felt like she finally understood the radical feminists in college who wore their hair cropped close and dressed in baggy jeans and wifebeaters. Why should a woman have to be judged for her body every single stupid time she left the house?

And so it was something of a natural progression that Hayden found herself at the edge of the Boston Common, having just departed the T, holding a black cotton triangle of cloth in her hands. She took a deep breath and quickly placed the scarf over her head, tying the ends under her chin. She knew what she looked like; she'd tried it on plenty of times at home, at first feeling sad, as though she'd lost something to the peasant-looking woman staring back at her, but with enough practice, and constant reminders of what the woman at that first *halaqa* had said—"this is beauty"—Hayden grew more comfortable. And now, scarf in place, she walked through the park, past the man with the accordion, over the bridge, toward the duck pond. A small boy who had been running in circles around two women stopped and looked at Hayden. After a minute, he went back to his circling. If that was the worst of it, Hayden figured it would be a snap.

She exited the Public Garden on the west side, heading toward Newbury Street. It was as good a time as any to do some window shopping. There was a Chanel boutique there, and while Fareeda had said that a proper Muslim woman shouldn't draw attention to herself or be showy, she hadn't said anything about skimping on quality.

In front of Cuoio, she saw him. Fadi. She stopped short and sucked in her breath. He was less than thirty feet away, holding several shopping bags in one hand and his cell phone to his ear with the other. He looked like a college kid with his faded jeans and flip-flops. He ended his call, shoved his phone into his pocket, and then shifted from one foot to another. He was waiting for someone, and Hayden bet she knew whom.

Incognito in her headscarf, Hayden pretended to look at the dresses in the window, watching out of her peripheral vision while Fadi tapped his foot and ran his fingers through his hair. He did not like waiting. Soon, a woman in a floral headscarf exited Cuoio, and Hayden's stomach seized. The woman was quite a bit shorter than Hayden, though perfectly proportioned—the kind of woman who shopped in the petite section and made men scramble to protect her. She was wearing a long khaki skirt and a fitted, long-sleeved shirt. When Fadi saw her, his demeanor changed. He smiled an enormous smile and slipped his arm around her tiny waist. He may not have liked waiting, but he apparently liked the woman he'd been waiting for.

Hayden felt a surge of anger. What right did those two have to be happy when they had caused her so much pain? Well, when *Fadi* had caused so much pain. The woman was really his victim, too. But there she was, looking happy and in love, slipping seamlessly into Hayden's spot. Like nothing had happened. Like *Hayden* had never happened.

She followed Fadi and his wife as they walked in the other direction. His arm was still around her waist, and every now and then she put her head on his shoulder. Hayden quickened her pace until she was just behind them. Without thinking, almost without processing it, she felt her hands reach out and shove Fadi. He lurched forward, disengaging from his wife's waist. Hayden was so startled at what she'd done that she pretended she had stumbled and propelled herself to the ground.

"Goodness, are you okay?" his wife asked. Hayden nodded without looking up. The woman knelt before her. "Are you sure?"

She nodded again. Fatima reached out her hands to help Hayden up. "Thank you," Hayden said. Her voice cracked. She looked at Fadi. It took a moment for the alarm to register on his face.

He recovered, saying, "I think she's okay, Fatima." Hayden remembered the first time she'd heard her name from Amra, back when she still thought she had a chance with him.

"Give her a minute to see." She turned to Hayden. "He's a doctor, so you're in good hands."

Hayden didn't want to think about all the parts of her that had been in his hands.

"She just stumbled," Fadi said. "I don't think we need to bring the gurney."

Hayden looked at him long enough for him to start shifting. "Your husband is right. I assume he is your husband?"

"Oh, yes. We wouldn't have been walking so close like that if he weren't," Fatima said.

"Of course," Hayden said with mock piety. "In any case, your *husband* is right. I'm fine. *Shukran*."

"Oh, you speak Arabic?" Fatima looked pleasantly surprised.

"Not really. I'm learning. Actually, I've just recently converted to Islam." Fadi's eyes narrowed as she said the last part.

"That's great! *Alhamdulillah,*" Fatima said. "Why don't I give you my phone number? I'm new to Boston and you're new to Islam. Maybe we can help each other out."

Hayden looked at Fadi. She didn't know that it was possible for him to blanch so white.

"That," Hayden said, "would be lovely."

A couple of hours later, Hayden's cell phone rang. She'd been expecting his call.

"What the hell are you doing, Hayden? Are you *following* me?" Fadi's voice was like ice.

"Assalaamu alaikum," Hayden said.

"I'm serious. How did you know we'd be shopping today? And why were you dressed like that?"

"I think it's a sin to refuse to return a fellow Muslim's greeting."

"Putting on a scarf doesn't make you a Muslim."

"You're right. But making the *Shahada* does. I converted several months ago. Right after our sordid affair, actually."

"You're kidding."

"I'm not." Hayden paused. "And I have you to thank. I first started thinking about converting when we were . . . well, *you know.*" Fadi didn't say anything. "I guess we'd better hope your wife doesn't ask how I came to Islam, right?"

"I don't know what you're talking about."

"That seems unlikely."

"Because we fooled around for a bit? *That's* why you converted?"

Hayden squeezed her eyes shut. "I think it was more than fooling around. And I think you think so, too. Maybe you have to pretend otherwise now, but we both know what it was."

"Right," Fadi said. "Let's think about it. The first time I saw you, you had on an extremely low-cut dress that showed everything except your nipples, and the third time I saw you we had sex. You're a lawyer. You weigh the evidence."

Everything in Hayden's body, all at once, started to burn.

"Stay away from my wife, Hayden."

"I can't make any promises."

"I'm not joking."

"Neither am I. Besides, your wife took my number, too. I'm assuming you never told her my name, since she didn't have some horrible moment of shock when I handed her my card. But don't forget that we know people in common, Fadi. And it can be a very small world. So if I were you, I might spend more time coming clean with my wife and less time harassing former lovers on the phone."

The line went dead. Hayden lay down on her bed and sobbed into her pillow. It shouldn't have been like this. She shouldn't be having such an acrid conversation with Fadi. She'd loved him. Maybe still did, if her initial reaction to seeing him was any indication. And now she was wearing a headscarf and listening to him tell her to stay away from his wife. She stared at her bedroom wall considering how they'd gotten to that point.

She knew it wasn't going to end well for at least one of them.

37

Amra had just come from her annual review. It was devastating. Eric revealed that she would not be considered for partner the following year, with all of her "part-time work" and the forthcoming family leave. Hank stopped by later with the "incredible news" that they were moving him up a year, and Amra knew: Hank was taking her partnership spot.

Once Hank left her office, she'd thought about going back to Eric and telling him what he was doing was illegal. That he couldn't punish her for being pregnant, that she was still working long hours and producing good results. That none of her clients had complained. Or had they? She was pretty sure Eric would have told her, but maybe not. Maybe there had been long conversations between Eric and the clients where he promised to get Hank more involved. Maybe there were scathing notations in Eric's scrawl in her personnel file. Eric was shrewd enough to cover his bases. As she sat in her office picturing it all, she grew weary. Not physically—she'd been exhausted since the first weeks of her pregnancy and was quite used to it—but mentally. She was tired of playing the nice girl at work, of putting up with all of Hank's subtle digs. And she was tired of pretending at home, sneaking around like someone having an affair, even working in the bathroom at night, hiding her laptop in the linen closet when Mateen woke, pretending she'd only been up for a minute. She was tired to her core. Tired enough to do something she'd never done before: She walked out of her office, with only her handbag—no computer, no briefcase, not a single sheet of paper—and drove to Mateen's old condo. She told no one that she was leaving or where she was going.

She opened the door quickly, slamming it behind her as though someone were chasing her. And somehow, leaning against the closed door, aware that no one knew where she was or how to find her, for the first time in a long time Amra felt as though she could breathe.

She stripped down to her underwear and bra and climbed in between the cool, cotton sheets. She pulled the puffy down comforter up to her neck, lying on her left side with her right hand on her stomach, and focused only on inhaling and exhaling. She'd gone too long without air.

When she woke, the condo was dark. She reached over and turned on the lamp, waiting for her eyes to adjust. She showered and put on the robe that Mateen kept on a large brass hook on the back of the bathroom door. She checked her cell phone. Eighteen messages. Most were from clients. Four were from Eric, with the last one asking where the hell she was and telling her that if she had to leave for another doctor appointment, she needed to let them know when she'd be back. Upon hearing his flinty voice, Amra was overwhelmed with an unfamiliar thought: *Maybe I won't ever be back.*

The last message was from Mateen. "*Salaam,* Amra *jaan*. Just wondering if my gorgeous wife and beautiful daughter are up for Szechuan food. Should be home by nine. Love you."

At the sound of his voice, and his reference to the baby as a girl—they'd opted not to find out, but he kept insisting that he knew—she smiled. She wasn't trying to get away from Mateen. She dialed his cell phone. He picked up on the first ring.

"Hey, gorgeous."

"Hey." Her voice caught in her throat.

"Amra? Are you okay? Is it the baby?"

"I'm fine. *We're* fine."

"Then what is it?"

"I miss you."

"How fortuitous. I'm almost home."

"Oh."

"Oh?" He laughed. "I thought you said you missed me."

"I do. Could you turn around and head for your condo?"

"Why would I do that?"

"Because your wife is lying on your bed wearing nothing but your robe and she needs you. *Now.*"

She met him at the door, pulling him in without saying a word, kissing him hungrily. He undid the robe and pushed it off her shoulders and down her back. He ran his hands over her full breasts and her protruding belly. And then he stood back and shook his head. "You've never looked more beautiful," he whispered. She led him to the bed and, as he made love to her, let the tears seep out—a mixture of love and longing and opening herself to him.

Afterward, while he held her, she told him about her day—the review, Eric, Hank, walking out. She wanted to tell him all of it, about the sneaked hours of work, the late nights after he'd gone to bed. But she just couldn't.

"Amra, you don't ever have to hide anything from me. Not ever. I love you for you. Type A, workaholic, the whole thing. Got it?"

"Got it," she said, and this time when he moved inside her, there were no tears.

38

After much soul-searching and prayer Fareeda said that Women for Islam had decided that Hayden would make the perfect speaker for their dinner. "Consider the simple power of your conversion," Fareeda said, drawing her hands together like a sorceress. "You had it all—a high-powered career, beautiful clothes, boyfriends"—at this last part, Fareeda stopped, closed her eyes, and whispered "*Astigfirullah*"—"but still you were seeking. And thanks to our almighty and merciful God, your past is wiped away. Now, you start fresh. It's a powerful narrative, don't you think?"

The best way to "start fresh" according to Fareeda was for Hayden to confess it all at the dinner. To show why *true* Islam was the only path to a good life, particularly in a libertine society like America.

"You think they have something on you, the girls who were born into Islam. But look at some of them," Fareeda said. "Your Zainab Mir, for starters. She's turned her back on it all. Mark my words: Our Creator will turn his back on her as well. He has no need for the ingrates and the degenerates. Not when he has good girls like you who have seen the light."

Hayden was both flattered and aghast at Fareeda's proposition.

The idea that she had something to teach other Muslim women—the ones who didn't smile at her when she went to the *masjid* or invite her to their parties on the one hand or the beautiful, superior Zainab Mirs of the world on the other—was, if she were honest, a satisfying taste of power that sweetened the more she considered it.

"Can I think about it?" she'd asked tentatively. Something about Fareeda's way with her always left her feeling like she needed to ask permission to have her own thoughts.

"Of course you may *pray* about it," Fareeda responded, "but I'll need an answer by tonight. We need to get the program printed and start advertising the dinner."

And so Hayden found herself standing before a roomful of women, most in *jilbabs,* the floor-length housecoat that ensured no one could see the slightest line of their bodies, all in *hijabs,* looking expectantly at her.

"*Assalaamu alaikum,*" she began, with an unfortunate shaking of her voice. "Thank you for coming tonight." She smoothed the paper with her notes. "My name is Hayden Palmer and I have recently found Islam." She paused for the applause she'd been sure would come. The room remained silent. She forced herself to continue. "I'm here tonight to share that journey with you and to emphasize why we need Islam in our lives and in this country so desperately. The purpose of Women for Islam is to see a return to the fundamentals and to stop the watering down and *Christianizing* of our faith."

Hayden took a deep breath and launched into a brief description of her life before Islam—the partying, the drinking, the going out with all the wrong guys. She did not specifically mention her sexual activity—she would have to see these people again, and while Fareeda assured her that all was forgiven with God, she wasn't so sure the stone-faced women staring her down would forgive so much as an openmouthed kiss—but she did allude to it. As she spoke, she realized that at least part of her words had started to take on the characteristic of truth, that she was no longer saying what Fareeda wanted her to say, but what simply *was*. Her life before made her sick to her stomach. She ended by saying how empty that life had left her and how much better her life was now.

After the enthusiastic applause, Fareeda embraced her. "Wonderful. Just wonderful. *Alhamdulillah*. I have to go make the rounds, but tomorrow, you will come to my house. I have a little surprise for you, *Insha'Allah*."

She wondered if it would be a new Qur'an or maybe something more frivolous, like a pair of earrings. She wished Fareeda had just brought the gift to the dinner instead of taking up her Sunday. The stress of worrying about speaking at the dinner had worn her down, and she'd been looking forward to a leisurely day at home. But, as usual, she couldn't say no to Fareeda.

She spent the night greeting strangers, retelling parts of her story. They particularly liked to hear about how dating had been miserable, nodding their knowing heads, chiming in that true love can only come *after* a marriage and anything before was just lust and would surely dissipate when the next attractive person came along. She couldn't help but think of Fadi and how she'd been so sure it was the real thing, how she was still sure she could have married him and loved him forever if he had only given her the chance.

Hayden rang Fareeda's bell at ten the next morning, as instructed. The door opened, but she couldn't see anyone.

"Assalaamu alaikum?" Hayden said, moving gingerly forward.

"Come," said Fareeda, from behind the door. "Hurry, I don't have my scarf."

It was the first time she'd seen Fareeda without her *hijab*. She had long, thinning hair that fell in a frizzy tangle almost to her waist. It wasn't what Hayden expected, but maybe other cultures didn't have rules about age and hair length.

Fareeda waved her into the living room and offered her some tea.

"I suppose you're wondering why I've brought you here bright and early on a Sunday morning," she said as she filled Hayden's cup.

Hayden smiled. She didn't want to look like she was in a hurry to get her gift. "It's always nice to spend time with you."

"Such a dear, aren't you." Fareeda took a scarf from the couch and covered her hair before sitting down. "Hayden, dear, I have a proposal for you."

"Okay," Hayden said, wondering what this had to do with her surprise.

Fareeda laughed. "You're so nonchalant! Let me clarify. I have an actual *proposal* for you. A marriage proposal."

Hayden was speechless.

"I know, I should have given you some warning. Now close your mouth; it's not like someone died."

"But who—I haven't met anyone—" Hayden struggled to say something coherent.

"Of course you haven't *met* anyone. You're a good Muslim girl now. And since your parents are, at least for the time, *kafirs,* I have taken it upon myself to find you a suitable husband. And"—Fareeda waved her hand in a flourish—"as luck would have it, my oldest son has just indicated he is ready to find a wife." She said it as though all of the fortunes of the world had culminated in that exact moment.

"Your son?"

"Abdullah Rahman. He is thirty years old and works as an engineer for a local software company. It's an excellent job, wonderful benefits. And he was almost a *hafiz,* came quite close, but God leads whom he will and sometimes these things are out of our human hands."

"A *hafiz*?"

"Yes, someone who has memorized the entire Qur'an. Goodness, you still do have a lot to learn, don't you?" Fareeda chuckled. "In any case, Abdullah Rahman will be a wonderful teacher for you."

"For me?" Hayden realized she was speaking in two-word questions. She cleared her throat. "It's not that I don't appreciate the thought, but I'm just not sure I'm ready—"

"Nonsense!" Fareeda's tone rattled the air. "Marriage is half of our faith, Hayden. And surely you will find no one better than my son."

"Oh, I know that. I wasn't questioning him. I was questioning myself."

"Well, no need. Now I'm thinking of a rather quick wedding. It's not like in America where you live together for a year and think it over. In Islam, once the parties are identified, we just do it. Like that Nike tagline, I suppose." She laughed again. "Wait here."

Hayden wondered if she should make a run for the door. She guessed Fareeda was fetching her son, and by then it would be too late to escape. But when Fareeda returned, she brought back a simple gold ring. "This is from Abdullah Rahman," she said solemnly, holding the ring in front of Hayden. "Go ahead, put it on."

"Doesn't he want to meet me?"

"He saw you come in. He'll come down after you accept the proposal."

It should have been preposterous, the idea that she would accept the proposal. Its vocalization should have shocked her. But Hayden was too tired to be shocked. It wasn't just Fadi, or the way her parents had treated the news about their breakup with knowing resignation, like they'd been planning to settle in for her spinsterhood all along. It was more than that. She thought about the absolute chronic fatigue of the past decade—the years when she'd stuck like a popped balloon in shriveled pieces to unkind men who only sometimes pretended to care. It had all culminated in that last, acerbic phone call with Fadi, so desperate to protect his wife. Who, Hayden wondered, would protect *her*?

She took a small, severing breath and placed Abdullah Rahman's ring on her finger.

. . .

Hayden entered her apartment carefully, like she was balancing a stack of books on her head and if she just remained still enough she could avoid renegade thoughts. She made it to her room in small, fluid steps and eased herself onto the bed, lying on her right side, her hands entwined between her bent legs. She could still feel the ring on her left hand but knew that the sensation would soon fade. That she would get used to it.

When Fareeda had gone to get her son, Hayden braced herself for ugly or fat or bald. Or all three. As it turned out, Abdullah Rahman was not bad looking: average height, a bit on the thin side, with thick brown hair and high cheekbones. He'd looked at her in serial stolen glances and, at Fareeda's prodding, greeted her. He said he liked children and was looking forward to a large family. He promised to be a good provider. He said it was okay if she wanted to quit her job. She was surprised to discover the idea didn't alarm her.

She'd thanked him for the ring and told him that she, too, wanted lots of children and that she'd think about her job. His smile was more genuine than his mother's and there was no harsh edge to his voice. He was not as good-looking as Fadi, but then again maybe he wasn't as duplicitous either.

Alone in her bed, Hayden thought of Amra's essentially arranged marriage. It had worked for her. Mateen seemed to treat her like a queen. Maybe it would work for Hayden, too. She pulled the covers over her and told herself that she was simply playing in a parallel universe; she could get out at any time. For the moment, however, she just wanted to sleep.

39

AMRA HAD, OF course, gone back to work after she and Mateen spent the weekend at his condo. That Monday morning, she'd casually strolled into Eric's office and told him that she had, in fact, left work early on Friday because of the pregnancy. She looked him clearly in the eye and said that, since her "condition" was protected, she was sure that he would understand. After that, she started leaving routinely at eight, making it home in time to have dinner with Mateen most nights, and then stretching out on the couch while they watched *Lost* or *Mad Men,* her legs on his lap, him rubbing her swollen ankles and feet. When they went to bed, she stayed put. And when Mateen asked her about taking a trip to Ithaca for the weekend to visit his cousin and his wife, Amra said yes, even though he wanted to leave at noon to beat the traffic.

On Friday, she came home early as promised and changed from her black suit into a long khaki skirt and a white maternity shirt. She tried not to think of Hank's enthusiastic smile when he'd told her to enjoy her weekend. Mateen appeared in the door and paused.

"What?" Amra looked at her outfit. "Is there a stain?"

"No. It's nothing. It's just—"

"It's just *what*?"

"Ahmad and his wife. They're pretty conservative."

"Okay."

"Your skirt has a slit in the back. I was just wondering if you'll be comfortable."

She looked at him for a moment. "I am, actually, extremely comfortable. That's why I put this on." She realized she was snapping at him. It wasn't his fault that Hank was under her skin. "Do you want me to change?"

He gave a sheepish smile. "Yes?"

"Fine," she said, "I'll go get the *burka*."

"Amra. Never mind. You look great."

"I'm kidding. It's fine. Give me two minutes." As she changed, she wondered how relaxing the weekend would be.

Amra dozed a bit in the car, waking when they were an hour outside of Ithaca.

"Hey, sleepyhead. How are you feeling?"

She stretched her arms and rolled her head without lifting it from the headrest. "Perfect."

"Me too," he said. He drove with his left hand and rested his right one on her leg. "Do you need to stop?"

"No, I'm okay."

He nodded. They drove in silence for a while and then Mateen asked about Zainab. "So, what's new with her superstar boyfriend? You haven't said much lately."

"Oh my God." Amra sat forward. "I can't believe I didn't tell you."

"Tell me what?"

"She's not seeing Taj anymore. She's seeing someone else."

"What happened with Taj?"

"They were just too different, I guess."

"Because Taj is a Muslim?"

"Mateen."

"Sorry." He changed lanes to pass the slow-moving minivan in front of them. "Okay, she's not seeing Taj. Who *is* she seeing?"

"Okay," Amra said. "Are you ready for this?"

"Lay it on me."

"You have to promise not to tell anyone."

"Who am I going to tell?"

"I don't know. Just promise."

He sighed. "Fine. I promise."

She paused for effect. "She's seeing Chase."

"Who?"

"*Chase*. The right-wing wack job who blasts her on his show all the time."

"The one who thinks she's an enemy of the state because of her religion?"

"That's the one."

Mateen's jaw clenched. "Why the hell would she date him?"

Amra fished her lip gloss out of her handbag. "I have no idea."

"I'm no fan of Taj Fareed, but to ditch him for some racist idiot? Come on, even for Zainab that's pretty impressive."

"What do you mean, 'even for Zainab'?"

"She's secular. I get that. But I never realized she was a self-hating Muslim."

"Zainab is the least self-hating anything I've ever met."

"How else can you explain her being attracted to someone like that? Seriously, Amra, I think you need to be careful where Zainab is concerned."

"You're kidding, right?"

He looked at her for a moment before focusing on the road again. "We're about to have a baby. We plan to raise her in a loving, Muslim home. I don't want anyone teaching her that she has anything to be ashamed of."

"Zainab would never teach her that."

"Maybe not explicitly," he said.

Amra didn't know what to say. She stared out her window and neither of them spoke again until they reached his cousin's home.

They pulled into the circular driveway just before six. Mateen shut off the car as a young couple emerged from the house. His cousin, Ahmad, was wearing white cotton *salwar kameez* and his wife had on an overcoat with a headscarf. Amra was glad she had changed.

"Assalaamu alaikum!" called Ahmad. He met them at the car while his wife stayed on the steps near the door. "Welcome, Mateen *bhai.* And this must be Amra. It's good to meet you."

"And it's lovely to meet you."

Ahmad turned to Mateen, shaking his hand. "Let me help you with your luggage. How was the drive?"

"*Alhamdulillah,*" Mateen said. Amra looked at him. She didn't think she'd ever heard him respond traditionally, even with his parents.

"Amra, go on and meet my wife, Lamya."

Amra walked up the stone path to the two-story colonial tucked neatly into the heavily wooded lot. She approached Lamya somewhat hesitantly. She was young, probably in her early twenties (or younger—Amra tried not to think about that) and seemed shy. They exchanged greetings, and Lamya showed Amra to her room without saying another word.

Ahmad announced that they would eat on the large deck that wrapped around the back of the house. A series of French doors provided access to the deck, one set from the living room, one from the kitchen, and another from what Amra assumed was the master suite. Through the sheer gauze curtains, Amra could see a large king-sized bed, twin desks, and a recumbent bike, which she assumed belonged to Ahmad. It was hard to imagine Lamya on a piece of exercise equipment.

Her movements were subdued, as though she didn't want to ripple any more air than was necessary.

Amra offered to help in the kitchen but Ahmad waved her away—"Not in your condition," he'd insisted—leaving her sitting alone at the wicker table while he and Mateen walked the grounds. Every now and then she could hear a snippet of their conversation punctuated by the sounds of Lamya in the kitchen clanking pots or working the blender. Amra felt rude sitting there, and once the men disappeared around the corner of the house she went into the kitchen and offered her assistance.

"*Jee nahin, nahin,*" Lamya said, waving her away.

Lamya served an Indian feast: the ubiquitous chicken *biryani,* lamb *vindaloo, palak paneer,* homemade potato *paratha,* beef kabobs. Serving dish after serving dish appeared, carted to the table by the diminutive Lamya, while Amra sat and Ahmad and Mateen stood on the edge of the deck. They ate like that as well, the men standing, the women sitting in a strained silence.

In bed, she told Mateen she felt bad about not helping. "Your cousin is so . . . *different* . . . from the rest of your family."

Mateen smiled. "You mean conservative."

"Yes."

"Well, he's different than my immediate family, although my mother is probably more conservative than you might think. She and her sister, Ahmad's mother, grew up in Mirpur. I think my aunt may have even worn a *burka* for a while. I know my grandmother did." He shrugged. "It's not like you don't have any conservative relatives."

"I know. It's just that you seem so close to him."

He laughed. "Should I steer clear of him because he follows Islam better than I do? Wouldn't that be as bad as him shunning me because I don't?"

"Is that what he does? Follows Islam better?"

"Technically, yes. I think that's obvious."

Amra sat up. "Because his wife is subservient?"

"What are you talking about?"

"Mateen, come on. She barely speaks above a whisper. She's covered from head to toe. She even wears the *socks*. And while she struggled to get that enormous dinner on the table, no one helped her."

"What socks?"

"You know, those thick beige socks." Mateen shook his head. Amra waved her hand. "It's not important. The socks are not important. What's important is that his wife had to wait on us hand and foot by herself."

"You offered to help. But they didn't want you to exert yourself because of the pregnancy."

"I'm not talking about me."

"So you wanted me to go do dishes with his ultra-conservative wife? That would have gone over well."

"Your cousin practically burst at the seams bragging about how he has never taken a dish to the sink. *Never.* Because he has her."

Mateen laughed. "Sounds like a pretty good gig to me."

She pulled away. "It's not funny."

"I'm teasing you." He frowned. "You used to know that."

"Well, you started it. You said they're better Muslims than we are."

"I didn't say 'we.' I said 'me.' "

"And what did you mean?"

"Nothing. Bad comparison." He chuckled. "What I should have said is that they're better Muslims than Zainab."

Amra stood up and pulled on her robe. "Zainab is my best friend whether you like it or not."

"Where are you going? You can't walk around their house like that in the middle of the night."

"Watch me," she said, and closed the door behind her.

. . .

Out on the deck the air felt like a cold cloth, palliating her nerves. She hadn't been able to find the switch for the outdoor lights, and when she heard branches snapping in the woods, she drew her robe closer around her, but she wasn't ready to go back inside. Not yet. She noticed movement in the master suite and realized she could see Ahmad and Lamya through a gap in the curtain panels.

Ahmad was sitting in a chair watching Lamya. She was wearing a black lace bra and matching panties. Her hair, which had been covered with the scarf, was long, falling past her shoulders in loose waves around her face. She was applying lotion to her hands and arms, working it into her elbows. Ahmad said something and Lamya laughed, and then flicked some lotion at him. He stood to embrace her and pulled back to look her in the face. Whatever he said caused Lamya to smile.

Amra turned away, giving them their privacy. She knew she should return to Mateen, but she needed a minute to collect her thoughts. And to process the fact that Lamya, with her overcoat and thick socks—or, to be accurate, *without* them—was having a better night than she was.

40

After much debate, Zainab agreed to go to a theater instead of renting another movie, provided Chase agreed to her conditions: She would choose the movie, they would arrive separately, he would join her only after the theater was dark. He'd wanted some assurances that it wouldn't be a chick flick. "You wish," she'd said, before telling him to be at the Chestnut Hill 7:10 showing of *The Visitor.*

Zainab saw him lingering in the lobby. Now that they weren't mortal enemies, she'd stopped resisting the thought: Chase Holland was extremely good-looking. More so than she'd been willing to admit the night he hit on her in D.C., when she'd qualified her assessment by the fact that he was white. She purchased a bottle of water and some Junior Mints, took a seat at the back of the theater, and texted him.

Left side, near the back.

That's it? Those are your directions? I might find you by the time the credits roll.

It's not that dark once your eyes adjust.

I'm starting to think that it would have been easier to just rent a movie again at one of our impressive homes.

Zainab smiled. *Easy is for wimps. And neo-cons.*

Ha. I saw you buy candy. Do you want anything else?

No thanks.

Ok. One other thing.

Yes?

You look incredible.

The previews ended and the theater grew quiet. She saw Chase take the stairs slowly, trying to find her in the darkened theater. She gave a little wave.

He sat down and leaned in, gesturing at the Junior Mints. "Any left?"

"A few." She pulled them protectively toward her chest. "You should have gotten your own."

"I don't want the mints." He moved his mouth close to her ear. "I want to hold your hand."

She tossed the box on the floor and slipped her hand into his.

"Good to know," he whispered, looking straight ahead.

"Good to know what?"

"That in the pecking order of your affection, I'm hovering somewhere above the Junior Mints."

When the movie let out, they took separate cabs to Chase's condo, where he produced a tray of miniature custards and a small butane torch.

"You're kidding, right?" Zainab said, gesturing at the torch. Chase just smiled and told her to lean back. With the white-blue flame, he heated the sugar on the custard until it bubbled and browned. He handed Zainab a fork.

"Okay, so I'm fairly impressed here," she said, waiting for the sugar to harden. "Is there anything you can't cook?"

"Funny you should ask." Chase pointed at the trash can. Zainab approached hesitantly. Inside, it was empty except for several small, golden, syrupy balls.

"Gulab jamun?"

He nodded.

"You made *gulab jamun*? And threw it away?"

"It was the *khoya*. I didn't reduce it enough."

"You made your own *khoya*?"

"I *tried* to make it."

Zainab shook her head "You know, they sell it at every single Indian grocer."

"It's not the same."

Zainab knew it wasn't the same, but Chase shouldn't have known. She just stared at him. "So basically you made two desserts for me, including spending, what—hours?—making *khoya*."

Chase took two of the custards to the table and sat down. "Well, I only meant to make one. So don't read too much into it."

Zainab joined him at the table. "Too late."

"Maybe I just like to cook."

"You made your own cheese."

"A fact I will deny if you choose to tell anyone."

"I'll still know."

"Okay." He pulled her into his lap. "Maybe I just like you."

"Was that so hard?"

"At least I say it."

She moved off his lap and into the adjacent chair. "This smells delicious," she said, sliding the crème brûlée toward her and taking a bite. It tasted even better than it smelled. "I'm almost glad the *gulab jamun* failed."

He started in on his own dessert. Zainab shifted in her seat. "So, what did you think of the movie?"

"Yeah," he said. "I'm not sure we should go there."

"Why?"

"I don't want to fight with you."

"It's a movie, Chase. I think I can handle it if you have a different opinion than I do."

He shrugged. "Fine. I thought it was a bit manipulative."

"In what way?"

"By making Tarek so likable. Who wouldn't want to let him stay in the country?"

"I'm guessing you."

He laughed. "Right, but not because he was an Arab. He was here illegally. So he's a great guy, so he can play the drums. He still shouldn't have been here."

"Well, obviously, *legally,* he shouldn't have. But I think the movie was making a larger point."

"Right. A pro–illegal immigrant point."

"Or maybe just a pro-humanity point."

Chase rolled his eyes.

"Think about it," Zainab said. "He shouldn't have been in Walter's apartment in the first place—"

"Exactly! Who would let total strangers stay with him in his apartment? So right away, I was like, yeah, right."

"—*but* Walter did let him stay and he was enriched because of it."

Chase laughed. "You did not just say enriched."

"I did."

"You sound like a politician."

Zainab shot him a look. "I'm just pointing out the metaphor that seems to have gone over your head."

"Okay," he said, "maybe I did miss the parallel 'uninvited guest makes the host better' subtext, but it still doesn't change anything. He shouldn't have been in Walter's apartment, and he shouldn't have been in the U.S."

"But it did change something. It changed Walter. A person he never would have known otherwise, from a totally different background and circumstance, changed his life, maybe even gave meaning to his life. Is that so hard to appreciate?"

Chase played with his napkin, creasing the corners. When he looked up, he shook his head. "No," he said. "It's not."

. . .

For the next couple of weeks, Zainab barely came up for air, fielding calls from the press, arranging town hall meetings, accompanying Eleanor almost everywhere—meet and greets in suburbs like Sudbury and Weston, a tour of Horizons for Homeless Children in Roxbury, a parade in Somerville. She had the sneaking suspicion that she was being put in charge of nearly every aspect of the campaign, but part of her liked it. She felt indispensable and somehow it grounded her. She had little time to see Chase, which he was nice enough not to complain about. She was able to get away one Saturday, early, for a discreet hike in Middlesex Fells, after which, while sitting on the rocks, Chase stared at her so intently that she became self-conscious. *"What?"* she finally said. He just shrugged and said he couldn't believe she was there.

Mostly, they talked on the phone, almost every night, at whatever ungodly hour she got home. She didn't mean to open up to him, and yet she found that in the dark under her covers with the phone propped between her ear and pillow there was an unexpected familiarity, a sense of being known. And so one night, with her eyes pressed shut and the knowledge that there was no going back, she told him about her parents, how her mother had caught her father cheating and swallowed a bottle of tranquilizers, how Zainab had come home from school to find the EMTs and the police and the aunties all gathered around her inconsolable father. "He kept pulling his hair, pacing the floor of our living room, reciting verses of the Qur'an," Zainab said. "But it was all a fucking show."

"How do you know?" Chase asked.

"He married the woman he was cheating on her with."

"Jesus," Chase said. "I'm sorry."

Zainab nodded in the dark.

"That means you have a stepmother."

"Technically. She's some Manhattan socialite. When my father started to forget things, she made arrangements for him to move into a nursing home."

"So you don't see him much."

"Actually, I do." She rolled on her back and bunched her pillow under her head. "I moved him up here. He has a small apartment in Natick with a home health-care aide."

"You're a better person than I am."

"Don't go getting all misty-eyed on me, Chase Holland. I'm just doing my duty."

"It's not nothing," he said. "Not everyone does it. I didn't do it." But when she pressed him, he said it wasn't the time. "Tonight is about your mother. The rest can wait."

The rest, as he'd called it, came out a week later, when Chase showed up at her door, late, drunk from a Cinco de Mayo party. He smelled of cigarette smoke and whiskey. She made him coffee, which he gulped with small, corresponding grimaces.

"It's his birthday," he finally said. "He would have been fifty-six."

Zainab didn't have to ask. "Your father."

"Yes." He pushed the coffee away and went to the window. Zainab stayed at the table, giving him his space. He turned back to her and apologized for barging in, saying he should go.

"I don't mind. Do you want to talk about it?"

He shook his head. "I don't want to use you like that."

"Like what?"

"Like a goddamned confessional."

"I won't take it that way."

"But I'll use you that way."

"Maybe you need to. I'm your friend, you know. It's okay."

"Is that what we are? Friends?" He looked even more despondent.

"I hope so. Is that such a bad thing?"

"It is if that's all we are."

"I didn't say that's all we are."

"Sorry. Don't mind me." He ran his hand through his hair, back and forth, as though wiping away grim thoughts. "Is there more coffee?"

"I can make some."

He nodded. "I want to be sober when I tell you."

"Then let's wait." Zainab went to the guest room and returned with the beige down comforter and two pillows. She led him to the couch, placing the pillows under his head and tucking the covers around him. "Get some sleep, okay?" He nodded and closed his eyes.

Zainab watched him for a bit, and then went to her room. She tried to read a memo about wind power on the Cape, but she couldn't focus. The air was thick with memories of childhoods that would never be redeemed. She'd always thought it was a father-daughter thing, but Chase looked as tormented as she'd been right after she'd learned the truth, when her father had announced his engagement to the white woman only a couple of months after her mother's funeral, and Layla Khan told everyone that her father had been unfaithful. Zainab had gone into a frenzy that day, screaming, ripping posters off her wall, emptying the bookshelf, stripping her clothes off their hangers. Afterward, she'd cleaned everything up, leaving no trace for her father to find. She never said a word to him, never let on that she knew. She maintained a cool exterior with him and his new wife, carefully navigating the years until she left for Smith to ensure their paths rarely crossed. She ate dinner and spent weekends at Amra's house and became involved in after-school activities like track and yearbook. When her father told her that her mother had had a sizable portfolio and that she'd left it all to Zainab, Zainab had refused to talk about it. Accepting the inheritance meant agreeing to take something in her mother's place. But when Amra pointed out that her father would get the money if she didn't take it, Zainab relented. She'd donated much of it to various charities; the rest she used to purchase things that reminded her of her mother—paintings by her mother's favorite artists, dresses from Nabeel & Aqeel, hand-sewn rugs.

At two, she gave up on the memo and shut off her light. She woke to Chase nudging her arm. She looked at the clock. "It's four thirty in the morning."

"I know. I'm sorry. It's just that—" He looked sheepish.

"What? It's just that what?" She tried not to sound irritated.

"I'm not drunk anymore."

She nodded. She turned on the bedside light and sat up. She drew her legs up so that her chin rested on her knees and motioned at the space in front of her. He sat down and took a deep breath. "Ready?"

Zainab nodded. "Ready."

"Okay, so my father was a solo attorney in our hometown in Iowa. Wills, tax returns, divorces, that kind of thing. Nothing too complex, but enough to carve out a pretty decent life. The problem was he hated it. He went to law school to please his father, but in his heart, he was a writer. He was always scribbling in this black notebook he carried around. He was working on a novel, called it his baby." Chase shook his head. "My mother hated when he talked about it. He said she was jealous of the time he spent on it. But that wasn't it. She was afraid he would make good on his promise to take a leave of absence from work to finish it."

"Why did that upset her so much?"

"Because she liked her lifestyle. She liked her Audi and her Chanel bag and the lunches at the country club. She wasn't so enamored with the whole starving-artist vibe."

Zainab nodded. "Did she work?"

Chase shook his head. "She never even went to college."

"So she relied on your dad to support her."

"One hundred percent. So one night, over beef Wellington when I was eleven, he just closed his practice."

"That's a nice little bombshell."

"Exactly."

"How did your mom react?"

"There was a lot of screaming and swearing. And accusations of abandonment. That was the kicker. Because he wasn't planning on leaving, but she made him go. So I'm thinking it will be like all the other kids whose parents got divorced, right, and that he'll take an apartment in town and I'll see him Tuesday nights for dinner and every other weekend. But then he calls an audible and moves to New York City. Fucking Avenue A. Ever been there?" Zainab nodded. Chase shifted. "I guess he thought he'd get in touch with his artsy side. At first I thought it would be cool, visiting New York a few times a year. But my mom wouldn't let me go. He came back to Iowa once or twice a year for a bit, but then when I was thirteen, he came to see me and my mom wouldn't let him in. I didn't know what was going on. I think I even called her a bitch. And then she told me he was high. Think about it: You're barely a teenager and you find out your dad is doing drugs? It was insane."

Zainab wasn't sure what to say. He smiled, a small half smile, and then, as though he read her mind, he told her she didn't have to say anything. "Not through any of this. Because it gets worse." She nodded for him to continue.

"Pretty soon it had been a few years since I'd seen him. My mom and I had to leave our house. We were living in a shitty apartment, I was wearing jeans with the fucking creases let down, everyone in town knew what had happened. The only thing that saved me from total social suicide was that I was athletic. But there was shame and I knew it and I was pissed. So I hopped on a bus and went to look for him. I had his address from some old letters he wrote my mother. I got to his apartment and was standing there knocking and knocking, like an idiot, like maybe he hadn't heard me the first fifty times. Finally, I sat in the hall to wait. This guy came home, his neighbor, all fucked up on something, and said, you're looking for Ted, right?

You're his kid, he said, right? And I said yes, I was his son and I was waiting for him to get home. And then he said he wasn't coming home. That he was at the hospice."

Zainab covered her mouth.

Chase nodded. "Yep, you guessed it. The AIDS hospice."

"Oh my God."

"Right? So this guy gives me the address. But I was too freaked out to go. I took the next bus home. I never even saw him. I asked my mom, and she confirmed it through pursed, mortified lips." Chase rubbed his hands together. "He died a few months later. I never spoke to him. I never said good-bye. After he passed away, my mom gave me a box of letters. Apparently he'd written to me every week since the day my mom wouldn't let him in. There were letters up until the week he died." Chase's voice broke. "He didn't know she didn't give me the letters. He must have thought I hated him."

Zainab pushed the covers away and wrapped her arms around him. He sat stiffly. "I'm fine," he said. "It's okay."

"It's okay not to be fine," she said, smoothing his face. And then, without thinking, she said, "I've got you." It was what her mother used to say when she'd woken from a bad dream or skinned her knee.

He put his hands over hers. "I haven't told anyone this. Ever."

"You were just a kid, Chase. You didn't do anything wrong."

"I don't know about that. But I do know that people would use the whole AIDS thing as a message. Just desserts for my father's moral failings."

"I don't think anyone would do that."

"The people I run with would."

Zainab resisted the urge to ask why he ran with them. "I'm glad you told me."

"Me too. It's good to finally tell someone," he said, then added with more certainty, "It's good to tell you."

Zainab nodded. She asked if he wanted to stay, gesturing at the other side of the bed.

"Nah. I think I'll get going."

"Are you sure? Maybe you shouldn't be alone."

"I kind of think I need to be." He let go of her hands and stood up.

"Hey," she said.

"Yes?"

"That's why you wanted to help the woman in Pakistan."

"I guess so." He shrugged. "It doesn't make up for anything."

She nodded. "Maybe. But it's not nothing."

41

Amra was still holding the invitation when Zainab picked her up. They were getting pedicures over lunch, and, while Amra was waiting outside her building, Hayden had approached and pressed the stiff white cardstock in her hands. "I'm getting married," she'd said abruptly, and then asked if Amra had time for lunch. "I was chasing you down the hall, but you got in the elevator before I could reach you. Didn't you hear me?"

Amra had apologized, saying she was preoccupied with work. It wasn't a lie; she and Eric had worked out a tense détente, and Hank was biding his time until the baby came when, no doubt, he would swoop down on her clients. He was probably hoping for a C-section, and the additional medical leave it would confer. And Mateen, after assuring her she could tell him anything, seemed almost irritable when she mentioned work lately, as though he was hoping that as her stomach grew, her proper mother instincts would kick in and she would quit her pesky little job.

She'd told Hayden that she was meeting Zainab and, before she caught herself, asked if Hayden wanted to join them. She knew Zainab wouldn't be happy. She had never warmed up to Hayden and thought the whole Fadi affair followed by her sudden conversion was "creepy." Still, Amra didn't want to be rude. At the mention of Zainab's name, though, Hayden's face clouded and she'd suddenly "remembered" a memo she needed to get to.

Zainab's car pulled alongside two parallel-parked cars and she gave a little wave. Amra stuck the invitation in her handbag and climbed in.

Zainab let out a chortle. "You're huge!"

"Thanks."

"You know what I mean," Zainab said. "You're just so pregnant."

"It is sort of a progressive condition."

"So I hear," Zainab said, shifting into gear.

While they soaked their feet and had their calves massaged, Amra noted that her ankles, previously of normal size, looked enormous next to Zainab's slim ankles and taut calves.

"You're still running," she moaned.

"Most days." Zainab had the decency to look guilty. "It's not the same without you?"

"Right." Amra rolled her eyes. "What's your best mile time these days?"

"Five fifty."

Amra sighed. "God, I miss running."

The manicurist accidentally kicked Amra's purse, knocking Hayden's invitation on the floor.

"What's that?" Zainab asked.

"Hayden's wedding invitation."

"Her what? Who's she marrying?"

Amra shrugged. "Some guy named Abdullah Rahman. At least that's what the invitation says."

"Let me see that." Zainab scanned the text. "Did you read this? The men and women are going to separate venues. Oh my God. It's not enough to just separate them at the hall, or to put the ubiquitous curtain down the center of the room. Now, men and women have to be in different buildings?" She laughed. "Are you going?"

Amra snatched the card back. "I don't know. It's pretty close to my due date. I feel bad, though, like I should be there to support her."

"In her shotgun marriage? To some guy who is clearly a fundamentalist freak?"

"Zainab."

"What?"

"You just sound so . . . I don't know. Harsh."

"Well, maybe that's because I *feel* harsh. And I'm not sure why you don't feel harsher."

Amra thought back to Mateen's cousin Ahmad, and his wife, Lamya. "I think we should let people make their own decisions."

"How enlightened of you," Zainab said. "Is this the new Amra, wife of Mateen, speaking?"

Amra stiffened. "What is that supposed to mean?"

"Nothing. Forget it. This is supposed to be relaxing, right?"

Amra searched for something to say, but Zainab had already pulled out her BlackBerry.

42

CHASE COULDN'T DECIDE if he liked sneaking around or if it was annoying the hell out of him. Most of the time, it felt sexy—meeting at out-of-the-way places, going out to Hopkinton or Concord for dinner. Of course, he didn't mind the nights at home either. He'd bought a copy of *The Art of Indian Vegetarian Cooking* and made *dosa* and *sambar* for Zainab, which he noticed she ordered whenever they saw it on a restaurant menu. When she said his *paratha* was as good as her mother's, he was sure she teared up. "Nonsense," she said. "I don't cry."

For the most part, he was just so damned glad, and still a bit incredulous, that Zainab even gave him the time of day. Discretion seemed like a small price to pay to be with her. Still, he missed the ease of dating someone publicly, missed being able to bring a woman to dinners and functions. And now the Boston chapter of the Conservative Women's Federation was having a black-tie affair, a huge blowout that Chase would be crazy to miss, and, like a petulant child, he was stewing over the fact that he couldn't bring Zainab.

The week before the event, when they were eating orzo-stuffed peppers on the small patio outside of his bedroom overlooking the scant patch of grass below, he put down his fork and stared at her.

"What?"

"Nothing." He shook his head. "I'm just thinking."

"About?"

"You, in a formal black dress."

"Okay," she said, leaning toward him. "Usually you don't tell a woman when you're fantasizing about her."

"I don't want it to be a fantasy," he said. "I'm sick of hiding."

"It is a bit tedious, I admit. But what does that have to do with a black dress?"

"The Republican women's thing I told you about. It's next weekend."

"Oh, that would be perfect, wouldn't it? All the local neo-cons, simultaneously aghast."

"I know. I *know*. It's a ridiculous thought. I just have this overwhelming desire to have you with me."

She looked at him for a moment. "How about a compromise."

"You don't compromise."

"Work with me here, Chase."

"Fine. What? You'll go in disguise? Wave at me from across the room? Pass within a scandalous ten yards of me?"

She covered his mouth with the tips of her fingers. "You'll go without me. You'll put in your little right-wing face time." She rolled her eyes. "And then you'll make an excuse after, say, an hour and hightail it to my place, where, if I'm feeling particularly generous, there might be a black dress involved."

Chase, decked out in an Armani tuxedo, headed into the Four Seasons Hotel with absolute clarity of purpose: He would stay an hour tops. Less if he could manage it.

At the bar, he got a vodka martini and joined some board members from the institute at a table. Two women from the Independent Women's Alliance joined them, along with Nadia Asad, who he hadn't seen since her talk the day he and Zainab had had coffee back when they were still enemies and he was dating Savannah. And when he'd already fallen for Zainab.

Nadia squeezed a chair between Chase and the guy next to him and focused her undivided attention on Chase, asking him about his show and his research. She all but batted her eyelashes, telling him he should really write a book and that writing hers had opened up a world of opportunities for her. "Don't tell anyone," she said, "but my agent is negotiating a cable news show as we speak." Chase thought of his own book with a twinge of jealousy. Nadia had the name recognition he needed. The thought, briefly, made him consider getting closer to her.

"You've got all of that radio experience," she said, placing her hand on his arm. "Maybe you can show me the ropes." Before he could respond, a photographer snapped their picture. Nadia flashed a smile in the camera's direction and said, "Ah the paparazzi. You know how it is." He wished.

"Excuse us," she said loudly to the table. "Chase and I are going to dance." He tried to protest, saying that he wasn't much of a dancer, but she looked him up and down and said she didn't believe a word of it. "I have a sense about these things," she said, and led him to the dance floor. The band had just finished a Celine Dion song, and he was hoping for something more up-tempo. But when the music started, he was doubly screwed. It was "Falling Slowly" from the indie film *Once,* the movie he and Zainab had rented on their first official date before she'd agreed to go anywhere in public together.

He cleared his throat. "I'm sorry. I really need to go."

"Come on. Just one dance." Nadia moved close and put her head on his shoulder. When the band reached the part about pointing the sinking boat home, about having a choice, Chase was sure he had never, in his entire life, felt a stronger pull to be somewhere other than where he was. And when they got to the knowing eyes, the inability to go back, he let the images of the night he and Zainab had first heard the song together wash over him: how she'd put the movie in and then joined him on the couch, sitting so close their shoulders touched; how, after the credits rolled, she'd turned to him, a question still in her eyes; how he'd answered with his lips on hers and never wanted the moment to end. Just then, another photographer snapped a series of pictures of Chase and Nadia, interrupting his thoughts. "Enough, okay?" he said. How many goddamned pictures did they need?

Chase thanked Nadia for the dance and then walked straight out of the ballroom. He'd made a mistake in coming. He didn't want to be anyplace he couldn't bring Zainab.

The next morning, emboldened, they went out for breakfast. Zainab wore black capri running pants, a Harvard tee shirt, and a Yankees baseball cap. "You can't wear that in Boston," Chase had told her, pointing at her hat, but she gave him a look that begged to differ. And after the previous night, when she'd met him at the door wearing a strapless black gown and led him to the balcony where they danced to Etta James on her iPod, he wasn't exactly in an arguing mood.

In the middle of their breakfast—her California omelet and coffee, his French toast and large OJ—Chase felt a wave of contentment that lasted until Zainab summoned the waitress to ask for the bill. When the girl walked away, Chase noticed the woman about to sit at the table next to them.

"Shit," he whispered.

"What's the matter?" Zainab said. "The propaganda gig isn't paying you enough to foot the bill?" She, of course, did not whisper. Out of his peripheral vision, he saw Eleanor Winthrop-Smith turn and look at them.

"Zainab?"

Zainab wiped her mouth calmly and stood to greet her boss,

strategically blocking Chase from Eleanor's sight. "Eleanor, how are you? I thought you'd be in D.C. until tonight."

"Yes, well, once you've seen one monument, you've seen them all. I did read the draft for the charter-school speech. Pitch-perfect. Perhaps you should be running instead?" Eleanor chuckled. "Now tell me, who are you here with, dear? I thought I kept you too busy for a social life." Eleanor shifted to see around Zainab.

Chase wondered if he should bolt. But Zainab, with characteristic poise, turned and gestured toward him. "Maybe you remember Charles Holland?"

A look of recognition passed over Eleanor's face. She squinted, and all Chase could think was mother lion. He cleared his throat. If anyone was going to lie to Zainab's boss, it was going to be him.

"Ms. Winthrop-Smith. How are you? When I ran into Zainab here I thought I'd take the pulse of the campaign. But don't worry. She keeps everything close to the vest." He forced a smile. "You've trained her well."

Eleanor eyed him warily. "Yes, well, I hope you weren't giving her too much grief. What you do on your despicable radio show is your business, but for God's sake, Zainab deserves to eat her breakfast in peace."

Chase nodded. "You're right. She does deserve at least that." When he looked at Eleanor, he feared that his voice had revealed too much. "I need to get going anyway. Zainab, I hope I didn't ruin your breakfast. Ms. Winthrop-Smith, it was nice to see you again."

He stopped at the counter and paid their bill. Outside, he rounded the corner and looked in the window. Zainab had joined Eleanor, and they were engaged in an animated conversation. He slumped against the front of the restaurant. So much for their plan to spend the day together. His phone vibrated.

"Chase speaking."

"Chase, it's Nadia. Have you checked out *The Daily Stalker*'s front page? I can't believe we're the top story!"

"What are you talking about?"

"You haven't seen it yet? I guess it's still early. I thought everyone started the day with Google Alerts." She laughed. "Anyway, are you near a computer?"

"No, but I've got my BlackBerry. Obviously."

"Right. Well, go look. Daily stalker dot com. I can't believe how fast they got the pictures up. Call me back after you've had a chance to look at it. Maybe we can celebrate being the toast of the town over lunch."

Even on his tiny phone screen, Chase could see enough to make his stomach turn. Four pictures of Nadia and him, including one with them dancing extremely close. The headline posed the question, "The New 'It Couple' of the Right?"

Chase closed his eyes. All he could think about was what Zainab would say if (he couldn't bring himself to think "when," holding out a sliver of hope that she might *not* see the pictures) she saw the article. He hadn't even told her Nadia had been there last night, remembering her visceral reaction when she'd heard Nadia speak. He could try to explain it away as part of their cover—that it would be easier if everyone thought he was, in fact, seeing Nadia—but in two of the pictures he looked like he adored Nadia. The photographer had captured with impressive clarity the longing in his eyes when the band played "Falling Slowly," when he'd been thinking of Zainab.

His phone vibrated again. He considered not answering but Nadia was a power player, and he didn't want to offend her. Plus, she might be able to help with his book. "Hey, Nadia."

"So? What do you think? Pretty outrageous, right?"

"Yeah, it's quite the spread. Listen, I need to run, but we'll catch up soon, okay?"

He hung up and stared at the pictures, wondering if he should tell Zainab or hope for the luck he never seemed to get.

43

Amra took her laptop on the patio after breakfast. Mateen was trying to figure out some new weed-cutting contraption requiring little plastic bands that did not want to stay in place. Between his swearing and her suggestions that they hire a lawn service, she attacked her e-mail. She read the work ones first, a series of back-and-forth communications between Hank and her client that he had been kind enough to copy her on. In the last one, the client said that she wouldn't agree to anything until she talked to Amra. She smiled. Hank may have replaced her in Eric's affections, but her clients still preferred her.

The first personal e-mail was from Rukan:

> Salaam, Amra. Oh my God, I'm not trying to be a busybody here, but is Zainab still seeing Chase? The reason I ask is: www.dailystalker.com/hotnewcouple. I tried to call her but her cell is going straight to voice mail. On a happier note, I met someone! Love, Rukan

Amra wasn't sure where to start—the link or the wonderful news that Rukan had met someone. But *The Daily Stalker* and Zainab together piqued her interest and she clicked on the link.

"Oh my God is right," Amra muttered.

"What's that?" Mateen looked up.

"Nothing. Just reading my e-mail." He nodded, revved up the tool, attempted to cut some weeds sticking up from in between the bricks on the walkway to the garden. It must have worked, because he gave her the thumbs-up.

Amra clicked REPLY.

> Salaam, Rukan. As far as I know, she is still seeing Chase. But frankly, it doesn't look like he's (just??) seeing her. She's probably working, but I'll try to reach her, too.
>
> And how dare you tease me with vague allusions to a new man. Call me soon—I want details! Love, Amra

She stood up and waved at Mateen, mouthing that she was going to take a shower. She figured now that his new toy was working, he'd be busy for a while. She tried Zainab's cell, but, just as Rukan said, it went straight to voice mail. She sighed. She'd been worried about Zainab from the moment she'd started dating Chase, not because Amra thought it meant Zainab hated being a Muslim, but because he just didn't seem like a good guy. What kind of a person made a living stirring up hatred against entire groups of people, and what could Zainab possibly see in a person like that?

She decided to make her statement to Mateen true and hop in the shower. She set her phone on the windowsill, just in case Zainab returned her call, and turned the dual showerheads on. She pulled off her shirt and then felt a pull in her stomach that brought her to her knees. She looked down to see red-tinged water coming from between her legs. She tried to think back to the childbirth class they took. She was pretty sure her water had just broken, but she didn't think it was supposed to be this bloody. Her stomach seized again, and she yelled for Mateen, her words coming out in a low, guttural tone she did not recognize. She yelled again but all she could hear was the motor of his weeder. She took a deep breath and used her cell phone to dial 911.

In the ambulance, Mateen held her arm with one of his hands and his head with the other. "I'm so sorry, Amra *jaan*. I'm so sorry I didn't hear you," he kept saying, as though it was his fault for not having bionic hearing. She nodded at him, trying to communicate her forgiveness; it hurt too much to talk. The wetness between her legs had turned thicker and redder before the paramedics got to her. When she'd asked if she was going to lose the baby, they'd just told her to relax. She did not take it as a good sign.

She woke in a darkened room, with an IV in place and a monitor beeping in the background. Mateen was stroking her hair. She opened and closed her eyes a few times, trying to focus. He looked so pale. And somber. And then she remembered the pain in her stomach, the ambulance, the blood. She tried to sit up.

"Where's my baby? What happened to my baby?"

"Amra, calm down, sweetheart. The baby is fine. They delivered her by emergency C-section. She's small, only about five pounds, but she's a fighter."

"She?"

"I told you."

"So you were right. Is she really okay?"

He smiled. "She's more than okay. She's got ten fingers and ten toes and she looks just like her beautiful mommy."

"Is that what I am? A mommy?"

"Of course. The best mommy ever. You were so strong on the way to the hospital." His voice cracked and his eyes became wet. "You did great, Amra. But now you need to rest."

"When can I see her?"

"Soon. I promise. Now get some sleep."

Amra tried to protest but her eyes were heavy. She felt a nurse take her vital signs and tried to ask for the baby, but she was too tired to get the words out.

Zainab rushed to the hospital still wearing her yoga pants and Yankees cap. She met Rukan in the lobby. Upstairs, Mateen told them Amra was sleeping, but he showed them pictures of the baby in the NICU.

"Amazing," Rukan said later, over coffee in the café. "I mean, Mateen was maybe thirty feet away from her and still she was all alone." *Sounds about right,* Zainab thought, but she bit her tongue. It wasn't the time to involve Rukan in her squabbles with Mateen.

She changed the subject. "So what's new with you?"

Rukan blushed. "Actually, there is something new. Or I guess I should say someone."

"That's great." Zainab leaned in eagerly. "So who is he?"

"He teaches at my school, eighth-grade math, and the kids adore him. He's tough with these really high expectations, but he's so cool that they all want to meet those expectations. And the girls probably all have crushes on him."

"So I assume he's good-looking."

"I think so," Rukan said, nodding.

Zainab could picture his type already. "So what's his name?"

"Dameer."

Zainab almost choked on her coffee. "Dameer? He's Muslim?"

Rukan laughed. "Yes, he's Muslim. Is that such a shock?"

"No. I'm sorry. Just when you said you met him at school and how everyone had a crush on him . . ." Zainab shrugged her shoulders. "I was picturing someone else."

"Someone like Adam."

"I'm sorry, Rook."

"It's okay. I can talk about all of that now. And believe me, Dameer is *nothing* like Adam. He might be the nicest guy I've ever met."

"That's wonderful. I can't wait to meet him."

"Soon. Not quite yet. I just need to be careful with this one."

Zainab nodded. "It sounds like you're serious."

Rukan smiled and looked down, running her fingers on the edge of the table. "So, how are things with Chase?"

"Good. Complicated. It's hard when you can't be seen in public or let anyone know."

Rukan nodded. "Zainab, you know I'd never do anything to hurt you, right?"

"I can't imagine you hurting anyone."

"Remember that, okay? Because I have to ask you something."

"Shoot."

"Have you seen stuff on the Internet about Chase and Nadia Asad?"

"What are you talking about?"

"I'll take that as a no." Rukan smoothed the napkin on her lap. "Apparently, they went to some conservative-prom thing last night and were all over each other."

Zainab thought back to the previous night. Chase had called from the car at nine and said he was on his way. Much earlier than she'd expected him. When she answered the door, he held her so tightly she almost couldn't breathe. "Not possible," she said.

"Zainab, there are pictures. It started on *The Daily Stalker,* but other places picked them up. They're being called the sweethearts of the right wing."

Zainab looked around the café at the somber hospital visitors, looking tired and stressed, and tried to process what Rukan was saying. She trusted Chase. But what about Charles Holland? She fished her BlackBerry out of her handbag. When she saw the pictures—Nadia's hand on his arm during dinner, the two of them dancing, Chase's expression—her face burned. "Who does he think he is? Who does he think *I* am? Someone's sloppy seconds?"

"I'm so sorry. I just thought you needed to know."

Zainab nodded. "Thank you for telling me. Now if you'll excuse me, I have something to take care of."

Zainab fumed all the way to the gym. *Nadia Asad.* The name ran through her mind over and over, except, of course, with the addition of her new middle name: *Nadia Fucking Asad.* Chase knew. He *knew* how she felt about her. That was their first real conversation, the time she'd reluctantly agreed to coffee. The first time she'd considered that maybe, just maybe, there was a human being in there after all. What an idiot she'd been. She pounded the punching bag until her hands went numb. She ran six miles. When a man approached asking if she wanted a spotter on the weights, she glared at him until he backed away. She stayed in the shower until the water singed her skin. And still she was out for blood.

Chase was sitting outside her door when she got home. She stepped over him. "What are you doing here?"

"I came to see you."

"How long have you been sitting there?"

He shrugged. "I don't know. A couple of hours."

She looked him up and down. His shirt was untucked and his hair was ruffled. "You look like shit."

"Thanks. Have you been with Eleanor this whole time?"

"Not that it's any of your business, but I've been at the hospital." When she saw his face, she held up her hand. "Amra. She had her baby." Zainab took out her keys. "I'd love to sit and chat, but I've got things to do."

"Zainab, we need to talk."

"Do we?"

"Yes."

"Well, I'm sure it can wait."

"You're serious? I've been sitting here for two hours and you're not even going to let me in?"

"What's the matter, wasn't your girlfriend available?"

"You're my girlfriend."

"Ha!" Zainab snorted. "That would be news to me, and to the rest of the free world."

"I don't care about the rest of the free world."

"Right. Just about one important person in the free world."

"Yes. And that would be you."

"Only if my name is Nadia Asad."

He slouched back against the wall. "So you know."

"I guess I do now."

He looked up hesitantly. "You saw the pictures?"

"They're stunning."

"Zainab."

"Chase."

"Can I explain?"

"Explain what? How your date went viral?"

"She wasn't my date. Yes, she was there last night and for some reason she attached herself to me like a parasite. But that's it. There's nothing else there."

"Why should I believe that? She's perfect for you. She's a right-wing nut and she hates Muslims. Looks to me like a match made in heaven."

"I don't hate Muslims."

"Well, not all of them, right? Some are pretty sexy, aren't they? Some are so sexy and exotic that you might want to get in their pants. But the rest of them? A bunch of evil savages trying to blow all of you 'real Americans' up."

He stood up. "I can't believe that's what you think of me. After everything. Yeah, Zainab, I was just trying to get in your pants. It was all about getting in your pants. I broke up with my fiancée because I couldn't stop thinking about getting in your pants. And that horseshit story about my dad? Made the whole thing up. You know, just to get in your pants. What took you so long to figure it out?"

She was surprised by his anger. And felt guilty about making him say that about his father. But she wasn't ready to concede. She tossed her hair over her shoulders. "I don't know. Momentary lapse in judgment."

He shook his head. "You've got it all figured out, don't you? Is it really that implausible? That she was just there, that when they took the photo of us dancing I was thinking of you, about how I wished I were dancing with you? That there is no way I could possibly be interested in her because I fucking fell in love with you months ago, when you'd barely give me the time of day, and that I can't imagine in my entire life I'll be interested in anyone else, ever?"

Zainab swallowed. "What did you just say?"

He glared at her. "I said that I love you."

"That's what I thought you said."

"I mean it, Zainab. I love you."

She nodded.

"Wait," he said. "You're not going to cry, are you?"

She shook her head. "I don't cry."

"Right." He moved closer to her, tentatively. He tilted her head up with his finger under her chin, until she met his gaze. "So you believe me?"

"I believe you," she whispered, right before his lips found hers. Later, when she was sure he was asleep, she whispered that she loved him, too.

44

AMRA CAME HOME five days after the birth; they brought Thanaa Huma Safa Syed home two weeks later. Amra's mother stayed in the beginning, cooking, washing clothes, walking with Thanaa when she was colicky. Once, when Amra was freshly showered and in her pajamas at three in the afternoon, her mother delivered Thanaa to nurse, and, as Amra watched her tiny daughter curl up in her arms, suckling peacefully, she thought, *I have everything I need right here.* It was the only time she could remember thinking such a thing.

A few weeks later, Amra invited Zainab and Rukan for lunch. Rukan called at the last minute and asked if she could bring Dameer. "Of course," Amra had said, trying to sound casual. But she'd been dying to meet Rukan's new friend ever since the cryptic e-mail just before she was rushed to the hospital. She felt both happy for and protective of Rukan. Her knowledge of what those wretched months after Adam called off the wedding had been like, coupled with her newly honed mothering instincts, meant Dameer had a rather high bar to clear.

Amra prepared *chole* and *paratha,* even though she'd told her friends she wouldn't fuss. Mateen had offered to pick up takeout. "I wish my mother had taught me how to cook," he'd said sheepishly, watching her flit around the kitchen in spurts between nursing Thanaa. "I need one of those baby slings," she declared with a laugh. Upon seeing Mateen's horrified face, she said, "Don't worry, I would never bring her near the stove." She wondered why she'd had to say anything at all. Even though he hadn't mentioned it, there was some lingering suspicion she sensed on Mateen's part, ever since she'd confessed all of her job stress, as though he half expected her at any moment to declare that while the baby had been fun, she really wasn't interested and would be returning to her 24-7 focus on her job. She caught herself in the perpetual mode of having to prove herself, making sure he noticed the adoring faces that she made at Thanaa, faces that started out as genuine expressions of love but morphed into some sort of performance art when he was around. She found it easier to care for the baby when Mateen was at work and no one was judging her abilities.

Mateen took out the ingredients for salad, the red leaf lettuce and cucumbers and bell peppers, and started to chop. "It's the least I can do," he said as Amra rolled out the *paratha*. "So what do we know about the object of Rukan's affection?"

"Dameer," Amra said. "His name is Dameer. And not much. Zainab said Rukan said he was nice and smart and gorgeous."

"So clearly she's taking after you," he teased. Amra was grateful for the playful mood. After their conversation the previous night, in which Amra tried to broach the subject of her return to work and Mateen had set his jaw and made himself busy with the newspaper, she'd worried that he wouldn't be in an entertaining mood. But he seemed fine. Overly fine, in fact.

"Yes, of course," Amra said, "but we all know he'll fall short of the original." Mateen kissed her on the nose and bent to rub Thanaa's head.

"Just think," he said, "someday Thanaa will be looking for a husband."

"Why don't we let her cut her first teeth before we worry about that?" But his words stirred something in Amra, some recognition that everything would change, that theirs was a temporary peace.

"*Assalaamu alaikum,*" Amra said, kissing Rukan and Zainab on the cheek while Mateen shook hands with Dameer. "Dameer, it's so nice to meet you. Thank you for coming with Rukan."

He handed Amra a bouquet of lilies. "Thanks for including me. I hope it's not an intrusion."

"Not at all," she said. She looked at Rukan and raised her eyebrows approvingly. Dameer was tall with thick, dark hair and the hint of a beard, slightly more than a shadow. But what she liked the most was how he looked at Rukan, partly eager, partly nervous. And Rukan looked at him with the kind of joy Amra wasn't sure she'd see again on her friend's face, at least not so soon.

They sat on the deck and drank lemonade, making small talk about Rukan and Dameer's jobs in the South Hadley school district. "How are the kids?" Amra asked, knowingly, when she heard he taught eighth grade.

"Great. You know, they think they know everything, but they're still fairly innocent. They can still be guided, if you're subtle about it."

"So," Zainab asked, looking at Amra, "speaking of work, when are you planning to return?"

Amra purposefully didn't look at Mateen. "I'm still figuring all that out," she said. Zainab looked like she wanted to say something, but mercifully did not. After an awkward silence, Dameer nudged Rukan and asked if she was ready to tell everyone.

"Tell us what?" Amra asked.

"We're engaged," Rukan said. There was no ostentatious ring, just a grinning couple. "The wedding will be in December. Just before New Year's," Rukan said.

Amra and Zainab rushed to hug her, while Mateen clapped Dameer on the back.

Twice during lunch, Amra left to nurse the baby. It was the only time she resented Dameer's presence. She couldn't exactly pull out her breast in front of him, but she was so hungry for time with her friends. The neighborhood women came, but with vapid small talk and platters of non-*halal* meat.

When she came back after the second time nursing, everyone was getting ready to leave. "So soon?" she asked, disappointed.

"Dameer and I have tickets to the Pioneer Valley Symphony in Noho," Rukan explained. Zainab said she had work to do.

Outside, Dameer asked where the property line was and Mateen led him around the back, no doubt pointing out the woods and the stone wall and explaining how the neighbors had had to put in an electric fence to keep their dog out of Amra and Mateen's yard.

Amra pulled Rukan close. "He's wonderful, Rukan. I mean that. I'm so happy for you."

"Thanks," Rukan said, looking at Dameer and Mateen. "We're both very fortunate."

After they left, Mateen started loading the dishwasher hastily, clanking the dishes together, turning the spraying water on high. "She can't wait to get you out the door, can she?" he said.

"Who?"

"Zainab. It's like she didn't even see the baby. She just saw you enslaved by her."

"What are you talking about?"

"I just think she's steering you in the wrong direction."

Amra folded her arms. "And what direction would that be?"

"Back to work." He scrubbed a plate with a copper sponge until it started to come apart in shreds. "Prematurely, I might add."

"I don't even know where to start." Amra took a deep breath. "First of all, Zainab doesn't make my decisions. I make them. And second, she *held* the baby. She brought her a gift, even though she already gave us a gift at the shower and after Thanaa was born. I think she *sees* the baby."

Mateen kept scrubbing.

"And as for steering me back to work, I tried to talk to you about this last night, but you'd have none of it. So maybe this is where we should start. When exactly do you think it would be acceptable for me to return to work?"

"I don't know an exact time. But I do think Thanaa deserves time with her mother."

"Which she's getting now and will continue to get after I return to work."

"So you're returning."

"Yes. Of course."

"Am I allowed to know when?"

"Mateen. Of course you are. I'm not saying we can't talk about it. Figure it out together."

"Fine. I'd say at least a year or two."

"A year or two?" Amra shook her head. "But even the unpaid leave would only take us to three months. That's all I'm guaranteed."

"I'm sure you could work it out with them. A leave of absence. People must do it all the time."

Amra could not, for the life of her, think of anyone in her firm or any other firm who had ever taken a leave of absence and returned.

"I have clients. Deals. I can't just walk away from that."

"But you can walk away from Thanaa."

"That's not fair. You go to work every day. Are you walking away?"

"I'm not her mother. I don't nurse her."

"I can pump my milk—"

"It's not the same."

She didn't know what to say. She had no idea he would take such a strong stance.

He approached her and took her hands. "I'm only saying this because I love you. You can't get this time back. You don't want to look back when she's eighteen and wish you'd been there. Eric will understand."

She shook her head. "I don't think so."

"Well, then maybe you're not as important to the firm as you thought."

Amra couldn't sleep that night. She tossed and turned thinking about Mateen and the baby and Eric and her job. Was it really a zero-sum game? Was it the age-old issue of not being able to have it all? But who got to decide? Mateen got up and went to work every day. No one judged him.

The next morning Zainab called. After they'd talked about how wonderful Dameer seemed, Amra decided to bite the bullet. "I'm thinking of taking a longer leave from work," she said.

"Longer? Like how long?" Disapproval registered in Zainab's voice.

"I'm really not sure. I need to see what they're willing to do."

"I think they're willing to do the three months, Amra. I mean, Hank has probably already pissed in a big perimeter around your deals."

"That's a lovely image."

"I'm not here to be lovely. I'm here to knock some sense into you." Zainab sighed. "How much control of your life are you willing to turn over to your husband?"

"That's not fair."

"No? I saw the way you panicked at your house yesterday when I asked about going back to work. You couldn't even look at him, like you were going to be in trouble. It was all very pathetic, actually."

"Great. Now it's you, too."

"Me too what?"

"You complain about Mateen and he complains about you. It puts me in a difficult position."

"Does it really? I've known you your whole life. I watched you slave away at Smith and Columbia and at your firm for five years. I can't just stand here and watch you throw it all away."

"Did it ever occur to you that I'm different than you? That I don't have to push the limits all the time? That maybe what Mateen wants, I want, too?" Amra felt a little guilty at this last part. She wasn't sure why, but she needed Zainab to think they were a more united front than, in fact, they were.

"No," Zainab said, "it never occurred to me and I don't believe it. God, you're acting like one of those women stuck under her man's thumb."

Amra paused. "I don't think you're really in a position to talk."

"Excuse me?"

Amra knew she shouldn't have said it, that she should back off. But she was tired of it. "I'm just saying that I'm not sure that you're in any position to lecture me, given that you're dating a man who rants to the public all day long about how he hates Muslims. At least I don't have to hide who I am with Mateen."

Zainab laughed. "Right. No hiding at all. Not even when you used to work in the bathroom at night."

Amra wished she hadn't told Zainab about that. "I can't do this, Zainab. I don't want to fight. Not with you, not with Mateen. I just need some peace and quiet." And she hung up. When her phone rang, she pushed IGNORE and went to pick up Thanaa, who had been crying during the entire phone call.

45

HAYDEN STOOD IN a red *gharara* hand-sewn by Fareeda, who was, for all practical purposes, taking on the dual roles of mother of the groom and mother of the bride. When Hayden told her own parents about her conversion and engagement to Abdullah Rahman, her mother had burst into tears and, after a muffled explanation to him, handed her father the phone. "Pumpkin," he began and then stopped. He hadn't called her that since she was in grade school. After a long silence—long enough for Hayden to wonder if he'd hung up—he told her he'd made some mistakes, but that she could always come home. Hayden ignored the wave of sadness she felt. What she was homesick for was a newlywed doctor, not her parents in Colorado.

As for Abdullah Rahman, he and Hayden had been talking on the phone—short, formal conversations in which he still had yet to show any semblance of a sense of humor. She'd made some jokes, mostly self-deprecating, but they seemed to go over his head. Still, he was polite and respectful and called every time he said he would.

As she looked in the mirror, her hair covered by the *dupatta,* her face colored with makeup—Fatima said it was perfectly permissible on her wedding day as long as she kept the *dupatta* low should she find herself in the company of men—she realized she looked like someone else, perhaps a friend of Amra's, getting married.

She straightened her shirt with her newly hennaed hands. When she saw Abdullah's initials near her wrist, she felt a rush of excitement. There was something tantalizing about the idea that this man, who spoke to her so formally and with whom she'd never spent a single second alone, would be permitted to have sex with her in a matter of hours. She remembered when Amra first explained the purpose of the henna—for a situation just like the one in which Hayden currently found herself—and how strange it had seemed. But now, it had a certain thrill about it. Of course, Hayden hadn't been intimate with a man in a long time, not since Fadi, but thoughts of Fadi were not going to get her in the mood for Abdullah Rahman.

Amra had recovered from her emergency delivery and had come to the *mehndi,* bringing little Thanaa with her, saying she was sorry that she wouldn't make it to the wedding. She only stayed for a bit, but they'd persuaded her to get the henna. Amra was so preoccupied with the baby sucking at the front of her light-green *kameez* that Hayden had had to remind her to ask for Mateen's initials in her design. "You always put what you want most, right?" Amra had nodded, but looked impatient as Fareeda's sister completed the design. She'd left soon after, kissing Hayden and wishing her well. Hayden was glad she hadn't showed up with Zainab. She wasn't sure how her mother-in-law-to-be would have reacted.

When Hayden's doorman called up to announce Fareeda, there to drive her to the wedding, Hayden took one last look in the mirror, grabbed her bags, and gently closed the door behind her.

The women gathered at Fareeda's house; the men were at the *masjid* with Abdullah Rahman and the imam. Fareeda's brother Bilal had agreed to be Hayden's representative. Fareeda imparted this information as if it were an honor, as if Bilal had had a hundred possible brides of his choosing and had deigned to pick Hayden.

At Fareeda's home, Hayden recognized only a few women from Women for Islam; the rest were nameless strangers dressed in bright Pakistani clothes, eyeing her suspiciously. At one point, a group of teenage girls approached and spoke animatedly to her, asking about where she'd gone to school, peppering their speech with "like" and "as if" and "OMG." They sounded like normal teenagers and reminded her of her younger self. She was both sad and relieved when they finally wandered away.

After an hour or so of awkward sitting, Bilal entered, asked her permission for the marriage, and left in order to communicate his findings to the imam and Abdullah Rahman. Soon the phone rang and Fareeda entered the room. "It's official. *Mubarak,* my new daughter. You and Abdullah Rahman are married!"

The food was served. Across town at the *masjid* she pictured an identical meal being enjoyed by the men. She ate her lamb and chicken and wondered if Abdullah Rahman was eating the same thing at that very moment and whether he was thinking about her. And about their first night together.

At eight, after dessert had been served and the girls had danced, people began to leave. Hayden's face hurt from the smile she'd forced, literally, for hours. When the last guests left, she started to help Fareeda clean up.

"*Nahin, beti.* There will be plenty of time for you to clean my house, but today is not that time. Go downstairs and prepare yourself for your new husband."

Hayden did as she was told. They'd all agreed that the basement bedroom with the wood paneling and shag carpet would afford the new couple the most privacy. She wasn't sure what Fareeda meant by prepare herself. She figured that Abdullah Rahman, who had not seen her all day, would want to see her in her wedding dress, but maybe it wasn't important. She had brought a long white silk nightgown in her suitcase, which, she noted, someone had completely emptied. She looked around the room, finding her shirts and suits in the closet, her toiletries inside the nightstand drawer. The nightgown was under the sweaters in the bureau.

There was a knock, and her stomach jolted. But it was only Fareeda, bringing a tray of sweets and mango *lassi*. "For you and Abdullah Rahman." She set the tray on the bed. "I'm glad you decided against the white nightclothes," she said pointedly.

"I wasn't sure what to do," Hayden confessed.

Fareeda took her hand. "I know this can all be a little awkward. We are all too aware that you have had prior . . . *experience*. But of course my son has not. So I think it is better if you do not come on too strong. I trust you understand?"

Hayden blushed. It wasn't like she'd brought sex toys. The nightgown went to the floor, for God's sake. But all she could do was nod.

"Good," Fareeda said. "One other thing. In Islam when a man and a woman have relations, they must take a full bath before they're clean to pray again. I know that with having only one full bathroom that could be awkward. Please don't worry. I won't pay any attention to your showering—when, how often, and so forth." Hayden felt that Fareeda was saying it specifically to let her know that, in fact, she would be listening to every drip of the shower, charting exactly when and how often Hayden and her husband made love.

Hayden was saved from having to figure out what to say by another knock at the door. It was Abdullah Rahman, looking serious.

"Assalaamu alaikum, beta," Fareeda gushed. "Come, greet your new wife. I will leave the two of you."

He closed the door and looked at the floor. Hayden wasn't sure what to say, or who was supposed to speak first. She had to admit he looked handsome in his knee-length coat and crisp white pants. Finally, he asked how her day was.

"Good. And yours?"

"Fine. The food was good."

"Yes."

He didn't say anything further. Hayden opened her hands on her lap, revealing the intricate henna design, hoping it would remind him that he was supposed to approach her and look for his initials. But he simply said he was going to take a shower.

As he gathered his clothes and left, Hayden worried that Fareeda would think it was her, *already,* taking her required full bath. But after the water stopped, she heard voices upstairs. She went to the bottom of the stairs and could hear Fareeda and Abdullah Rahman talking in the kitchen. She listened for a bit as they discussed some distant cousins who had traveled all the way from Arizona to attend the wedding and the remarks the imam had made to the men. Hayden thought Fareeda would send Abdullah Rahman down, giving him the push he needed, or that he, who had apparently never so much as kissed a woman, would be in a rush to finally be with her. But they gave no sign of letting up. Hayden brushed her teeth in the small half bath in the basement, located her sweatpants and a tee shirt, and went to bed, alone.

When Hayden's henna had nearly faded, three weeks and two days from the wedding ceremony, Abdullah Rahman made his move. He'd come home late, as had Hayden, pushing the family dinner back to eight o'clock, an unpopular development with Fareeda, who had announced, from the beginning, that she would continue preparing the meals—"just until you learn how to make proper Pakistani food"—provided Hayden cleaned the kitchen afterward. Hayden was sure that Fareeda was creating unnecessary mess when she cooked; in those first few newlywed days when Fareeda wouldn't let Hayden do a thing, Fareeda would meticulously wipe any stray spattering of turmeric or clump of pureed vegetables off the laminate countertops immediately. But now Hayden would find dried food everywhere, wiping powdered spices from every corner and crevice in the kitchen, struggling to get the yellow stains off the white counters.

She was scrubbing burned rice out of a large pot when Abdullah Rahman pushed away from the table and went to shower—he always showered after work, though apparently not for his wife. Fareeda had excused herself halfway through dinner, citing a headache. After his shower, she expected Abdullah Rahman to go read, as he did every night, but instead he came into the kitchen and shyly said, "*Salaam*."

"*Wa alaikum asalaam*," she said without looking up from the pot. She made a mental note to remember to buy copper sponges on her way home from work the following day. She was getting nowhere with the pot, which, she suspected, was the idea.

"So, I was wondering," Abdullah Rahman began, "if maybe I could see your henna. I forgot to look earlier." He shrugged nonchalantly. "It's part of the wedding tradition. It might even be required."

So that's how it would be. Even now that it was permissible, he wouldn't let himself appear interested. She realized that Fareeda did not understand her son in the least. The entire success of the marriage appeared to rest on Hayden's ability to "come on strong."

She put the pot on the drying rack and wiped her hands on the poplin dishcloth hanging on the stove handle. And then, very deliberately, she walked over to Abdullah Rahman and displayed her hands. She was sure he would be unable to locate his initials in the faded design, but she let him have a good look. He did not, she noted, touch her hands. Was that not the point of the charade?

A fit of coughing emanated from Fareeda's room. "Abdullah Rahman," Hayden said, leaning close to him, "why don't we go downstairs so that you can have a better look?" Without so much as a glance back, she walked to their room. She could hear him follow behind her on the creaky stairs. She waited for him to close the door and very slowly removed her clothes.

She saw him swallow hard, but he didn't move. She lowered herself onto the bed and held out her hands. "Come, find your initials." And, as if awakening from a long slumber, he was there, on her, pulling at his own clothes, telling her she was beautiful.

When he slept, finally, she clambered up the stairs, let the bathroom door slam, flushed the toilet, turned on the shower, and "accidentally" dropped the shampoo and, a few minutes later, the conditioner. So there, she thought, as she pictured Fareeda on the other side of the wall, knowing full well that her son had already showered. She thought it again the next day when Abdullah Rahman came home with two gold bracelets and let Fareeda choose first: *So there.* Her mother-in-law might talk to him late into the night and get the best jewelry, but Hayden was the one who'd made him say, "Oh God, oh God, oh God" for hours.

46

In the small interstice between when the headline first flashed across the bottom of her television and when the vapid early-morning anchorman read the story, Zainab allowed herself a selfish thought: *Please don't let them be Muslim*. But the news reader betrayed her: The men were American converts. The woman was of Pakistani descent. They all were younger than twenty years old, followers of some radical Muslim cleric, and together they'd planned to blow up Fenway Park. In the shower, Zainab mentally drafted Eleanor's statement. But when Zainab reached her, Eleanor didn't want to discuss the statement. Instead, in a curt voice, Eleanor told her to be at the office in twenty minutes.

Across the antique pedestal desk from Eleanor, Zainab realized that, for perhaps the first time, she couldn't read her boss. She smoothed her hair, tucking it behind her ears, and waited for Eleanor to speak.

"Zainab, I'm sure you're wondering why I wanted to see you so early."

"I assume it's about our response to the bombing attempt."

"Yes. I have Jim working on the campaign's statement—"

"Jim?" Jim hadn't written a significant statement for the campaign in months.

"Yes, Jim. I think under the circumstances, it will be easier."

"I don't understand."

"Well, when people ask—and they *will* ask—if your background played a part in our response, we can nip all of that in the bud by saying that you had nothing to do with it."

"Isn't our response going to be a condemnation?"

"Of course," Eleanor said. "But if I know Fred Whitaker, he'll be advocating civil-liberty infringements, if you will, that I can't and won't support. So our position may seem weaker, in comparison. I just don't want anyone to blame you for that."

Zainab tried to think of the good of the campaign. Eleanor wasn't taking a swipe at her; she was trying to prevent others from doing so. "Okay, so I guess I'll lie low on this one."

"Not exactly," Eleanor said. "We still have to deal with your role."

"My role?"

"The woman they arrested was Pakistani. You are Pakistani. We have to address that unfortunate coincidence before Fred does."

"But it has nothing to do with me."

"I *know* it has nothing to do with you." Eleanor leaned forward, setting her hands on the desk. Her oversized gold bangles clanked against the wood. "But talk radio has made mincemeat out of your heritage." She looked at Zainab pointedly. "And don't forget the pieces you willingly participated in."

She meant Darby's article and the piece in *Vanity Fair*. Zainab wanted to point out that she had done both with Eleanor's avid encouragement, that Eleanor had pressed her to participate for the exposure it would bring to the campaign. But she knew Eleanor would simply point out that things had changed.

"Zainab, dear, I know you don't condone this sort of thing. But other people don't know that. So, first, Jim will put together a statement reiterating what I've already said to the news outlets. This is terrorism, we condemn it, and we stand with the people of Boston and all Americans in confronting this sort of evil wherever we may find it." Eleanor pursed her lips. "And I'm afraid you're going to need to make a statement of your own."

"I don't understand."

"You'll need to distance yourself from the people who did this."

Zainab didn't know what to say. "What exactly are you asking me to do?"

"I want you to make a simple statement acknowledging that you are, indeed, of Pakistani descent. No, wait." Eleanor narrowed her eyes. "That you are an *American* of Pakistani descent, and the fact that your parents are Muslim doesn't prevent you from abhorring these cowardly and terroristic acts."

Zainab's spine stretched, until she was sitting as tall as possible. "I'm Muslim, too. Not just my parents."

"Well, technically, I suppose you're right. But you've said you're not terribly practicing."

"So a Catholic who only goes to church on Christmas isn't really a Catholic?"

"Zainab, really. I'm not trying to debate you. I'm on your side. I need you on this campaign. We can't leave it all to Jim, for God's sake. And this will all blow over, sooner rather than later with any luck, but for now, we need to be politically astute. The primary is in three weeks. I'm just trying to distance you from it all as much as possible, as fast as possible."

That word again. *Distance.* As though Zainab were standing in the middle of the conspiracy, alongside the bumbling terrorists, and all that the situation required was remoteness.

Zainab cleared her throat. "But you just said that it has nothing to do with me. If I distance myself from it, won't that imply that it *does* have something to do with me?"

"You're being too logical. The voters of the Commonwealth are not going to be feeling logical at this moment. They will be operating on pure emotion. And our opponents are going to capitalize on that emotion." Eleanor raised her left eyebrow. "Including, no doubt, your boyfriend."

"I'm sorry?"

Eleanor tilted her head. "Now is not the time to be coy, Zainab."

She wondered how long Eleanor had known. "Chase wouldn't do that."

"He's already done it."

"That was before."

Eleanor scoffed. "Before what? Before he became infatuated with a beautiful Muslim woman? Don't be naive. He won't have a choice. Not if he wants to keep his cushy job and that lucrative book contract I hear he's about to be offered."

For a moment Zainab said nothing, but the irony was, apparently, lost on Eleanor.

Hank broke the news about the Fenway plot to Amra, hovering in her doorway, flipping a pencil through his fingers.

"That's horrible," she said, launching her Web browser dismissively.

"Hey, Amra?"

"Yes?"

"You're Pakistani, right?"

In the middle of her conference call, Amra's cell phone vibrated. It was Zainab. They hadn't talked since their fight about Mateen and her return to work. Still, with the city reacting and Hank making insinuations, she wanted to hear her friend's voice. She muted the conference call—they were stuck on a disagreement about venue, which fortunately Amra's client had no position on—and greeted Zainab.

"I'm on a call so I only have a second," she cautioned.

"Then I'll be brief," Zainab said. "I quit my job."

"You what? Why?"

"Eleanor, it turns out, is a politician."

"You quit your job on a political campaign because your boss is a politician?" Amra rubbed her forehead. "Help me out here, Zainab."

Zainab was quiet for a minute. "She wanted me to issue a statement about the Fenway thing."

"You issue statements all the time."

"Not for the campaign. For me, personally."

And there it was. Just like Hank, except public and infantilizing and worse. "I'm so sorry," Amra said. "I know how much your job meant to you. Tell me what I can do."

"Find me a new job?" Zainab laughed. "I'm kidding. I'll be fine. Look, you need to get back to your call. I'll be in touch soon."

In the kitchen, Amra transferred the containers of *ma po* tofu and the Szechuan shrimp from the white paper bag to the island countertop, which was already overflowing with nursing paraphernalia—flattened plastic storage bags, suction cups, breast shields. Mateen sighed and tossed two coiled plastic tubes onto the built-in desk.

"Those were sterile," Amra said, knowing they'd have to be boiled again before she could pump her milk.

Mateen just looked at her, and Amra could read his mind: *If you weren't returning to work so prematurely, we wouldn't need all of this crap.* She changed the subject. "Zainab quit her job today," she said, before she could think better of it. She stiffened her back, like a shield.

"Why would she do that?"

"Eleanor wanted her to apologize for the Fenway Park bombing plot." She purposefully made it sound worse than what Eleanor had actually proposed.

"You mean say she condemned it."

"I guess so."

"And instead of doing that, she quit."

"Yes."

"Is she so embarrassed of being a Muslim that she can't even issue a simple statement saying that this is not Islam?"

"I don't think that was her thinking," Amra said. "I think she thought it should be obvious to everyone that she would condemn it, that there is something wrong with the person asking her to condemn it."

"In an ideal world, yes. But we don't live in an ideal world. And I think it would have gone a long way, that it would have helped lots of Muslims who are not famous and powerful, if Zainab had stuck up for them."

Amra couldn't argue. It would have been helpful. But it also would have been harmful to Zainab. She couldn't say that to Mateen, of course. He would twist it to make Zainab look selfish. She took out the plates and silverware. "It's a difficult time for everyone, Mateen. Let's not pile on."

"It might have been less difficult if she had stuck her neck out."

"Can we talk about something else?"

He shrugged. "Fine. Did you call Eric today?"

Amra thought about stalling, but there was no point. The answer wasn't going to change. "No," she said, "but I will."

"When?"

"Soon."

"Don't mind me," Mateen said. "I'll just be over here holding my breath."

She scooped the bean curd onto their plates. "I said I'd talk to him and I will."

"So do it."

She set the spoon down. "What part of 'I will' don't you understand?"

Mateen got up and grabbed the cordless phone. "The part where you never actually do it." He set the phone on the counter. "How about now, Amra. How about doing it right now?"

"I'm sure he's left for home by now."

"So call his cell."

"Is that an order?"

"More like me calling your bluff."

She took a deep breath. "I said I'd do it and I will, but on my own terms and not with you"—she waved her arms—"hovering over me like my keeper."

"Ah, and here it comes. It's like Zainab has her hand in your back telling you how oppressed you are with your real, live Muslim husband. Maybe that could be her new career. Zainab Mir, grand puppeteer."

Amra's face burned. "This has nothing to do with Zainab. This is about us. You and me and our baby."

"For me it is. I'm not sure what it's about for you."

"That's not fair."

"Really? I'll tell you what's not fair. I gave up my whole life in L.A., took an enormous career risk, moved across the country, and have been killing myself to make a go of this office. I did all that for you, to make a life and have a family with you, and what did you give up, Amra? What have you had to sacrifice?"

She didn't know what to say. She couldn't believe he thought of it that way—as a quid pro quo. He'd never, in all of their fights, thrown the move in her face.

He ran his hands through his hair. "I'm tired of the one-way street. If I'd known how selfish you were going to be—" He stopped and stared at the floor.

It was like she'd been clubbed in the stomach. "Finish it, Mateen. If you'd known how selfish I was going to be, what? You wouldn't have moved here? You wouldn't have married me?"

"I didn't say that."

She nodded. "But that's the truth, right?" She couldn't blame him. She had not been upfront about how important her job was to her. She'd misrepresented herself, because she wanted him so much. Pared down to its most fundamental form, she had lied to him.

"There's no point in looking back, Amra. It is what it is." He looked defeated. Her anger dissipated. When she'd first seen him after so many years at her parents' home that dreadful night in the sari, he'd been larger than life. Confident. On top of the world. And now, she'd turned him into the unhappy man slumped against their kitchen counter.

"You're right," she said. "We can't go back. But maybe we can't go forward either."

He looked at her. "What are you saying?"

She closed her eyes tightly, to keep the tears back. "I'm saying what you're thinking. That maybe we need some time."

The words were a bluff, a straw man for him to knock down. To tell her she was being ridiculous, that she was overemotional from the baby. That the last thing he wanted was time away from her. But instead he picked up his keys and his phone. "I'll be at the condo in Brookline," he said. "I'll call you about seeing Thanaa."

She made it until she heard the garage door rise before dropping to the floor, her face pressed against the cool ceramic tile, struggling to breathe.

Amra's mother, who'd come on the 8:00 A.M. shuttle, sat with the baby, cooing to her, whispering grandmotherly love into her ear, while Amra made the tea. Blackcurrant, with honey and condensed milk. Her father had been making it for her mother every morning since they were married forty years earlier.

Amra brought the tea, placing the cup and saucer on the far end of the coffee table, out of the way of Thanaa's arms and legs. She forced a smile. "So how is work, *Ammi*?"

Her mother looked at her. "Work is fine, *beti*. But I'm not here to talk about work."

Amra feigned ignorance. She hadn't told anyone that Mateen had moved out.

"Mateen's mother called me yesterday." Her mother let the import of her words sink in. So he had already confided in his mother. He'd only been gone for a couple of days. Now Amra feared that he must be thinking of it as a more permanent situation. She could see no other reason why he would tell his mother something so enormous and alarming. She knew there was no escaping the conversation to come, but still, she tried to buy some time. "That's nice. How is she?"

"Amra. *Beti.* I know."

And just like that, Amra crumpled. She cried hard enough that her mother put Thanaa in the bouncy seat and joined Amra on the couch, stroking her arm. "There, there. Let it all out. And then we can try to sort through it, *Insha'Allah.*"

Her mother's words were like salve. There was something still sort-out-able. *Insha'Allah.* She took the tissue her mother offered and wiped her face.

"Now tell me," her mother said, smoothing Amra's hair, "what happened?"

"What did his mother tell you?"

"It doesn't matter. I want to hear from my daughter."

She took a breath. "We've been fighting for months. About my job. About working and having a baby."

Her mother frowned. "Mateen knew you had an important career when he married you. It's not realistic to think someone will completely change after marriage. If you want something different, you marry someone different."

Amra nodded. "He thought he was marrying someone different."

"I don't understand."

She sighed. "I never told him how important my job was. I hid how much I worked and how much I was willing to sacrifice to make partner."

"I'm sure he could surmise as much with the firm you're at."

"I think it's a matter of degree. And it's not his fault. I kept it from him on purpose."

"Why?"

And finally, she told the truth, to her mother and to herself: "Because I didn't think he'd marry me if he knew."

Her mother nodded. "But that should have been his choice," she said gently. "You made the choice for him and so he is naturally feeling frustrated."

"Frustrated is putting it politely."

Her mother smiled. "Yes, I suppose it is."

Amra wiped the reappearing tears. Her mother kept her arm around her.

"Please, *Ammi*. You have to tell me what his mother said. I haven't spoken to him since he left. I can't eat; I can't sleep. I need to know what he's thinking."

"Safa said the two of you hit a difficult patch, and you both needed some time to think." Her mother laughed. "And then she told me to call her next week so we can plot to fix everything."

Amra smiled. A few years ago, the idea would have made her roll her eyes. But now she found it comforting, the idea of their mothers at work, the women who knew them better than anyone and who had brought them together in the first place, fixing it all, bandaging their hurt, wiping away the muddy mess into which they'd gotten themselves.

"Did she say how Mateen was?"

"She said he's not himself. That she's never seen him like this."

Amra didn't know how to read that. "Never seen him like this" could mean lots of things, including anger and resentment.

"Enough about Mateen," her mother said. "How are *you*?"

"A mess," she confided. "And confused. I thought I knew what I wanted. I've always had a plan."

Her mother nodded. "Plans can change, what we want can shift, sometimes without our realizing it. But that should be because we want it to, because we choose it, not because someone chooses it for us."

"But what if you can't tell?" Amra asked. "What if your thoughts are so blurred that you can't tell anymore what you want and what someone you love wants?"

"Then you think some more. And talk it out with people you trust."

Amra nodded. She looked at Thanaa, bouncing blissfully, unaware that her parents had made such a mess of things. "I love her," she said.

"Of course you do! No one has said that you don't."

"I just wasn't expecting to have to give up everything. Not so soon. I thought children would come *after* I made partner. When I'd have more pull at work."

"But here she is."

"So now I'm supposed to give up everything?"

"Not everything, *beti*. But you will have to make decisions you weren't planning on making yet. We all do."

Amra sighed.

"I know what you're thinking," her mother said. "That I stayed home with you and therefore I'll judge you." Her mother took a sip of her tea. "You're wrong. It's not the same. My job was more flexible than yours. And there were other factors as well."

"What other factors?"

"I never told you this because I didn't want to scare you. I didn't want you to worry that you'd inherit my condition. I had six miscarriages before you came. We'd given up trying. You were unexpected, and I didn't even see a doctor in the beginning, because I was sure that I was going to lose you, too. But I didn't and, *Alhamdulillah,* there you were. So precious, my miracle baby. They couldn't have gotten me back to work even with a gun to my head."

Amra thought about the fierce love that she'd always felt from her mother. She hadn't known it was born, in part, out of loss, inexorably tied to the mourning for six unborn siblings. What a luxury the accidental appearance of Thanaa must have seemed like to her mother, pregnant the first time she'd made love, and how selfish she must seem to be treating her like a burden.

As if she could read her mind, her mother said, "I'm glad it wasn't so hard for you. And my difficulties have nothing to do with your decision."

Amra nodded, but she wasn't so sure about that.

47

IN THE AFTERMATH of the failed bombing attempt, Zainab became practically unreachable. She didn't answer her phone and when Chase texted her, she responded with short, truncated messages, saying she'd be in touch. At first, he wondered if she was mad about his show. In his defense, he had tried to keep the discussion aboveboard, focusing on the people involved, inserting "radical Islam" into his commentary, cutting off the most combative of callers. He'd mentioned the Winthrop-Smith campaign statement as often as he cited Fred Whitaker's, and had even thrown in the Democrat's for good measure. Possibly, Zainab was just busy with the upcoming primary. Still, he missed her. After a week of silence, he showed up at her apartment with a dozen roses.

When she answered the door, she just looked at him. He raised the bouquet, like a peace offering. "Hey," he said. "I've missed you."

She leaned against the doorway. "Sorry. I've had some things to take care of."

"Can I come in for a second?"

She stepped back to allow his entry. He looked around her living room, expecting to see papers everywhere, the last chaotic gasp of the campaign. Instead, it was spotless. He set the flowers on the console table and stood awkwardly just inside the door.

"So," he said, "everything got a bit crazy last week."

"Yes."

"And just before the primary. It will be interesting to see how it impacts the election."

She looked at him. "Well, the Republicans are certainly milking it for all it's worth."

"Some on the left, too. It's hard to blame them, right? They planned to blow up Fenway Park, for Christ's sake. You have to give them credit. It doesn't get more American than baseball."

"I don't give them any credit."

"It was a figure of speech, Zainab."

She plopped on the couch. She did not, he noticed, ask him to sit down. "I quit my job," she said.

"You *what*?"

"Quit," she said. "My job."

No wonder the place was so clean. "What the hell . . . when?"

"A few days ago."

"You weren't going to tell me?"

"I just did."

"Because of the terrorism thing? That doesn't sound like Eleanor."

She shook her head. "She didn't make me quit. It was my decision."

"I understand not wanting to harm the campaign. But I still can't believe she took your resignation."

"It wasn't like that. It wasn't some selfless act." Zainab waved her hand. "She wanted me to make a statement. Personally."

Chase took a deep breath and blew it out in one long sigh. "I'm sorry."

"You're not going to tell me how stupid that is? That I couldn't just make some stupid statement condemning an utterly condemnable act?"

"No. I'm not going to say that."

She nodded and then closed her eyes.

"Zainab?"

"I'm sorry. I'm just so tired, you know? I'm just so fucking exhausted. I worked my ass off for that campaign. For Eleanor. But it wasn't enough. It's never enough. And that's the point, right? To make sure that no Muslim is ever really accepted. We're all suspect. Even the so-called liberal people will still make the connection between Muslims and terrorists. After all, they've been trained well." She didn't need to say who had done the training. No wonder she hadn't taken his calls. "And what's the end game, Chase? To get us all to leave?"

"No one wants you to leave. I don't want you to leave."

"Right, you just don't want to be seen with me."

He stepped toward her. "That's not fair," he said. "We both decided that because of our careers we shouldn't create the appearance of a conflict of interest."

"Is that what we decided?"

"Yes."

"And now?"

"What do you mean?"

"Well, there really isn't a conflict anymore, is there?"

"No, there's not." He paused. "So let's go somewhere tomorrow night. Wherever you want. Lumière or Via Matta. Anywhere. Your choice."

"I'll think about it."

He gestured as though he'd been wounded in the chest. "So the truth is you don't want to be seen with me."

"I'm not sure," she said. "Let me think about it, okay?"

He could feel her slipping away. Her tone was flat, distant, like it wouldn't matter if he fell off the face of the earth. He knelt before her and put his head in her lap. She didn't move. He looked up and took her stone-cold hands in his. "Well, think about this, too, Zainab Mir."

"Yes?"

"If we're going to spend the rest of our lives together, you're going to have to be seen with me sooner or later."

For a minute, the look in her eyes remained cool, unchanged, and her hands stayed limp in his. But somehow, she seemed to resuscitate, tightening her grip, the look in her eyes softening.

"Oh my God," he said. "Are you crying?"

She laughed and wiped under her eyes. "I don't cry."

"That's too bad."

"Why?"

"Because you look so beautiful when you do."

They spent the night on the couch, Zainab sleeping fitfully in his arms, Chase watching her for fear that if he closed his eyes she might disappear. They stayed that way until dawn, when he made *paratha* and *dal* for her before leaving for the studio. He kissed Zainab goodbye and told her that he was serious about dinner.

At the studio, he read the usual assortment of e-mails, many of which posed the question, "Why do we let them in our country?" and the corollary, "How can we get rid of them?" Chase felt his stomach turn. He could imagine the e-mail he'd get after he and Zainab went public.

His producer came in. "The lines are still going nuts. The message from the top is that you need to take it up a notch, egg them on, do what you can to get them riled up. They think last week was something of a missed opportunity on your part." Chase nodded, but his mind was racing, trying to figure out how to walk the line between appeasing the guys he worked for and still being able to face Zainab.

His first caller said that while he was not a bigot, he didn't see how the government had any choice but to intern all Muslim Americans, because "while not all Muslims are terrorists, all terrorists are Muslims" and it was the only way "we can be sure we got the ones who are going to blow us up." Chase reminded him of the Japanese internment, which was widely refuted by history, and pointed out that interning all six million American Muslims would make the United States no better than the people it was fighting, that important American values and Constitutional principles were at stake.

"First of all, where'd you get your figures, Charles? CAIR? Six million, my fat ass. And second, those freedoms you speak of are for the rest of us," the caller said. "Not for some goddamned towel heads who only come here to kill us."

At the commercial break, Brad McFadden, the program director, burst in. "What the hell was that? Bringing up the Japanese thing? What is this, Air fucking America? NPR?"

Chase shook his head.

"Look, maybe you've had some epiphany between the legs of that hot Muslim girl I hear you're screwing. Maybe you'd rather make love than war. Fine. Kumba-fucking-ya. But do it on your own time. In this studio, you play to our audience, or we won't have one, got it? And if you can't, I got a hundred up-and-coming guys who will be happy to take your place. And your paycheck. And that little book deal you have in the works. Are we clear?"

Chase went back to the calls and let other people do most of the talking. He didn't try to calm them down, but he didn't add much of his own opinion. During the last commercial break, Brad slipped him some copy. In bold letters at the top, underlined in thick black lines, it said, "Read this, word for word." He skimmed the first few lines of the text. It was a call for registration for Muslim Americans, arguing that loyal American Muslims should have no problem helping the government weed out the bad seeds. He felt a wave of relief. It was essentially what he'd said to Taj Fareed in their debate. Meaning Zainab had heard it before and shouldn't be shocked. He just needed to get through this show and have a chance to think, to figure out what to do next. He would quit, of that he was certain—he couldn't even register Brad's comments about Zainab or he was liable to do something to get himself both fired and arrested—but better that he leave on his own terms, when there was still some hope of salvaging his career. It wouldn't do him any good to get blacklisted. He said he'd read the statement.

"You'd better," Brad warned.

But the text grew more ominous as he read it to his listeners, ending with the assertion that loyal Americans need not worry about infringing the rights of people who come here only to abuse the Constitution for their own purposes, who do not believe that other people's lives have value, who prefer to be slaves to their vengeful god. As he finished and watched the phone lines light up like fireflies, Chase knew he'd been wrong, that there was something worse than being blacklisted.

Before he left the studio he vomited, first in the trash can in the hall and then in the men's room on the first floor. He needed to get to Zainab's place and tell her everything. That he'd just been playing a role. That he was going to quit. But then he rounded the corner of the building and there she was: Zainab, hair loose, blowing across her face. She was wearing the same clothes he'd left her in. She just stared.

"Zainab!" he yelled, and ran across the street. She didn't move, not even when he stood right in front of her.

"I caught your show."

He nodded. "Can we go somewhere to talk?" She flinched when he touched her shoulder. "Please. Let me explain."

"That's a rich thought, since I came here to explain something to *you*. Although," she said, looking up and down the street, "this might be a bit public for you. You know how these witch hunts work, right? There's always that pesky little guilt-by-association thing."

He swallowed hard. "I was reading copy, Zainab. They made me say it."

She nodded. "I wanted to see your face when you said that."

He knew he looked like a coward. She had chosen on principle just days earlier and now he had chosen on something else and, he imagined, revealed himself rather fully to her. "I made a mistake. An enormous mistake. But I swear, Zainab, on my father's grave that I will make it up to you. I will find a way to make this right."

"There isn't one."

"There has to be. I'll do whatever it takes."

"Listen to me. You need to listen carefully, because this is the last thing I'm ever going to say to you."

He shook his head. "No—"

"Listen to me."

"I'll give you some time. As much as you need."

She put her hands on his shoulders and leaned close. He took a deep breath, burying his face in her hair. She smelled like his future, a mix of fragrant shampoo and the lentil soup he'd made her for breakfast. She brought her lips next to his ear. "Charles Holland," she whispered, "if you ever contact me again I'll call the police and have Amra file a restraining order."

He took a step back, as if her words had physical force. He felt, for the first time, what his father must have felt at some point in the hospice: the cold futility of future efforts. He watched his foot kick a small stone and looked at her. "No second chances, right?"

"I'm glad you understand," she said, and walked away.

48

Zainab arrived first. "I'm meeting someone," she told the hostess. At the table she instinctively reached for her BlackBerry and caught herself. She was no longer employed, no longer wedded to the crisis mode of the campaign. In the days after she'd quit, she'd tried to keep up with the barrage of calls and e-mails. She did her best to respond, especially to the media, for Eleanor's sake. Eleanor had not fired Zainab or wanted her to quit. She had merely asked something eminently reasonable that Zainab could not do. She said as much to the reporters who called, telling them it was entirely her decision. When Darby called, Zainab told her to get the message out that Eleanor had wanted her to stay. "What's the real reason you left?" Darby had asked, intuitively, but Zainab refused to explain further. She couldn't, when she hadn't said it out loud to anyone, including Eleanor.

"Zainab, *Assalaamu alaikum*." It was May al-Ansari, in a bright pink scarf and matching Kate Spade purse.

"Wa alaikum asalaam," Zainab said, standing and kissing May on each cheek. "I love your bag."

May laughed. "I know. It's hard to be in a bad mood when you're carrying something so darned cheerful."

Zainab couldn't imagine May ever being in a bad mood. She said as much out loud. May shook her head. "I have my days. Just ask my husband."

After they ordered, Zainab sipped her water, not sure how to begin. "This is harder than I intended," she confessed.

"What is?"

"To explain why I invited you here."

May nodded. "I'm a pretty good listener, if that helps."

"Maybe I don't even know exactly why I wanted to talk to you," Zainab said. "It has to do with the Fenway terrorist plot and quitting my job."

May nodded. "I heard about that. I'm sorry."

"It was my decision. Eleanor wanted me to stay."

"But you didn't."

"She wanted me to issue a statement condemning the attack."

May shook her head. "That happens too much. As if every Muslim must condemn every abhorrent thing any other Muslim does. And yet . . ." May bit her lip. "Don't take this the wrong way, but I still think it's important for us to do. Maybe I'm naive, but I keep thinking that if we do it enough, someday we'll be done. People will switch from assuming that we don't condemn it to knowing that we do. It will become one of those 'of course' types of things."

"I know. I get that. But still—"

"You couldn't."

Zainab nodded.

"I know people who feel the same way. My good friend, Jamila Duchamps, a professor at Brown, refuses to say a word about it. The most she will say is, 'It doesn't have anything to do with me.' I don't think she's alone in that sentiment." May gestured at Zainab and smiled. "Obviously."

"That's pretty much what I told Eleanor."

"I'm sure she understood."

Zainab waited for the waiter to set down their salads. "The thing is, it wasn't the truth. Not entirely anyway."

"I'm not sure I understand."

Zainab took a deep breath. "All my life, I've been a Muslim. And I've been reflexively defensive in that capacity. I don't want bad things said about my faith because I don't want bad things said about me."

"Naturally."

"So of course I hoped they wouldn't turn out to be Muslims. The terrorists. But when they did, instead of rushing into defensive mode, I felt like I needed a nap." May laughed. Zainab leaned forward. "Seriously. Because as tired as I am of America asking me to prove my loyalty, I am absolutely exhausted by Muslims. Why should I put myself out there, when they won't do the same for me?" Zainab stabbed a piece of baby spinach with her fork. "Muslims have judged me; criticized what I wear, who I am friends with; even questioned my sexuality." She took a breath. "Muslims talk a big game about how revolutionary the Qur᾿an is on women's rights, and it may well be, but they have failed miserably in carrying forward that egalitarian impulse. It is utterly lost on them how harmful their 'separate but equal' doctrine has been for women. And so many women collaborate in their own oppression." She waved her hand. "America has not forced me, *yet,* to pray in filthy, segregated basement rooms with the prayer piped in over the voices of screaming children. America has not forced me to enter separate doors. America has never told me not to be seen or heard. But Muslims have." Zainab paused, gauging May's reaction. It had all come out a bit more vitriolic and, from the looks on the faces of those dining nearby, louder than she'd intended.

"You've been hurt, Zainab," May said. "And you're saying you've had enough."

Zainab nodded. "So when Eleanor wanted me to condemn the attack, which was really a way of saying, hey, I'm not a terrorist, not all Muslims are terrorists, I just couldn't do it. I couldn't put myself out there for a community who wouldn't do the same for me." She sighed. "So I'm mad at America and the people who stir up hatred. But I'm equally mad at Muslims."

"Perfectly understandable. I suspect you're in good company."

"Then why do I feel so alone?"

May smiled. "Because you're carving out a third space. An honest space. And that takes guts. Not everyone will agree with you. And even among those who do, not all will have the courage to stand with you." May dipped some lettuce in her vinaigrette. "Revolution is a lonely thing, Zainab."

Zainab laughed. "Is that what this is?"

May put her fork down. "I know you know that Muslims are not Islam. The men and women who tell you to go to the unkempt basement of the mosque are just people. They are not God. But when enough people stay quiet, maybe they start to think they are. Or at least believe that they speak for Him."

"Well, how do you convince them they're wrong?"

"I'm not sure you do. I'm not sure that's our job. Maybe our job is simply to make sure they don't intimidate us into suppressing our own beliefs." May paused. "How many Muslim feminists do you actually know? Women or men."

"Besides you and Taj? None. I guess I think of it as more of an academic enterprise. Not a community."

"Maybe you can help us make it one." May reached into her purse and pulled out a shiny postcard-sized flyer. It announced a woman-led prayer on August 23 in Cambridge. "They've been occurring with more frequency," May said. "We still get a lot of protesters, of course. But I'd love for you to come."

Zainab took the flyer and put it in her handbag carefully, as if transporting precious cargo.

49

FAREEDA CALLED THE Woman for Islam meeting to order. "On the one hand," she said, "this is a tricky time for us. We want to come out in condemnation of the bombing attempt. We have to do that, or no one will ever take us seriously."

Hayden wondered if that was a good enough reason to condemn it. She thought there were probably better ones. She looked around Fareeda's living room in the hopes of finding a like mind. Abdullah Rahman had said that Muslims should never take innocent life, but he wondered if the threesome had been entrapped. He said he didn't know enough to take a stand.

"But there are more pressing matters at hand," Fareeda continued. "We all know that it is a constant struggle to lead an Islamic life in this country. We know that the *kafir* will constantly put temptations in plain view, either purposefully, to lead us astray, or inadvertently, as a by-product of their tainted lives." She looked pointedly at Hayden when she said this last part. "But there are threats from within as well. And it is our job to counter those threats."

Fareeda scanned the room, letting it sink in, this notion of enemies within. She was silent long enough that the women started looking at each other, as though they weren't quite sure what to make of the idea. Or possibly, Hayden thought, looking for the internal threats.

"Now, what I am about to pass out to you may be troubling. In fact, it *should be* troubling to any decent Muslim, but nonetheless we must face it head-on."

Hayden was expecting some sort of adult-content material or maybe a copy of the article she'd come across alleging that the citizens of Pakistan consumed the most Internet porn. Instead, Fareeda passed out stiff cards, giving one to each woman. They were invitations to a prayer service, led by a woman.

"What we have here, sisters, is an attempt to *corrupt* our faith, to change it to accommodate perverse, Western notions of feminism." She said the word *feminism* as though it tasted like milk left too long on the counter. "We are not Christians. We do not change or accommodate. We follow the word of God and the *Sunnah* of our Beloved Prophet, peace and blessings be upon him, and that is it."

A young woman in a white scarf raised her hand. "But what can we do?"

"Ah, that is the question, isn't it." Fareeda nodded, surveying the room. "That is something for each of us to answer for ourselves. Some of us will have one response; some might have another. What is important is that we stand up to this blasphemy, in whatever way we feel called." She cocked her head. "As for me, I will stand outside of that abomination and protest until there is no voice or breath left in me. The rest of you will have to decide for yourselves what lengths you are willing to go to for your Creator."

50

THE CURTAINS WERE failing miserably in their one and only job, which was to keep Chase's room dark enough for him to sleep off his hangover and delay the time at which he would need to start drinking again. He opened one eye—the left one since the right one was pushed into the pillow along with his nose and half of his mouth—and looked at the clock. 11:15. He started to push himself up, but his head throbbed in protest. Instead, he reached over to the bedside table and groped for his phone. Sixteen messages. He scrolled through the recent calls just to be sure. Zainab, of course, had not called.

He dragged himself to the bathroom, then to the kitchen, where he drank, rapidly, two glasses of water and took a third one to the couch. Once he hydrated, he'd have his way with the remaining vodka.

He turned on the television and lowered the volume. He watched part of a *Seinfeld* rerun and caught the back end of a story on death-row inmates. He kept flipping and, at one point, thought he saw Nadia Asad. "It means 'lion,'" Zainab once said, referring to Nadia's last name. "Could that be any more *appropriate*?"

He backed up a few channels. Sure enough, it was Nadia being interviewed on the local FOX affiliate's noontime show. The bottom of the screen read, "Controversial Prayer." He turned up the volume.

"But isn't it a good step?" the reporter, a young woman with big hair, asked. "Doesn't it benefit us all if Muslims modernize?"

"Well, that's a separate issue. The question here is who is behind this so-called feminist prayer. And I think if we dig deep, we will find the names of apologists for Islam, including people like Taj Fareed and May al-Ansari."

The reporter frowned. "I'm not sure I follow you."

"These people are vested in *normalizing* the image of Islam in the West. Making it compatible with our notions of equality, particularly for women. But we all know that Islam oppresses every woman in its path. A woman-led Muslim prayer is a fiction. Most Muslim women around the world would face death for participating in such a thing. That's why events like this—and notice how much they are publicizing it—are so dangerous. They create a false impression and lead to complacency on the part of decent Americans."

The reporter nodded. Her hair, Chase noted, did not move. "So what you're saying is, why didn't they just hold their prayer without making it such a spectacle?"

"Exactly!" Nadia pumped her fist. "If people want to worship God, what do they do? They retreat to their houses of worship and pray. They do not call Fox News and CNN and MSNBC."

"And I understand that you have a protest planned?"

Nadia looked straight into the camera. Straight, Chase felt, at him.

"Yes. We will be standing outside of the event to protest this subterfuge. And we will be praying for the innocent women who suffer at the hands of Islam and who would be threatened with death if they tried to pull off something like this in their own countries."

Chase closed his eyes, thinking of how he must have sounded to Zainab. He shut the television off and took the remaining vodka to his bedroom.

51

WHEN AMRA AND Mateen took a break, it seemed she and Zainab did, too. They hadn't talked since Zainab announced her resignation. Part of Amra didn't mind; she didn't want to hear Zainab gloat about Mateen's moving out. She was surprised, then, to find a small envelope with Zainab's handwriting in the mail. It was an announcement of a "Celebration of the Female in Islam"—a prayer to be led by a Muslim woman. On the back of the card, she saw Zainab's careful script:

> *I don't know what has happened; craziness abounds. Still, come. Please. Love, Zainab*

Amra had heard of similar events, although not frequently. It was widely accepted in Islam that only men could lead the prayers in mixed congregations. She hadn't really questioned it. But there was Zainab's plaintive "please come." It was an odd request from Zainab, who rarely prayed, who'd watched Amra perform the five daily prayers and observe Ramadan when they were roommates at Smith, giving strict instructions not to wake her when Amra rose for *fajr,* the early morning prayer, or for *suhoor,* the predawn meal. But she was also fiercely protective, chastising anyone who dared to eat or drink in front of Amra while she fasted. Zainab, while not practicing, had always supported Amra. And now, she thought, it was time to support her friend.

After she e-mailed Zainab, she went on her laptop and learned that, because of a bomb threat, the venue had been changed from its original location to a local Unitarian church. Amra had already been wary of taking Thanaa along; there was no way she could bring her with the threat of violence. She called Mateen to ask him to switch weekends with her.

"I'll have to check my schedule. It wasn't my planned day."

"I know, but something has come up."

"Can I ask what?"

She paused. "A prayer in Cambridge."

"On a Saturday?"

"It's a celebration of women and Islam. A woman named Sameera Khan is going to lead the prayer."

"So you're going to a prayer for women but you can't take your daughter."

She closed her eyes. "It's not just for women."

"I'm sorry?"

"It's a woman-led prayer. But anyone can go."

"Women can't lead men—" He sucked in air, interrupting himself. "Let me guess. Zainab is somehow involved."

"She invited me."

"Of course." And then: "Is this what you plan to teach Thanaa?"

"I don't know. Maybe. Would that be so horrible? To teach her that men and women are equal?"

"It's not about equality. It's about what is permitted."

"Well, some scholars, including some male scholars, support it."

"I'd like to see that."

"So look it up," she said curtly. "I didn't call you to fight about this. I just wanted to know if you could watch Thanaa."

"I'll let you know," he said and hung up without saying good-bye.

52

Zainab was going to be late to the prayer. Somehow she thought May would understand. As she was heading out the door, she got a Google Alert on her phone about Nadia Asad. She'd signed up for them, with all of the embarrassing modus operandi of an insecure teenage girl, when Nadia and Chase became an Internet item. She almost deleted the alert, but curiosity got the better of her and she looked at the headline: *Ex-Muslim Activist Fabricated Past.* She read, with her mouth agape, how Nadia was not raised in Dearborn, Michigan, but in the suburbs of Atlanta, that there was no uncle, no pregnancy, simply parents who wanted to return with their daughter to India. Nadia had a boyfriend and a spot on the cheerleading squad, so she threatened to accuse her father of trying to marry her off under threat of an honor killing. Her parents left, and she stayed in the United States with her best friend's Baptist family. In college, she fabricated a provocative past, joined the Young Republicans, and made a name for herself writing anti-immigrant and anti-Islam editorials.

Zainab sat down. She thought of all the strife, all the anti-Muslim fervor Nadia whipped up with her incendiary book. All because a petulant teenager didn't want to leave her friends. Zainab felt the weight of Nadia Asad's—what was the word?—"perfidy" settle over her. Then she laughed. *The Perfidy of Nadia Asad.* Maybe someone would write the book.

She grabbed her keys and headed out the door.

53

In the end, Mateen claimed a conflict, and Rukan agreed to watch Thanaa. Amra kissed her friend and her daughter good-bye, trying to ignore her jangled nerves. She wished she and Zainab were driving together, but Zainab had insisted on meeting her there.

When she reached Cambridge, she had to make a series of left turns to reach the church. The police had roped off the nearest intersection, and she had to park several blocks away. Amra could hear the shouting as soon as she stepped out of the car. When she got closer, she spied two groups of protestors partitioned by uniformed officers. On one side were Western-clothed men and women, maybe twenty or so total, chanting, over and over, "Islam oppresses women," and holding signs warning those who walked by not to believe the "farce." On the other side of the police-created demilitarized zone, a bit farther from where Amra approached, stood a dozen or so women, all in *hijab,* some in *niqab,* and twice as many men. She had to squint to read their signs, but soon wished she hadn't. "*Kafirs,*" they said, or "You are the reason there are more women than men in Hell," or "Mixed gender prayer today, hellfire tomorrow." She met the gaze of a young man, no more than twenty, who poured hatred from his eyes. His sign said simply "Dogs." She rushed for the stairs. At the top, she saw women, both with and without headscarves, and a few young artsy-looking men entering the church. An elderly man with a white beard and a *kufi* held the door. He waited for Amra before following her in. She teared up at the sight of him and had to stop herself from hugging him.

Inside, the atmosphere was completely different. The room the church provided was quiet and serene. Vases with lilies sat on pedestals flanking the doorway. A mix of prayer rugs covered the floor. People sat in groups—women sat on the right, men sat on the left, and in the middle they sat together. Some in the crowd spoke softly among themselves, some were reading the Qur'an, some fingered wooden beads while their lips moved silently in prayer. She recognized Sameera Khan, who was at the front of the room, from the Internet. She was shorter than Amra had pictured, but she sported the same cropped hairstyle and wide, friendly eyes that warmed the space and belied the hatred outside.

Amra sat near the front, in the middle, setting her purse down optimistically to hold a place for Zainab. She removed the scarf from her purse. She knew no one would make her wear it, and that was enough. She tied it beneath her chin, cupped her hands, and prayed to God to keep them safe.

"*Assalaamu alaikum,* sisters and brothers." Sameera stood at the front and welcomed them. Her voice was surprisingly forceful for her diminutive size. "*Insha'Allah,* we will get started in just a few moments. Please, move forward if you can. We don't want to turn anyone away."

The crowd shifted, scooting forward. Amra turned and was surprised to see that the room had filled. Four police officers stood in the back of the room. She craned her neck to look for Zainab, and then she saw him. Mateen. He was in the back, on the men's side, staring at her. He gave half a smile and shrugged.

A young woman with glasses and a blue scarf began the call to prayer. At first, her voice was shaky, but soon rose to a loud, lyrical cry. During the *khutbah,* Sameera spoke of commonalities, of how many different kinds of people had come to pray together, how the Unitarian community had provided such a lovely venue, and thanked its members for the beautiful decorations. "As you can see, we've united some unlikely groups outside as well," she said, to laughter, "so we're bringing all kinds of people together today." She recited some of the Qur'an, a verse Amra knew well, about the believing men and women, and spoke about how God didn't have to specify women in that passage. "Most religious texts do not. Many political documents do not. All *men* are created equal, right? It can't be an accident, the Qur'anic inclusion." She went on to remind them to be patient with critics, to love and serve God, to remember him so that he would remember them. She concluded by saying that she hoped they would all have the chance to pray together again soon. Amra lingered to introduce herself. Afterward, when she turned, she saw Mateen waiting for her. As they approached the large double doors leading to the outside, the yelling grew louder.

"Are you ready?" Mateen asked. Amra nodded. He went first, pushing the door open, holding her arm, rushing her through the crowd. "Where are you parked?" he asked. She pointed and he followed her to her car.

She fished her keys out of her purse and looked at him. "So this was your conflict?"

He gestured at the crowd. "I couldn't leave you to the wolves."

"I'm a big girl, Mateen," she said. "And I'm not your responsibility." The *anymore* hung between them.

He nodded and stuffed his hands in his pockets. "Right. You're right." He leaned close to her. "But you do know that if anything happened to you I would die, right?"

She didn't know what to say. Or how long she could hold back the tears.

"Take care, Amra," he whispered. He kissed her on the forehead and then walked away.

Hayden's voice was hoarse from yelling, but it was the good kind of hoarse. The kind that signified productivity, that meant her God-given voice had been put to good use. She stretched her neck to see if anyone else was coming. It looked as though most of the people inside had left, although she hadn't seen the prayer leader yet. Fareeda had given them all a picture of Sameera Khan, "just in case." Fareeda had not finished her thought and no one had asked. Hayden figured that Sameera must have left through a back entrance and was surprised to realize she was glad.

Suddenly, a commotion erupted and people started yelling again, back and forth, the anti-Islamic protestors and Hayden's group. The crowd had grown considerably, and Hayden estimated that there must have been at least a hundred protestors, maybe more. She raised her sign, the one she'd carefully lettered with the words "Women-Led Prayer Is Against Islamic Law." Simple and respectful. She'd made it at the gathering the night before, which had been like a party, all of the women chatting and laughing while children ran between them in Fareeda's basement. Hayden finally felt like she belonged. And she and Abdullah Rahman got along surprisingly well. It wasn't the kind of crazy infatuation she'd felt with Fadi, but he was solid and stable and, at least when his mother wasn't around, quite solicitous of Hayden.

In the middle of the commotion, while the police tried to hold the groups apart, Fareeda nudged Hayden with her elbow. "Look," she said, pointing toward the curb. "It's Zainab Mir." Zainab tried to weave through the crowd, but the police yelled for her to turn back.

"The blasphemy is over!" a man yelled at Zainab. "Go beg Allah for forgiveness, you swine!" A woman from the other group yelled for the man to go back to his third world country.

"Get out of my way," Zainab said, trying to push through the crowd. Hayden wanted to tell her it was over, but she would have had to shout and her voice, which had performed so spectacularly earlier, refused to cooperate. As more men blocked Zainab's path, the police tried to push through the crowd. And then, almost in slow motion, Hayden saw Zainab fall. The crowd was on her, pushing and kicking. Just before the police got to her, Hayden saw a man spit.

Additional officers arrived to disperse the crowd. Fareeda tried to pull Hayden's arm, but she couldn't move. Someone must have called an ambulance because at some point EMTs were tending to Zainab, placing a brace around her neck, lifting her onto a stretcher. When they moved her, Hayden saw the blood on the sidewalk. She should have been startled by the amount, but for some reason she wasn't. An officer told her not to leave the scene; he needed to ask her some questions. She nodded, asked if she could make a call. "You're not under arrest," he said. Hayden wondered if he meant *yet*.

It had been several months since she'd dialed the number, but she still knew it by heart. "Zainab's been hurt," she said. "I'm not sure where they're taking her. I thought you should know." She hung up without waiting for Amra to say anything.

54

THE NURSE ANNOUNCED a male visitor. She said he didn't give his name and asked if Zainab was up to it.

"Is he white?"

"Excuse me?" The nurse looked uncertain.

"The visitor. Is he white?"

"I don't think . . . no. He looks . . . well, like *you*."

She traced around the edges of the fact that it was not Chase. Her initial feeling had been hope, and she hated herself for that fleeting, mutinous thought. There was a gentle tapping at the door. Mateen poked his head in.

"Mateen? What are you doing here?"

He took a step in and stood awkwardly between the IV stand and the chair that turned into a bed, should someone feel so invested that he could not leave her side.

"I heard on the news. I just wanted to—" He looked at her and made what Zainab considered a valiant effort at not seeming horrified. He rubbed his hand over his face. "God, Zainab, are you okay?"

She shrugged. "A couple of broken ribs, a few superficial facial fractures. Lots of bruising. They say I'll look good as new in a couple months, give or take. It's mostly swelling." She'd looked in the mirror, despite the nurses advising her to wait a day or two. "It could have been worse."

"Small comfort," he said.

"That's exactly what your wife said."

"She was here?"

"She's still here. They had to fix one of my dressings. She went to get tea."

Mateen shifted.

"It's okay to sit down, you know."

He did, sitting stiffly on the edge of the chair. Zainab imagined how much worse she looked up close.

"Who the hell did this to you?"

"The police aren't sure. The two groups of protestors were already going at it when I got there." She sneered. "Nothing to bring the anti-Muslim forces and the fundamentalists together like a big scary woman leading a prayer."

"Can I do anything? I'm sure Amra will want you to come home with us—" He seemed to catch himself. "With her. You shouldn't be alone right now."

"Neither should Amra."

He looked away. "Come on. Cut me some slack."

"Why? Because I've known you since we were little? She's my best friend." He didn't say anything. "It's Amra, for God's sake," Zainab said. "*Amra*. Who the hell could hurt Amra?"

"She hurt me, too."

"By taking her job seriously and hanging out with me?"

He sighed. "It wasn't you. It was what I thought you represented."

"Which is?"

"You know, turning your back on your culture and your religion. I think you threw the baby out with the bathwater."

She adjusted the IV tubing. "I think that's fair." He looked surprised. "What?" she said, "I can't admit that I'm not perfect? But that has nothing to do with Amra. Remember her? The one who actually practices her religion? Working hard, wanting to be partner, that's not un-Islamic. Not unless you're living in the dark ages."

"It was like she didn't need me. Definitely not to support her—"

Zainab couldn't help it; she laughed.

"Is that funny?"

"No, sorry. But think about it. You were just about the most eligible bachelor we knew. Smart, maddeningly good-looking, successful. I never would have pegged you as insecure."

"I'm not. Or I wasn't until I saw Amra again after all those years. From the second I walked into her parents' place that night and saw her—she was mortified, you know, that her mother had put her in those clothes and I knew she was mortified, and it was so damn endearing. And I knew it that night. I knew she was the one."

"Yet you broke it off when she wouldn't move."

"It was a blow. I admit that," he said. "My pride was wounded enough for me to try to move on. But I couldn't. So when I gave up everything and came, I was always looking for some sign that she was just as committed. And it seemed easier to believe if she was entrenched in our culture and traditions. I mean, come on, Zainab, you know me. I don't even pray regularly. But there I was, riding her all of the time for hanging out with you. I could have just as easily warned her about hanging out with me." He smiled, but it faded quickly. "She knew I was committed. She knew I wouldn't leave her."

As gently as possible, Zainab said, "But you did."

"I know." He put his head in his hands.

"Mateen?"

"Yeah?"

"Get the hell out of here."

He looked up. "I'm sorry?"

She forced a smile through her swollen lips. "Go find your wife and tell her everything you just told me."

. . .

After Mateen left, Zainab closed her eyes. It occurred to her, unhappily, that she was as culpable as Mateen where Amra was concerned. She'd known Amra wasn't happy, but she refused to consider that maybe Amra had changed. So she'd wanted to be partner all her life. What if now she wanted something else more? In her sterile room, alone, Zainab finally admitted she'd been trying to keep Amra boxed in, just like Mateen, for her own reasons. They both needed her so damn much—Mateen, who was head-over-heels in love with her, and Zainab, for whom Amra had become her only real family. They both thought they could lose her at any moment. And in trying to keep her, they'd both failed her miserably.

There was a gentle tap on the door. It was May, peeking in. "*As-salaamu alaikum,* Zainab. Are you up for a visit? I promise not to stay more than a minute."

"Please, come in."

May approached the bed and touched Zainab's hand lightly. She shook her head. "I can't help but feel responsible, Zainab. I am so sorry this happened to you, at something I encouraged you to attend."

"If it's anyone's fault, it's mine, for being habitually late." She smiled. "I'm really sorry I missed it. My friend said it was beautiful."

"It was," May said. "So how are you doing?"

"I think the medicine is keeping me from knowing."

May nodded. "You'll tell me if there's anything I can do, right? We've all spoken to the police. The *Globe* is covering it. I heard Darby Tate from *The New York Times* is on her way up here, so it will be all over the news." May bit her lip. "We're going to catch the people who did this to you."

Zainab sighed. "I wish I could remember more. I can't even give them decent descriptions."

"I think maybe it's a blessing that you can't remember more."

Zainab had thought the same thing. She didn't remember anything after the crowd descended. When she'd tried to bring back the images, she felt an overwhelming sense of vertigo. She changed the subject. "So did you hear about Nadia Asad? How she made it all up?"

May nodded. "Actually, I already knew. Or suspected. Rumors have been going around for months about all of that. I debated her once, at Boston College, and I think she was terrified I would bring it up."

"Why didn't you?"

"Because it happened to someone."

"No, it didn't."

May smiled. "Let me try to explain. Nadia represented a position that needs representation. I don't agree with the conclusions she drew from what she claimed happened to her, but I understand them. Some women are married off at young ages, not just in Islam, but sometimes in Islam. Some children are forced to have sex with their dramatically older husbands. That is a pain I cannot imagine, and if Nadia had been telling the truth, I would understand why she blamed the religion."

"But she wasn't telling the truth."

"She wasn't telling *her* truth, but she was telling *someone's* truth. I'm always in favor of more speaking of truth, rather than less. How else can we address pain and suffering? If I had simply said, 'This never happened to you,' then where does the conversation go? I am sure there are others, who *have* suffered what is essentially child rape, who conflate their abuse with my faith. Nadia provided a way for me to talk to those people without them having to come forward. Does that make sense?"

Zainab nodded. "It does, but it's so far removed from my first instinct, which was always just to crush her, given the opportunity."

May laughed and leaned in conspiratorially. "I had that instinct, too. Especially when I suspected she was lying. But I had to remember the women who were silent, the young girls in any religion who are living out the nightmare she described. Plus, I felt sorry for her."

Zainab shook her head. "Impossible."

"Think about it. Once you start down a path like that, your whole livelihood is contingent on this role you're playing—your reputation, your social network, your paycheck. She must have been under a tremendous amount of pressure to keep it up. Everything she had was the result of smoke and mirrors." May shrugged. "I wouldn't want to live like that."

Zainab fingered the bedsheets. "I don't know how to say this without sounding idiotic, but you're just so amazing."

"I don't think that sounds idiotic at all," May said and winked. "And for what it's worth, the feeling is quite mutual."

Zainab felt her eyes closing.

"Get some rest," May said. "*Insha'Allah,* I'll see you soon."

55

THE DAY AFTER Darby's story appeared in the *Times,* Chase sent her the e-mail. He had no idea what she would do with it. It was possible she would simply delete it or tell him where to shove it. Instead, she left him a voice mail saying that the *Globe* was on board as well for the Sunday edition. With the headline "An Open Letter to My Listeners" alongside an update on the investigation into the attack on Zainab, they both ran it word for word:

> Most of you who are familiar with my work probably know me as an avid conservative, as someone who fights for the personal freedoms of Americans and for the values that made this country great.
>
> It's equally possible you know me as someone who has impugned an entire religion and said hyperbolic things about Muslims involving phrases like "enemy of the state" and "evil" and "forced registration."
>
> I said these things in part in response to the horror of September 11 and future threats by Al-Qaeda and its ilk. I still believe those are serious threats. But other threats exist in this country as well, threats that find their genesis largely in my political party, threats that I, for pecuniary gain, helped to foment.

Last week, a woman named Zainab Mir was attacked by a crowd of Muslim radicals and right-wing bigots protesting a woman-led Islamic prayer in Cambridge. She is an American citizen of Pakistani and Indian descent who suffered multiple broken bones and other injuries for daring to exercise her Constitutional rights.

Zainab Mir is a smart, talented woman who previously served as communications director for Eleanor Winthrop-Smith's senatorial campaign. She worked tirelessly in that role and adhered to the highest ethical and professional standards. She was fiercely loyal to her candidate, wrote passionate, brilliant speeches that always made Ms. Winthrop-Smith look the better for having hired her, and never let cynicism rule her day.

Zainab is also the kind of woman who cares for an ailing father, who has earned lifelong friends, who would listen patiently in the middle of the night to a professional opponent she barely knew confess that his father died of AIDS and admit that he was too much of a coward to say good-bye, and still look at him as though there were some good inside. If her beloved mother, who taught her to love art and literature and to see beauty in an often tragic world, were alive today, she would be overcome with pride.

I understand the impulse to hate Muslims because of the actions of terrorists who act in the name of Islam. I appreciate the emotion involved in that calculus. I walked in those knee-jerk shoes.

But consider this: If you hate Muslims because of Osama Bin Laden or the twelve men who attacked us on September 11, you should also love Muslims because of people like Zainab Mir.

And if you have been stupid enough in the past to say one thing publicly and another privately, hoping that the woman you love—a woman with as much integrity and self-respect as Zainab Mir—would overlook your political expediency and moral bankruptcy, you should say you're sorry. And if she, quite reasonably, won't let you say it to her face, you should shout it from the hills or paint it across the sky or publish it in the most well-read paper in the world and hope it reaches her eyes or ears, and maybe, Insha'Allah, God willing, her heart.

I'm sorry, Zainab. I meant everything I said to you.

Is it so implausible?

56

Zainab watched Amra with the baby, how she raised her eyebrows when she talked to her, as though she wanted to take all of her in, how she smoothed her fuzzy little head while Thanaa slept in her arms. *She's a good mother,* Zainab thought and, knowing something about how important having a good mother was, kicked herself for giving Amra so much grief when she'd been unsure about returning to work. Perhaps it wasn't all Mateen.

Rukan had brought takeout from Gourmet India and Amra had furnished dessert, a decadent-looking chocolate cake. They both said they'd spend the night if she wanted. She knew they were trying to distract her, perhaps even keep her from turning on the television at all or checking online for the Republican senatorial primary results. Plus, they were dying to know her reaction to Chase's op-ed.

"So, I assume you read it?" Amra asked.

Rukan poured the tea. "I think it's just about the most romantic thing I've ever seen."

"Careful. I'll tell Dameer you said that," Zainab teased. But she wasn't ready to talk about Chase. She looked at her watch.

Amra noticed. "Trying to get rid of us?"

"Of course not."

"You must be getting tired," Amra said. "We shouldn't have stayed so long."

"Don't be ridiculous," Zainab said. "It's good to have company. I was just thinking the election returns might be coming in."

Zainab noticed a look pass between Amra and Rukan.

"It's okay. It was my decision to quit, remember?" She flicked on the television. The early returns showed Fred and Eleanor in a dead heat.

When Zainab started yawning, Amra said she and Rukan should get going. "Are you sure you're going to be okay?" she whispered when she hugged Zainab.

"Yes, *go*." Zainab shooed them out the door and got ready for bed. And then she took her comforter and curled up on the couch, thinking about where she'd thought she'd be that night—at the Four Seasons Hotel with Eleanor, sending secret texts to Chase, meeting him after the festivities. She thought of the people who had taken all of it from her: the Three Stooges of terrorists and the country that wanted her to apologize for them.

In the end, Eleanor lost 52–48. Zainab left her a message expressing her condolences on the loss and congratulating her on a tough and decent campaign. She was surprised when Eleanor called back, almost instantly. She didn't want to talk about the campaign. "The sweatshop deal is done," she said. "So, like you, I can go back to my principles. If you ever need anything, Zainab, promise you'll contact me. Just say the word, and I'll make any call you want on your behalf. In fact, I hear there might be something in the White House speechwriters' office if things go the right way in November."

Zainab thanked her and hung up. It was too early to think about the future. For tonight, it was enough to focus on the women that Eleanor had saved, women for whom in her own way Eleanor had been willing to risk it all and who were about to get another shot at a decent life.

57

HAYDEN STARED AT the celing while Abdullah Rahman slept. She'd grown used to his snoring and, after the first restless nights, found it reassuring to fall asleep to the soft, steady sound of his obstructed breath. It calmed her, somehow, after a frenzied day at work or a run-in with his mother. In spite of Fareeda's difficult personality, Abdullah Rahman had turned out to be kind and generous, if a bit simple, often massaging Hayden's feet at night, bringing her small gifts, teaching her about his faith and culture patiently. He'd never made her feel stupid for not knowing something, never judged her for her past.

When the police wanted to question her after the protest, Abdullah Rahman stayed by her side, holding her hand through the interrogation. Hayden had told them she was sure it was the anti-Muslim side who'd started the attack, although when pressed she'd been forced to admit that she really hadn't seen everything. When the officer let her go, he told her to be careful whom she associated with. In the car, Abdullah Rahman called it a witch hunt, telling her not to give any of it a second thought.

She'd tried to follow his advice, but then there was the publicity and the investigation and the letter by some talk-radio guy in the newspaper—they'd all morphed Zainab into some sort of *hero*—and Hayden found that the more she tried to forget about the protest, the more she focused on it. She had never been a fan of Zainab's, but Hayden was no monster. She would not wish those injuries on an enemy, let alone the friend of a friend. Even if that friend was brash and more than a little stuck up.

She adjusted the comforter carefully, making sure it stayed tucked around Abdullah Rahman. He was not to blame for any of it. He had done his best. But she could not say the same for Fareeda, or Women for Islam, or, in the end, herself. By trying to hide in the unfamiliar landscape of Islam, she had used both Abdullah Rahman and the faith he held dear. She understood that now.

It was time to leave them both alone.

Hayden kissed her husband lightly on the cheek, placed her wedding ring on the bedside table, and slipped out the door with the suitcase she'd brought the day they married and a plane ticket home to Colorado.

58

THEY WALKED ALONG the Charles River and found a bench near the Esplanade.

"I can't believe you're sitting here," Chase said.

Zainab shrugged. "Stranger things have happened."

"Maybe." He studied her face. "How are you, really? I mean, is everything healing okay?"

"I'm a little sore," she said. "Good thing I vetoed that modeling career."

"I think you could still give them a run for their money." He tossed a stone into the water and shook his head. "How did everything get so out of control?"

"I wish I knew."

He nodded and they were quiet for a minute. Then he asked about the campaign. "So Eleanor wasn't able to do it without you."

"She did alright. She kept it close."

"I heard about what she's doing with the sweatshops. That's why you couldn't tell me."

She nodded and thought back to that first, unexpected dinner, when she'd been surprised that he appreciated her art. "Eleanor was willing to lose the election for something she believed in," she said.

"Sounds like someone I know." Chase shifted in his seat. "So, what's next for you?"

"I've got some offers. *Salon*. *Vanity Fair*." Zainab wrinkled her nose. "There might be a thing in the White House. You know, the speechwriters' office."

"A thing?" He laughed. "So you're going to be in the White House. I can say I knew you when."

"It's just a possibility."

"Mark my words."

Zainab looked out over the water. "What about you? You know, now that your name is mud in the right-wing whack-job circles."

"Actually, I'm going to Karachi."

"Karachi, *Pakistan*?"

"*Jee*," he said and smiled. "You know that doctor you called? I'm helping him set up a clinic to treat HIV patients discreetly. I've got a buddy who's a big-shot infectious-disease guy at Mass General. He's coming along to get us started."

"I don't know what to say."

"I know." He sighed. "I'm the king of making up for things when it's way too late."

"It's not too late for the people you're going to help."

He nodded. "I hope not."

"You'll be the next Greg Mortenson. I can say I knew you when."

"Touché." He smiled halfheartedly.

"How long will you be there?"

"I'm not sure. It's sort of open-ended right now."

"Maybe I'll write an article about you. You know, if I don't go to the White House."

He nodded. "Guaranteed exclusive. Full access. Day or night." He stared straight ahead. "For the rest of my life."

A small, tugging feeling caught in Zainab's throat.

Chase leaned forward. "I know you're not big on second chances, and I sure as hell don't deserve one. But when I get back . . ."

"Chase."

"I know. It doesn't exactly have happy ending written all over it."

She let his words hang between them. She stared at the water lapping against the edge of the river. The wind had picked up and the seagulls struggled against its force. "I should go," she said, standing. He nodded and slumped against the back of the bench. She made it as far as the large oak tree and stopped. She turned and took a shoestring breath. "Hey, Chase."

"Yeah?"

"That whole happy-ending thing?"

He nodded.

"It's not so implausible." Before he could answer, she turned around, letting the breeze push her toward home.

59

RUKAN LOOKED STUNNING in her lavender Banarasi *gharara*. She'd wanted something unexpected, "anything but the ubiquitous red," she'd insisted, and Amra knew she wanted to look as different as possible from the last time she'd put on such a dress. Amra pinned the *dupatta* in place and hooked the gold *tikka* in Rukan's hair, adjusting it on her forehead. As they lined up in the hallway of the Liberty Hotel—Amra, Zainab, and Dameer's younger sister, each with their white bouquets—Amra couldn't help but think of Rukan's last wedding, which held sour memories for her as well. It was the night she and Mateen had broken up, when she'd been unwilling to move to the West Coast. It was also the night Hayden had met Fadi, setting in motion a string of events that in her wildest dreams Amra could not have imagined. It was possible, she now knew, to break a heart so completely that it was ready to receive anything just to fill it up.

After she was certain Zainab was going to be okay that wretched day at the hospital, Amra had had time to process the phone call from Hayden, to piece together the fact that Hayden had witnessed the attack and had been part of the acrid mob outside the church. Amra would have to come to terms with how she should have done more, earlier, when Hayden first converted, to support her friend. She would carry that little piece of guilt, especially when she saw Zainab's scars, for the rest of her life. It was a reminder to reach out to others more, to be less consumed by her own struggles.

As they waited in the hallway, Zainab nudged her. "They're ready," she said, and they headed for the elevator, the three women in the bridesmaids' pink, Rukan flanked by her beaming parents. Amra looked at Zainab. The makeup artist had promised she could "erase" the scars, but Zainab said to leave them. "They make me look more interesting," she'd said, "or at least like someone you don't want to mess with." Amra laughed and said another small prayer of thanks that the mob that broke Zainab's body had done nothing to her spirit. Things were back to normal between the two of them. Zainab had confessed her jealousy of Mateen and supported Amra's decision to take a one-year leave of absence from her job. "I'm going back," Amra had said emphatically, and Zainab nodded like she believed her. And Amra had listened, really listened, for the first time when Zainab spoke about Chase—how the parts they'd each lost so catastrophically as children healed a bit in each other's presence, how their jagged edges somehow fit together in the important spots. When Amra had finished Zainab's henna the night before, she handed her the cone. "Just in case you want to add something," she'd said and hugged Zainab tight.

From the back of the hall, Amra could see Mateen sitting with her parents, holding Thanaa. During his scheduled visits, they'd started to talk, tentatively at first, about what had gone wrong. The rushing into things, the not being fully honest, their insecurities. The last time he visited, he'd stayed for dinner and kissed her gently before leaving. Amra had noticed that he, too, was still wearing his wedding ring.

As the procession began, Amra looked down at her hands, covered in florid strokes, and thought about how they had been a canvas